THE PICTURE OF
DORIAN GRAY

DE PROFUNDIS

THE MODERN LIBRARY
OF THE WORLD'S BEST BOOKS

The publisher will be placed to send upon request, an
illustrated folder setting forth the purpose and scope of
THE MODERN LIBRARY, and listing each volume
in the series. Every reader of books will find titles he has
been looking for, handsomely printed in unabridged
editions, and at an unusually low price.

THE PICTURE OF
DORIAN GRAY

◆

DE PROFUNDIS

BY OSCAR WILDE

THE

MODERN LIBRARY

NEW YORK

Random House IS THE PUBLISHER OF

THE MODERN LIBRARY

BENNETT A. CERF · DONALD S. KLOPFER · ROBERT K. HAAS

Manufactured in the United States of America
By H. Wolff

THE ARTIST'S PREFACE

DURING the Spring of 1884 Oscar Wilde was often in the studio. One of my sitters was a young gentleman of such peculiar beauty that his friends had nicknamed him "The Radiant Youth." Each afternoon Wilde watched the work advance, enchanting us, meanwhile, with brilliant talk, until, at last, the portrait was finished and its original had gone his ways—rejoicing, without doubt, to be at liberty.

Now, the beauty of "Dorian" was of that kind which depends on colour and expression for its charm. His hair was bright and wavy; the ruddiness of health suffused his cheeks; his eyes sparkled with wholesome fun, good humour, and high thoughts. He was the sort of boy who makes the world seem jolly even when the east wind blows. Goodness and merriment radiated from him visibly; the darkest room appeared to glow and brighten when he entered it.

"What a pity such a glorious creature should ever grow old," sighed Wilde.

"Yes, it is indeed," said I. "How delightful it would be if 'Dorian' could remain exactly as he is, while the *portrait* aged and withered in his stead. I wish it might be so!"

And that was all. I occupied myself with the picture for perhaps a quarter of an hour, during which Wilde smoked reflectively, but uttered not one word. He arose, presently, and sauntered to the door, merely nodding as he left the room.

Family affairs called me, by-and-by, from London. I saw no more of either Wilde or "Gray."

One day, years afterward, this book fell into my hands,
I cannot remember where or how, although it startled me
to find the germ, sown carelessly in idle talk, expanded by
the writer's art into "The Picture of Dorian Gray." Wilde
must have brooded long upon the theme. "The Radiant
Youth" was, to be sure, the very opposite of Wilde's bad
hero; but such was the author's love of paradox that this
antithesis of character was just the thing to fascinate his
poet's mind, from which the following pages grew.

BASIL HALLWARD.

THE PREFACE

THE artist is the creator of beautiful things.
   To reveal art and conceal the artist is art's aim. The critic is he who can translate into another manner or a new material his impression of beautiful things.
   The highest, as the lowest, form of criticism is a mode of autobiography.
Those who find ugly meanings in beautiful things are corrupt without being charming. This is a fault.
   Those who find beautiful meanings in beautiful things are the cultivated. For these there is hope.
They are the elect to whom beautiful things means only Beauty.
   There is no such thing as a moral or an immoral book. Books are well written, or badly written. That is all.
The nineteenth century dislike of Realism is the rage of Caliban seeing his own face in a glass.
   The nineteenth century dislike of Romanticism is the rage of Caliban not seeing his own face in a glass.
The moral life of man forms part of the subject-matter of the artist, but the morality of art consists in the perfect use of an imperfect medium. No artist desires to prove anything. Even things that are true can be proved.
   No artist has ethical sympathies. An ethical sympathy in an artist is an unpardonable mannerism of style.
   No artist is ever morbid. The artist can express everything.

Thought and language are to the artist instruments of an art.

Vice and virtue are to the artist materials for an art. From the point of view of form, the type of all the arts is the art of the musician. From the point of view of feeling, the actor's craft is the type.

All art is at once surface and symbol.

Those who go beneath the surface do so at their peril.

Those who read the symbol do so at their peril. It is the spectator, and not life, that art really mirrors.

Diversity of opinion about a work of art shows that the work is new, complex, and vital.

When critics disagree the artist is in accord with himself.

We can forgive a man for making a useful thing as long as he does not admire it. The only excuse for making a useless thing is that one admires it intensely.

All art is quite useless.

OSCAR WILDE.

THE PICTURE OF DORIAN GRAY

CHAPTER I

THE studio was filled with the rich odour of roses, and when the light summer wind stirred amidst the trees of the garden, there came through the open door the heavy scent of the lilac, or the more delicate perfume of the pink-flowering thorn.

From the corner of the divan of Persian saddle-bags on which he was lying, smoking, as was his custom, innumerable cigarettes, Lord Henry Wotton could just catch the gleam of the honey-sweet and honey-coloured blossoms of a laburnum, whose tremulous branches seemed hardly able to bear the burden of a beauty so flame-like as theirs; and now and then the fantastic shadows of birds in flight flitted across the long tussore-silk curtains that were stretched in front of the huge window, producing a kind of momentary Japanese effect, and making him think of those pallid jade-faced painters of Tokio who, through the medium of an art that is necessarily immobile, seek to convey the sense of swiftness and motion. The sullen murmur of the bees shouldering their way through the long unmown grass, or circling with monotonous insistence round the dusty gilt horns of the straggling woodbine, seemed to make the stillness more oppressive. The dim roar of London was like the bourdon note of a distant organ.

In the centre of the room, clamped to an upright easel, stood the full-length portrait of a young man of extraordinary personal beauty, and in front of it, some little distance away, was sitting the artist himself, Basil Hallward, whose sudden disappearance some years ago caused, at the time, such public excitement, and gave rise to so many strange conjectures.

As the painter looked at the gracious and comely form he had so skilfully mirrored in his art, a smile of pleasure passed across his face, and seemed about to linger there. But he suddenly started up, and, closing his eyes, placed his fingers upon the lids, as though he sought to imprison within his brain some curious dream from which he feared he might awake.

"It is your best work, Basil, the best thing you have ever done," said Lord Henry, languidly. "You must certainly send it next year to the Grosvenor. The Academy is too large and too vulgar. Whenever I have gone there, there have been either so many people that I have not been able to see the pictures, which was dreadful, or so many pictures that I have not been able to see the people, which was worse. The Grosvenor is really the only place."

"I don't think I shall send it anywhere," he answered, tossing his head back in that odd way that used to make his friends laugh at him at Oxford. "No: I won't send it anywhere."

Lord Henry elevated his eyebrows, and looked at him in amazement through the thin blue wreaths of smoke that curled up in such fanciful whorls from his heavy opium-tainted cigarette. "Not send it anywhere? My dear fellow, why? Have you any reason? What odd chaps you painters are! You do anything in the world to gain a reputation. As soon as you have one, you seem to want to throw it away. It is silly of you, for there is only one thing in the world worse than being talked about, and that is not being talked about. A portrait like this would set you far above all the young men in England, and make the old men quite jealous, if old men are ever capable of any emotion."

"I know you will laugh at me," he replied, "but I really can't exhibit it. I have put too much of myself into it."

Lord Henry stretched himself out on the divan and laughed.

"Yes, I knew you would; but it is quite true, all the same."

"Too much of yourself in it! Upon my word, Basil, I didn't know you were so vain; and I really can't see any resemblance between you, with your rugged strong face and your coal-black hair, and this young Adonis, who looks as if he was made out of ivory and rose-leaves. Why, my dear Basil, he is a Narcissus, and you—well, of course you have an intellectual expression, and all that. But beauty, real beauty, ends where an intellectual expression begins. Intellect is in itself a mode of exaggeration, and destroys the harmony of any face. The moment one sits down to think, one becomes all nose, or all forehead, or something horrid. Look at the successful men in any of the learned professions. How perfectly hideous they are! Except, of course, in the Church. But then in the Church they don't think. A bishop keeps on saying at the age of eighty what he was told to say when he was a boy of eighteen, and as a natural consequence he always looks absolutely delightful. Your mysterious young friend, whose name you have never told me, but whose picture really fascinates me, never thinks. I feel quite sure of that. He is some brainless, beautiful creature, who should be always here in winter when we have no flowers to look at, and always here in summer when we want something to chill our intelligence. Don't flatter yourself, Basil: you are not in the least like him."

"You don't understand me, Harry," answered the artist. "Of course I am not like him. I know that perfectly well. Indeed, I should be sorry to look like him. You shrug your shoulders? I am telling you the truth. There is a fatality about all physical and intellectual distinction, the sort of fatality that seems to dog through history the faltering steps of kings. It is better not to be different from one's fellows. The ugly and the stupid have the best of it in this world. They can sit at their ease and gape at the play. If they know nothing of victory, they are at least spared the knowledge of defeat. They live as we all should live, undisturbed, indifferent, and without disquiet. They neither bring ruin upon others, nor ever receive it from alien hands. Your rank and wealth, Harry; my brains, such as they are—my art, whatever it may be worth; Dorian Gray's good looks—we shall all suffer for what the gods have given us, suffer terribly."

"Dorian Gray? Is that his name?" asked Lord Henry, walking across the studio towards Basil Hallward.

"Yes, that is his name. I didn't intend to tell it to you."

"But why not?"

"Oh, I can't explain. When I like people immensely I never tell their names to anyone. It is like surrendering a part of them. I have grown to love secrecy. It seems to be the one thing that can make modern life mysterious or marvellous to us. The commonest thing is delightful if one only hides it. When I leave town now I never tell my people where I am going. If I did, I would lose all my pleasure. It is a silly habit, I daresay, but somehow it seems to bring a great deal of romance into one's life. I suppose you think me awfully foolish about it?"

"Not at all," answered Lord Henry, "not at all, my dear Basil. You seem to forget that I am married, and the one charm of marriage is that it makes a life of deception absolutely necessary for both parties. I never know where my wife is, and my wife never knows what I am doing. When we meet—we do meet occasionally, when we dine out together, or go down to the Duke's—we tell each other the most absurd stories with the most serious faces. My wife is very good at it—much better, in fact, than I am. She never gets confused over her dates, and I always do. But when she does find me out, she makes no row at all. I sometimes wish she would; but she merely laughs at me."

"I hate the way you talk about your married life, Harry," said Basil Hallward, strolling towards the door that led into the garden. "I believe that you are really a very good husband, but that you are thoroughly ashamed of your own virtues. You are an extraordinary fellow. You never say a moral thing, and you never do a wrong thing. Your cynicism is simply a pose."

"Being natural is simply a pose, and the most irritating pose I know," cried Lord Henry, laughing; and the two young men went out into the garden together, and ensconced themselves on a long bamboo seat that stood in the shade of a tall laurel bush. The sunlight slipped over the polished leaves. In the grass, white daisies were tremulous.

After a pause, Lord Henry pulled out his watch. "I am afraid I must be going, Basil," he murmured, "and before I go, I insist on your answering a question I put to you some time ago."

"What was that?" said the painter, keeping his eyes fixed on the ground.

"You know quite well."

"I do not, Harry."

"Well, I will tell you what it is. I want you to explain to me why you won't exhibit Dorian Gray's picture. I want the real reason."

"I told you the real reason."

"No, you did not. You said it was because there was too much of yourself in it. Now, that is childish."

"Harry," said Basil Hallward, looking him straight in the face, "every portrait that is painted with feeling is a portrait of the artist, not of the sitter. The sitter is merely the accident, the occasion. It is not he who is revealed by the painter; it is rather the painter who, on the coloured canvas, reveals himself. The reason I will not exhibit this picture is that I am afraid that I have shown in it the secret of my own soul."

Lord Henry laughed. "And what is that?" he asked.

"I will tell you," said Hallward; but an expression of perplexity came over his face.

"I am all expectation, Basil," continued his companion, glancing at him.

"Oh, there is really very little to tell, Harry," answered the painter; "and I am afraid you will hardly understand it. Perhaps you will hardly believe it."

Lord Henry smiled, and, leaning down, plucked a pink-petalled daisy from the grass, and examined it. "I am quite sure I shall understand it," he replied, gazing intently at the little golden white-feathered disk, "and as for believing things, I can believe anything, provided that it is quite incredible."

The wind shook some blossoms from the trees, and the heavy lilac-blooms, with their clustering stars, moved to and fro in the languid air. A grasshopper began to chirrup by the wall, and like a blue thread a long thin dragon-fly floated past on its brown gauze wings. Lord Henry felt as if he could hear Basil Hallward's heart beating, and wondered what was coming.

"The story is simply this," said the painter after some time. "Two months ago I went to a crush at Lady Brandon's. You know we poor artists have to show ourselves in society from time to time, just to remind the public that we are not savages. With an evening coat and a white tie, as you told me once, anybody, even a stockbroker, can gain a reputation for being civilised. Well, after I had been in the room about ten minutes, talking to huge overdressed dowagers and tedious

Academicians, I suddenly became conscious that someone was looking at me. I turned halfway round, and saw Dorian Gray for the first time. When our eyes met, I felt that I was growing pale. A curious sensation of terror came over me. I knew that I had come face to face with someone whose mere personality was so fascinating that, if I allowed it to do so, it would absorb my whole nature, my whole soul, my very art itself. I did not want any external influence in my life. You know yourself, Harry, how independent I am by nature. I have always been my own master; had at least always been so, till I met Dorian Gray. Then——but I don't know how to explain it to you. Something seemed to tell me that I was on the verge of a terrible crisis in my life. I had a strange feeling that Fate had in store for me exquisite joys and exquisite sorrows. I grew afraid, and turned to quit the room. It was not conscience that made me do so; it was a sort of cowardice. I take no credit to myself for trying to escape."

"Conscience and cowardice are really the same things, Basil. Conscience is the trade-name of the firm. That is all."

"I don't believe that, Harry, and I don't believe you do either. However, whatever was my motive—and it may have been pride, for I used to be very proud—I certainly struggled to the door. There, of course, I stumbled against Lady Brandon. 'You are not going to run away so soon, Mr. Hallward?' she screamed out. You know her curiously shrill voice?"

"Yes; she is a peacock in everything but beauty," said Lord Henry, pulling the daisy to bits with his long, nervous fingers.

"I could not get rid of her. She brought me up to Royalties, and people with Stars and Garters, and elderly ladies with gigantic tiaras and parrot noses. She spoke of me as her dearest friend. I had only met her once before, but she took it into her head to lionise me. I believe some picture of mine made a great success at the time, at least had been chatted about in the penny newspapers, which is the nineteenth-century standard of immortality. Suddenly I found myself face to face with the young man whose personality had so strangely stirred me. We were quite close, almost touching. Our eyes met again. It was reckless of me, but I asked Lady Brandon to introduce me to him. Perhaps it was not so reckless, after all. It was simply inevitable. We would have spoken to each other without any introduction. I am sure of that. Dorian told me so afterwards. He, too, felt that we were destined to know each other."

"And how did Lady Brandon describe this wonderful young man?" asked his companion. "I know she goes in for giving a rapid *précis* of all her guests. I remember her bringing me up to a truculent and red-faced old gentleman covered all over with orders and ribbons, and hissing into my ear, in a tragic whisper which must have been perfectly audible to everybody in the room, the most astounding details. I simply fled. I like to find out people for myself. But Lady Brandon treats her guests exactly as an auctioneer treats his goods. She either explains them entirely away, or tells one everything about them except what one wants to know."

"Poor Lady Brandon! You are hard on her, Harry!" said Hallward, listlessly.

"My dear fellow, she tried to found a *salon,* and only succeeded in opening a restaurant. How could I admire her? But tell me, what did she say about Mr. Dorian Gray?"

"Oh, something like, 'Charming boy—poor dear mother and I absolutely inseparable. Quite forget what he does—afraid he—doesn't do anything—oh, yes, plays the piano—or is it the violin, dear Mr. Gray?' Neither of us could help laughing, and we became friends at once."

"Laughter is not at all a bad beginning for a friendship, and it is far the best ending for one," said the young lord, plucking another daisy.

Hallward shook his head. "You don't understand what

friendship is, Harry," he murmured—"or what enmity is, for that matter. You like everyone; that is to say, you are indifferent to everyone."

"How horribly unjust of you!" cried Lord Henry, tilting his hat back, and looking up at the little clouds that, like ravelled skeins of glossy white silk, were drifting across the hollowed turquoise of the summer sky. "Yes; horribly unjust of you. I make a great difference between people. I choose my friends for their good looks, my acquaintances for their good characters, and my enemies for their good intellects. A man cannot be too careful in the choice of his enemies. I have not got one who is a fool. They are all men of some intellectual power, and consequently they all appreciate me. Is that very vain of me? I think it is rather vain."

"I should think it was, Harry. But according to your category, I must be merely an acquaintance."

"My dear old Basil, you are much more than an acquaintance."

"And much less than a friend. A sort of brother, I suppose?"

"Oh, brothers! I don't care for brothers. My elder brother won't die, and my younger brothers seem never to do anything else."

"Harry!" exclaimed Hallward, frowning.

"My dear fellow, I am not quite serious. But I can't help detesting my relations. I suppose it comes from the fact that none of us can stand other people having the same faults as ourselves. I quite sympathise with the rage of the English democracy against what they call the vices of the upper orders. The masses feel that drunkenness, stupidity, and immorality should be their own special property, and that if anyone of us makes an ass of himself he is poaching on their preserves. When poor Southwark got into the Divorce Court, their indignation was quite magnificent. And yet I don't suppose that ten per cent. of the proletariat live correctly."

"I don't agree with a single word that you have said, and, what is more, Harry, I feel sure you don't either."

Lord Henry stroked his pointed brown beard, and tapped the toe of his patent-leather boot with a tasselled ebony cane. "How English you are, Basil! That is the second time you have made that observation. If one puts forward an idea to a true Englishman—always a rash thing to do—he never dreams of considering whether the idea is right or wrong. The only thing he considers of any importance is whether one believes it oneself. Now, the value of an idea has nothing whatsoever to do with the sincerity of the man who expresses it. Indeed, the probabilities are that the more insincere the man is, the more purely intellectual will the idea be, as in that case it will not be coloured by either his wants, his desires, or his prejudices. However, I don't propose to discuss politics, sociology, or metaphysics with you. I like persons better than principles, and I like persons with no principles better than anything else in the world. Tell me more about Mr. Dorian Gray. How often do you see him?"

"Every day. I couldn't be happy if I didn't see him every day. He is absolutely necessary to me."

"How extraordinary! I thought you would never care for anything but your art."

"He is all my art to me now," said the painter, gravely. "I sometimes think, Harry, that there are only two eras of any importance in the world's history. The first is the appearance of a new medium for art, and the second is the appearance of a new personality for art also. What the invention of oil-painting was to the Venetians, the face of Antinoüs was to late Greek sculpture, and the face of Dorian Gray will some day be to me. It is not merely that I paint from him, draw from him, sketch from him. Of course I have done all that. But he is much more to me than a model or a sitter. I won't tell you that I am dissatisfied with what I have done of him, or that his beauty is such that Art cannot express it. There is nothing that Art cannot express, and I know that the work I have done, since I met Dorian Gray, is good work, is the best work of my life. But in some curious way—I wonder will you understand me?—his personality has suggested to me an entirely new manner in art, an entirely new mode of style. I see things differently. I think of them differently. I can now recreate life in a way that was hidden from me before. 'A dream of form in days of thought:—who is it who says that? I forget; but it is what Dorian Gray has been to me. The merely visible presence of this lad—for he seems to me little more than a lad, though he is really over twenty—his merely visible presence—ah! I wonder can you realise all that that means? Unconsciously he defines for me the lines of a fresh school, a school that is to have in it all the passion of the romantic spirit, all the perfection of the spirit that is Greek. The harmony of soul and body—how much that is! We in our madness have separated the two, and have invented a realism that is vulgar, an ideality that is void. Harry! if you only knew what Dorian Gray is to me! You remember that landscape of mine, for which Agnew offered me such a huge price, but which I would not part with? It is one of the best things I have ever done. And why is it so? Because, while I was painting it, Dorian Gray sat beside me. Some subtle influence passed from him to me, and for the first time in my life I saw in the plain woodland the wonder I had always looked for, and always missed."

"Basil, this is extraordinary! I must see Dorian Gray."

Hallward got up from the seat, and walked up and down the garden. After some time he came back. "Harry," he said, "Dorian Gray is to me simply a motive in art. You might see nothing in him. I see everything in him. He is never more present in my work than when no image of him is there. He is a suggestion, as I have said, of a new manner. I find in him the curves of certain lines, in the loveliness and subtleties of certain colours. That is all."

"Then why won't you exhibit his portrait?" asked Lord Henry.

"Because, without intending it, I have put into it some expression of all this curious artistic idolatry, of which, of course, I have never cared to speak to him. He knows nothing about it. He shall never know anything about it. But the world might guess it; and I will not bare my soul to their shallow prying eyes. My heart shall never be put under their microscope. There is too much of myself in the thing, Harry —too much of myself!"

"Poets are not so scrupulous as you are. They know how useful passion is for publication. Nowadays a broken heart will run to many editions."

"I hate them for it," cried Hallward. "An artist should create beautiful things, but should put nothing of his own life into them. We live in an age when men treat art as if it were meant to be a form of autobiography. We have lost the abstract sense of beauty. Some day I will show the world what it is; and for that reason the world shall never see my portrait of Dorian Gray."

"I think you are wrong, Basil, but I won't argue with you. It is only the intellectually lost who ever argue. Tell me, is Dorian Gray very fond of you?"

The painter considered for a few moments. "He likes me," he answered, after a pause; "I know he likes me. Of course I flatter him dreadfully. I find a strange pleasure in saying things to him that I know I shall be sorry for having said. As a rule, he is charming to me, and we sit in the studio and talk of a thousand things. Now and then, however, he is horribly thoughtless, and seems to take a real delight in giving me pain. Then I feel, Harry, that I have given away my whole soul to someone who treats it as if it were a flower to put in his coat, a bit of decoration to charm his vanity, an ornament for a summer's day."

"Days in summer, Basil, are apt to linger," murmured Lord Henry. "Perhaps you will tire sooner than he will. It is a sad thing to think of, but there is no doubt that Genius lasts longer than Beauty. That accounts for the fact that we all take such pains to over-educate ourselves. In the wild struggle for existence, we want to have something that endures, and so we fill our minds with rubbish and facts, in the silly hope of keeping our place. The thoroughly well-informed man— that is the modern ideal. And the mind of the thoroughly well-informed man is a dreadful thing. It is like a bric-à-brac shop, all monsters and dust, with everything priced above its proper value. I think you will tire first, all the same. Some day you will look at your friend, and he will seem to you to be a little out of drawing, or you won't like his tone of colour, or something. You will bitterly reproach him in your own heart, and seriously think that he has behaved very badly to you. The next time he calls, you will be perfectly cold and indifferent. It will be a great pity, for it will alter you. What you have told me is quite a romance, a romance of art one might call it, and the worst of having a romance of any kind is that it leaves one so unromantic."

"Harry, don't talk like that. As long as I live, the personality of Dorian Gray will dominate me. You can't feel what I feel. You change too often."

"Ah, my dear Basil, that is exactly why I can feel it. Those who are faithful know only the trivial side of love: it is the faithless who know love's tragedies." And Lord Henry struck a light on a dainty silver case, and began to smoke a cigarette with a self-conscious and satisfied air, as if he had summed up the world in a phrase. There was a rustle of chirruping sparrows in the green lacquer leaves of the ivy and the blue cloud-shadows chased themselves across the grass like swallows. How pleasant it was in the garden! And how delightful other people's emotions were!—much more delightful than their ideas, it seemed to him. One's own soul, and the passions of one's friends—those were the fascinating things in life. He pictured to himself with silent amusement the tedious luncheon that he had missed by staying so long with Basil Hallward. Had he gone to his aunt's he would have been sure to have met Lord Goodbody there, and the whole conversation would have been about the feeding of the poor, and the necessity for model lodging-houses. Each class would have preached the importance of those virtues, for whose exercise there was no necessity in their own lives. The rich would have spoken on the value of thrift, and the idle grown eloquent over the dignity of labour. It was charming to have escaped all that! As he thought of his aunt, an idea seemed to strike him, He turned to Hallward and said: "My dear fellow, I have just remembered."

"Remembered what, Harry?"

"Where I heard the name of Dorian Gray."

"Where was it?" asked Hallward, with a slight frown.

"Don't look so angry, Basil. It was at my aunt, Lady Agatha's. She told me she had discovered a wonderful young man, who was going to help her in the East End, and that his name was Dorian Gray. I am bound to state that she never told me he was good-looking. Women have no appreciation of good looks; at least, good women have not. She said that he was very earnest, and had a beautiful nature. I at once pictured to myself a creature with spectacles and lank hair, horribly freckled, and tramping about on huge feet. I wish I had known it was your friend."

"I am very glad you didn't, Harry."

"Why?"

"I don't want you to meet him."

"You don't want me to meet him?"

"No."

"Mr. Dorian Gray is in the studio, sir," said the butler, coming into the garden.

"You must introduce me now," cried Lord Henry, laughing.

The painter turned to his servant, who stood blinking in the sunlight. "Ask Mr. Gray to wait, Parker: I shall be in in a few moments." The man bowed, and went up the walk.

Then he looked at Lord Henry. "Dorian Gray is my dearest friend," he said. "He has a simple and beautiful nature. Your aunt was quite right in what she said of him. Don't spoil him. Don't try to influence him. Your influence would be bad. The world is wide, and has many marvellous people in it. Don't take away from me the one person who gives to my art whatever charm it possesses; my life as an artist depends on him. Mind, Harry, I trust you." He spoke very slowly and the words seemed wrung out of him almost against his will.

"What nonsense you talk!" said Lord Henry, smiling, and, taking Hallward by the arm, he almost led him into the house.

CHAPTER II

AS they entered they saw Dorian Gray. He was seated at the piano, with his back to them, turning over the pages of a volume of Schumann's "Forest Scenes." "You must lend me these, Basil," he cried. "I want to learn them. They are perfectly charming."

"That entirely depends on how you sit to-day, Dorian."

"Oh, I am tired of sitting, and I don't want a life-sized portrait of myself," answered the lad, swinging round on the music-stool, in a wilful, petulant manner. When he caught sight of Lord Henry, a faint blush coloured his cheeks for a moment, and he started up. "I beg your pardon, Basil, but I didn't know you had anyone with you."

"This is Lord Henry Wotton, Dorian, an old Oxford friend of mine. I have just been telling him what a capital sitter you were, and now you have spoiled everything."

"You have not spoiled my pleasure in meeting you, Mr Gray," said Lord Henry, stepping forward and extending his hand. "My aunt has often spoken to me about you. You are one of her favourites, and, I am afraid one of her victims also."

"I am in Lady Agatha's black books at present," answered Dorian, with a funny look of penitence. "I promised to go to a club in Whitechapel with her last Tuesday, and I really forgot all about it. We were to have played a duet together —three duets, I believe. I don't know what she will say to me. I am far too frightened to call."

"Ah. I will make your peace with my aunt. She is quite devoted to you. And I don't think it really matters about your not being there. The audience probably thought it was a duet. When Aunt Agatha sits down to the piano she makes quite enough noise for two people."

"That is very horrid to her, and not very nice to me," answered Dorian, laughing.

Lord Henry looked at him. Yes, he was certainly wonderfully handsome, with his finely-curved scarlet lips, his frank blue eyes, his crisp gold hair. There was something in his face that made one trust him at once. All the candour of youth was there, as well as youth's passionate purity. One felt that he had kept himself unspotted from the world. No wonder Basil Hallward worshipped him.

"You are too charming to go in for philanthropy, Mr. Gray—far too charming." And Lord Henry flung himself down on the divan, and opened his cigarette-case.

The painter had been busy mixing his colours and getting his brushes ready. He was looking worried, and when he heard Lord Henry's last remark he glanced at him, hesitated for a moment, and then said: "Harry, I want to finish this picture to-day. Would you think it awfully rude of me if I asked you to go away?"

Lord Henry smiled, and looked at Dorian Gray. "Am I to go, Mr. Gray?" he asked.

"Oh, please don't, Lord Henry. I see that Basil is in one of his sulky moods; and I can't bear him when he sulks. Besides, I want you to tell me why I should not go in for philanthropy."

"I don't know that I shall tell you that, Mr. Gray. It is so tedious a subject that one would have to talk seriously about it. But I certainly shall not run away, now that you have asked me to stop. You don't really mind, Basil, do you? You have often told me that you liked your sitters to have someone to chat to."

Hallward bit his lip. "If Dorian wishes it, of course you

must stay. Dorian's whims are laws to everybody, except himself."

Lord Henry took up his hat and gloves. "You are very pressing, Basil, but I am afraid I must go. I have promised to meet a man at the Orleans. Good-bye, Mr. Gray. Come and see me some afternoon in Curzon Street. I am nearly always at home at five o'clock. Write to me when you are coming. I should be sorry to miss you."

"Basil," cried Dorian Gray, "if Lord Henry Wotton goes I shall go too. You never open your lips while you are painting, and it is horribly dull standing on a platform and trying to look pleasant. Ask him to stay. I insist upon it."

"Stay, Harry, to oblige Dorian, and to oblige me," said Hallward, gazing intently at his picture. "It is quite true, I never talk when I am working, and never listen either, and it must be dreadfully tedious for my unfortunate sitters. I beg you to stay."

"But what about my man at the Orleans?"

The painter laughed. "I don't think there will be any difficulty about that. Sit down again, Harry. And now, Dorian, get up on the platform, and don't move about too much, or pay any attention to what Lord Henry says. He has a very bad influence over all his friends, with the single exception of myself."

Dorian Gray stepped up on the dais, with the air of a young Greek martyr, and made a little *moue* of discontent to Lord Henry, to whom he had rather taken a fancy. He was so unlike Basil. They made a delightful contrast. And he had such a beautiful voice. After a few moments he said to him: "Have you really a very bad influence, Lord Henry? As bad as Basil says?"

"There is no such thing as a good influence, Mr. Gray. All influence is immoral—immoral from the scientific point of view."

"Why?"

"Because to influence a person is to give him one's own soul. He does not think his natural thoughts, or burn with his natural passions. His virtues are not real to him. His sins, if there are such things as sins, are borrowed. He becomes an echo of someone else's music, an actor of a part that has not been written for him. The aim of life is self-development. To realise one's nature perfectly—that is what each of us is here for. People are afraid of themselves, nowadays. They have forgotten the highest of all duties, the duty that one owes to one's self. Of course they are charitable. They feed the hungry, and clothe the beggar. But their own souls starve, and are naked. Courage has gone out of our race. Perhaps we never really had it. The terror of society, which is the basis of morals, the terror of God, which is the secret of religion—these are the two things that govern us. And yet——"

"Just turn your head a little more to the right, Dorian, like a good boy," said the painter, deep in his work, and conscious only that a look had come into the lad's face that he had never seen there before.

"And yet," continued Lord Henry, in his low, musical voice, and with that graceful wave of the hand that was always so characteristic of him, and that he had even in his Eton days, "I believe that if one man were to live out his life fully and completely, were to give form to every feeling, expression to every thought, reality to every dream—I believe that the world would gain such a fresh impulse of joy that we would forget all the maladies of mediævalism, and return to the Hellenic ideal—to something finer, richer, than the Hellenic ideal, it may be. But the bravest man amongst us is afraid of himself. The mutilation of the savage has its tragic survival in the self-denial that mars our lives. We are punished for our refusals. Every impulse that we strive to strangle broods in the mind, and poisons us. The body sins once, and has done with its sin, for action is a mode of purification. Nothing remains then but the recollection of a pleasure, or the luxury of a regret. The only way to get rid of a temptation is to yield to it. Resist it, and your soul grows sick with longing for the things it has forbidden to itself, with desire for what its monstrous laws have made monstrous and unlawful. It has been said that the great events of the world take place in the brain. It is in the brain, and the brain only, that the great sins of the world take place also. You, Mr. Gray, you your- self, with your rose-red youth and your rose-white boyhood, you have had passions that have made you afraid, thoughts that have filled you with terror, day-dreams and sleeping dreams whose mere memory might stain your cheek with shame——"

"Stop!" faltered Dorian Gray, "stop! you bewilder me. I don't know what to say. There is some answer to you, but I cannot find it. Don't speak. Let me think. Or, rather, let me try not to think."

For nearly ten minutes he stood there, motionless, with parted lips, and eyes strangely bright. He was dimly con- scious that entirely fresh influences were at work within him. Yet they seemed to him to have come really from him- self. The few words that Basil's friend had said to him— words spoken by chance, no doubt, and with willful para- dox in them—had touched some secret chord that had never been touched before, but that he felt was now vibrating and throbbing to curious pulses.

Music had stirred him like that. Music had troubled him many times. But music was not articulate. It was not a new world, but rather another chaos, that it created in us. Words! Mere words! How terrible they were! How clear, and vivid, and cruel! One could not escape from them. And yet what a subtle magic there was in them! They seemed to be able to give a plastic form to formless things, and to have a music of their own as sweet as that of viol or of lute. Mere words! Was there anything so real as words?

Yes; there had been things in his boyhood that he had not understood. He understood them now. Life suddenly became fiery-coloured to him. It seemed to him that he had been walking in fire. Why had he not known it?

With his subtle smile, Lord Henry watched him. He knew the precise psychological moment when to say nothing. He felt intensely interested. He was amazed at the sudden impression that his words had produced, and, remembering a book that he had read when he was sixteen, a book which had revealed to him much that he had not known before, he wondered whether Dorian Gray was passing through a similar experience. He had merely shot an arrow into the air. Had it hit the mark? How fascinating the lad was!

Hallward painted away with that marvellous bold touch of his, that had the true refinement and perfect delicacy that in art, at any rate, comes only from strength. He was unconscious of the silence.

"Basil, I am tired of standing," cried Dorian Gray, suddenly. "I must go out and sit in the garden. The air is stifling here."

"My dear fellow, I am so sorry. When I am painting, I can't think of anything else. But you never sat better. You were perfectly still. And I have caught the effect I wanted— the half-parted lips, and the bright look in the eyes. I don't know what Harry has been saying to you, but he has certainly made you have the most wonderful expression. I suppose he has been paying you compliments. You mustn't believe a word that he says."

"He has certainly not been paying me compliments. Perhaps that is the reason that I don't believe anything he has told me."

"You know you believe it all," said Lord Henry, looking at him with his dreamy, languorous eyes. "I will go out to the garden with you. It is horribly hot in the studio. Basil, let us have something iced to drink, something with strawberries in it."

"Certainly, Harry. Just touch the bell, and when Parker comes I will tell him what you want. I have got to work up this background, so I will join you later on. Don't keep Dorian too long. I have never been in better form for painting than I am to-day. This is going to be my masterpiece. It is my masterpiece as it stands."

Lord Henry went out to the garden, and found Dorian Gray burying his face in the great cool lilac-blossoms, feverishly drinking in their perfume as if it had been wine. He came close to him, and put his hand upon his shoulder. "You are quite right to do that," he murmured. "Nothing can cure the soul but the senses, just as nothing can cure the senses but the soul."

The lad started and drew back. He was bare-headed, and the leaves had tossed his rebellious curls and tangled all their gilded threads. There was a look of fear in his eyes, such as people have when they are suddenly awakened. His finely-chiselled nostrils quivered, and some hidden nerve shook the scarlet of his lips and left them trembling.

"Yes," continued Lord Henry, "that is one of the great secrets of life—to cure the soul by means of the senses, and the senses by means of the soul. You are a wonderful creation. You know more than you think you know, just as you know less than you want to know."

Dorian Gray frowned and turned his head away. He could not help liking the tall, graceful young man who was standing by him. His romantic olive-coloured face and worn expression interested him. There was something in his low, languid voice that was absolutely fascinating. His cool, white, flower-like hands, even, had a curious charm. They moved, as he spoke, like music, and seemed to have a language of their own. But he felt afraid of him, and ashamed of being afraid. Why had it been left for a stranger to reveal him to himself? He had known Basil Hallward for months, but the friendship between them had never altered him. Suddenly there had to come someone across his life who seemed to have disclosed to him life's mystery. And, yet, what was there to be afraid of? He was not a schoolboy or a girl. It was absurd to be frightened.

"Let us go and sit in the shade," said Lord Henry. "Parker has brought out the drinks, and if you stay any longer in this glare you will be quite spoiled, and Basil will never paint you again. You really must not allow yourself to become sunburnt. It would be unbecoming."

"What can it matter?" cried Dorian Gray, laughing, as he sat down on the seat at the end of the garden.

"It should matter everything to you, Mr. Gray."

"Why?"

"Because you have the most marvellous youth, and youth is the one thing worth having."

"I don't feel that, Lord Henry."

"No, you don't feel it now. Some day, when you are old and wrinkled and ugly, when thought has seared your forehead with its lines, and passion branded your lips with its hideous fires, you will feel it, you will feel it terribly. Now, wherever you go, you charm the world. Will it always be so? . . . You have a wonderfully beautiful face, Mr. Gray. Don't frown. You have. And Beauty is a form of Genius— is higher, indeed, than Genius, as it needs no explanation. It is of the great facts of the world, like sunlight, or springtime, or the reflection in dark waters of that silver shell we call the moon. It cannot be questioned. It has its divine right of sovereignty. It makes princes of those who have it. You

smile? Ah! when you have lost it you won't smile. . . .
People say sometimes that Beauty is only superficial. That
may be so. But at least it is not superficial as Thought is. To
me, Beauty is the wonder of wonders. It is only shallow
people who do not judge by appearances. The true mystery
of the world is the visible, not the invisible. . . . Yes, Mr.
Gray, the gods have been good to you. But what the gods
give they quickly take away. You have only a few years in
which to live really, perfectly, and fully. When your youth
goes, your beauty will go with it, and then you will suddenly
discover that there are no triumphs left for you, or have to
content yourself with those mean triumphs that the memory
of your past will make more bitter than defeats. Every month
as it wanes brings you nearer to something dreadful. Time
is jealous of you, and wars against your lilies and your roses.
You will become sallow, and hollow-cheeked, and dull-eyed.
You will suffer horribly. . . . Ah! realise your youth while
you have it. Don't squander the gold of your days, listening
to the tedious, trying to improve the hopeless failure, or
giving away your life to the ignorant, the common, and the
vulgar. These are the sickly aims, the false ideals, of our age.
Live! Live the wonderful life that is in you! Let nothing be
lost upon you. Be always searching for new sensations. Be
afraid of nothing. . . . A new Hedonism—that is what our
century wants. You might be its visible symbol. With your
personality there is nothing you could not do. The world
belongs to you for a season. . . . The moment I met you I
saw that you were quite unconscious of what you really are,
of what you really might be. There was so much in you that
charmed me that I felt I must tell you something about
yourself. I thought how tragic it would be if you were wasted.
For there is such a little time that your youth will last—such
a little time. The common hill-flowers wither, but they blossom again. The laburnum will be as yellow next June as it is

now. In a month there will be purple stars on the clematis, and year after year the green night of its leaves will hold its purple stars. But we never get back our youth. The pulse of joy that beats in us at twenty, becomes sluggish. Our limbs fail, our senses rot. We degenerate into hideous puppets, haunted by the memory of the passions of which we were too much afraid, and the exquisite temptations that we had not the courage to yield to. Youth! Youth! There is absolutely nothing in the world but youth!"

Dorian Gray listened, open-eyed and wondering. The spray of lilac fell from his hand upon the gravel. A furry bee came and buzzed round it for a moment. Then it began to scramble all over the oval stellated globe of the tiny blossoms. He watched it with that strange interest in trivial things that we try to develop when things of high import make us afraid, or when we are stirred by some new emotion for which we cannot find expression, or when some thought that terrifies us lays sudden siege to the brain and calls on us to yield. After a time the bee flew away. He saw it creeping into the stained trumpet of a Tyrian convolvulus. The flower seemed to quiver, and then swayed gently to and fro.

Suddenly the painter appeared at the door of the studio, and made staccato signs for them to come in. They turned to each other, and smiled.

"I am waiting," he cried. "Do come in. The light is quite perfect, and you can bring your drinks."

They rose up, and sauntered down the walk together. Two green-and-white butterflies fluttered past them, and in the pear-tree at the corner of the garden a thrush began to sing.

"You are glad to have met me, Mr. Gray," said Lord Henry, looking at him.

"Yes, I am glad now. I wonder shall I always be glad?"

"Always! That is a dreadful word. It makes me shudder when I hear it. Women are so fond of using it. They spoil

every romance by trying to make it last forever. It is a meaningless word, too. The only difference between a caprice and
a life-long passion is that the caprice lasts a little longer."

As they entered the studio, Dorian Gray put his hand upon
Lord Henry's arm. "In that case, let our friendship be a
caprice," he murmured, flushing at his own boldness, then
stepped up on the platform and resumed his pose.

Lord Henry flung himself into a large wicker armchair,
and watched him. The sweep and dash of the brush on the
canvas made the only sound that broke the stillness, except
when, now and then, Hallward stepped back to look at his
work from a distance. In the slanting beams that streamed
through the open doorway the dust danced and was golden.
The heavy scent of the roses seemed to brood over everything.

After about a quarter of an hour Hallward stopped painting, looked for a long time at Dorian Gray, and then for
a long time at the picture, biting the end of one of his huge
brushes, and frowning. "It is quite finished," he cried at last,
and stooping down he wrote his name in long vermilion
letters on the left-hand corner of the canvas.

Lord Henry came over and examined the picture. It was
certainly a wonderful work of art, and a wonderful likeness
as well.

"My dear fellow, I congratulate you most warmly," he
said. "It is the finest portrait of modern times. Mr. Gray,
come over and look at yourself."

The lad started, as if awakened from some dream. "Is it
really finished?" he murmured, stepping down from the
platform.

"Quite finished," said the painter. "And you have sat splen-
didly to-day. I am awfully obliged to you."

"That is entirely due to me," broke in Lord Henry. "Isn't
it, Mr. Gray?"

Dorian made no answer, but passed listlessly in front of his picture, and turned towards it. When he saw it he drew back, and his cheeks flushed for a moment with pleasure. A look of joy came into his eyes, as if he had recognised himself for the first time. He stood there motionless and in wonder, dimly conscious that Hallward was speaking to him, but not catching the meaning of his words. The sense of his own beauty came on him like a revelation. He had never felt it before. Basil Hallward's compliments had seemed to him to be merely the charming exaggerations of friendship. He had listened to them, laughed at them, forgotten them. They had not influenced his nature. Then had come Lord Henry Wotton with his strange panegyric on youth, his terrible warning of its brevity. That had stirred him at the time, and now, as he stood gazing at the shadow of his own loveliness, the full reality of the description flashed across him. Yes, there would be a day when his face would be wrinkled and wizen, his eyes dim and colourless, the grace of his figure broken and deformed. The scarlet would pass away from his lips, and the gold steal from his hair. The life that was to make his soul would mar his body. He would become dreadful, hideous, and uncouth.

As he thought of it, a sharp pang of pain struck through him like a knife, and made each delicate fibre of his nature quiver. His eyes deepened into amethyst, and across them came a mist of tears. He felt as if a hand of ice had been laid on his heart.

"Don't you like it?" cried Hallward at last, stung a little by the lad's silence, not understanding what it meant.

"Of course he likes it," said Lord Henry. "Who wouldn't like it? It is one of the greatest things in modern art. I will give you anything you like to ask for it. I must have it."

"It is not my property, Harry."

"Whose property is it?"

"Dorian's, of course," answered the painter.

"He is a very lucky fellow."

"How sad it is!" murmured Dorian Gray, with his eyes still fixed upon his own portrait. "How sad it is! I shall grow old, and horrible, and dreadful. But this picture will remain always young. It will never be older than this particular day of June. . . . If it were only the other way! If it were I who was to be always young, and the picture that was to grow old! For that—for that—I would give everything! Yes, there is nothing in the whole world I would not give! I would give my soul for that!"

"You would hardly care for such an arrangement, Basil," cried Lord Henry, laughing. "It would be rather hard lines on your work."

"I should object very strongly, Harry," said Hallward.

Dorian Gray turned and looked at him. "I believe you would, Basil. You like your art better than your friends. I am no more to you than a green bronze figure. Hardly as much, I daresay."

The painter stared in amazement. It was so unlike Dorian to speak like that. What had happened? He seemed quite angry. His face was flushed and his cheeks burning.

"Yes," he continued, "I am less to you than your ivory Hermes or your silver Faun. You will like them always. How long will you like me? Till I have my first wrinkle, I suppose. I know, now, that when one loses one's good looks, whatever they may be, one loses everything. Your picture has taught me that. Lord Henry Wotton is perfectly right. Youth is the only thing worth having. When I find that I am grow- ing old, I shall kill myself."

Hallward turned pale, and caught his hand. "Dorian! Dorian!" he cried, "don't talk like that. I have never had such a friend as you, and I shall never have such another.

You are not jealous of material things, are you?—you who are finer than any of them!"

"I am jealous of everything whose beauty does not die. I am jealous of the portrait you have painted of me. Why should it keep what I must lose? Every moment that passes takes something from me, and gives something to it. Oh, if it were only the other way! If the picture could change, and I could be always what I am now! Why did you paint it? It will mock me some day—mock me horribly!" The hot tears welled into his eyes; he tore his hand away, and, flinging himself on the divan, he buried his face in the cushions, as though he was praying.

"This is your doing, Harry," said the painter, bitterly.

Lord Henry shrugged his shoulders. "It is the real Dorian Gray—that is all."

"It is not."

"If it is not, what have I to do with it?"

"You should have gone away when I asked you," he muttered.

"I stayed when you asked me," was Lord Henry's answer.

"Harry, I can't quarrel with my two best friends at once, but between you both you have made me hate the finest piece of work I have ever done, and I will destroy it. What is it but canvas and colour? I will not let it come across our three lives and mar them."

Dorian Gray lifted his golden head from the pillow, and with pallid face and tear-stained eyes looked at him, as he walked over to the deal painting-table that was set beneath the high curtained window. What was he doing there? His fingers were straying about among the litter of tin tubes and dry brushes, seeking for something. Yes, it was for the long palette-knife, with its thin blade of lithe steel. He had found it at last. He was going to rip up the canvas.

With a stifled sob the lad leaped from the couch, and,

rushing over to Hallward, tore the knife out of his hand, and flung it to the end of the studio. "Don't, Basil, don't!" he cried. "It would be murder!"

"I am glad you appreciate my work at last, Dorian," said the painter, coldly, when he had recovered from his surprise. "I never thought you would."

"Appreciate it? I am in love with it, Basil. It is part of myself. I feel that."

"Well, as soon as you are dry, you shall be varnished, and framed, and sent home. Then you can do what you like with yourself." And he walked across the room and rang the bell for tea. "You will have tea, of course, Dorian? And so will you, Harry? Or do you object to such simple pleasures?"

"I adore simple pleasures," said Lord Henry. "They are the last refuge of the complex. But I don't like scenes, except on the stage. What absurd fellows you are, both of you! I wonder who it was defined man as a rational animal. It was the most premature definition ever given. Man is many things, but he is not rational. I am glad he is not, after all: though I wish you chaps would not squabble over the picture. You had much better let me have it, Basil. This silly boy doesn't really want it, and I really do."

"If you let anyone have it but me, Basil, I shall never forgive you!" cried Dorian Gray; "and I don't allow people to call me a silly boy."

"You know the picture is yours, Dorian. I gave it to you before it existed."

"And you know you have been a little silly, Mr. Gray, and that you don't really object to being reminded that you are extremely young."

"I should have objected very strongly this morning, Lord Henry."

"Ah! this morning! You have lived since then."

There came a knock at the door, and the butler entered

with a laden tea-tray and set it down upon a small Japanese table. There was a rattle of cups and saucers and the hissing of a fluted Georgian urn. Two globe-shaped china dishes were brought in by a page. Dorian Gray went over and poured out the tea. The two men sauntered languidly to the table, and examined what was under the covers.

"Let us go to the theatre to-night," said Lord Henry. "There is sure to be something on, somewhere. I have promised to dine at White's, but it is only with an old friend, so I can send him a wire to say that I am ill, or that I am prevented from coming in consequence of a subsequent engagement. I think that would be a rather nice excuse: it would have all the surprise of candour."

"It is such a bore putting on one's dress-clothes," muttered Hallward. "And, when one has them on, they are so horrid."

"Yes," answered Lord Henry, dreamily, "the costume of the nineteenth century is detestable. It is so sombre, so depressing. Sin is the only real colour-element left in modern life."

"You really must not say things like that before Dorian, Harry."

"Before which Dorian? The one who is pouring out tea for us, or the one in the picture?"

"Before either."

"I should like to come to the theatre with you, Lord Henry," said the lad.

"Then you shall come; and you will come too, Basil, won't you?"

"I can't really. I would sooner not. I have a lot of work to do."

"Well, then, you and I will go alone, Mr. Gray."

"I should like that awfully."

The painter bit his lip and walked over, cup in hand, to the picture. "I shall stay with the real Dorian," he said, sadly.

"Is it the real Dorian?" cried the original of the portrait, strolling across to him. "Am I really like that?"

"Yes; you are just like that."

"How wonderful, Basil!"

"At least you are like it in appearance. But it will never alter," sighed Hallward. "That is something."

"What a fuss people make about fidelity!" exclaimed Lord Henry. "Why, even in love it is purely a question for physiology. It has nothing to do with our own will. Young men want to be faithful, and are not; old men want to be faithless, and cannot: that is all one can say."

"Don't go to the theatre to-night, Dorian," said Hallward. "Stop and dine with me."

"I can't, Basil."

"Why?"

"Because I have promised Lord Henry Wotton to go with him."

"He won't like you the better for keeping your promises. He always breaks his own. I beg you not to go."

Dorian Gray laughed and shook his head.

"I entreat you."

The lad hesitated, and looked over at Lord Henry, who was watching them from the tea-table with an amused smile.

"I must go, Basil," he answered.

"Very well," said Hallward; and he went over and laid down his cup on the tray. "It is rather late, and, as you have to dress, you had better lose no time. Good-bye, Harry. Good-bye, Dorian. Come and see me soon. Come to-morrow."

"Certainly."

"You won't forget?"

"No, of course not," cried Dorian.

"And . . . Harry!"

"Yes, Basil?"

"Remember what I asked you, when we were in the garden this morning"

"I have forgotten it."

"I trust you."

"I wish I could trust myself," said Lord Henry, laughing. "Come, Mr. Gray, my hansom is outside, and I can drop you at your own place. Good-bye, Basil. It has been a most interesting afternoon."

As the door closed behind them, the painter flung himself down on a sofa, and a look of pain came into his face.

"Remember that I asked you where you were in the
ernoon, and
"I have to once
I was
with people and more people there

CHAPTER III

AT half-past twelve next day Lord Henry Wotton strolled
from Curzon Street over to the Albany to call on his
uncle, Lord Fermor, a genial if somewhat rough-mannered
old bachelor, whom the outside world called selfish because
it derived no particular benefit from him, but who was considered generous by Society as he fed the people who amused
him. His father had been our ambassador at Madrid when
Isabella was young, and Prim unthought of, but had retired
from the Diplomatic Service in a capricious moment of annoyance at not being offered the Embassy at Paris, a post
to which he considered that he was fully entitled by reason
of his birth, his indolence, the good English of his despatches,
and his inordinate passion for pleasure. The son, who had
been his father's secretary, had resigned along with his chief,
somewhat foolishly as was thought at the time, and on suc-
ceeding some months later to the title, had set himself to the
serious study of the great aristocratic art of doing absolutely
nothing. He had two large town houses, but preferred to live
in chambers, as it was less trouble, and took most of his meals
at his club. He paid some attention to the management of his
collieries in the Midland counties, excusing himself for this
taint of industry on the ground that the one advantage of
having coal was that it enabled a gentleman to afford the
decency of burning wood on his own hearth. In politics he
was a Tory, except when the Tories were in office, during
which period he roundly abused them for being a pack of
Radicals. He was a hero to his valet, who bullied him, and a
terror to most of his relations, whom he bullied in turn.

Only England could have produced him, and he always said that the country was going to the dogs. His principles were out of date, but there was a good deal to be said for his prejudices.

When Lord Henry entered the room, he found his uncle sitting in a rough shooting coat, smoking a cheroot, and grumbling over "The Times." "Well, Harry," said the old gentleman, "what brings you out so early? I thought you dandies never got up till two, and were not visible till five."

"Pure family affection, I assure you, Uncle George. I want to get something out of you."

"Money, I suppose," said Lord Fermor, making a wry face. "Well, sit down and tell me all about it. Young people, nowadays, imagine that money is everything."

"Yes," murmured Lord Henry, settling his buttonhole in his coat; "and when they grow older they know it. But I don't want money. It is only people who pay their bills who want that, Uncle George, and I never pay mine. Credit is the capital of a younger son, and one lives charmingly upon it. Besides, I always deal with Dartmoor's tradesmen, and consequently they never bother me. What I want is information; not useful information, of course; useless information."

"Well, I can tell you anything that is in an English Blue-book, Harry, although those fellows nowadays write a lot of nonsense. When I was in the Diplomatic, things were much better. But I hear they let them in now by examination. What can you expect? Examinations, sir, are pure humbug from beginning to end. If a man is a gentleman, he knows quite enough, and if he is not a gentleman, whatever he knows is bad for him."

"Mr. Dorian Gray does not belong to Blue-books, Uncle George," said Lord Henry, languidly.

"Mr. Dorian Gray? Who is he?" asked Lord Fermor, knitting his bushy white eyebrows.

"That is what I have come to learn, Uncle George. Or rather, I know who he is. He is the last Lord Kelso's grandson. His mother was a Devereux; Lady Margaret Devereux. I want you to tell me about his mother. What was she like? Whom did she marry? You have known nearly everybody in your time, so you might have known her. I am very much interested in Mr. Gray at present. I have only just met him."

"Kelso's grandson!" echoed the old gentleman.—"Kelso's grandson! . . . Of course. . . . I knew his mother intimately. I believe I was at her christening. She was an extraordinarily beautiful girl, Margaret Devereux; and made all the men frantic by running away with a penniless young fellow; a mere nobody, sir, a subaltern in a foot regiment, or something of that kind. Certainly. I remember the whole thing as if it happened yesterday. The poor chap was killed in a duel at Spa, a few months after the marriage. There was an ugly story about it. They said Kelso got some rascally adventurer, some Belgian brute, to insult his son-in-law in public; paid him, sir, to do it, paid him; and that the fellow spitted his man as if he had been a pigeon. The thing was hushed up, but, egad, Kelso ate his chop alone at the club for some time afterwards. He brought his daughter back with him, I was told, and she never spoke to him again. Oh, yes; it was a bad business. The girl died too; died within a year. So she left a son, did she? I had forgotten that. What sort of boy is he? If he is like his mother he must be a good-looking chap."

"He is very good-looking," assented Lord Henry.

"I hope he will fall into proper hands," continued the old man. "He should have a pot of money waiting for him if Kelso did the right thing by him. His mother had money too. All the Selby property came to her, through her grandfather. Her grandfather hated Kelso, thought him a mean dog. He was, too. Came to Madrid once when I was there. Egad, I was ashamed of him. The Queen used to ask me about the English noble who was always quarrelling with the cabmen about their fares. They made quite a story of it. I didn't dare to show my face at Court for a month. I hope he treated his grandson better than he did the jarvies."

"I don't know," answered Lord Henry. "I fancy that the boy will be well off. He is not of age yet. He has Selby, I know. He told me so. And . . . his mother was very beautiful?"

"Margaret Devereux was one of the loveliest creatures I ever saw, Harry. What on earth induced her to behave as she did, I never could understand. She could have married anybody she chose. Carlington was mad after her. She was romantic, though. All the women of that family were. The men were a poor lot, but, egad! the women were wonderful Carlington went on his knees to her. Told me so himself. She laughed at him, and there wasn't a girl in London at the time who wasn't after him. And by the way, Harry, talking about silly marriages, what is this humbug your father tells me about Dartmoor wanting to marry an American? Ain't English girls good enough for him?"

"It is rather fashionable to marry Americans just now, Uncle George."

"I'll back English women against the world, Harry," said Lord Fermor, striking the table with his fist.

"The betting is on the Americans."

"They don't last, I am told," muttered his uncle.

"A long engagement exhausts them, but they are capital at a steeplechase. They take things flying. I don't think Dartmoor has a chance."

"Who are her people?" grumbled the old gentleman. "Has she got any?"

Lord Henry shook his head. "American girls are as clever at concealing their parents as English women are at concealing their past," he said, rising to go.

"They are pork-packers, I suppose?"

"I hope so, Uncle George, for Dartmoor's sake. I am told that pork-packing is the most lucrative profession in America, after politics."

"Is she pretty?"

"She behaves as if she was beautiful. Most American women do. It is the secret of their charm."

"Why can't these American women stay in their own country? They are always telling us that it is the Paradise for women."

"It is. That is the reason why, like Eve, they are so excessively anxious to get out of it," said Lord Henry. "Goodbye, Uncle George. I shall be late for lunch, if I stop any longer. Thanks for giving me the information I wanted. I always like to know everything about my new friends, and nothing about my old ones."

"Where are you lunching, Harry?"

"At Aunt Agatha's. I have asked myself and Mr. Gray. He is her latest *protégé.*"

"Humph! tell your Aunt Agatha, Harry, not to bother me any more with her charity appeals. I am sick of them. Why, the good woman thinks that I have nothing to do but to write cheques for her silly fads."

"All right, Uncle George, I'll tell her, but it won't have any effect. Philanthropic people lose all sense of humanity. It is their distinguishing characteristic."

The old gentleman growled approvingly, and rang the bell for his servant. Lord Henry passed up the low arcade into Burlington Street, and turned his steps in the direction of Berkeley Square.

So that was the story of Dorian Gray's parentage. Crudely

as it had been told to him, it had yet stirred him by its suggestion of a strange, almost modern romance. A beautiful
woman risking everything for a mad passion. A few wild
weeks of happiness cut short by a hideous, treacherous crime.
Months of voiceless agony, and then a child born in pain.
The mother snatched away by death, the boy left to solitude and the tyranny of an old and loveless man. Yes; it was
an interesting background. It posed the lad, made him more
perfect as it were. Behind every exquisite thing that existed,
there was something tragic. Worlds had to be in travail,
that the meanest flower might blow. . . . And how charming he had been at dinner the night before, as, with startled
eyes and lips parted in frightened pleasure, he had sat opposite to him at the club, the red candle-shades staining to a
richer rose the wakening wonder of his face. Talking to him
was like playing upon an exquisite violin. He answered to
every touch and thrill of the bow. . . . There was something terribly enthralling in the exercise of influence. No
other activity was like it. To project one's soul into some
gracious form, and let it tarry there for a moment; to hear
one's own intellectual views echoed back to one with all the
added music of passion and youth; to convey one's temperament into another as though it were a subtle fluid or a
strange perfume; there was a real joy in that—perhaps the
most satisfying joy left to us in an age so limited and vulgar
as our own, an age grossly carnal in its pleasures, and grossly
common in its aims. . . . He was a marvellous type, too,
this lad, whom by so curious a chance he had met in Basil's
studio; or could be fashioned into a marvellous type, at any
rate. Grace was his, and the white purity of boyhood, and
beauty such as old Greek marbles kept for us. There was
nothing that one could not do with him. He could be made
a Titan or a toy. What a pity it was that such beauty was
destined to fade! . . . And Basil? From a psychological

point of view, how interesting he was! The new manner in art, the fresh mode of looking at life, suggested so strangely by the merely visible presence of one who was unconscious of it all; the silent spirit that dwelt in dim woodland, and walked unseen in an open field, suddenly showing herself, Dryad-like and not afraid, because in his soul who sought for her there had been wakened that wonderful vision to which alone are wonderful things revealed; the mere shapes and patterns of things becoming, as it were, refined, and gaining a kind of symbolical value, as though they were themselves patterns of some other and more perfect form whose shadow they made real: how strange it all was! He remembered something like it in history. Was it not Plato, that artist in thought, who had first analysed it? Was it not Buonarotti who had carved it in the coloured marbles of a sonnet-sequence? But in our own century it was strange. . . . Yes; he would try to be to Dorian Gray what, without knowing it, the lad was to the painter who had fashioned the wonderful portrait. He would seek to dominate him— had already, indeed, half done so. He would make that wonderful spirit his own. There was something fascinating in this son of Love and Death.

Suddenly he stopped, and glanced up at the houses. He found that he had passed his aunt's some distance, and, smiling to himself, turned back. When he entered the somewhat sombre hall the butler told him that they had gone in to lunch. He gave one of the footmen his hat and stick, and passed into the dining-room.

"Late as usual, Harry," cried his aunt, shaking her head at him.

He invented a facile excuse, and having taken the vacant seat next to her, looked round to see who was there. Dorian bowed to him shyly from the end of the table, a flush of pleasure stealing into his cheek. Opposite was the Duchess of

Harley; a lady of admirable good-nature and good temper, much liked by everyone who knew her, and of those ample architectural proportions that in women who are not Duchesses are described by contemporary historians as stoutness. Next to her sat, on her right, Sir Thomas Burdon, a Radical member of Parliament, who followed his leader in public life, and in private life followed the best cooks, dining with the Tories, and thinking with the Liberals, in accordance with a wise and well-known rule. The post on her left was occupied by Mr. Erskine of Treadley, an old gentleman of considerable charm and culture, who had fallen, however, into bad habits of silence, having, as he explained once to Lady Agatha, said everything that he had to say before he was thirty. His own neighbour was Mrs. Vandeleur, one of his aunt's oldest friends, a perfect saint amongst women, but so dreadfully dowdy that she reminded one of a badly bound hymn-book. Fortunately for him she had on the other side Lord Faudel, a most intelligent middle-aged mediocrity, as bald as a Ministerial statement in the House of Commons, with whom she was conversing in that intensely earnest manner which is the one unpardonable error, as he remarked once himself, that all really good people fall into, and from which none of them ever quite escape.

"We are talking about poor Dartmoor, Lord Henry," cried the Duchess, nodding pleasantly to him across the table. "Do you think he will really marry this fascinating young person?"

"I believe she has made up her mind to propose to him, Duchess."

"How dreadful!" exclaimed Lady Agatha. "Really, some one should interfere."

"I am told, on excellent authority, that her father keeps an American dry-goods store," said Sir Thomas Burdon, looking supercilious.

"My uncle has already suggested pork-packing, Sir Thomas."

"Dry-goods! What are American dry-goods?" asked the Duchess, raising her large hands in wonder, and accentuating the verb.

"American novels," answered Lord Henry, helping himself to some quail.

The Duchess looked puzzled.

"Don't mind him, my dear," whispered Lady Agatha. "He never means anything that he says."

"When America was discovered," said the Radical member, and he began to give some wearisome facts. Like all people who try to exhaust a subject, he exhausted his listeners. The Duchess sighed, and exercised her privilege of interruption. "I wish to goodness it never had been discovered at all!" she exclaimed. "Really, our girls have no chance nowadays. It is most unfair."

"Perhaps, after all, America never has been discovered," said Mr. Erskine. "I myself would say that it had merely been detected."

"Oh! but I have seen specimens of the inhabitants," answered the Duchess, vaguely. "I must confess that most of them are extremely pretty. And they dress well, too. They get all their dresses in Paris. I wish I could afford to do the same."

"They say that when good Americans die they go to Paris," chuckled Sir Thomas, who had a large wardrobe of Humour's cast-off clothes.

"Really! And where do bad Americans go to when they die?" inquired the Duchess.

"They go to America," murmured Lord Henry. Sir Thomas frowned. "I am afraid that your nephew is prejudiced against that great country," he said to Lady Agatha. "I have travelled all over it, in cars provided by the directors, who, in such matters, are extremely civil. I assure you that it is an education to visit it."

"But must we really see Chicago in order to be educated?" asked Mr. Erskine, plaintively. "I don't feel up to the journey."

Sir Thomas waved his hand. "Mr. Erskine of Treadley has the world on his shelves. We practical men like to see things, not to read about them. The Americans are an extremely interesting people. They are absolutely reasonable. I think that is their distinguishing characteristic. Yes, Mr. Erskine, an absolutely reasonable people. I assure you there is no nonsense about the Americans."

"How dreadful!" cried Lord Henry. "I can stand brute force, but brute reason is quite unbearable. There is something unfair about its use. It is hitting below the intellect."

"I do not understand you," said Sir Thomas, growing rather red.

"I do, Lord Henry," murmured Mr. Erskine, with a smile.

"Paradoxes are all very well in their way. . . ." rejoined the Baronet.

"Was that a paradox?" asked Mr. Erskine. "I did not think so. Perhaps it was. Well, the way of paradoxes is the way of truth. To test Reality we must see it on the tight-rope. When the Verities become acrobats we can judge them."

"Dear me!" said Lady Agatha, "how you men argue! I am sure I never can make out what you are talking about. Oh! Harry, I am quite vexed with you. Why do you try to persuade our nice Mr. Dorian Gray to give up the East End? I assure you he would be quite invaluable. They would love his playing."

"I want him to play to me," cried Lord Henry, smiling, and he looked down the table and caught a bright answering glance.

"But they are so unhappy in Whitechapel," continued Lady Agatha.

"I can sympathise with everything, except suffering," said Lord Henry, shrugging his shoulders. "I cannot sympathise with that. It is too ugly, too horrible, too distressing. There is something terribly morbid in the modern sympathy with pain. One should sympathise with the colour, the beauty, the joy of life. The less said about life's sores the better."

"Still, the East End is a very important problem," remarked Sir Thomas, with a grave shake of the head.

"Quite so," answered the young lord. "It is the problem of slavery, and we try to solve it by amusing the slaves."

The politician looked at him keenly. "What change do you propose, then?" he asked.

Lord Henry laughed. "I don't desire to change anything in England except the weather," he answered. "I am quite content with philosophic contemplation. But, as the nineteenth century has gone bankrupt through an over-expenditure of sympathy, I would suggest that we should appeal to Science to put us straight. The advantage of the emotions is that they lead us astray, and the advantage of Science is that it is not emotional."

"But we have such grave responsibilities," ventured Mrs. Vandeleur, timidly.

"Terribly grave," echoed Lady Agatha.

Lord Henry looked over at Mr. Erskine. "Humanity takes itself too seriously. It is the world's original sin. If the caveman had known how to laugh, History would have been different."

"You are really very comforting," warbled the Duchess. "I have always felt rather guilty when I came to see your dear aunt, for I take no interest at all in the East End. For the future I shall be able to look her in the face without a blush."

"A blush is very becoming, Duchess," remarked Lord Henry.

"Only when one is young," she answered. "When an old woman like myself blushes, it is a very bad sign. Ah! Lord Henry, I wish you would tell me how to become young again."

He thought for a moment. "Can you remember any great error that you committed in your early days, Duchess?" he asked, looking at her across the table.

"A great many, I fear," she cried.

"Then commit them over again," he said, gravely. "To get back one's youth, one has merely to repeat one's follies."

"A delightful theory!" she exclaimed. "I must put it into practice."

"A dangerous theory!" came from Sir Thomas's tight lips. Lady Agatha shook her head, but could not help being amused. Mr. Erskine listened.

"Yes," he continued, "that is one of the great secrets of life. Nowadays most people die of a sort of creeping common sense, and discover when it is too late that the only things one never regrets are one's mistakes."

A laugh ran round the table.

He played with the idea, and grew willful; tossed it into the air and transformed it; let it escape and recaptured it; made it iridescent with fancy, and winged it with paradox. The praise of folly, as he went on, soared into a philosophy, and Philosophy herself became young, and catching the mad music of Pleasure, wearing, one might fancy, her wine-stained robe and wreath of ivy, danced like a Bacchante over the hills of life, and mocked the slow Silenus for being sober. Facts fled before her like frightened forest things. Her white feet trod the huge press at which wise Omar sits, till the seething grape-juice rose round her bare limbs in waves of purple bubbles, or crawled in red foam over the vat's black.

dripping, sloping sides. It was an extraordinary improvisation. He felt that the eyes of Dorian Gray were fixed on him, and the consciousness that amongst his audience there was one whose temperament he wished to fascinate, seemed to give his wit keenness, and to lend colour to his imagination. He was brilliant, fantastic, irresponsible. He charmed his listeners out of themselves, and they followed his pipe laughing. Dorian Gray never took his gaze off him, but sat like one under a spell, smiles chasing each other over his lips, and wonder growing grave in his darkening eyes.

At last, liveried in the costume of the age, Reality entered the room in the shape of a servant to tell the Duchess that her carriage was waiting. She wrung her hands in mock despair. "How annoying!" she cried. "I must go. I have to call for my husband at the club, to take him to some absurd meeting at Willis's Rooms, where he is going to be in the chair. If I am late, he is sure to be furious, and I couldn't have a scene in this bonnet. It is far too fragile. A harsh word would ruin it. No, I must go, dear Agatha. Good-bye, Lord Henry, you are quite delightful, and dreadfully demoralising. I am sure I don't know what to say about your views. You must come and dine with us some night. Tuesday? Are you disengaged Tuesday?"

"For you I would throw over anybody, Duchess," said Lord Henry, with a bow.

"Ah! that is very nice, and very wrong of you," she cried; "so mind you come;" and she swept out of the room, followed by Lady Agatha and the other ladies.

When Lord Henry had sat down again, Mr. Erskine moved round, and taking a chair close to him, placed his hand upon his arm.

"You talk books away," he said; "why don't you write one?"

"I am too fond of reading books to care to write them, Mr.

Erskine. I should like to write a novel certainly; a novel that would be as lovely as a Persian carpet, and as unreal. But there is no literary public in England for anything except newspapers, primers, and encyclopædias. Of all people in the world the English have the least sense of the beauty of literature."

"I fear you are right," answered Mr. Erskine. "I myself used to have literary ambitions, but I gave them up long ago. And now, my dear young friend, if you will allow me to call you so, may I ask if you really meant all that you said to us at lunch?"

"I quite forget what I said," smiled Lord Henry. "Was it all very bad?"

"Very bad indeed. In fact I consider you extremely dangerous, and if anything happens to our good Duchess we shall all look on you as being primarily responsible. But I should like to talk to you about life. The generation into which I was born was tedious. Some day, when you are tired of London, come down to Treadley, and expound to me your philosophy of pleasure over some admirable Burgundy I am fortunate enough to possess."

"I shall be charmed. A visit to Treadley would be a great privilege. It has a perfect host, and a perfect library."

"You will complete it," answered the old gentleman, with a courteous bow. "And now I must bid good-bye to your excellent aunt. I am due at the Athenæum. It is the hour when we sleep there."

"All of you, Mr. Erskine?"

"Forty of us, in forty arm-chairs. We are practising for an English Academy of Letters."

Lord Henry laughed, and rose. "I am going to the Park,' he cried.

As he was passing out of the door Dorian Gray touched him on the arm. "Let me come with you," he murmured.

"But I thought you had promised Basil Hallward to go and see him," answered Lord Henry.

"I would sooner come with you; yes, I feel I must come with you. Do let me. And you will promise to talk to me all the time? No one talks so wonderfully as you do."

"Ah! I have talked quite enough for to-day," said Lord Henry, smiling. "All I want now is to look at life. You may come and look at it with me, if you care to."

CHAPTER IV

ONE afternoon, a month later, Dorian Gray was reclining in a luxurious arm-chair, in the little library of Lord Henry's house in Mayfair. It was, in its way, a very charming room, with its high-panelled wainscoting of olive-stained oak, its cream-coloured frieze and ceiling of raised plaster-work, and its brick-dust felt carpet strewn with silk long-fringed Persian rugs. On a tiny satinwood table stood a statuette by Clodion, and beside it lay a copy of "Les Cent Nouvelles," bound for Margaret of Valois by Clovis Eve, and powdered with the gilt daisies that Queen had selected for her device. Some large blue china jars and parrot-tulips were ranged on the mantelshelf, and through the small leaded panels of the window streamed the apricot-coloured light of a summer day in London.

Lord Henry had not yet come in. He was always late on principle, his principle being that punctuality is the thief of time. So the lad was looking rather sulky, as with listless fingers he turned over the pages of an elaborately-illustrated edition of "Manon Lescaut," that he had found in one of the bookcases. The formal monotonous ticking of the Louis Quatorze clock annoyed him. Once or twice he thought of going away.

At last he heard a step outside, and the door opened. "How late you are, Harry!" he murmured.

"I am afraid it is not Harry, Mr. Gray," answered a shrill voice.

He glanced quickly round, and rose to his feet. "I beg your pardon. I thought——"

"You thought it was my husband. It is only his wife. You must let me introduce myself. I know you quite well by your photographs. I think my husband has got seventeen of them."

"Not seventeen, Lady Henry?"

"Well, eighteen, then. And I saw you with him the other night at the Opera." She laughed nervously as she spoke, and watched him with her vague forget-me-not eyes. She was a curious woman, whose dresses always looked as if they had been designed in a rage and put on in a tempest. She was usually in love with somebody, and, as her passion was never returned, she had kept all her illusions. She tried to look picturesque, but only succeeded in being untidy. Her name was Victoria, and she had a perfect mania for going to church.

"That was at 'Lohengrin,' Lady Henry, I think?"

"Yes; it was at dear 'Lohengrin.' I like Wagner's music better than anybody's. It is so loud that one can talk the whole time without other people hearing what one says. That is a great advantage: don't you think so, Mr. Gray?"

The same nervous staccato laugh broke from her thin lips, and her fingers began to play with a long tortoise-shell paper-knife.

Dorian smiled, and shook his head: "I am afraid I don't think so, Lady Henry. I never talk during music, at least, during good music. If one hears bad music, it is one's duty to drown it in conversation."

"Ah! that is one of Harry's views, isn't it, Mr. Gray? I always hear Harry's views from his friends. It is the only way I get to know of them. But you must not think I don't like good music. I adore it, but I am afraid of it. It makes me too romantic. I have simply worshipped pianists—two at a time, sometimes, Harry tells me. I don't know what it is about them. Perhaps it is that they are foreigners. They all are, ain't they? Even those that are born in England become foreigners after a time, don't they? It is so clever of them, and such a compliment to art. Makes it quite cosmo-politan, doesn't it? You have never been to any of my parties, have you, Mr. Gray? You must come. I can't afford orchids, but I spare no expense in foreigners. They make one's rooms look so picturesque. But here is Harry!—Harry, I came in to look for you, to ask you something—I forget what it was—and I found Mr. Gray here. We have had such a pleasant chat about music. We have quite the same ideas. No; I think our ideas are quite different. But he has been most pleasant. I am so glad I've seen him."

"I am charmed, my love, quite charmed," said Lord Henry, elevating his dark crescent-shaped eyebrows and looking at them both with an amused smile. "So sorry I am late, Dorian. I went to look after a piece of old brocade in Wardour Street, and had to bargain for hours for it. Nowadays people know the price of everything, and the value of nothing."

"I am afraid I must be going," exclaimed Lady Henry, breaking an awkward silence with her silly sudden laugh. "I have promised to drive with the Duchess. Good-bye, Mr. Gray. Good-bye, Harry. You are dining out, I suppose? So am I. Perhaps I shall see you at Lady Thornbury's."

"I daresay, my dear," said Lord Henry, shutting the door behind her, as, looking like a bird of paradise that had been out all night in the rain, she flitted out of the room, leaving a faint odour of frangipanni. Then he lit a cigarette, and flung himself down on the sofa.

"Never marry a woman with straw-coloured hair, Dorian," he said, after a few puffs.

"Why, Harry?"

"Because they are so sentimental."

"But I like sentimental people."

"Never marry at all, Dorian. Men marry because they are tired; women, because they are curious; both are disappointed."

"I don't think I am likely to marry, Henry. I am too much in love. That is one of your aphorisms. I am putting it into practice, as I do everything that you say."

"Who are you in love with?" asked Lord Henry, after a pause.

"With an actress," said Dorian Gray, blushing.

Lord Henry shrugged his shoulders. "That is a rather commonplace *début*."

"You would not say so if you saw her, Harry."

"Who is she?"

"Her name is Sibyl Vane."

"Never heard of her."

"No one has. People will some day, however. She is a genius."

"My dear boy, no woman is a genius. Women are a decorative sex. They never have anything to say, but they say it charmingly. Women represent the triumph of matter over mind, just as men represent the triumph of mind over morals."

"Harry, how can you?"

"My dear Dorian, it is quite true. I am analysing women at the present, so I ought to know. The subject is not so abstruse as I thought it was. I find that, ultimately, there are only two kinds of women, the plain and the coloured. The plain women are very useful. If you want to gain a reputation for respectability, you have merely to take them down to supper. The other women are very charming. They commit one mistake, however. They paint in order to try and look young. Our grandmothers painted in order to try and talk brilliantly. *Rouge* and *esprit* used to go together. That is all over now. As long as a woman can look ten years younger than her own daughter, she is perfectly satisfied. As for conversation, there are only five women in London worth talking to, and two of these can't be admitted into decent society. However, tell me about your genius. How long have you known her?"

"Ah! Harry, your views terrify me."

"Never mind that. How long have you known her?"

"About three weeks."

"And where did you come across her?"

"I will tell you, Harry; but you mustn't be unsympathetic about it. After all, it never would have happened if I had not met you. You filled me with a wild desire to know everything about life. For days after I met you, something seemed to throb in my veins. As I lounged in the Park, or strolled down Piccadilly, I used to look at every one who passed me, and wonder, with a mad curiosity, what sort of lives they led. Some of them fascinated me. Others filled me with terror. There was an exquisite poison in the air. I had a passion for sensations. . . . Well, one evening about seven o'clock, I determined to go out in search of some adventure. I felt that this grey, monstrous London of ours, with its myriads of people, its sordid sinners, and its splendid sins, as you once phrased it, must have something in store for me. I fancied a thousand things. The mere danger gave me a sense of delight. I remembered what you had said to me on that wonderful evening when we first dined together, about the search for beauty being the real secret of life. I don't know what I expected, but I went out and wandered eastward, soon losing my way in a labyrinth of grimy streets and black, grassless squares. About half-past eight I passed by an absurd little theatre, with great flaring gas-jets and gaudy play-bills. A hideous Jew, in the most amazing waistcoat I ever beheld in my life, was standing at the entrance, smoking a vile cigar. He had greasy ringlets, and an enormous diamond blazed in the centre of a soiled shirt. 'Have a box, my Lord?' he said, when he saw me, and he took off his hat with an air of gorgeous servility. There

was something about him, Harry, that amused me. He was
such a monster. You will laugh at me, I know, but I really
went in and paid a whole guinea for the stage-box. To the
present day I can't make out why I did so; and yet if I
hadn't—my dear Harry, if I hadn't, I should have missed
the greatest romance of my life. I see you are laughing. It
is horrid of you!"

"I am not laughing, Dorian; at least I am not laughing at
you. But you should not say the greatest romance of your
life. You should say the first romance of your life. You will
always be loved, and you will always be in love with love.
A *grande passion* is the privilege of people who have nothing
to do. That is the one use of the idle classes of a country.
Don't be afraid. There are exquisite things in store for you.
This is merely the beginning."

"Do you think my nature so shallow?" cried Dorian Gray,
angrily.

"No; I think your nature so deep."

"How do you mean?"

"My dear boy, the people who love only once in their lives
are really the shallow people. What they call their loyalty,
and their fidelity, I call either the lethargy of custom or their
lack of imagination. Faithfulness is to the emotional life
what consistency is to the life of the intellect—simply a confession of failures. Faithfulness! I must analyse it some day.
The passion for property is in it. There are many things that
we would throw away if we were not afraid that others
might pick them up. But I don't want to interrupt you. Go
on with your story."

"Well, I found myself seated in a horrid little private
box, with a vulgar drop-scene staring me in the face. I
looked out from behind the curtain, and surveyed the house.
It was a tawdry affair, all Cupids and cornucopias, like a
third-rate wedding cake. The gallery and pit were fairly

full, but the two rows of dingy stalls were quite empty, and there was hardly a person in what I suppose they called the dress-circle. Women went about with oranges and ginger-beer, and there was a terrible consumption of nuts going on."

"It must have been just like the palmy days of the British Drama."

"Just like, I should fancy, and very depressing. I began to wonder what on earth I should do, when I caught sight of the play-bill. What do you think the play was, Harry?"

"I should think, 'The Idiot Boy, or Dumb but Innocent.' Our fathers used to like that sort of piece, I believe. The longer I live, Dorian, the more keenly I feel that whatever was good enough for our fathers is not good enough for us. In art, as in politics, *les grandpères ont toujours tort.*"

"This play was good enough for us, Harry. It was 'Romeo and Juliet.' I must admit that I was rather annoyed at the idea of seeing Shakespeare done in such a wretched hole of a place. Still, I felt interested, in a sort of way. At any rate, I determined to wait for the first act. There was a dreadful orchestra, presided over by a young Hebrew who sat at a cracked piano, that nearly drove me away, but at last the drop-scene was drawn up, and the play began. Romeo was a stout elderly gentleman, with corked eyebrows, a husky tragedy voice, and a figure like a beer-barrel. Mercutio was almost as bad. He was played by the low-comedian, who had introduced gags of his own and was on most friendly terms with the pit. They were both as grotesque as the scenery, and that looked as if it had come out of a country-booth. But Juliet! Harry, imagine a girl, hardly seventeen years of age, with a little flower-like face, a small Greek head with plaited coils of dark-brown hair, eyes that were violet wells of passion, lips that were like the petals of a rose. She was the loveliest thing I had ever seen in my life. You said to me once that pathos left you unmoved, but that beauty, mere beauty, could fill your eyes with tears. I tell you, Harry, I could hardly see this girl for the mist of tears that came across me. And her voice—I never heard such a voice. It was very low at first, with deep mellow notes, that seemed to fall singly upon one's ear. Then it became a little louder, and sounded like a flute or a distant hautbois. In the garden-scene it had all the tremulous ecstasy that one hears just before dawn when nightingales are singing. There were moments, later on, when it had the wild passion of violins. You know how a voice can stir one. Your voice and the voice of Sibyl Vane are two things that I shall never forget. When I close my eyes, I hear them, and each of them says something different. I don't know which to follow. Why should I not love her? Harry, I do love her. She is everything to me in life. Night after night I go to see her play. One evening she is Rosalind, and the next evening she is Imogen. I have seen her die in the gloom of an Italian tomb, sucking the poison from her lover's lips. I have watched her wandering through the forest of Arden, disguised as a pretty boy in hose and doublet and dainty cap. She has been mad, and has come into the presence of a guilty king, and given him rue to wear, and bitter herbs to taste of. She has been innocent, and the black hands of jealousy have crushed her reed-like throat. I have seen her in every age and in every costume. Ordinary women never appeal to one's imagination. They are limited to their century. No glamour ever transfigures them. One knows their minds as easily as one knows their bonnets. One can always find them. There is no mystery in any of them. They ride in the Park in the morning, and chatter at tea-parties in the afternoon. They have their stereotyped smile, and their fashionable manner. They are quite obvious. But an actress! How different an actress is! Harry! why didn't you tell me that the only thing worth loving is an actress?"

"Because I have loved so many of them, Dorian."

"Oh, yes, horrid people with dyed hair and painted faces."

"Don't run down dyed hair and painted faces. There is an extraordinary charm in them, sometimes," said Lord Henry.

"I wish now I had not told you about Sibyl Vane."

"You could not have helped telling me, Dorian. All through your life you will tell me everything you do."

"Yes, Harry, I believe that is true. I cannot help telling you things. You have a curious influence over me. If I ever did a crime, I would come and confess it to you. You would understand me."

"People like you—the willful sunbeams of life—don't commit crimes, Dorian. But I am much obliged for the compliment, all the same. And now tell me—reach me the matches, like a good boy: thanks—what are your actual relations with Sibyl Vane?"

Dorian Gray leaped to his feet, with flushed cheeks and burning eyes. "Harry! Sibyl Vane is sacred!"

"It is only the sacred things that are worth touching, Dorian," said Lord Henry, with a strange touch of pathos in his voice. "But why should you be annoyed? I suppose she will belong to you some day. When one is in love, one always begins by deceiving one's self, and one always ends by deceiving others. That is what the world calls a romance. You know her, at any rate, I suppose?"

"Of course I know her. On the first night I was at the theatre, the horrid old Jew came round to the box after the performance was over, and offered to take me behind the scenes and introduce me to her. I was furious with him, and told him that Juliet had been dead for hundreds of years, and that her body was lying in a marble tomb in Verona. I think, from his blank look of amazement, that he was under the impression that I had taken too much champagne, or something."

"I am not surprised."

"Then he asked me if I wrote for any of the newspapers. I told him I never even read them. He seemed terribly disappointed at that, and confided to me that all the dramatic critics were in a conspiracy against him, and that they were every one of them to be bought."

"I should not wonder if he was quite right there. But, on the other hand, judging from their appearance, most of them cannot be at all expensive."

"Well, he seemed to think they were beyond his means," laughed Dorian. "By this time, however, the lights were being put out in the theatre, and I had to go. He wanted me to try some cigars that he strongly recommended. I declined. The next night, of course, I arrived at the place again. When he saw me he made me a low bow, and assured me that I was a munificent patron of art. He was a most offensive brute, though he had an extraordinary passion for Shakespeare. He told me once with an air of pride, that his five bankruptcies were entirely due to 'The Bard,' as he insisted on calling him. He seemed to think it a distinction."

"It was a distinction, my dear Dorian—a great distinction. Most people become bankrupt through having invested too heavily in the prose of life. To have ruined one's self over poetry is an honour. But when did you first speak to Miss Sibyl Vane?"

"The third night. She had been playing Rosalind. I could not help going round. I had thrown her some flowers, and she had looked at me; at least I fancied that she had. The old Jew was persistent. He seemed determined to take me behind, so I consented. It was curious my not wanting to know her, wasn't it?"

"No; I don't think so."

"My dear Harry, why?"

"I will tell you some other time. Now I want to know about the girl."

"Sibyl? Oh, she was so shy, and so gentle. There is something of a child about her. Her eyes opened wide in exquisite wonder when I told her what I thought of her performance, and she seemed quite unconscious of her power. I think we were both rather nervous. The old Jew stood grinning at the doorway of the dusty greenroom, making elaborate speeches about us both, while we stood looking at each other like children. He would insist on calling me 'My Lord,' so I had to assure Sibyl that I was not anything of the kind. She said quite simply to me, 'You look more like a prince. I must call you Prince Charming.'"

"Upon my word, Dorian, Miss Sibyl knows how to pay compliments."

"You don't understand her, Harry. She regarded me merely as a person in a play. She knows nothing of life. She lives with her mother, a faded tired woman who played Lady Capulet in a sort of magenta dressing-wrapper on the first night, and looks as if she had seen better days."

"I know that look. It depresses me," murmured Lord Henry, examining his rings.

"The Jew wanted to tell me her history, but I said it did not interest me."

"You were quite right. There is always something infinitely mean about other people's tragedies."

"Sibyl is the only thing I care about. What is it to me where she came from? From her little head to her little feet, she is absolutely and entirely divine. Every night of my life I go to see her act, and every night she is more marvellous."

"That is the reason, I suppose, that you never dine with me now. I thought you must have some curious romance on hand. You have; but it is not quite what I expected."

"My dear Harry, we either lunch or sup together every

day, and I have been to the Opera with you several times," said Dorian, opening his blue eyes in wonder.

"You always come dreadfully late."

"Well, I can't help going to see Sibyl play," he cried, "even if it is only for a single act. I get hungry for her presence; and when I think of the wonderful soul that is hidden away in that little ivory body, I am filled with awe."

"You can dine with me to-night, Dorian, can't you?"

He shook his head. "To-night she is Imogen," he answered, "and to-morrow night she will be Juliet."

"When is she Sibyl Vane?"

"Never."

"I congratulate you."

"How horrid you are! She is all the great heroines of the world in one. She is more than an individual. You laugh, but I tell you she has genius. I love her and I must make her love me. You, who know all the secrets of life, tell me how to charm Sibyl Vane to love me! I want to make Romeo jealous. I want the dead lovers of the world to hear our laughter, and grow sad. I want a breath of our passion to stir their dust into consciousness, to wake their ashes into pain. My God, Harry, how I worship her!" He was walking up and down the room as he spoke. Hectic spots of red burned on his cheeks. He was terribly excited.

Lord Henry watched him with a subtle sense of pleasure. How different he was now from the shy, frightened boy he had met in Basil Hallward's studio! His nature had developed like a flower, had borne blossoms of scarlet flame. Out of its secret hiding-place had crept his Soul, and Desire had come to meet it on the way.

"And what do you propose to do?" said Lord Henry, at last.

"I want you and Basil to come with me some night and see her act. I have not the slightest fear of the result. You are certain to acknowledge her genius. Then we must get her out of the Jew's hands. She is bound to him for three years—at least for two years and eight months—from the present time. I shall have to pay him something, of course. When all that is settled, I shall take a West End theatre and bring her out properly. She will make the world as mad as she has made me."

"That would be impossible, my dear boy."

"Yes, she will. She has not merely art, consummate art-instinct, in her, but she has personality also; and you have often told me that it is personalities, not principles, that move the age."

"Well, what night shall we go?"

"Let me see. To-day is Tuesday. Let us fix to-morrow. She plays Juliet to-morrow."

"All right. The Bristol at eight o'clock; and I will get Basil."

"Not eight, Harry, please. Half-past six. We must be there before the curtain rises. You must see her in the first act, where she meets Romeo."

"Half-past six! What an hour! It will be like having a meat-tea, or reading an English novel. It must be seven. No gentleman dines before seven. Shall you see Basil between this and then? Or shall I write to him?"

"Dear Basil! I have not laid eyes on him for a week. It is rather horrid of me, as he has sent me my portrait in the most wonderful frame, specially designed by himself, and, though I am a little jealous of the picture for being a whole month younger than I am, I must admit that I delight in it. Perhaps you had better write to him. I don't want to see him alone. He says things that annoy me. He gives me good advice."

Lord Henry smiled. "People are very fond of giving away

what they need most themselves. It is what I call the depth of generosity."

"Oh, Basil is the best of fellows, but he seems to me to be just a bit of a Philistine. Since I have known you, Harry, I have discovered that."

"Basil, my dear boy, puts everything that is charming in him into his work. The consequence is that he has nothing left for life but his prejudices, his principles, and his common-sense. The only artists I have ever known, who are personally delightful, are bad artists. Good artists exist simply in what they make, and consequently are perfectly uninteresting in what they are. A great poet, a really great poet, is the most unpoetical of all creatures. But inferior poets are absolutely fascinating. The worse their rhymes are, the more picturesque they look. The mere fact of having published a book of second-rate sonnets makes a man quite irresistible. He lives the poetry that he cannot write. The others write the poetry that they dare not realise."

"I wonder is that really so, Harry?" said Dorian Gray, putting some perfume on his handkerchief out of a large gold-topped bottle that stood on the table. "It must be, if you say it. And now I am off. Imogen is waiting for me. Don't forget about to-morrow. Good-bye."

As he left the room, Lord Henry's heavy eyelids drooped, and he began to think. Certainly few people had ever interested him so much as Dorian Gray, and yet the lad's mad adoration of some one else caused him not the slightest pang of annoyance or jealousy. He was pleased by it. It made him a more interesting study. He had been always enthralled by the methods of natural science, but the ordinary subject-matter of that science had seemed to him trivial and of no import. And so he had begun by vivisecting himself, as he had ended by vivisecting others. Human life—that appeared to him the one thing worth investigating. Compared to it there was nothing else of any value. It was true that as one watched life in its curious crucible of pain and pleasure, one could not wear over one's face a mask of glass, nor keep the sulphurous fumes from troubling the brain, and making the imagination turbid with monstrous fancies and misshapen dreams. There were poisons so subtle that to know their properties one had to sicken of them. There were maladies so strange that one had to pass through them if one sought to understand their nature. And, yet, what a great reward one received! How wonderful the whole world became to one! To note the curious hard logic of passion, and the emotional coloured life of the intellect—to observe where they met, and where they separated, at what point they were in unison, and at what point they were at discord—there was a delight in that! What matter what the cost was? One could never pay too high a price for any sensation.

He was conscious—and the thought brought a gleam of pleasure into his brown agate eyes—that it was through certain words of his, musical words said with musical utterance, that Dorian Gray's soul had turned to this white girl and bowed in worship before her. To a large extent the lad was his own creation. He had made him premature. That was something. Ordinary people waited till life disclosed to them its secrets, but to the few, to the elect, the mysteries of life were revealed before the veil was drawn away. Sometimes this was the effect of art, and chiefly of the art of literature, which dealt immediately with the passions and the intellect. But now and then a complex personality took the place and assumed the office of art; was indeed, in its way, a real work of art, Life having its elaborate masterpieces, just as poetry has, or sculpture, or painting.

Yes, the lad was premature. He was gathering his harvest while it was yet spring. The pulse and passion of youth were in him, but he was becoming self-conscious. It was delightful to watch him. With his beautiful face, and his beautiful soul, he was a thing to wonder at. It was no matter how it all ended, or was destined to end. He was like one of those gracious figures in a pageant or a play, whose joys seem to be remote from one, but whose sorrows stir one's sense of beauty, and whose wounds are like red roses.

Soul and body, body and soul—how mysterious they were! There was animalism in the soul, and the body had its moments of spirituality. The senses could refine, and the intellect could degrade. Who could say where the fleshly impulse ceased, or the physical impulse began? How shallow were the arbitrary definitions of ordinary psychologists! And yet how difficult to decide between the claims of the various schools! Was the soul a shadow seated in the house of sin? Or was the body really in the soul, as Giordano Bruno thought? The separation of spirit from matter was a mystery, and the union of spirit with matter was a mystery also.

He began to wonder whether we could ever make psychology so absolute a science that each little spring of life would be revealed to us. As it was, we always misunderstood ourselves, and rarely understood others. Experience was of no ethical value. It was merely the name men gave to their mistakes. Moralists had, as a rule, regarded it as a mode of warning, had claimed for it a certain ethical efficacy in the formation of character, had praised it as something that taught us what to follow and showed us what to avoid. But there was no motive power in experience. It was as little of an active cause as conscience itself. All that it really demonstrated was that our future would be the same as our past, and that the sin we had done once, and with loathing, we would do many times, and with joy.

It was clear to him that the experimental method was the only method by which one could arrive at any scientific analysis of the passions; and certainly Dorian Gray was a subject made to his hand, and seemed to promise rich and fruit-ful results. His sudden mad love for Sibyl Vane was a psycho-logical phenomenon of no small interest. There was no doubt that curiosity had much to do with it, curiosity and the de-sire for new experiences; yet it was not a simple but rather a very complex passion. What there was in it of the purely sensuous instinct of boyhood had been transformed by the workings of the imagination, changed into something that seemed to the lad himself to be remote from sense, and was for that very reason all the more dangerous. It was the pas-sions about whose origin we deceived ourselves that tyran-nised most strongly over us. Our weakest motives were those of whose nature we were conscious. It often happened that when we thought we were experimenting on others we were really experimenting on ourselves.

While Lord Henry sat dreaming on these things, a knock came to the door, and his valet entered, and reminded him it was time to dress for dinner. He got up and looked out into the street. The sunset had smitten into scarlet gold the upper windows of the houses opposite. The panes glowed like plates of heated metal. The sky above was like a faded rose. He thought of his friend's young fiery-coloured life, and wondered how it was all going to end.

When he arrived home, about half-past twelve o'clock, he saw a telegram lying on the hall table. He opened it, and found it was from Dorian Gray. It was to tell him that he was engaged to be married to Sibyl Vane.

CHAPTER V

"MOTHER, mother, I am so happy!" whispered the girl, burying her face in the lap of the faded, tired-looking woman who, with back turned to the shrill intrusive light, was sitting in the one armchair that their dingy sitting room contained. "I am so happy!" she repeated, "and you must be happy too!"

Mrs. Vane winced, and put her thin bismuth-whitened hands on her daughter's head. "Happy!" she echoed, "I am only happy, Sibyl, when I see you act. You must not think of anything but your acting. Mr. Isaacs has been very good to us, and we owe him money."

The girl looked up and pouted. "Money, mother?" she cried, "what does money matter? Love is more than money."

"Mr. Isaacs has advanced us fifty pounds to pay off our debts, and to get a proper outfit for James. You must not forget that, Sibyl. Fifty pounds is a very large sum. Mr. Isaacs has been most considerate."

"He is not a gentleman, mother, and I hate the way he talks to me," said the girl, rising to her feet, and going over to the window.

"I don't know how we could manage without him," answered the elder woman, querulously.

Sibyl Vane tossed her head and laughed. "We don't want him any more, mother. Prince Charming rules life for us now." Then she paused. A rose shook in her blood, and shadowed her cheeks. Quick breath parted the petals of her lips. They trembled. Some southern wind of passion swept over her, and stirred the dainty folds of her dress. "I love him," she said, simply.

"Foolish child! foolish child!" was the parrot-phrase flung in answer. The waving of crooked, false-jewelled fingers gave grotesqueness to the words.

The girl laughed again. The joy of a caged bird was in her voice. Her eyes caught the melody, and echoed it in radiance; then closed for a moment, as though to hide their secret. When they opened, the mist of a dream had passed across them.

Thin-lipped wisdom spoke at her from the worn chair, hinted at prudence, quoted from that book of cowardice whose author apes the name of common sense. She did not listen. She was free in her prison of passion. Her prince, Prince Charming, was with her. She had called on Memory to remake him. She had sent her soul to search for him, and it had brought him back. His kiss burned again upon her mouth. Her eyelids were warm with his breath.

Then Wisdom altered its method and spoke of espial and discovery. This young man might be rich. If so, marriage should be thought of. Against the shell of her ear broke the waves of worldly cunning. The arrows of craft shot by her. She saw the thin lips moving, and smiled.

Suddenly she felt the need to speak. The wordy silence troubled her. "Mother, mother," she cried, "why does he love me so much? I know why I love him. I love him because he is like what Love himself should be. But what does he see in me? I am not worthy of him. And yet—why, I cannot tell—though I feel so much beneath him, I don't feel humble. I feel proud, terribly proud. Mother, did you love my father as I love Prince Charming?"

The elder woman grew pale beneath the coarse powder that daubed her cheeks, and her dry lips twitched with a spasm of pain. Sibyl rushed to her, flung her arms round her neck, and kissed her. "Forgive me, mother. I know it pains you to talk about our father. But it only pains you because you loved him so much. Don't look so sad. I am as happy to-day as you were twenty years ago. Ah! let me be happy for ever!"

"My child, you are far too young to think of falling in love. Besides, what do you know of this young man? You don't even know his name. The whole thing is most inconvenient, and really, when James is going away to Australia, and I have so much to think of, I must say that you should have shown more consideration. However, as I said before, if he is rich. . . ."

"Ah! Mother, mother, let me be happy!"

Mrs. Vane glanced at her, and with one of those false theatrical gestures that so often become a mode of second nature to a stage-player, clasped her in her arms. At this moment the door opened, and a young lad with rough brown hair came into the room. He was thick-set of figure, and his hands and feet were large, and somewhat clumsy in movement. He was not so finely bred as his sister. One would hardly have guessed the close relationship that existed between them. Mrs. Vane fixed her eyes on him, and intensified the smile. She mentally elevated her son to the dignity of an audience. She felt sure that the *tableau* was interesting.

"You might keep some of your kisses for me, Sibyl, I think," said the lad, with a good-natured grumble.

"Ah! but you don't like being kissed, Jim," she cried. "You are a dreadful old bear." And she ran across the room and hugged him.

James Vane looked into his sister's face with tenderness. "I want you to come out with me for a walk, Sibyl. I don't suppose I shall ever see this horrid London again. I am sure I don't want to."

"My son, don't say such dreadful things," murmured Mrs.

Vane, taking up a tawdry theatrical dress, with a sigh, and beginning to patch it. She felt a little disappointed that he had not joined the group. It would have increased the theatrical picturesqueness of the situation.

"Why not, mother? I mean it."

"You pain me, my son. I trust you will return from Australia in a position of affluence. I believe there is no society of any kind in the Colonies, nothing that I would call society; so when you have made your fortune you must come back and assert yourself in London."

"Society!" muttered the lad. "I don't want to know anything about that. I should like to make some money to take you and Sibyl off the stage. I hate it."

"Oh, Jim!" said Sibyl, laughing, "how unkind of you! But are you really going for a walk with me? That will be nice! I was afraid you were going to say good-bye to some of your friends—to Tom Hardy, who gave you that hideous pipe, or Ned Langton, who makes fun of you for smoking it. It is very sweet of you to let me have your last afternoon. Where shall we go? Let us go to the Park."

"I am too shabby," he answered, frowning. "Only swell people go to the Park."

"Nonsense, Jim," she whispered, stroking the sleeve of his coat.

He hesitated for a moment. "Very well," he said at last, "but don't be too long dressing." She danced out of the door. One could hear her singing as she ran upstairs. Her little feet pattered overhead.

He walked up and down the room two or three times. Then he turned to the still figure in the chair. "Mother, are my things ready?" he asked.

"Quite ready, James," she answered, keeping her eyes on her work. For some months past she had felt ill at ease when she was alone with this rough, stern son of hers. Her shallow secret nature was troubled when their eyes met. She used to wonder if he suspected anything. The silence, for he made no other observation, became intolerable to her. She began to complain. Women defend themselves by attacking, just as they attack by sudden and strange surrenders. "I hope you will be contented, James, with your sea-faring life," she said. "You must remember that it is your own choice. You might have entered a solicitor's office. Solicitors are a very respectable class, and in the country often dine with the best families."

"I hate offices, and I hate clerks," he replied. "But you are quite right. I have chosen my own life. All I say is, watch over Sibyl. Don't let her come to any harm. Mother, you must watch over her."

"James, you really talk very strangely. Of course I watch over Sibyl."

"I hear a gentleman comes every night to the theatre, and goes behind to talk to her. Is that right? What about that?"

"You are speaking about things you don't understand, James. In the profession we are accustomed to receive a great deal of most gratifying attention. I myself used to receive many bouquets at one time. That was when acting was really understood. As for Sibyl, I do not know at present whether her attachment is serious or not. But there is no doubt that the young man in question is a perfect gentleman. He is always most polite to me. Besides, he has the appearance of being rich, and the flowers he sends are lovely."

"You don't know his name, though," said the lad, harshly.

"No," answered his mother, with a placid expression in her face. "He has not yet revealed his real name. I think it is quite romantic of him. He is probably a member of the aristocracy."

James Vane bit his lip. "Watch over Sibyl, mother," he cried, "watch over her."

"My son, you distress me very much. Sibyl is always under my special care. Of course, if this gentleman is wealthy, there is no reason why she should not contract an alliance with him. I trust he is one of the aristocracy. He has all the appearance of it, I must say. It might be a most brilliant marriage for Sibyl. They would make a charming couple. His good looks are really quite remarkable; everybody notices them."

The lad muttered something to himself, and drummed on the window-pane with his coarse fingers. He had just turned round to say something, when the door opened, and Sibyl ran in.

"How serious you both are!" she cried. "What is the matter?"

"Nothing," he answered. "I suppose one must be serious sometimes. Goodbye, mother; I will have my dinner at five o'clock. Everything is packed, except my shirts, so you need not trouble."

"Goodbye, my son," she answered, with a bow of strained stateliness.

She was extremely annoyed at the tone he had adopted with her, and there was something in his look that had made her feel afraid.

"Kiss me, mother," said the girl. Her flower-like lips touched the withered cheek, and warmed its frost.

"My child! my child!" cried Mrs. Vane, looking up to the ceiling in search of an imaginary gallery.

"Come, Sibyl," said her brother, impatiently. He hated his mother's affectations.

They went out into the flickering wind-blown sunlight, and strolled down the dreary Euston Road. The passers-by glanced in wonder at the sullen, heavy youth, who, in coarse ill-fitting clothes, was in the company of such a graceful, refined-looking girl. He was like a common gardener walking with a rose.

Jim frowned from time to time when he caught the inquisitive glance of some stranger. He had that dislike of being stared at which comes on geniuses late in life, and never leaves the commonplace. Sibyl, however, was quite unconscious of the effect she was producing. Her love was trembling in laughter on her lips. She was thinking of Prince Charming, and, that she might think of him all the more, she did not talk of him but prattled on about the ship in which Jim was going to sail, about the gold he was certain to find, about the wonderful heiress whose life he was to save from the wicked, red-shirted bushrangers. For he was not to remain a sailor, or a super-cargo, or whatever he was going to be. Oh, no! A sailor's existence was dreadful. Fancy being cooped up in a horrid ship, with the hoarse, hump-backed waves trying to get in, and a black wind blowing the masts down, and tearing the sails into long screaming ribands! He was to leave the vessel at Melbourne, bid a polite goodbye to the captain, and go off at once to the gold-fields. Before a week was over he was to come across a large nugget of pure gold, the largest nugget that had ever been discovered, and bring it down to the coast in a waggon guarded by six mounted policemen. The bushrangers were to attack them three times, and be defeated with immense slaughter. Or, no. He was not to go to the gold-fields at all. They were horrid places, where men got intoxicated, and shot each other in bar-rooms, and used bad language. He was to be a nice sheep-farmer, and one evening, as he was riding home, he was to see the beautiful heiress being carried off by a robber on a black horse, and give chase, and rescue her. Of course she would fall in love with him, and he with her, and they would get married, and come home, and live in an immense house in London. Yes, there were delightful things in store for him. But he must be very good, and not lose his temper, or spend his money foolishly. She was only a year older than he was, but she knew so much more of life. He must be sure, also, to write to her by every mail, and to say his prayers each night before he went to sleep. God was very good, and would watch over him. She would pray for him, too, and in a few years he would come back quite rich and happy.

The lad listened sulkily to her, and made no answer. He was heart-sick at leaving home.

Yet it was not this alone that made him gloomy and morose. Inexperienced though he was, he had still a strong sense of the danger of Sibyl's position. This young dandy who was making love to her could mean her no good. He was a gentleman, and he hated him for that, hated him through some curious race-instinct for which he could not account, and which for that reason was all the more dominant within him. He was conscious also of the shallowness and vanity of his mother's nature, and in that saw infinite peril for Sibyl and Sibyl's happiness. Children begin by loving their parents; as they grow older they judge them; sometimes they forgive them.

His mother! He had something on his mind to ask of her, something that he had brooded on for many months of silence. A chance phrase that he had heard at the theatre, a whispered sneer that had reached his ears one night as he waited at the stage-door, had set loose a train of horrible thoughts. He remembered it as if it had been the lash of a hunting-crop across his face. His brows knit together into a wedge-like furrow, and with a twitch of pain he bit his under-lip.

"You are not listening to a word I am saying, Jim," cried Sibyl, "and I am making the most delightful plans for your future. Do say something."

"What do you want me to say?"

"Oh! that you will be a good boy, and not forget us," she answered, smiling at him.

He shrugged his shoulders. "You are more likely to forget me, than I am to forget you, Sibyl."

She flushed. "What do you mean, Jim?" she asked.

"You have a new friend, I hear. Who is he? Why have you not told me about him? He means you no good."

"Stop, Jim!" she exclaimed. "You must not say anything against him. I love him."

"Why, you don't even know his name," answered the lad. "Who is he? I have a right to know."

"He is called Prince Charming. Don't you like the name? Oh! you silly boy! you should never forget it. If you only saw him, you would think him the most wonderful person in the world. Some day you will meet him: when you come back from Australia. You will like him so much. Everybody likes him, and I . . . love him. I wish you could come to the theatre to-night. He is going to be there, and I am to play Juliet. Oh! how I shall play it! Fancy, Jim, to be in love and play Juliet! To have him sitting there! To play for his delight! I am afraid I may frighten the company, frighten or enthrall them. To be in love is to surpass one's self. Poor dreadful Mr. Isaacs will be shouting 'genius' to his loafers at the bar. He has preached me as a dogma; to-night he will announce me as a revelation. I feel it. And it is all his, his only, Prince Charming, my wonderful lover, my god of graces. But I am poor beside him. Poor? What does that matter? When poverty creeps in at the door, love flies in through the window. Our proverbs want re-writing. They were made in winter, and it is summer now; spring-time for me, I think, a very dance of blossoms in blue skies."

"He is a gentleman," said the lad, sullenly.

"A Prince!" she cried, musically. "What more do you want?"

"He wants to enslave you."

"I shudder at the thought of being free."

"I want you to beware of him."

"To see him is to worship him, to know him is to trust him."

"Sibyl, you are mad about him."

She laughed, and took his arm. "You dear old Jim, you talk as if you were a hundred. Some day you will be in love yourself. Then you will know what it is. Don't look so sulky. Surely you should be glad to think that, though you are going away, you leave me happier than I have ever been before. Life has been hard for us both, terribly hard and difficult. But it will be different now. You are going to a new world, and I have found one. Here are two chairs; let us sit down and see the smart people go by."

They took their seats amidst a crowd of watchers. The tulip-beds across the road flamed like throbbing rings of fire. A white dust, tremulous cloud of orris-root it seemed, hung in the panting air. The brightly-coloured parasols danced and dipped like monstrous butterflies.

She made her brother talk of himself, his hopes, his prospects. He spoke slowly and with effort. They passed words to each other as players at a game pass counters. Sibyl felt oppressed. She could not communicate her joy. A faint smile curving that sullen mouth was all the echo she could win. After some time she became silent. Suddenly she caught a glimpse of golden hair and laughing lips, and in an open carriage with two ladies Dorian Gray drove past.

She started to her feet. "There he is!" she cried.

"Who?" said Jim Vane.

"Prince Charming," she answered, looking after the victoria.

He jumped up, and seized her roughly by the arm. "Show him to me. Which is he? Point him out. I must see him!"

he exclaimed; but at that moment the Duke of Berwick's four-in-hand came between, and when it had left the space clear, the carriage had swept out of the Park.

"He is gone," murmured Sibyl, sadly. "I wish you had seen him."

"I wish I had, for as sure as there is a God in heaven, if he ever does you any wrong I shall kill him."

She looked at him in horror. He repeated his words. They cut the air like a dagger. The people round began to gape. A lady standing close to her tittered.

"Come away, Jim; come away," she whispered. He followed her doggedly, as she passed through the crowd. He felt glad at what he had said.

When they reached the Achilles Statue she turned round. There was pity in her eyes that became laughter on her lips. She shook her head at him. "You are foolish, Jim, utterly foolish; a bad-tempered boy, that is all. How can you say such horrible things? You don't know what you are talking about. You are simply jealous and unkind. Ah! I wish you would fall in love. Love makes people good, and what you said was wicked."

"I am sixteen," he answered, "and I know what I am about. Mother is no help to you. She doesn't understand how to look after you. I wish now that I was not going to Australia at all. I have a great mind to chuck the whole thing up. I would, if my articles hadn't been signed."

"Oh, don't be so serious, Jim. You are like one of the heroes of those silly melodramas mother used to be so fond of acting in. I am not going to quarrel with you. I have seen him, and oh! to see him is perfect happiness. We won't quarrel. I know you would never harm anyone I love, would you?"

"Not as long as you love him, I suppose," was the sullen answer.

"I shall love him for ever!" she cried.

"And he?"

"For ever, too!"

"He had better."

She shrank from him. Then she laughed and put her hand on his arm. He was merely a boy.

At the Marble Arch they hailed an omnibus, which left them close to their shabby home in the Euston Road. It was after five o'clock, and Sibyl had to lie down for a couple of hours before acting. Jim insisted that she should do so. He said that he would sooner part with her when their mother was not present. She would be sure to make a scene, and he detested scenes of every kind.

In Sibyl's own room they parted. There was jealousy in the lad's heart, and a fierce, murderous hatred of the stranger who, as it seemed to him, had come between them. Yet, when her arms were flung round his neck, and her fingers strayed through his hair, he softened, and kissed her with real affection. There were tears in his eyes as he went downstairs.

His mother was waiting for him below. She grumbled at his unpunctuality, as he entered. He made no answer, but sat down to his meagre meal. The flies buzzed round the table, and crawled over the stained cloth. Through the rumble of omnibuses, and the clatter of street-cabs, he could hear the droning voice devouring each minute that was left to him.

After some time, he thrust away his plate, and put his head in his hands. He felt that he had a right to know. It should have been told to him before, if it was as he suspected. Leaden with fear, his mother watched him. Words dropped mechanically from her lips. A tattered lace handkerchief twitched in her fingers. When the clock struck six, he got up, and went to the door. Then he turned back, and looked at her. Their eyes met. In hers he saw a wild appeal for mercy. It enraged him.

"Mother, I have something to ask you," he said. Her eyes wandered vaguely about the room. She made no answer. "Tell me the truth. I have a right to know. Were you married to my father?"

She heaved a deep sigh. It was a sigh of relief. The terrible moment, the moment that night and day, for weeks and months, she had dreaded, had come at last, and yet she felt no terror. Indeed in some measure it was a disappointment to her. The vulgar directness of the question called for a direct answer. The situation had not been gradually led up to. It was crude. It reminded her of a bad rehearsal.

"No," she answered, wondering at the harsh simplicity of life.

"My father was a scoundrel then?" cried the lad, clenching his fists.

She shook her head. "I knew he was not free. We loved each other very much. If he had lived, he would have made provision for us. Don't speak against him, my son. He was your father, and a gentleman. Indeed he was highly connected."

An oath broke from his lips. "I don't care for myself," he exclaimed, "but don't let Sibyl . . . It is a gentleman, isn't it, who is in love with her, or says he is? Highly connected, too, I suppose."

For a moment a hideous sense of humiliation came over the woman. Her head drooped. She wiped her eyes with shaking hands. "Sibyl has a mother," she murmured; "I had none."

The lad was touched. He went towards her, and stooping down he kissed her. "I am sorry if I have pained you by asking about my father," he said, "but I could not help it. I must go now. Good-bye. Don't forget that you will only have one child now to look after, and believe me that if this man wrongs my sister, I will find out who he is, track him down, and kill him like a dog. I swear it."

The exaggerated folly of the threat, the passionate gesture that accompanied it, the mad melodramatic words, made life seem more vivid to her. She was familiar with the atmosphere. She breathed more freely, and for the first time for many months she really admired her son. She would have liked to have continued the scene on the same emotional scale, but he cut her short. Trunks had to be carried down, and mufflers looked for. The lodging-house drudge bustled in and out. There was the bargaining with the cabman. The moment was lost in vulgar details. It was with a renewed feeling of disappointment that she waved the tattered lace handkerchief from the window, as her son drove away. She was conscious that a great opportunity had been wasted. She consoled herself by telling Sibyl how desolate she felt her life would be, now that she had only one child to look after. She remembered the phrase. It had pleased her. Of the threat she said nothing. It was vividly and dramatically expressed. She felt that they would all laugh at it some day.

CHAPTER VI

"I SUPPOSE you have heard the news, Basil?" said Lord Henry that evening, as Hallward was shown into a little private room at the Bristol where dinner had been laid for three.

"No, Harry," answered the artist, giving his hat and coat to the bowing waiter. "What is it? Nothing about politics, I hope? They don't interest me. There is hardly a single person in the House of Commons worth painting; though many of them would be the better for a little whitewashing."

"Dorian Gray is engaged to be married," said Lord Henry, watching him as he spoke.

Hallward started, and then frowned. "Dorian engaged to be married!" he cried. "Impossible!"

"It is perfectly true."

"To whom?"

"To some little actress or other."

"I can't believe it. Dorian is far too sensible."

"Dorian is far too wise not to do foolish things now and then, my dear Basil."

"Marriage is hardly a thing that one can do now and then, Harry."

"Except in America," rejoined Lord Henry, languidly. "But I didn't say he was married. I said he was engaged to be married. There is a great difference. I have a distinct remembrance of being married, but I have no recollection at all of being engaged. I am inclined to think that I never was engaged."

"But think of Dorian's birth, and position, and wealth. It

would be absurd for him to marry so much beneath him."

"If you want to make him marry this girl tell him that, Basil. He is sure to do it, then. Whenever a man does a thoroughly stupid thing, it is always from the noblest motives."

"I hope the girl is good, Harry. I don't want to see Dorian tied to some vile creature, who might degrade his nature and ruin his intellect."

"Oh, she is better than good—she is beautiful," murmured Lord Henry, sipping a glass of vermouth and orange-bitters. "Dorian says she is beautiful; and he is not often wrong about things of that kind. Your portrait of him has quickened his appreciation of the personal appearance of other people. It has had that excellent effect, amongst others. We are to see her to-night, if that boy doesn't forget his appointment."

"Are you serious?"

"Quite serious, Basil. I should be miserable if I thought I should ever be more serious than I am at the present moment."

"But do you approve of it, Harry?" asked the painter, walking up and down the room, and biting his lip. "You can't approve of it, possibly. It is some silly infatuation."

"I never approve, or disapprove, of anything now. It is an absurd attitude to take towards life. We are not sent into the world to air our moral prejudices. I never take any notice of what common people say, and I never interfere with what charming people do. If a personality fascinates me, whatever mode of expression that personality selects is absolutely delightful to me. Dorian Gray falls in love with a beautiful girl who acts Juliet, and proposes to marry her. Why not? If he wedded Messalina he would be none the less interesting. You know I am not a champion of marriage. The real drawback to marriage is that it makes one unselfish. And unselfish people are colourless. They lack in-

dividuality. Still, there are certain temperaments that marriage makes more complex. They retain their egotism, and
add to it many other egos. They are forced to have more than
one life. They become more highly organised, and to be
highly organised is, I should fancy, the object of man's
existence. Besides, every experience is of value, and, whatever one may say against marriage, it is certainly an experience. I hope that Dorian Gray will make this girl his wife,
passionately adore her for six months, and then suddenly
become fascinated by someone else. He would be a wonderful study."

"You don't mean a single word of all that, Harry; you
know you don't. If Dorian Gray's life were spoiled, no one
would be sorrier than yourself. You are much better than you
pretend to be."

Lord Henry laughed. "The reason we all like to think so
well of others is that we are all afraid of ourselves. The basis
of optimism is sheer terror. We think that we are generous
because we credit our neighbour with the possession of those
virtues that are likely to be a benefit to us. We praise the
banker that we may overdraw our account, and find good
qualities in the highwayman in the hope that he may spare
our pockets. I mean everything that I have said. I have the
greatest contempt for optimism. As for a spoiled life, no life
is spoiled but one whose growth is arrested. If you want to
mar a nature, you have merely to reform it. As for marriage,
of course that would be silly, but there are other and more
interesting bonds between men and women. I will certainly
encourage them. They have the charm of being fashionable.
But here is Dorian himself. He will tell you more than I can."

"My dear Harry, my dear Basil, you must both congratulate me!" said the lad, throwing off his evening cape with its
satin-lined wings and shaking each of his friends by the hand
in turn. "I have never been so happy. Of course it is sudden;

all really delightful things are. And yet it seems to me to be the one thing I have been looking for all my life." He was flushed with excitement and pleasure, and looked extraordinarily handsome.

"I hope you will always be very happy, Dorian," said Hallward, "but I don't quite forgive you for not having let me know of your engagement. You let Harry know."

"And I don't forgive you for being late for dinner," broke in Lord Henry, putting his hand on the lad's shoulder, and smiling as he spoke. "Come, let us sit down and try what the new *chef* here is like, and then you will tell us how it all came about."

"There is really not much to tell," cried Dorian, as they took their seats at the small round table. "What happened was simply this. After I left you yesterday evening, Harry, I dressed, had some dinner at that little Italian restaurant in Rupert Street you introduced me to, and went down at eight o'clock to the theatre. Sibyl was playing Rosalind. Of course the scenery was dreadful, and the Orlando absurd. But Sibyl! You should have seen her! When she came on in her boy's clothes she was perfectly wonderful. She wore a moss-coloured velvet jerkin with cinnamon sleeves, slim brown cross-gartered hose, a dainty little green cap with a hawk's feather caught in a jewel, and a hooded cloak lined with dull red. She had never seemed to me more exquisite. She had all the delicate grace of that Tanagra figurine that you have in your studio, Basil. Her hair clustered round her face like dark leaves round a pale rose. As for her acting— well, you shall see her to-night. She is simply a born artist. I sat in the dingy box absolutely enthralled. I forgot that I was in London and in the nineteenth century. I was away with my love in a forest that no man had ever seen. After the performance was over I went behind, and spoke to her. As we were sitting together, suddenly there came into her eyes a look that I had never seen there before. My lips moved towards hers. We kissed each other. I can't describe to you what I felt at that moment. It seemed to me that all my life had been narrowed to one perfect point of rose-coloured joy. She trembled all over, and shook like a white narcissus. Then she flung herself on her knees and kissed my hands. I feel that I should not tell you all this, but I can't help it. Of course our engagement is a dead secret. She has not even told her own mother. I don't know what my guardians will say. Lord Radley is sure to be furious. I don't care. I shall be of age in less than a year, and then I can do what I like. I have been right, Basil, haven't I, to take my love out of poetry, and to find my wife in Shakespeare's plays? Lips that Shakespeare taught to speak have whispered their secret in my ear. I have had the arms of Rosalind around me, and kissed Juliet on the mouth."

"Yes, Dorian, I suppose you were right," said Hallward, slowly.

"Have you seen her to-day?" asked Lord Henry.

Dorian Gray shook his head. "I left her in the forest of Arden, I shall find her in an orchard in Verona."

Lord Henry sipped his champagne in a meditative manner. "At what particular point did you mention the word marriage, Dorian? And what did she say in answer? Perhaps you forgot all about it."

"My dear Harry, I did not treat it as a business transaction, and I did not make any formal proposal. I told her that I loved her, and she said she was not worthy to be my wife. Not worthy! Why, the whole world is nothing to me compared with her."

"Women are wonderfully practical," murmured Lord Henry—"much more practical than we are. In situations of that kind we often forget to say anything about marriage, and they always remind us."

Hallward laid his hand upon his arm. "Don't, Harry. You have annoyed Dorian. He is not like other men. He would never bring misery upon anyone. His nature is too fine for that."

Lord Henry looked across the table. "Dorian is never annoyed with me," he answered. "I asked the question for the best reason possible, for the only reason, indeed, that excuses one for asking any question—simple curiosity. I have a theory that it is always the women who propose to us, and not we who propose to the women. Except, of course, in middle-class life. But then the middle classes are not modern."

Dorian Gray laughed, and tossed his head. "You are quite incorrigible, Harry; but I don't mind. It is impossible to be angry with you. When you see Sibyl Vane you will feel that the man who could wrong her would be a beast, a beast without a heart. I cannot understand how anyone can wish to shame the thing he loves. I love Sibyl Vane. I want to place her on a pedestal of gold, and to see the world worship the woman who is mine. What is marriage? An irrevocable vow. You mock at it for that. Ah! don't mock. It is an irrevocable vow that I want to take. Her trust makes me faithful, her belief makes me good. When I am with her, I regret all that you have taught me. I become different from what you have known me to be. I am changed, and the mere touch of Sibyl Vane's hand makes me forget you and all your wrong, fascinating, poisonous, delightful theories."

"And those are . . . ?" asked Lord Henry, helping himself to some salad.

"Oh, your theories about life, your theories about love, your theories about pleasure. All your theories, in fact, Harry."

"Pleasure is the only thing worth having a theory about," he answered, in his slow, melodious voice. "But I am afraid I cannot claim my theory as my own. It belongs to Nature not to me. Pleasure is Nature's test, her sign of approval. When we are happy we are always good, but when we are good we are not always happy."

"Ah, but what do you mean by good?" cried Basil Hallward.

"Yes," echoed Dorian, leaning back in his chair, and looking at Lord Henry over the heavy clusters of purple-lipped irises that stood in the centre of the table, "what do you mean by good, Harry?"

"To be good is to be in harmony with one's self," he replied, touching the thin stem of his glass with his pale, fine-pointed fingers. "Discord is to be forced to be in harmony with others. One's own life—that is the important thing. As for the lives of one's neighbours, if one wishes to be a prig or a Puritan, one can flaunt one's moral views about them, but they are not one's concern. Besides, Individualism has really the higher aim. Modern morality consists in accepting the standard of one's age. I consider that for any man of culture to accept the standard of his age is a form of the grossest immorality."

"But, surely, if one lives merely for one's self, Harry, one pays a terrible price for doing so?" suggested the painter.

"Yes, we are overcharged for everything nowadays. I should fancy that the real tragedy of the poor is that they can afford nothing but self-denial. Beautiful sins, like beautiful things, are the privilege of the rich."

"One has to pay in other ways but money."

"What sort of ways, Basil?"

"Oh! I should fancy in remorse, in suffering, in . . . well, in the consciousness of degradation."

Lord Henry shrugged his shoulders. "My dear fellow, mediæval art is charming, but mediæval emotions are out of date. One can use them in fiction, of course. But then the only things that one can use in fiction are the things that one has

ceased to use in fact. Believe me, no civilised man ever regrets
a pleasure, and no uncivilised man ever knows what a pleasure is."

"I know what pleasure is," cried Dorian Gray. "It is to
adore someone."

"That is certainly better than being adored," he answered,
toying with some fruits. "Being adored is a nuisance. Women
treat us just as Humanity treats its gods. They worship us,
and are always bothering us to do something for them."

"I should have said that whatever they ask for they had
first given to us," murmured the lad, gravely. "They create
Love in our natures. They have a right to demand it back."

"That is quite true, Dorian," cried Hallward.

"Nothing is ever quite true," said Lord Henry.

"This is," interrupted Dorian. "You must admit, Harry,
that women give to men the very gold of their lives."

"Possibly," he sighed, "but they invariably want it back
in such very small change. That is the worry. Women, as
some witty Frenchman once put it, inspire us with the desire
to do masterpieces, and always prevent us from carrying
them out."

"Harry, you are dreadful! I don't know why I like you so
much."

"You will always like me, Dorian," he replied. "Will you
have some coffee, you fellows?—Waiter, bring coffee, and
fine-champagne, and some cigarettes. No: don't mind the
cigarettes; I have some. Basil, I can't allow you to smoke
cigars. You must have a cigarette. A cigarette is the perfect
type of the perfect pleasure. It is exquisite, and it leaves one
unsatisfied. What more can one want? Yes, Dorian, you will
always be fond of me. I represent to you all the sins you have
never had the courage to commit."

"What nonsense you talk, Harry!" cried the lad, taking a
light from a fire-breathing silver dragon that the waiter had

placed on the table. "Let us go down to the theatre. When Sibyl comes on the stage you will have a new ideal of life. She will represent something to you that you have never known."

"I have known everything," said Lord Henry, with a tired look in his eyes, "but I am always ready for a new emotion. I am afraid, however, that, for me at any rate, there is no such thing. Still, your wonderful girl may thrill me. I love acting. It is so much more real than life. Let us go. Dorian, you will come with me. I am so sorry, Basil, but there is only room for two in the brougham. You must follow us in a hansom."

They got up and put on their coats, sipping their coffee standing. The painter was silent and preoccupied. There was a gloom over him. He could not bear this marriage, and yet it seemed to him to be better than many other things that might have happened. After a few minutes, they all passed downstairs. He drove off by himself, as had been arranged, and watched the flashing lights of the little brougham in front of him. A strange sense of loss came over him. He felt that Dorian Gray would never again be to him all that he had been in the past. Life had come between them. . . . His eyes darkened, and the crowded, flaring streets became blurred to his eyes. When the cab drew up at the theatre, it seemed to him that he had grown years older.

CHAPTER VII

FOR some reason or other, the house was crowded that night, and the fat Jew manager who met them at the door was beaming from ear to ear with an oily, tremulous smile. He escorted them to their box with a sort of pompous humility, waving his fat jewelled hands, and talking at the top of his voice. Dorian Gray loathed him more than ever. He felt as if he had come to look for Miranda and had been men by Caliban. Lord Henry, upon the other hand, rather liked him. At least he declared he did, and insisted on shaking him by the hand, and assuring him that he was proud to meet a man who had discovered a real genius and gone bankrupt over a poet. Hallward amused himself with watching the faces in the pit. The heat was terribly oppressive, and the huge sunlight flamed like a monstrous dahlia with petals of yellow fire. The youths in the gallery had taken off their coats and waistcoats and hung them over the side. They talked to each other across the theatre, and shared their oranges with the tawdry girls who sat beside them. Some women were laughing in the pit. Their voices were horribly shrill and discordant. The sound of the popping corks came from the bar.

"What a place to find one's divinity in!" said Lord Henry.

"Yes!" answered Dorian Gray. "It was here I found her, and she is divine beyond all living things. When she acts you will forget everything. These common, rough people, with their coarse faces and brutal gestures, become quite different when she is on the stage. They sit silently and watch her. They weep and laugh as she wills them to do. She makes them as responsive as a violin. She spiritualises them, and one feels that they are of the same flesh and blood as one's self."

"The same flesh and blood as one's self! Oh, I hope not!" exclaimed Lord Henry, who was scanning the occupants of the gallery through his opera-glass.

"Don't pay any attention to him, Dorian," said the painter. "I understand what you mean, and I believe in this girl. Anyone you love must be marvellous, and any girl that has the effect you describe must be fine and noble. To spiritualise one's age—that is something worth doing. If this girl can give a soul to those who have lived without one, if she can create the sense of beauty in people whose lives have been sordid and ugly, if she can strip them of their selfishness and lend them tears for sorrows that are not their own, she is worthy of all your adoration, worthy of the adoration of the world. This marriage is quite right. I did not think so at first, but I admit it now. The gods made Sibyl Vane for you. Without her you are incomplete."

"Thanks, Basil," answered Dorian Gray, pressing his hand. "I knew that you would understand me. Harry is so cynical, he terrifies me. But here is the orchestra. It is quite dreadful, but it only lasts for about five minutes. Then the curtain rises, and you will see the girl to whom I am going to give all my life, to whom I have given everything that is good in me."

A quarter of an hour afterwards, amidst an extraordinary turmoil of applause, Sibyl Vane stepped on to the stage. Yes, she was certainly lovely to look at—one of the loveliest creatures, Lord Henry thought, that he had ever seen. There was something of the fawn in her shy grace and startled eyes. A faint blush, like the shadow of a rose in a mirror of silver, came to her cheeks as she glanced at the crowded, enthusiastic house. She stepped back a few paces, and her lips seemed to tremble. Basil Hallward leaped to his feet and began to applaud. Motionless, and as one in a dream, sat Dorian Gray, gazing at her. Lord Henry peered through his glasses, murmuring, "Charming! charming!"

The scene was the hall of Capulet's house, and Romeo in his pilgrim's dress had entered with Mercutio and his other friends. The band, such as it was, struck up a few bars of music, and the dance began. Through the crowd of ungainly, shabbily-dressed actors, Sibyl Vane moved like a creature from a finer world. Her body swayed, while she danced, as a plant sways in the water. The curves of her throat were the curves of a white lily. Her hands seemed to be made of cool ivory.

Yet she was curiously listless. She showed no sign of joy when her eyes rested on Romeo. The few words she had to speak—

"Good pilgrim, you do wrong your hand too much,
Which mannerly devotion shows in this;
For saints have hands that pilgrims' hands do touch,
And palm to palm is holy palmers' kiss—"

with the brief dialogue that follows, were spoken in a thoroughly artificial manner. The voice was exquisite, but from the point of view of tone it was absolutely false. It was wrong in colour. It took away all the life from the verse. It made the passion unreal.

Dorian Gray grew pale as he watched her. He was puzzled and anxious. Neither of his friends dared to say anything to him. She seemed to them to be absolutely incompetent. They were horribly disappointed.

Yet they felt that the true test of any Juliet is the balcony scene of the second act. They waited for that. If she failed there, there was nothing in her.

She looked charming as she came out in the moonlight. That could not be denied. But the staginess of her acting was unbearable, and grew worse as she went on. Her gestures became absurdly artificial. She over-emphasised everything that she had to say. The beautiful passage—

"Thou knowest the mask of night is on my face,
Else would a maiden blush bepaint my cheek
For that which thou hast heard me speak to-night- "

was declaimed with the painful precision of a schoolgirl who has been taught to recite by some second-rate professor of elocution. When she leaned over the balcony and came to those wonderful lines—

"Although I joy in thee,
I have no joy of this contract to-night:
It is too rash, too unadvised, too sudden;
Too like the lightning, which doth cease to be
Ere one can say, 'It lightens.' Sweet, good-night!
This bud of love by summer's ripening breath
May prove a beauteous flower when next we meet—"

she spoke the words as though they conveyed no meaning to her. It was not nervousness. Indeed, so far from being nervous, she was absolutely self-contained. It was simply bad art. She was a complete failure.

Even the common, uneducated audience of the pit and gallery lost their interest in the play. They got restless, and began to talk loudly and to whistle. The Jew manager, who was standing at the back of the dress-circle, stamped and swore with rage. The only person unmoved was the girl herself.

When the second act was over there came a storm of hisses, and Lord Henry got up from his chair and put on his coat. "She is quite beautiful, Dorian," he said, "but she can't act. Let us go."

"I am going to see the play through," answered the lad, in a hard, bitter voice. "I am awfully sorry that I have made you waste an evening, Harry. I apologise to you both."

"My dear Dorian, I should think Miss Vane was ill," interrupted Hallward. "We will come some other night."

"I wish she were ill," he rejoined. "But she seems to me to be simply callous and cold. She has entirely altered. Last night she was a great artist. This evening she is merely a commonplace, mediocre actress."

"Don't talk like that about anyone you love, Dorian. Love is a more wonderful thing than Art."

"They are both simply forms of imitation," remarked Lord Henry. "But do let us go. Dorian, you must not stay here any longer. It is not good for one's morals to see bad acting. Besides, I don't suppose you will want your wife to act. So what does it matter if she plays Juliet like a wooden doll? She is very lovely, and if she knows as little about life as she does about acting, she will be a delightful experience. There are only two kinds of people who are really fascinating —people who know absolutely everything, and people who know absolutely nothing. Good heavens, my dear boy, don't look so tragic! The secret of remaining young is never to have an emotion that is unbecoming. Come to the club with Basil and myself. We will smoke cigarettes and drink to the beauty of Sibyl Vane. She is beautiful. What more can you want?"

"Go away, Harry," cried the lad. "I want to be alone. Basil, you must go. Ah! can't you see that my heart is breaking?" The hot tears came to his eyes. His lips trembled, and, rushing to the back of the box, he leaned up against the wall, hiding his face in his hands.

"Let us go, Basil," said Lord Henry, with a strange tenderness in his voice; and the two young men passed out together.

A few moments afterwards the footlights flared up, and the curtain rose on the third act. Dorian Gray went back to his seat. He looked pale, and proud, and indifferent. The play dragged on, and seemed interminable. Half of the audience went out, tramping in heavy boots and laughing. The whole thing was a *fiasco*. The last act was played to almost empty benches. The curtain went down on a titter, and some groans.

As soon as it was over, Dorian Gray rushed behind the scenes into the greenroom. The girl was standing there alone, with a look of triumph on her face. Her eyes were lit with an exquisite fire. There was a radiance about her. Her parted lips were smiling over some secret of their own.

When he entered, she looked at him, and an expression of infinite joy came over her. "How badly I acted to-night, Dorian!" she cried.

"Horribly!" he answered, gazing at her in amazement—"horribly! It was dreadful. Are you ill? You have no idea what it was. You have no idea what I suffered."

The girl smiled. "Dorian," she answered, lingering over his name with long-drawn music in her voice, as though it were sweeter than honey to the red petals of her mouth—"Dorian, you should have understood. But you understand now, don't you?"

"Understand what?" he asked, angrily.

"Why I was so bad to-night. Why I shall always be bad. Why I shall never act well again."

He struggled his shoulders. "You are ill, I suppose. When you are ill you shouldn't act. You make yourself ridiculous. My friends were bored. I was bored."

She seemed not to listen to him. She was transfigured with joy. An ecstasy of happiness dominated her.

"Dorian, Dorian," she cried, "before I knew you, acting was the one reality of my life. It was only in the theatre that

I lived. I thought that it was all true. I was Rosalind one night, and Portia the other. The joy of Beatrice was my joy, and the sorrows of Cordelia were mine also. I believed in everything. The common people who acted with me seemed to me to be godlike. The painted scenes were my world. I knew nothing but shadows, and I thought them real. You came— oh, my beautiful love!—and you freed my soul from prison. You taught me what reality really is. To-night, for the first time in my life, I saw through the hollowness, the sham, the silliness of the empty pageant in which I had always played. To-night, for the first time, I became conscious that the Romeo was hideous, and old, and painted, that the moon-light in the orchard was false, that the scenery was vulgar, and that the words I had to speak were unreal, were not my words, were not what I wanted to say. You had brought me something higher, something of which all art is but a reflection. You had made me understand what love really is. My love! my love! Prince Charming! Prince of life! I have grown sick of shadows. You are more to me than all art can ever be. What have I to do with the puppets of a play? When I came on to-night, I could not understand how it was that everything had gone from me. I thought that I was going to be wonderful. I found that I could do nothing. Suddenly it dawned on my soul what it all meant. The knowledge was exquisite to me. I heard them hissing, and I smiled. What could they know of love such as ours? Take me away, Dorian --take me away with you, where we can be quite alone. I hate the stage. I might mimic a passion that I do not feel, but I cannot mimic one that burns me like fire. Oh, Dorian, Dorian, you understand now what it signifies? Even if I could do it, it would be profanation for me to play at being in love. You have made me see that."

He flung himself down on the sofa, and turned away his face. "You have killed my love," he muttered.

She looked at him in wonder, and laughed. He made no answer. She came across to him, and with her little fingers stroked his hair. She knelt down and pressed his hands to her lips. He drew them away, and a shudder ran through him.

Then he leaped up, and went to the door. "Yes," he cried, "you have killed my love. You used to stir my imagination. Now you don't even stir my curiosity. You simply produce no effect. I loved you because you were marvellous, because you had genius and intellect, because you realised the dreams of great poets and gave shape and substance to the shadows of art. You have thrown it all away. You are shallow and stupid. My God! how mad I was to love you! What a fool I have been! You are nothing to me now. I will never see you again. I will never think of you. I will never mention your name. You don't know what you were to me, once. Why, once . . . Oh, I can't bear to think of it! I wish I had never laid eyes upon you! You have spoiled the romance of my life. How little you can know of love, if you say it mars your art! Without your art you are nothing. I would have made you famous, splendid, magnificent. The world would have worshipped you, and you would have borne my name, What are you now? A third-rate actress with a pretty face."

The girl grew white, and trembled. She clenched her hands together, and her voice seemed to catch in her throat. "You are not serious, Dorian?" she murmured. "You are acting."

"Acting! I leave that to you. You do it so well," he answered bitterly.

She rose from her knees, and, with a piteous expression of pain in her face, came across the room to him. She put her hand upon his arm, and looked into his eyes. He thrust her back. "Don't touch me!" he cried.

A low moan broke from her, and she flung herself at his feet, and lay there like a trampled flower. "Dorian, Dorian, don't leave me!" she whispered. "I am so sorry I didn't act well. I was thinking of you all the time. But I will try—indeed, I will try. It came so suddenly across me, my love for you. I think I should never have known it if you had not kissed me—if we had not kissed each other. Kiss me again, my love. Don't go away from me. I couldn't bear it. Oh! don't go away from me. My brother . . . No; never mind. He didn't mean it. He was in jest. . . . But you, oh! can't you forgive me for to-night? I will work so hard, and try to improve. Don't be cruel to me because I love you better than anything in the world. After all, it is only once that I have not pleased you. But you are quite right, Dorian. I should have shown myself more of an artist. It was foolish of me; and yet I couldn't help it. Oh, don't leave me, don't leave me." A fit of passionate sobbing choked her. She crouched on the floor like a wounded thing, and Dorian Gray, with his beautiful eyes, looked down at her, and his chiselled lips curled in exquisite disdain. There is always something ridiculous about the emotions of people whom one has ceased to love. Sibyl Vane seemed to him to be absurdly melodramatic. Her tears and sobs annoyed him.

"I am going," he said at last, in his calm, clear voice. "I don't wish to be unkind, but I can't see you again. You have disappointed me."

She wept silently, and made no answer, but crept nearer Her little hands stretched blindly out, and appeared to be seeking for him. He turned on his heel, and left the room. In a few moments he was out of the theatre.

Where he went to he hardly knew. He remembered wandering through dimly-lit streets, past gaunt black-shadowed archways and evil-looking houses. Women with hoarse voices and harsh laughter had called after him. Drunkards had reeled by cursing, and chattering to themselves like monstrous apes. He had seen grotesque children huddled upon doorsteps, and heard shrieks and oaths from gloomy courts.

As the dawn was just breaking he found himself close to Covent Garden. The darkness lifted, and, flushed with faint fires, the sky hollowed itself into a perfect pearl. Huge carts filled with nodding lilies rumbled slowly down the polished empty street. The air was heavy with the perfume of the flowers, and their beauty seemed to bring him an ano-dyne for his pain. He followed into the market, and watched the men unloading their waggons. A white-smocked carter offered him some cherries. He thanked him, and wondered why he refused to accept any money for them, and began to eat them listlessly. They had been plucked at midnight, and the coldness of the moon had entered into them. A long line of boys carrying crates of striped tulips, and of yellow and red roses, defiled in front of him, threading their way through the huge jade-green piles of vegetables. Under the portico, with its grey sunbleached pillars, loitered a troop of draggled bareheaded girls, waiting for the auction to be over. Others crowded round the swinging doors of the coffee-house in the Piazza. The heavy cart-horses slipped and stamped upon the rough stones, shaking their bells and trappings. Some of the drivers were lying asleep on a pile of sacks. Iris-necked, and pink-footed, the pigeons ran about picking up seeds.

After a little while, he hailed a hansom, and drove home. For a few moments he loitered upon the doorstep, looking round at the silent Square with its blank, close-shuttered win-dows, and its staring blinds. The sky was pure opal now, and the roofs of the houses glistened like silver against it. From some chimney opposite a thin wreath of smoke was rising. It curled, a violet riband, through the nacre-coloured air.

In the huge gilt Venetian lantern, spoil of some Doge's barge, that hung from the ceiling of the great oak-panelled hall of entrance, lights were still burning from three flickering jets: thin blue petals of flame they seemed, rimmed with white fire. He turned them out, and, having thrown his hat and cape on the table, passed through the library towards the door of his bedroom, a large octagonal chamber on the ground floor that, in his new-born feeling for luxury, he had just had decorated for himself, and hung with some curious Renaissance tapestries that had been discovered stored in a disused attic at Selby Royal. As he was turning the handle of the door, his eye fell upon the portrait Basil Hallward had painted of him. He started back as if in surprise. Then he went on into his own room, looking somewhat puzzled. After he had taken the buttonhole out of his coat, he seemed to hesitate. Finally he came back, went over to the picture, and examined it. In the dim arrested light that struggled through the cream-coloured silk blinds, the face appeared to him to be a little changed. The expression looked different. One would have said that there was a touch of cruelty in the mouth. It was certainly strange.

He turned round, and, walking to the window, drew up the blind. The bright dawn flooded the room, and swept the fantastic shadows into dusky corners, where they lay shuddering. But the strange expression that he had noticed in the face of the portrait seemed to linger there, to be more intensified even. The quivering, ardent sunlight showed him the lines of cruelty round the mouth as clearly as if he had been looking into a mirror after he had done some dreadful thing.

He winced, and, taking up from the table an oval glass framed in ivory Cupids, one of Lord Henry's many presents to him, glanced hurriedly into its polished depths. No line like that warped his red lips. What did it mean?

He rubbed his eyes, and came close to the picture, and examined it again. There were no signs of any change when he looked into the actual painting, and yet there was no doubt that the whole expression had altered. It was not a mere fancy of his own. The thing was horribly apparent.

He threw himself into a chair, and began to think. Suddenly there flashed across his mind what he had said in Basil Hallward's studio the day the picture had been finished. Yes, he remembered it perfectly. He had uttered a mad wish that he himself might remain young, and the portrait grow old; that his own beauty might be untarnished, and the face on the canvas bear the burden of his passions and his sins; that the painted image might be seared with the lines of suffering and thought, and that he might keep all the delicate bloom and loveliness of his then just conscious boyhood. Surely his wish had not been fulfilled? Such things were impossible. It seemed monstrous even to think of them. And, yet, there was the picture before him, with the touch of cruelty in the mouth.

Cruelty! Had he been cruel? It was the girl's fault, not his. He had dreamed of her as a great artist, had given his love to her because he had thought her great. Then she had disappointed him. She had been shallow and unworthy. And, yet, a feeling of infinite regret came over him, as he thought of her lying at his feet sobbing like a little child. He remembered with what callousness he had watched her. Why had he been made like that? Why had such a soul been given to him? But he had suffered also. During the three terrible hours that the play had lasted, he had lived centuries of pain, æon upon æon of torture. His life was well worth hers. She had marred him for a moment, if he had wounded her for an age. Besides, women were better suited to bear sorrow than men. They lived on their emotions. They only thought of their emotions. When they took lovers, it was merely to have someone with whom they could have scenes. Lord Henry had told him that, and Lord Henry knew what women were. Why should he trouble about Sibyl Vane? She was nothing to him now.

But the picture? What was he to say of that? It held the secret of his life, and told his story. It had taught him to love his own beauty. Would it teach him to loathe his own soul? Would he ever look at it again?

No; it was merely an illusion wrought on the troubled senses. The horrible night that he had passed had left phantoms behind it. Suddenly there had fallen upon his brain that tiny scarlet speck that makes men mad. The picture had not changed. It was folly to think so.

Yet it was watching him, with its beautiful marred face and its cruel smile. Its bright hair gleamed in the early sunlight. Its blue eyes met his own. A sense of infinite pity, not for himself, but for the painted image of himself, came over him. It had altered already, and would alter more. Its gold would wither into grey. Its red and white roses would die. For every sin that he committed, a stain would fleck and wreck its fairness. But he would not sin. The picture, changed or unchanged, would be to him the visible emblem of conscience. He would resist temptation. He would not see Lord Henry any more—would not, at any rate, listen to those subtle poisonous theories that in Basil Hallward's garden had first stirred within him the passion for impossible things. He would go back to Sibyl Vane, make her amends, marry her, try to love her again. Yes, it was his duty to do so. She must have suffered more than he had. Poor child! He had been selfish and cruel to her. The fascination that she had exercised over him would return. They would be happy together. His life with her would be beautiful and pure.

He got up from his chair, and drew a large screen right in front of the portrait, shuddering as he glanced at it. "How horrible!" he murmured to himself, and he walked across to the window and opened it. When he stepped out on the grass, he drew a deep breath. The fresh morning air seemed to drive away all his sombre passions. He thought only of Sibyl. A faint echo of his love came back to him. He repeated her name over and over again. The birds that were singing in the dew-drenched garden seemed to be telling the flowers about her.

CHAPTER VIII

IT was long past noon when he awoke. His valet had crept several times on tiptoe into the room to see if he was stirring, and had wondered what made his young master sleep so late. Finally his bell sounded, and Victor came softly in with a cup of tea, and a pile of letters, on a small tray of old Sèvres china, and drew back the olive-satin curtains, with their shimmering blue lining, that hung in front of the three tall windows.

"Monsieur has well slept this morning," he said, smiling.

"What o'clock is it, Victor?" asked Dorian Gray, drowsily.

"One hour and a quarter, Monsieur."

How late it was! He sat up, and, having sipped some tea, turned over his letters. One of them was from Lord Henry, and had been brought by hand that morning. He hesitated for a moment, and then put it aside. The others he opened listlessly. They contained the usual collection of cards, invitations to dinner, tickets for private views, programmes of charity concerts, and the like, that are showered on fashionable young men every morning during the season. There was a rather heavy bill, for a chased silver Louis-Quinze toilet-set, that he had not yet the courage to send on to his guardians, who were extremely old-fashioned people and did not realise that we live in an age when unnecessary things are our only necessities; and there were several very courteously worded communications from Jermyn Street money lenders offering to advance any sum of money at a moment's notice and at the most reasonable rates of interest.

After about ten minutes he got up, and, throwing on a

elaborate dressing-gown of silk-embroidered cashmere wool, passed into the onyx-paved bathroom. The cool water refreshed him after his long sleep. He seemed to have forgotten all that he had gone through. A dim sense of having taken part in some strange tragedy came to him once or twice, but there was the unreality of a dream about it.

As soon as he was dressed, he went into the library and sat down to a light French breakfast, that had been laid out for him on a small round table close to the open window. It was an exquisite day. The warm air seemed laden with spices. A bee flew in, and buzzed round the blue-dragon bowl that, filled with sulphur-yellow roses, stood before him. He felt perfectly happy.

Suddenly his eye fell upon the screen that he had placed in front of the portrait, and he started.

"Too cold for Monsieur?" asked his valet, putting an omelette on the table. "I shut the window?"

Dorian shook his head. "I am not cold," he murmured.

Was it all true? Had the portrait really changed? Or had it been simply his own imagination that had made him see a look of evil where there had been a look of joy? Surely a painted canvas could not alter? The thing was absurd. It would serve as a tale to tell Basil some day. It would make him smile.

And, yet, how vivid was his recollection of the whole thing! First in the dim twilight, and then in the bright dawn, he had seen the touch of cruelty round the warped lips. He almost dreaded his valet leaving the room. He knew that when he was alone he would have to examine the portrait. He was afraid of certainty. When the coffee and cigarettes had been brought and the man turned to go, he felt a wild desire to tell him to remain. As the door was closing behind him he called him back. The man stood waiting for his orders. Dorian looked at him for a moment. "I am not at home to anyone, Victor," he said, with a sigh. The man bowed and retired.

Then he rose from the table, lit a cigarette, and flung himself down on a luxuriously-cushioned couch that stood facing the screen. The screen was an old one, of gilt Spanish leather, stamped and wrought with a rather florid Louis-Quatorze pattern. He scanned it curiously, wondering if ever before it had concealed the secret of a man's life.

Should he move it aside, after all? Why not let it stay there? What was the use of knowing? If the thing was true, it was terrible. If it was not true, why trouble about it? But what if, by some fate or deadlier chance, eyes other than his spied behind, and saw the horrible change? What should he do if Basil Hallward came and asked to look at his own picture? Basil would be sure to do that. No; the thing had to be examined, and at once. Anything would be better than this dreadful state of doubt.

He got up, and locked both doors. At least he would be alore when he looked upon the mask of his shame. Then he drew the screen aside, and saw himself face to face. It was perfectly true. The portrait had altered.

As he often remembered afterwards, and always with no small wonder, he found himself at first gazing at the portrait with a feeling of almost scientific interest. That such a change should have taken place was incredible to him. And yet it was a fact. Was there some subtle affinity between the chemical atoms, that shaped themselves into form and colour on the canvas, and the soul that was within him? Could it be that what that soul thought, they realized?— that what it dreamed, they made true? Or was there some other, more terrible reason? He shuddered, and felt afraid, and, going back to the couch, lay there, gazing at the picture in sickened horror.

One thing, however, he felt that it had done for him

It had made him conscious how unjust, how cruel, he had been to Sibyl Vane. It was not too late to make reparation for that. She could still be his wife. His unreal and selfish love would yield to some higher influence, would be transformed into some nobler passion, and the portrait that Basil Hallward had painted of him would be a guide to him through life, would be to him what holiness is to some, and conscience to others, and the fear of God to us all. There were opiates for remorse, drugs that could lull the moral sense to sleep. But here was a visible symbol of the degradation of sin. Here was an ever-present sign of the ruin men brought upon their souls.

Three o'clock struck, and four, and the half-hour rang its double chime, but Dorian Gray did not stir. He was trying to gather up the scarlet threads of life, and to weave them into a pattern; to find his way through the sanguine labyrinth of passion through which he was wandering. He did not know what to do, or what to think. Finally, he went over to the table, and wrote a passionate letter to the girl he had loved, imploring her forgiveness, and accusing himself of madness. He covered page after page with wild words of sorrow, and wilder words of pain. There is a luxury in self-reproach. When we blame ourselves we feel that no one else has a right to blame us. It is the confession, not the priest, that gives us absolution. When Dorian had finished the letter, he felt that he had been forgiven.

Suddenly there came a knock on the door, and he heard Lord Henry's voice outside. "My dear boy, I must see you. Let me in at once. I can't bear your shutting yourself up like this."

He made no answer at first, but remained quite still. The knocking still continued, and grew louder. Yes, it was better to let Lord Henry in, and to explain to him the new life he was going to lead, to quarrel with him if it became necessary to quarrel, to part if parting was inevitable. He jumped up, drew the screen hastily across the picture, and unlocked the door.

"I am so sorry for it all, Dorian," said Lord Henry, as he entered. "But you must not think too much about it."

"Do you mean about Sibyl Vane?" asked the lad.

"Yes, of course," answered Lord Henry, sinking into a chair, and slowly pulling off his yellow gloves. "It is dreadful, from one point of view, but it was not your fault. Tell me, did you go behind and see her, after the play was over?"

"Yes."

"I felt sure you had. Did you make a scene with her?"

"I was brutal, Harry—perfectly brutal. But it is all right now. I am not sorry for anything that has happened. It has taught me to know myself better."

"Ah, Dorian, I am so glad you take it in that way! I was afraid I would find you plunged in remorse, and tearing that nice curly hair of yours."

"I have got through all that," said Dorian, shaking his head, and smiling. "I am perfectly happy now. I know what conscience is, to begin with. It is not what you told me it was. It is the divinest thing in us. Don't sneer at it, Harry, any more—at least not before me. I want to be good. I can't bear the idea of my soul being hideous."

"A very charming artistic basis for ethics, Dorian! I congratulate you on it. But how are you going to begin?"

"By marrying Sibyl Vane."

"Marrying Sibyl Vane!" cried Lord Henry, standing up, and looking at him in perplexed amazement. "But, my dear Dorian——"

"Yes, Harry, I know what you are going to say. Something dreadful about marriage. Don't say it. Don't ever say things of that kind to me again. Two days ago I asked Sibyl to marry me. I am not going to break my word to her. She is to be my wife!"

"Your wife! Dorian! . . . Didn't you get my letter? I wrote to you this morning, and sent the note down, by my own man."

"Your letter? Oh, yes, I remember. I have not read it yet, Harry. I was afraid there might be something in it that I wouldn't like. You cut life to pieces with your epigrams."

"You know nothing then?"

"What do you mean?"

Lord Henry walked across the room, and, sitting down by Dorian Gray, took both his hands in his own, and held them tightly. "Dorian," he said, "my letter—don't be frightened—was to tell you that Sibyl Vane is dead."

A cry of pain broke from the lad's lips, and he leaped to his feet, tearing his hands away from Lord Henry's grasp. "Dead! Sibyl dead! It is not true! It is a horrible lie! How dare you say it?"

"It is quite true, Dorian," said Lord Henry, gravely. "It is in all the morning papers. I wrote down to you to ask you not to see anyone till I came. There will have to be an inquest, of course, and you must not be mixed up in it. Things like that make a man fashionable in Paris. But in London people are so prejudiced. Here, one should never make one's début with a scandal. One should reserve that to give an interest to one's old age. I suppose they don't know your name at the theatre? If they don't, it is all right. Did anyone see you going round to her room? That is an important point."

Dorian did not answer for a few moments. He was dazed with horror. Finally he stammered in a stifled voice: "Harry, did you say an inquest? What did you mean by that? Did Sibyl——? Oh, Harry, I can't bear it! But be quick. Tell me everything at once."

"I have no doubt it was not an accident, Dorian, though it must be put in that way to the public. It seems that as she was leaving the theatre with her mother, about half-past twelve or so, she said she had forgotten something upstairs. They waited some time for her, but she did not come down again. They ultimately found her lying dead on the floor of her dressing-room. She had swallowed something by mistake, some dreadful thing they use at theatres. I don't know what it was, but it had either prussic acid or white lead in it. I should fancy it was prussic acid, as she seems to have died instantaneously."

"Harry, Harry, it is terrible!" cried the lad.

"Yes; it is very tragic, of course, but you must not get yourself mixed up in it. I see by 'The Standard' that she was seventeen. I should have thought she was almost younger than that. She looked such a child, and seemed to know so little about acting. Dorian, you mustn't let this thing get on your nerves. You must come and dine with me, and afterwards we will look in at the Opera. It is a Patti night, and everybody will be there. You can come to my sister's box. She has got some smart women with her."

"So I have murdered Sibyl Vane," said Dorian Gray, half to himself—"murdered her as surely as if I had cut her little throat with a knife. Yet the roses are not less lovely for all that. The birds sing just as happily in my garden. And tonight I am to dine with you, and then go on to the Opera, and sup somewhere, I suppose, afterwards. How extraordinarily dramatic life is! If I had read all this in a book, Harry, I think I would have wept over it. Somehow, now that it has happened actually, and to me, it seems far too wonderful for tears. Here is the first passionate love-letter I have ever written in my life. Strange, that my first passionate love-letter should have been addressed to a dead girl. Can they feel, I wonder, those white silent people we call the dead?

Sibyl! Can she feel, or know, or listen? Oh, Harry, how I loved her once! It seems years ago to me now. She was everything to me. Then came that dreadful night—was it really only last night?—when she played so badly, and my heart almost broke. She explained it all to me. It was terribly pathetic. But I was not moved a bit. I thought her shallow. Suddenly something happened that made me afraid. I can't tell you what it was, but it was terrible. I said I would go back to her. I felt I had done wrong. And now she is dead. My God! my God! Harry, what shall I do? You don't know the danger I am in, and there is nothing to keep me straight. She would have done that for me. She had no right to kill herself. It was selfish of her."

"My dear Dorian," answered Lord Henry, taking a cigarette from his case, and producing a gold-latten matchbox, "the only way a woman can ever reform a man is by boring him so completely that he loses all possible interest in life. If you had married this girl you would have been wretched. Of course you would have treated her kindly. One can always be kind to people about whom one cares nothing. But she would have soon found out that you were absolutely indifferent to her. And when a woman finds that out about her husband, she either becomes dreadfully dowdy, or wears very smart bonnets that some other woman's husband has to pay for. I say nothing about the social mistake, which would have been abject, which, of course, I would not have allowed, but I assure you that in any case the whole thing would have been an absolute failure."

"I suppose it would," muttered the lad, walking up and down the room, and looking horribly pale. "But I thought it was my duty. It is not my fault that this terrible tragedy has prevented my doing what was right. I remember your saying once that there is a fatality about good resolutions—that they are always made too late. Mine certainly were."

"Good resolutions are useless attempts to interfere with scientific laws. Their origin is pure vanity. Their result is absolutely nil. They give us, now and then, some of those luxurious sterile emotions that have a certain charm for the weak. That is all that can be said for them. They are simply cheques that men draw on a bank where they have no account."

"Harry," cried Dorian Gray, coming over and sitting down beside him, "why is it that I cannot feel this tragedy as much as I want to? I don't think I am heartless. Do you?"

"You have done too many foolish things during the last fortnight to be entitled to give yourself that name, Dorian," answered Lord Henry, with his sweet, melancholy smile.

The lad frowned. "I don't like that explanation, Harry," he rejoined, "but I am glad you don't think I am heartless. I am nothing of the kind. I know I am not. And yet I must admit that this thing that has happened does not affect me as it should. It seems to me to be simply like a wonderful ending to a wonderful play. It has all the terrible beauty of a Greek tragedy, a tragedy in which I took a great part, but by which I have not been wounded."

"It is an interesting question," said Lord Henry, who found an exquisite pleasure in playing on the lad's unconscious egotism—"an extremely interesting question. I fancy that the true explanation is this. It often happens that the real tragedies of life occur in such an inartistic manner that they hurt us by their crude violence, their absolute incoherence, their absurd want of meaning, their entire lack of style. They affect us just as vulgarity affects us. They give us an impression of sheer brute force, and we revolt against that. Sometimes, however, a tragedy that possesses artistic elements of beauty crosses our lives. If these elements of beauty are real, the whole thing simply appeals to our sense of dramatic effect. Suddenly we find that we are no longer the actors, but the spectators of the play. Or rather we are both. We watch ourselves, and the mere wonder of the spectacle enthralls us. In the present case, what is it that has really happened? Someone has killed herself for love of you. I wish that I had ever had such an experience. It would have made me in love with love for the rest of my life. The people who have adored me—there have not been very many, but there have been some—have always insisted on living on, long after I had ceased to care for them, or they to care for me. They have become stout and tedious, and when I meet them they go in at once for reminiscences. That awful memory of woman! What a fearful thing it is! And what an utter intellectual stagnation it reveals! One should absorb the colour of life, but one should never remember its details. Details are always vulgar."

"I must sow poppies in my garden," sighed Dorian.

"There is no necessity," rejoined his companion. "Life has always poppies in her hands. Of course, now and then things linger. I once wore nothing but violets all through one season, as a form of artistic mourning for a romance that would not die. Ultimately, however, it did die. I forget what killed it. I think it was her proposing to sacrifice the whole world for me. That is always a dreadful moment. It fills one with the terror of eternity. Well—would you believe it?—a week ago, at Lady Hampshires, I found myself seated at dinner next the lady in question, and she insisted on going over the whole thing again, and digging up the past, and raking up the future. I had buried my romance in a bed of asphodel. She dragged it out again, and assured me that I had spoiled her life. I am bound to state that she ate an enormous dinner, so I did not feel any anxiety. But what a lack of taste she showed! The one charm of the past is that it is the past. But women never know when the curtain has fallen. They always want a sixth act, and as soon as the interest of the play is entirely over they propose to continue it. If they were allowed their own way, every comedy would have a tragic ending, and every tragedy would culminate in a farce. They are charmingly artificial, but they have no sense of art. You are more fortunate than I am. I assure you, Dorian, that not one of the women I have known would have done for me what Sibyl Vane did for you. Ordinary women always console themselves. Some of them do it by going in for sentimental colours. Never trust a woman who wears mauve, whatever her age may be, or a woman over thirty-five who is fond of pink ribbons. It always means that they have a history. Others find a great consolation in suddenly discovering the good qualities of their husbands. They flaunt their conjugal felicity in one's face, as if it were the most fascinating of sins. Religion consoles some. Its mysteries have all the charm of a flirtation, a woman once told me; and I can quite understand it. Besides, nothing makes one so vain as being told that one is a sinner. Conscience makes egotists of us all. Yes; there is really no end to the consolations that women find in modern life. Indeed, I have not mentioned the most important one."

"What is that, Harry?" said the lad, listlessly.

"Oh, the obvious consolation. Taking someone else's admirer when one loses one's own. In good society that always whitewashes a woman. But really, Dorian, how different Sibyl Vane must have been from all the women one meets! There is something to me quite beautiful about her death. I am glad I am living in a century when such wonders happen. They make one believe in the reality of the things we all play with, such as romance, passion, and love."

"I was terribly cruel to her. You forget that."

"I am afraid that women appreciate cruelty, downright cruelty, more than anything else. They have wonderfully primitive instincts. We have emancipated them, but they remain slaves looking for their masters, all the same. They love being dominated. I am sure you were splendid. I have never seen you really and absolutely angry, but I can fancy how delightful you looked. And, after all, you said something to me the day before yesterday that seemed to me at the time to be merely fanciful, but that I see now was absolutely true, and it holds the key to everything."

"What was that, Harry?"

"You said to me that Sibyl Vane represented to you all the heroines of romance—that she was Desdemona one night, and Ophelia the other; that if she died as Juliet, she came to life as Imogen."

"She will never come to life again now," muttered the lad, burying his face in his hands.

"No, she will never come to life. She has played her last part. But you must think of that lonely death in the tawdry dressing-room simply as a strange lurid fragment from some Jacobean tragedy, as a wonderful scene from Webster, or Ford, or Cyril Tourneur. The girl never really lived, and so she has never really died. To you at least she was always a dream, a phantom that flitted through Shakespeare's plays and left them lovelier for its presence, a reed through which Shakespeare's music sounded richer and more full of joy. The moment she touched actual life, she marred it, and it marred her, and so she passed away. Mourn for Ophelia, if you like. Put ashes on your head because Cordelia was strangled. Cry out against Heaven because the daughter of Brabantio died. But don't waste your tears over Sibyl Vane. She was less real than they are."

There was a silence. The evening darkened in the room. Noiselessly, and with silver feet, the shadows crept in from the garden. The colours faded wearily out of things.

After some time Dorian Gray looked up. "You have explained me to myself, Harry," he murmured, with something of a sigh of relief. "I felt all that you have said, but somehow I was afraid of it, and I could not express it to myself. How well you know me! But we will not talk again of what has happened. It has been a marvellous experience. That is all. I wonder if life has still in store for me anything as marvellous."

"Life has everything in store for you, Dorian. There is nothing that you, with your extraordinary good looks, will not be able to do."

"But suppose, Harry, I became haggard, and old, and wrinkled? What then?"

"Ah, then," said Lord Henry, rising to go—"then, my dear Dorian, you would have to fight for your victories. As it is, they are brought to you. No, you must keep your good looks. We live in an age that reads too much to be wise, and that thinks too much to be beautiful. We cannot spare you. And now you had better dress, and drive down to the club. We are rather late, as it is."

"I think I shall join you at the Opera, Harry. I feel too tired to eat anything. What is the number of your sister's box?"

"Twenty-seven, I believe. It is on the grand tier. You will see her name on the door. But I am sorry you won't come and dine."

"I don't feel up to it," said Dorian, listleslsy. "But I am awfully obliged to you for all that you have said to me. You are certainly my best friend. No one has ever understood me as you have."

"We are only at the beginning of our friendship, Dorian," answered Lord Henry, shaking him by the hand. "Good-bye. I shall see you before nine-thirty, I hope. Remember, Patti is singing."

As he closed the door behind him, Dorian Gray touched the bell, and in a few minutes Victor appeared with the lamps and drew the blinds down. He waited impatiently for him to go. The man seemed to take an interminable time over everything.

As soon as he had left, he rushed to the screen, and drew it back. No; there was no further change in the picture. It had received the news of Sibyl Vane's death before he had known of it himself. It was conscious of the events of life as they occurred. The vicious cruelty that marred the fine lines of the mouth had, no doubt, appeared at the very moment that the girl had drunk the poison, whatever it was. Or was it indifferent to results? Did it merely take cognizance of what passed within the soul? He wondered, and hoped that some day he would see the change taking place before his very eyes, shuddering as he hoped it.

Poor Sibyl! what a romance it had all been! She had often mimicked death on the stage. Then Death himself had touched her, and taken her with him. How had she played that dreadful last scene? Had she cursed him, as she died? No; she had died for love of him, and love would always be a sacrament to him now. She had atoned for everything, by the sacrifice she had made of her life. He would not think any more of what she had made him go through, on that horrible night at the theatre. When he thought of her, it would be as a wonderful tragic figure sent on to the world's stage to show the supreme reality of Love. A wonderful tragic figure? Tears came to his eyes as he remembered her childlike look, and winsome fanciful ways, and shy tremulous grace. He brushed them away hastily, and looked again at the picture.

He felt that the time had really come for making his choice. Or had his choice already been made? Yes, life had decided that for him—life, and his own infinite curiosity about life. Eternal youth, infinite passion, pleasures subtle and secret, wild joys and wilder sins—he was to have all these things.

The portrait was to bear the burden of his shame: that was all.

A feeling of pain crept over him as he thought of the desecration that was in store for the fair face on the canvas. Once, in boyish mockery of Narcissus, he had kissed, or feigned to kiss, those painted lips that now smiled so cruelly at him. Morning after morning he had sat before the portrait, wondering at its beauty, almost enamoured of it, as it seemed to him at times. Was it to alter now with every mood to which he yielded? Was it to become a monstrous and loathsome thing, to be hidden away in a locked room, to be shut out from the sunlight that had so often touched to brighter gold the waving wonder of its hair? The pity of it! the pity of it!

For a moment he thought of praying that the horrible sympathy that existed between him and the picture might cease. It had changed in answer to a prayer; perhaps in answer to a prayer it might remain unchanged. And, yet, who, that knew anything about Life, would surrender the chance of remaining always young, however fantastic that chance might be, or with what fateful consequences it might be fraught? Besides, was it really under his control? Had it indeed been prayer that had produced the substitution? Might there not be some curious scientific reason for it all? If thought could exercise its influence upon a living organism, might not thought exercise an influence upon dead and inorganic things? Nay, without thought or conscious desire, might not things external to ourselves vibrate in unison with our moods and passions, atom calling to atom in secret love of strange affinity? But the reason was of no importance. He would never again tempt by a prayer any terrible power. If the picture was to alter, it was to alter. That was all. Why inquire too closely into it?

For there would be a real pleasure in watching it. He

would be able to follow his mind into its secret places. This portrait would be to him the most magical of mirrors. As it had revealed to him his own body, so it would reveal to him his own soul. And when winter came upon it, he would still be standing where spring trembles on the verge of summer. When the blood crept from its face, and left behind a pallid mask of chalk with leaden eyes, he would keep the glamour of boyhood. Not one blossom of his loveliness would ever fade. Not one pulse of his life would ever weaken. Like the gods of the Greeks, he would be strong, and fleet, and joyous. What did it matter what happened to the coloured image on the canvas? He would be safe. That was every-thing.

He drew the screen back into its former place in front of the picture, smiling as he did so, and passed into his bed-room, where his valet was already waiting for him. An hour later he was at the Opera, and Lord Henry was leaning over his chair.

CHAPTER IX

AS he was sitting at breakfast next morning, Basil Hall-ward was shown into the room.

"I am so glad I have found you, Dorian," he said, gravely. "I called last night, and they told me you were at the Opera. Of course I knew that was impossible. But I wish you had left word where you had really gone to. I passed a dreadful evening, half afraid that one tragedy might be followed by another. I think you might have telegraphed for me when you heard of it first. I read of it quite by chance in a late edition of 'The Globe,' that I picked up at the club. I came here at once, and was miserable at not finding you. I can't tell you how heart-broken I am about the whole thing. I know that you must suffer. But where were you? Did you go down and see the girl's mother? For a moment I thought of following you there. They gave the address in the paper. Somewhere in the Euston Road, isn't it? But I was afraid of intruding upon a sorrow that I could not lighten. Poor woman! What a state she must be in! And her only child, too! What did she say about it all?"

"My dear Basil, how do I know?" murmured Dorian Gray, sipping some pale-yellow wine from a delicate gold-beaded bubble of Venetian glass, and looking dreadfully bored. "I was at the Opera. You should have come on there. I met Lady Gwendolyn, Harry's sister, for the first time. We were in her box. She is perfectly charming; and Patti sang divinely. Don't talk about horrid subjects. If one doesn't talk about a thing, it has never happened. It is simply expression, as Harry says, that gives reality to things. I may mention that she was not the woman's only child. There is a son, a charming fellow, I believe. But he is not on the stage. He is a sailor, or something. And now, tell me about yourself and what you are painting."

"You went to the Opera?" said Hallward, speaking very slowly, and with a strained touch of pain in his voice. "You went to the Opera while Sibyl Vane was lying dead in some sordid lodging? You can talk to me of other women being charming, and of Patti singing divinely, before the girl you loved has even the quiet of a grave to sleep in? Why, man, there are horrors in store for that little white body of hers!"

"Stop, Basil! I won't hear it!" cried Dorian, leaping to his feet. "You must not tell me about things. What is done is done. What is past is past."

"You call yesterday the past?"

"What has the actual lapse of time got to do with it? It is only shallow people who require years to get rid of an emotion. A man who is master of himself can end a sorrow as easily as he can invent a pleasure. I don't want to be at the mercy of my emotions. I want to use them, to enjoy them, and to dominate them."

"Dorian, this is horrible! Something has changed you completely. You look exactly the same wonderful boy who, day after day, used to come down to my studio to sit for his picture. But you were simple, natural, and affectionate then. You were the most unspoiled creature in the whole world. Now, I don't know what has come over you. You talk as if you had no heart, no pity in you. It is all Harry's influence. I see that."

The lad flushed up, and, going to the window, looked out for a few moments on the green, flickering, sunlashed garden. "I owe a great deal to Harry, Basil," he said, at last—"more than I owe to you. You only taught me to be vain."

"Well, I am punished for that, Dorian—or shall be some day."

"I don't know what you mean, Basil," he exclaimed, turning round. "I don't know what you want. What do you want?"

"I want the Dorian Gray I used to paint," said the artist, sadly.

"Basil," said the lad, going over to him, and putting his hand on his shoulder, "you have come too late. Yesterday when I heard that Sibyl Vane had killed herself——"

"Killed herself! Good heavens! is there no doubt about that?" cried Hallward, looking up at him with an expression of horror.

"My dear Basil! Surely you don't think it was a vulgar accident? Of course she killed herself."

The elder man buried his face in his hands. "How fearful," he muttered, and a shudder ran through him.

"No," said Dorian Gray, "there is nothing fearful about it. It is one of the great romantic tragedies of the age. As a rule, people who act lead the most commonplace lives. They are good husbands, or faithful wives, or something tedious. You know what I mean—middle-class virtue, and all that kind of thing. How different Sibyl was! She lived her finest tragedy. She was always a heroine. The last night she played—the night you saw her—she acted badly because she had known the reality of love. When she knew its unreality, she died, as Juliet might have died. She passed again into the sphere of art. There is something of the martyr about her. Her death has all the pathetic uselessness of martyrdom, all its wasted beauty. But, as I was saying, you must not think I have not suffered. If you had come in yesterday at a particular moment—about half-past five, perhaps, or a quarter to six—you would have found me in tears. Even Harry, who was here, who brought me the news, in fact, had no idea what I was going through. I suffered immensely. Then it passed away. I cannot repeat an emotion. No one can, except sentimentalists. And you are awfully unjust, Basil. You come down here to console me. That is charming of you. You find me consoled, and you are furious. How like a sympathetic person! You remind me of a story Harry told me about a certain philanthropist who spent twenty years of his life in trying to get some grievance redressed, or some unjust law altered—I forget exactly what it was. Finally he succeeded, and nothing could exceed his disappointment. He had absolutely nothing to do, almost died of ennui, and became a confirmed misanthrope. And besides, my dear old Basil, if you really want to console me, teach me rather to forget what has happened, or to see it from the proper artistic point of view. Was it not Gautier who used to write about *la consolation des arts?* I remember picking up a little vellum-covered book in your studio one day and chancing on that delightful phrase. Well, I am not like that young man you told me of when we were down at Marlow together, the young man who used to say that yellow satin could console one for all the miseries of life. I love beautiful things that one can touch and handle. Old brocades, green bronzes, lacquer-work, carved ivories, exquisite surroundings, luxury, pomp, there is much to be got from all these. But the artistic temperament that they create, or at any rate reveal, is still more to me. To become the spectator of one's own life, as Harry says, is to escape the suffering of life. I know you are surprised at my talking to you like this. You have not realised how I have developed. I was a school-boy when you knew me. I am a man now. I have new passions, new thoughts, new ideas. I am different, but you must not like me less. I am changed, but you must always be my friend. Of course I am very fond of Harry. But I know that you are better than he is. You are not stronger—you are too much afraid of life—but you are better. And how happy we used to be together! Don't leave me, Basil, and don't quarrel with me. I am what I am. There is nothing more to be said."

The painter felt strangely moved. The lad was infinitely dear to him, and his personality had been the great turning point in his art. He could not bear the idea of reproaching him any more. After all, his indifference was probably merely a mood that would pass away. There was so much in him that was good, so much in him that was noble.

"Well, Dorian," he said, at length, with a sad smile, "I won't speak to you again about this horrible thing, after to-day. I only trust your name won't be mentioned in connection with it. The inquest is to take place this afternoon. Have they summoned you?"

Dorian shook his head and a look of annoyance passed over his face at the mention of the word "inquest." There was something so crude and vulgar about everything of the kind. "They don't know my name," he answered.

"But surely she did?"

"Only my Christian name, and that I am quite sure she never mentioned to anyone. She told me once that they were all rather curious to learn who I was, and that she invariably told them my name was Prince Charming. It was pretty of her. You must do me a drawing of Sibyl, Basil. I should like to have something more of her than the memory of a few kisses and some broken pathetic words."

"I will try and do something, Dorian, if it would please you. But you must come and sit to me yourself again. I can't get on without you."

"I can never sit to you again, Basil. It is impossible!" he exclaimed, starting back.

The painter stared at him. "My dear boy, what nonsense!" he cried. "Do you mean to say you don't like what I did of you? Where is it? Why have you pulled the screen in front of it? Let me look at it. It is the best thing I have ever done.

Do take the screen away, Dorian. It is simply disgraceful of your servant hiding my work like that. I felt the room looked different as I came in."

"My servant has nothing to do with it, Basil. You don't imagine I let him arrange my room for me? He settles my flowers for me sometimes—that is all. No; I did it myself. The light was too strong on the portrait."

"Too strong! Surely not, my dear fellow? It is an admirable place for it. Let me see it." And Hallward walked towards the corner of the room.

A cry of terror broke from Dorian Gray's lips, and he rushed between the painter and the screen. "Basil," he said, looking very pale, "you must not look at it. I don't wish you to."

"Not look at my own work! you are not serious. Why shouldn't I look at it?" exclaimed Hallward, laughing.

"If you try to look at it, Basil, on my word of honour I will never speak to you again as long as I live. I am quite serious. I don't offer any explanation, and you are not to ask for any. But, remember, if you touch this screen, everything is over between us."

Hallward was thunderstruck. He looked at Dorian Gray in absolute amazement. He had never seen him like this before. The lad was actually pallid with rage. His hands were clenched, and the pupils of his eyes were like disks of blue fire. He was trembling all over.

"Dorian!"

"Don't speak!"

"But what is the matter? Of course I won't look at it if you don't want me to," he said, rather coldly, turning on his heel, and going over towards the window. "But, really, it seems rather absurd that I shouldn't see my own work. especially as I am going to exhibit it in Paris in the autumn.

I shall probably have to give it another coat of varnish before that, so I must see it some day, and why not to-day?"

"To exhibit it? You want to exhibit it?" exclaimed Dorian Gray, a strange sense of terror creeping over him. Was the world going to be shown his secret? Were people to gape at the mystery of his life? That was impossible. Something— he did not know what—had to be done at once.

"Yes; I don't suppose you will object to that. George Petit is going to collect all my best pictures for a special exhibition in the Rue de Sèze, which will open the first week in October. The portrait will only be away a month. I should think you could easily spare it for that time. In fact, you are sure to be out of town. And if you keep it always behind a screen, you can't care much about it."

Dorian Gray passed his hand over his forehead. There were beads of perspiration there. He felt that he was on the brink of a horrible danger. "You told me a month ago that you would never exhibit it," he cried. "Why have you changed your mind? You people who go in for being consistent have just as many moods as others have. The only difference is that your moods are rather meaningless. You can't have for- gotten that you assured me most solemnly that nothing in the world would induce you to send it to any exhibition. You told Harry exactly the same thing." He stopped suddenly, and a gleam of light came into his eyes. He remembered that Lord Henry had said to him once, half seriously and half in jest, "If you want to have a strange quarter of an hour, get Basil to tell you why he won't exhibit your picture. He told me why he wouldn't, and it was a revelation to me." Yes, perhaps Basil, too, had his secret. He would ask him and try.

"Basil," he said, coming over quite close, and looking him straight in the face, "we have each of us a secret. Let me know yours and I shall tell you mine. What was your reason for refusing to exhibit my picture?"

The painter shuddered in spite of himself. "Dorian, if I told you, you might like me less than you do, and you would certainly laugh at me. I could not bear your doing either of those two things. If you wish me never to look at your picture again, I am content. I have always you to look at. If you wish the best work I have ever done to be hidden from the world, I am satisfied. Your friendship is dearer to me than any fame or reputation."

"No, Basil, you must tell me," insisted Dorian Gray. "I think I have a right to know." His feeling of terror had passed away, and curiosity had taken its place. He was determined to find out Basil Hallward's mystery.

"Let us sit down, Dorian," said the painter, looking troubled. "Let us sit down. And just answer me one question. Have you noticed in the picture something curious?—something that probably at first did not strike you, but that revealed itself to you suddenly?"

"Basil!" cried the lad, clutching the arms of his chair with trembling hands, and gazing at him with wild, startled eyes.

"I see you did. Don't speak. Wait till you hear what I have to say. Dorian, from the moment I met you, your personality had the most extraordinary influence over me. I was dominated, soul, brain, and power by you. You became to me the visible incarnation of that unseen ideal whose memory haunts us artists like an exquisite dream. I worshipped you. I grew jealous of everyone to whom you spoke. I wanted to have you all to myself. I was only happy when I was with you. When you were away from me you were still present in my art. . . . Of course I never let you know anything about this. It would have been impossible. You would not have understood it. I hardly understood it myself. I only knew that I had seen perfection face to face, and that the world had become wonderful to my eyes—too wonderful, perhaps, for in such mad worships there is peril, the peril

of losing them, no less than the peril of keeping them. . . .
Weeks and weeks went on, and I grew more and more absorbed in you. Then came a new development. I had drawn
you as Paris in dainty armour, and as Adonis with hunts-
man's cloak and polished boar-spear. Crowned with heavy
lotus-blossoms you had sat on the prow of Adrian's barge,
gazing across the green turbid Nile. You had leant over the
still pool of some Greek woodland, and seen in the water's
silent silver the marvel of your own face. And it had all
been what art should be, unconscious, ideal, and remote. One
day, a fatal day I sometimes think, I determined to paint a
wonderful portrait of you as you actually are, not in the
costume of dead ages, but in your own dress and in your own
time. Whether it was the Realism of the method, or the
mere wonder of your own personality, thus directly pre-
sented to me without mist or veil, I cannot tell. But I know
that as I worked at it, every flake and film of colour seemed
to me to reveal my secret. I grew afraid that others would
know of my idolatry. I felt, Dorian, that I had told too much,
that I had put too much of myself into it. Then it was that
I resolved never to allow the picture to be exhibited. You
were a little annoyed; but then you did not realise all that
it meant to me. Harry, to whom I talked about it, laughed
at me. But I did not mind that. When the picture was finished, and I sat alone with it, I felt that I was right. . . .
Well, after a few days the thing left my studio, and as soon
as I had got rid of the intolerable fascination of its presence
it seemed to me that I had been foolish in imagining that I
had seen anything in it, more than that you were extremely
good-looking, and that I could paint. Even now I cannot
help feeling that it is a mistake to think that the passion one
feels in creation is ever really shown in the work one creates.
Art is always more abstract than we fancy. Form and colour
tell us of form and colour—that is all. It often seems to me

that art conceals the artist far more completely than it ever reveals him. And so when I got this offer from Paris I determined to make your portrait the principal thing in my exhibition. It never occurred to me that you would refuse. I see now that you were right. The picture cannot be shown. You must not be angry with me, Dorian, for what I have told you. As I said to Harry, once, you are made to be worshipped."

Dorian Gray drew a long breath. The colour came back to his cheeks, and a smile played about his lips. The peril was over. He was safe for the time. Yet he could not help feeling infinite pity for the painter who had just made this strange confession to him, and wondered if he himself would ever be so dominated by the personality of a friend. Lord Henry had the charm of being very dangerous. But that was all. He was too clever and too cynical to be really fond of. Would there ever be someone who would fill him with a strange idolatry? Was that one of the things that life had in store?

"It is extraordinary to me, Dorian," said Hallward, "that you should have seen this in the portrait. Did you really see it?"

"I saw something in it," he answered, "something that seemed to me very curious."

"Well, you don't mind my looking at the thing now?"

Dorian shook his head. "You must not ask me that, Basil. I could not possibly let you stand in front of that picture."

"You will some day, surely?"

"Never."

"Well, perhaps you are right. And now good-bye, Dorian. You have been the one person in my life who has really influenced my art. Whatever I have done that is good, I owe it to you. Ah! you don't know what it cost me to tell you all that I have told you."

"My dear Basil," said Dorian, "what have you told me? Simply that you felt that you admired me too much. That is not even a compliment."

"It was not intended as a compliment. It was a confession. Now that I have made it, something seems to have gone out of me. Perhaps one should never put one's worship into words."

"It was a very disappointing confession."

"Why, what did you expect, Dorian? You didn't see anything else in the picture, did you? There was nothing else to see?"

"No; there was nothing else to see. Why do you ask? But you mustn't talk about worship. It is foolish. You and I are friends, Basil, and we must always remain so."

"You have got Harry," said the painter, sadly.

"Oh, Harry!" cried the lad, with a ripple of laughter. "Harry spends his days in saying what is incredible, and his evenings in doing what is improbable. Just the sort of life I would like to lead. But still I don't think I would go to Harry if I were in trouble. I would sooner go to you, Basil."

"You will sit to me again?"

"Impossible!"

"You spoil my life as an artist by refusing, Dorian. No man came across two ideal things. Few come across one."

"I can't explain it to you, Basil, but I must never sit to you again. There is something fatal about a portrait. It has a life of its own. I will come and have tea with you. That will be just as pleasant."

"Pleasanter for you, I am afraid," murmured Hallward, regretfully. "And now good-bye. I am sorry you won't let me look at the picture once again. But that can't be helped. I quite understand what you feel about it."

As he left the room, Dorian Gray smiled to himself. Poor

Basil! how little he knew of the true reason! And how strange it was that, instead of having been forced to reveal his own secret, he had succeeded, almost by chance, in wresting a secret from his friend! How much that strange confession explained to him! The painter's absurd fits of jealousy, his wild devotion, his extravagant panegyrics, his curious reticences—he understood them all now, and he felt sorry. There seemed to him to be something tragic in a friendship so coloured by romance.

He sighed, and touched the bell. The portrait must be hidden away at all costs. He could not run such a risk of discovery again. It had been mad of him to have allowed the thing to remain, even for an hour, in a room to which any of his friends had access.

CHAPTER X

WHEN his servant entered, he looked at him steadfastly, and wondered if he had thought of peering
behind the screen. The man was quite impassive, and waited
for his orders. Dorian lit a cigarette, and walked over to the
glass and glanced into it. He could see the reflection of
Victor's face perfectly. It was like a placid mask of servility.
There was nothing to be afraid of, there. Yet he thought it
best to be on his guard.

Speaking very slowly, he told him to tell the housekeeper
that he wanted to see her, and then to go to the frame-maker
and ask him to send two of his men round at once. It seemed
to him that as the man left the room his eyes wandered in
the direction of the screen. Or was that merely his own fancy?

After a few moments, in her black silk dress, with old-
fashioned thread mittens on her wrinkled hands, Mrs. Leaf
bustled into the library. He asked her for the key of the
schoolroom.

"The old schoolroom, Mr. Dorian?" she exclaimed. "Why
it is full of dust. I must get it arranged, and put straight before you go into it. It is not fit for you to see, sir. It is not,
indeed."

"I don't want it put straight, Leaf. I only want the key."

"Well, sir, you'll be covered with cobwebs if you go into it.
Why, it hasn't been opened for nearly five years, not since
his lordship died."

He winced at the mention of his grandfather. He had hateful memories of him. "That does not matter," he answered.
"I simply want to see the place—that is all. Give me the key."

"And here is the key, sir," said the old lady, going over the contents of her bunch with tremulously uncertain hands. "Here is the key. I'll have it off the bunch in a moment. But you don't think of living up there, sir, and you so comfortable here?"

"No, no," he cried, petulantly. "Thank you, Leaf. That will do."

She lingered for a few moments, and was garrulous over some detail of the household. He sighed, and told her to manage things as she thought best. She left the room, wreathed in smiles.

As the door closed, Dorian put the key in his pocket, and looked round the room. His eye fell on a large, purple satin coverlet heavily embroidered with gold, a splendid piece of late seventeenth-century Venetian work that his grandfather had found in a convent near Bologna. Yes, that would serve to wrap the dreadful thing in. It had perhaps served often as a pall for the dead. Now it was to hide something that had a corruption of its own, worse than the corruption of death itself—something that would breed horrors and yet would never die. What the worm was to the corpse, his sins would be to the painted image on the canvas. They would mar its beauty, and eat away its grace. They would defile it, and make it shameful. And yet the thing would still live on. It would be always alive.

He shuddered, and for a moment he regretted that he had not told Basil the true reason why he had wished to hide the picture away. Basil would have helped him to resist Lord Henry's influence, and the still more poisonous influences that came from his own temperament. The love that he bore him —for it was really love—had nothing in it that was not noble and intellectual. It was not that mere physical admiration of beauty that is born of the senses, and that dies when the senses tire. It was such love as Michael Angelo had known, and

Montaigne, and Winckelmann, and Shakespeare himself. Yes, Basil could have saved him. But it was too late now. The past could always be annihilated. Regret, denial, or forgetfulness could do that. But the future was inevitable. There were passions in him that would find their terrible outlet, dreams that would make the shadow of their evil real.

He took up from the couch the great purple-and-gold texture that covered it, and, holding it in his hands, passed behind the screen. Was the face on the canvas viler than before? It seemed to him that it was unchanged; and yet his loathing of it was intensified. Gold hair, blue eyes, and rose-red lips—they all were there. It was simply the expression that had altered. That was horrible in its cruelty. Compared to what he saw in it of censure or rebuke, how shallow Basil's reproaches about Sibyl Vane had been!—how shallow, and of what little account! His own soul was looking out at him from the canvas and calling him to judgment. A look of pain came across him, and he flung the rich pall over the picture. As he did so, a knock came to the door. He passed out as his servant entered.

"The persons are here, Monsieur."

He felt that the man must be got rid of at once. He must not be allowed to know where the picture was being taken to. There was something sly about him, and he had thoughtful, treacherous eyes. Sitting down at the writing-table, he scribbled a note to Lord Henry, asking him to send him round something to read, and reminding him that they were to meet at eight-fifteen that evening.

"Wait for an answer," he said, handing it to him, "and show the men in here."

In two or three minutes there was another knock, and Mr. Hubbard himself, the celebrated frame-maker of South Audley Street, came in with a somewhat rough-looking young assistant. Mr. Hubbard was a florid, red-whiskered little man, whose admiration for art was considerably tempered by the inveterate impecuniosity of most of the artists who dealt with him. As a rule, he never left his shop. He waited for people to come to him. But he always made an exception in favour of Dorian Gray. There was something about Dorian that charmed everybody. It was a pleasure even to see him.

"What can I do for you, Mr. Gray?" he said, rubbing his fat freckled hands. "I thought I would do myself the honour of coming round in person. I have just got a beauty of a frame, sir. Picked it up at a sale. Old Florentine. Came from Fonthill, I believe. Admirably suited for a religious subject, Mr. Gray."

"I am so sorry you have given yourself the trouble of coming round, Mr. Hubbard. I shall certainly drop in and look at the frame—though I don't go in much at present for religious art—but to-day I only want a picture carried to the top of the house for me. It is rather heavy, so I thought I would ask you to lend me a couple of your men."

"No trouble at all, Mr. Gray. I am delighted to be of any service to you. Which is the work of art, sir?"

"This," replied Dorian, moving the screen back. "Can you move it, covering and all, just as it is? I don't want it to get scratched going upstairs."

"There will be no difficulty, sir," said the genial framemaker, beginning, with the aid of his assistant, to unhook the picture from the long brass chains by which it was suspended. "And, now, where shall we carry it to, Mr. Gray?"

"I will show you the way, Mr. Hubbard, if you will kindly follow me. Or perhaps you had better go in front. I am afraid it is right at the top of the house. We will go up by the front staircase, as it is wider."

He held the door open for them, and they passed out into the hall and began the ascent. The elaborate character of the frame had made the picture extremely bulky, and now and then, in spite of the obsequious protests of Mr. Hubbard, who had the true tradesman's spirited dislike of seeing a gentleman doing anything useful, Dorian put his hand to it so as to help them.

"Something of a load to carry, sir," gasped the little man, when they reached the top landing. And he wiped his shiny forehead.

"I am afraid it is rather heavy," murmured Dorian, as he unlocked the door that opened into the room that was to keep for him the curious secret of his life and hide his soul from the eyes of men.

He had not entered the place for more than four years— not, indeed, since he had used it first as a play-room when he was a child, and then as a study when he grew somewhat older. It was a large, well-proportioned room, which had been specially built by the last Lord Kelso for the use of the little grandson whom, for his strange likeness to his mother, and also for other reasons, he had always hated and desired to keep at a distance. It appeared to Dorian to have but little changed. There was the huge Italian *cassone,* with its fantastically-painted panels and its tarnished gilt mouldings, in which he had so often hidden himself as a boy. There the satinwood bookcase filled with his dog-eared schoolbooks. On the wall behind it was hanging the same ragged Flemish tapestry, where a faded king and queen were playing chess in a garden, while a company of hawkers rode by, carrying hooded birds on their gauntleted wrists. How well he remembered it all!! Every moment of his lonely childhood came back to him as he looked round. He recalled the stainless purity of his boyish life, and it seemed horrible to him that it was here the fatal portrait was to be hidden away. How little he had thought, in those dead days, of all that was in store for him!

But there was no other place in the house so secure from prying eyes as this. He had the key, and no one else could enter it. Beneath its purple pall, the face painted on the canvas could grow bestial, sodden, and unclean. What did it matter? No one could see it. He himself would not see it. Why should he watch the hideous corruption of his soul? He kept his youth—that was enough. And, besides, might not his nature grow finer, after all? There was no reason that the future should be so full of shame. Some love might come across his life, and purify him, and shield him from those sins that seemed to be already stirring in spirit and in flesh—those curious unpictured sins whose very mystery lent them their subtlety and their charm. Perhaps, some day, the cruel look would have passed away from the scarlet sensitive mouth, and he might show to the world Basil Hallward's masterpiece.

No; that was impossible. Hour by hour, and week by week, the thing upon the canvas was growing old. It might escape the hideousness of sin, but the hideousness of age was in store for it. The cheeks would become hollow or flaccid. Yellow crow's-feet would creep round the fading eyes and make them horrible. The hair would lose its brightness, the mouth would gape or droop, would be foolish or gross, as the mouths of old men are. There would be the wrinkled throat, the cold, blue-veined hands, the twisted body, that he remembered in the grandfather who had been so stern to him in his boyhood. The picture had to be concealed. There was no help for it.

"Bring it in, Mr. Hubbard, please," he said, wearily, turning round. "I am sorry I kept you so long. I was thinking of something else."

"Always glad to have a rest, Mr. Gray," answered the frame-maker, who was still gasping for breath. "Where shall we put it, sir?"

"Oh, anywhere. Here: this will do. I don't want to have it hung up. Just lean it against the wall. Thanks."

"Might one look at the work of art, sir?"

Dorian started. "It would not interest you, Mr. Hubbard," he said, keeping his eye on the man. He felt ready to leap upon him and fling him to the ground if he dared to lift the gorgeous hanging that concealed the secret of his life. "I shan't trouble you any more now. I am much obliged for your kindness in coming round."

"Not at all, not at all, Mr. Gray. Ever ready to do anything for you, sir." And Mr. Hubbard tramped downstairs, followed by the assistant, who glanced back at Dorian with a look of shy wonder in his rough, uncomely face. He had never seen anyone so marvellous.

When the sound of their footsteps had died away, Dorian locked the door, and put the key in his pocket. He felt safe now. No one would ever look upon the horrible thing. No eye but his would ever see his shame.

On reaching the library he found that it was just after five o'clock, and that the tea had been already brought up. On a little table of dark perfumed wood thickly encrusted with nacre, a present from Lady Radley, his guardian's wife, a pretty professional invalid, who had spent the preceding winter in Cairo, was lying a note from Lord Henry, and beside it was a book bound in yellow paper, the cover slightly torn and the edges soiled. A copy of the third edition of "The St. James's Gazette" had been placed on the tea-tray. It was evident that Victor had returned. He wondered if he had met the men in the hall as they were leaving the house, and had wormed out of them what they had been doing. He would be sure to miss the picture—had no doubt missed it already, while he had been laying the tea-things. The screen had not been set back, and a blank space was visible on the wall. Perhaps some night he might find him creeping up-

stairs and trying to force the door of the room. It was a horrible thing to have a spy in one's house. He had heard of rich
men who had been blackmailed all their lives by some servant
who had read a letter, or overheard a conversation, or picked
up a card with an address, or found beneath a pillow a
withered flower or a shred of crumpled lace.

He sighed, and, having poured himself out some tea,
opened Lord Henry's note. It was simply to say that he sent
him round the evening paper, and a book that might interest him, and that he would be at the club at eight-fifteen. He
opened "The St. James's" languidly, and looked through it.
A red pencil-mark on the fifth page caught his eye. It drew
attention to the following paragraph:

> "INQUEST ON AN ACTRESS—An inquest was held this
> morning at the Bell Tavern, Hoxton Road, by Mr. Danby,
> the District Coroner, on the body of Sibyl Vane, a young
> actress recently engaged at the Royal Theatre, Holborn.
> A verdict of death by misadventure was returned. Con-
> siderable sympathy was expressed for the mother of the
> deceased, who was greatly affected during the giving of
> her own evidence, and that of Dr. Birrell, who had made
> the post-mortem examination of the deceased."

He frowned, and, tearing the paper in two, went across
the room and flung the pieces away. How ugly it all was!
And how horribly real ugliness made things! He felt a little
annoyed with Lord Henry for having sent him the report.
And it was certainly stupid of him to have marked it with
red pencil. Victor might have read it. The man knew more
than enough English for that.

Perhaps he had read it, and had begun to suspect something. And, yet, what did it matter? What had Dorian Gray
to do with Sibyl Vane's death? There was nothing to fear.
Dorian Gray had not killed her.

His eye fell on the yellow book that Lord Henry had sent him. What was it, he wondered. He went towards the little pearl-coloured octagonal stand, that had always looked to him like the work of some strange Egyptian bees that wrought in silver, and taking up the volume, flung himself into an armchair, and began to turn over the leaves. After a few minutes he became absorbed. It was the strangest book that he had ever read. It seemed to him that in exquisite raiment, and to the delicate sound of flutes, the sins of the world were passing in dumb show before him. Things that he had dimly dreamed of were suddenly made real to him. Things of which he had never dreamed were gradually revealed.

It was a novel without a plot, and with only one character, being, indeed, simply a psychological study of a certain young Parisian, who spent his life trying to realise in the nineteenth century all the passions and modes of thought that belonged to every century except his own, and to sum up, as it were, in himself the various moods through which the world-spirit had ever passed, loving for their mere artificiality those renunciations that men have unwisely called virtue, as much as those natural rebellions that wise men still call sin. The style in which it was written was that curious jewelled style, vivid and obscure at once, full of argot and of archaisms, of technical expressions and of elaborate paraphrases, that characterises the work of some of the finest artists of the French school of *Symbolistes*. There were in it metaphors as monstrous as orchids, and as subtle in colour. The life of the senses was described in the terms of mystical philosophy. One hardly knew at times whether one was reading the spiritual ecstasies of some mediæval saint or the morbid confessions of a modern sinner. It was a poisonous book. The heavy odour of incense seemed to cling about its pages and to trouble the brain. The mere cadence of the sentences, the subtle monotony of their music, so full as it was of com-

plex refrains and movements elaborately repeated, produced in the mind of the lad, as he passed from chapter to
chapter, a form of reverie, a malady of dreaming, that made
him unconscious of the falling day and creeping shadows.

Cloudless, and pierced by one solitary star, a copper green
sky gleamed through the windows. He read on by its wan
light till he could read no more. Then, after his valet had reminded him several times of the lateness of the hour, he got
up, and, going into the next room, placed the book on the
little Florentine table that always stood at his bedside, and
began to dress for dnner.

It was almost nine o'clock before he reached the club,
where he found Lord Henry sitting alone, in the morning-
room, looking very much bored.

"I am so sorry, Harry," he cried, "but really it is entirely
your fault. That book you sent me so fascinated me that I
forgot how the time was going."

"Yes: I thought you would like it," replied his host, rising
from his chair.

"I didn't say I liked it, Harry. I said it fascinated me. There
is a great difference."

"Ah, you have discovered that?" murmured Lord Henry.
And they passed into the dining-room.

CHAPTER XI

FOR years, Dorian Gray could not free himself from the influence of this book. Or perhaps it would be more accurate to say that he never sought to free himself from it. He procured from Paris no less than nine large-paper copies of the first edition, and had them bound in different colours, so that they might suit his various moods and the changing fancies of a nature over which he seemed, at times, to have almost entirely lost control. The hero, the wonderful young Parisian, in whom the romantic and the scientific temperaments were so strangely blended, became to him a kind of prefiguring type of himself. And, indeed, the whole book seemed to him to contain the story of his own life, written before he had lived it.

In one point he was more fortunate than the novel's fantastic hero. He never knew—never, indeed, had any cause to know—that somewhat grotesque dread of mirrors, and polished metal surfaces, and still water, which came upon the young Parisian so early in his life, and was occasioned by the sudden decay of a beauty that had once, apparently, been so remarkable. It was with an almost cruel joy—and perhaps in nearly every joy, as certainly in every pleasure, cruelty has its place—that he used to read the latter part of the book, with its really tragic, if somewhat over-emphasised, account of the sorrow and despair of one who had himself lost what in others, and in the world, he had most dearly valued.

For the wonderful beauty that had so fascinated Basil Hallward, and many others besides him, seemed never to leave him. Even those who had heard the most evil things against him, and from time to time strange rumours about his mode of life crept through London and became the chatter of the clubs, could not believe anything to his dishonour when they saw him. He had always the look of one who had kept himself unspotted from the world. Men who talked grossly became silent when Dorian Gray entered the room. There was something in the purity of his face that rebuked them. His mere presence seemed to recall to them the memory of the innocence that they had tarnished. They wondered how one so charming and graceful as he was could have escaped the stain of an age that was at once sordid and sensual.

Often, on returning home from one of those mysterious and prolonged absences that gave rise to such strange conjecture among those who were his friends, or thought that they were so, he himself would creep upstairs to the locked room, open the door with the key that never left him now, and stand, with a mirror, in front of the portrait that Basil Hallward had painted of him, looking now at the evil and ageing face on the canvas, and now at the fair young face that laughed back at him from the polished glass. The very sharpness of the contrast used to quicken his sense of pleasure. He grew more and more enamoured of his own beauty, more and more interested in the corruption of his own soul. He would examine with minute care, and sometimes with a monstrous and terrible delight, the hideous lines that seared the wrinkling forehead, or crawled around the heavy sensual mouth, wondering sometimes which were the more horrible, the signs of sin or the signs of age. He would place his white hands beside the coarse bloated hands of the picture, and smile. He mocked the misshapen body and the failing limbs.

There were moments, indeed, at night, when, lying sleepless in his own delicately-scented chamber, or in the sordid room of the little ill-famed tavern near the Docks, which, under an assumed name, and in disguise, it was his habit to frequent, he would think of the ruin he had brought upon his soul, with a pity that was all the more poignant because it was purely selfish. But moments such as these were rare. That curiosity about life which Lord Henry had first stirred in him, as they sat together in the garden of their friend, seemed to increase with gratification. The more he knew, the more he desired to know. He had mad hungers that grew more ravenous as he fed them.

Yet he was not really reckless, at any rate in his relations to society. Once or twice every month during the winter, and on each Wednesday evening while the season lasted, he would throw open to the world his beautiful house and have the most celebrated musicians of the day to charm his guests with the wonders of their art. His little dinners, in the settling of which Lord Henry always assisted him, were noted as much for the careful selection and placing of those invited, as for the exquisite taste shown in the decoration of the table, with its subtle symphonic arrangements of exotic flowers, and embroidered cloths, and antique plate of gold and silver. Indeed, there were many, especially among the very young men, who saw, or fancied that they saw, in Dorian Gray the true realisation of a type of which they had often dreamed in Eton or Oxford days, a type that was to combine something of the real culture of the scholar with all the grace and distinction and perfect manner of a citizen of the world. To them he seemed to be of the company of those whom Dante describes as having sought to "make themselves perfect by the worship of beauty." Like Gautier, he was one for whom "the visible world existed."

And, certainly, to him Life itself was the first, the greatest of the arts, and for it all the other arts seemed to be but a preparation. Fashion, by which what is really fantastic becomes for a moment universal, and Dandyism, which, in its own way, is an attempt to assert the absolute modernity of beauty, had, of course, their fascination for him. His mode of dressing, and the particular styles that from time to time he affected, had their marked influence on the young exquisites of the Mayfair balls and Pall Mall club windows, who copied him in everything that he did, and tried to reproduce the accidental charm of his graceful, though to him only half-serious, fopperies.

For, while he was but too ready to accept the position that was almost immediately offered to him on his coming of age, and found, indeed, a subtle pleasure in the thought that he might really become to the London of his own day what to imperial Neronian Rome the author of the "Satyricon" once had been, yet in his inmost heart he desired to be something more than a mere *arbiter elegantiarum,* to be consulted on the wearing of a jewel, or the knotting of a necktie, or the conduct of a cane. He sought to elaborate some new scheme of life that would have its reasoned philosophy and its ordered principles, and find in the spiritualising of the senses its highest realisation.

The worship of the senses has often, and with much justice, been decried, men feeling a natural instinct of terror about passions and sensations that seem stronger than themselves, and that they are conscious of sharing with the less highly organised forms of existence. But it appeared to Dorian Gray that the true nature of the senses had never been understood, and that they had remained savage and animal merely because the world had sought to starve them into submission or to kill them by pain, instead of aiming at making them elements of a new spirituality, of which a fine instinct for beauty was to be the dominant characteristic. As he looked back upon man moving through History, he was haunted by a feeling of loss. So much had been surrendered! and to such little purpose! There had been mad wilful rejections, monstrous forms of self-torture and self-denial, whose origin was fear, and whose result was a degradation infinitely more terrible than that fancied degradation from which, in their ignorance, they had sought to escape, Nature, in her wonderful irony, driving out the anchorite to feed with the wild animals of the desert and giving to the hermit the beasts of the field as his companions.

Yes: there was to be, as Lord Henry had prophesied, a new Hedonism that was to recreate life, and to save it from that harsh, uncomely puritanism that is having, in our own day, its curious revival. It was to have its service of the intellect, certainly; yet, it was never to accept any theory or system that would involve the sacrifice of any mode of passionate experience. Its aim, indeed, was to be experience itself, and not the fruits of experience, sweet or bitter as they might be. Of the asceticism that deadens the senses, as of the vulgar profligacy that dulls them, it was to know nothing. But it was to teach man to concentrate himself upon the moments of a life that is itself but a moment.

There are few of us who have not sometimes wakened before dawn, either after one of those dreamless nights that make us almost enamoured of death, or one of those nights of horror and misshapen joy, when through the chambers of the brain sweep phantoms more terrible than reality itself, and instinct with that vivid life that lurks in all grotesques, and that lends to Gothic art its enduring vitality, this art being, one might fancy, especially the art of those whose minds have been troubled with the malady of reverie. Gradually white fingers creep through the curtains, and they appear to tremble. In black fantastic shapes, dumb shadows crawl into the corners of the room, and crouch there. Outside, there is the stirring of birds among the leaves, or the sound of men going forth to their work, or the sigh and sob of the wind coming down from the hills, and wandering

round the silent house, as though it feared to wake the sleep-
ers, and yet must needs call forth sleep from her purple cave.
Veil after veil of thin dusky gauze is lifted, and by degrees
the forms and colours of things are restored to them, and we
watch the dawn remaking the world in its antique pattern.
The wan mirrors get back their mimic life. The flameless
tapers stand where we had left them, and beside them lies the
half-cut book that we had been studying, or the wired flower
that we had worn at the ball, or the letter that we had been
afraid to read, or that we had read too often. Nothing seems
to us changed. Out of the unreal shadows of the night comes
back the real life that we had known. We have to resume it
where we had left off, and there steals over us a terrible
sense of the necessity for the continuance of energy in the
same wearisome round of stereotyped habits, or a wild longing, it may be, that our eyelids might open some morning
upon a world that had been refashioned anew in the darkness for our pleasure, a world in which things would have
fresh shapes and colours, and be changed, or have other
secrets, a world in which the past would have little or no
place, or survive, at any rate, in no conscious form of obliga-
tion or regret, the remembrance even of joy having its bitterness, and the memories of pleasure their pain.

It was the creation of such worlds as these that seemed to
Dorian Gray to be the true object, or amongst the true objects, of life; and in his search for sensations that would be at
once new and delightful, and possess that element of strangeness that is so essential to romance, he would often adopt
certain modes of thought that he knew to be really alien to
his nature, abandon himself to their subtle influences, and
then, having, as it were, caught their colour and satisfied his
intellectual curiosity, leave them with that curious indifference that is not incompatible with a real ardour of tem-

perament, and that indeed, according to certain modern psychologists, is often a condition of it.

It was rumoured of him once that he was about to join the Roman Catholic communion; and certainly the Roman ritual had always a great attraction for him. The daily sacrifice, more awful really than all the sacrifices of the antique world, stirred him as much by its superb rejection of the evidence of the senses as by the primitive simplicity of its elements and the eternal pathos of the human tragedy that it sought to symbolise. He loved to kneel down on the cold marble pavement, and watch the priest, in his stiff flowered vestment, slowly and with white hands moving aside the veil of the tabernacle, or raising aloft the jewelled lantern-shaped monstrance with that pallid wafer that at times, one would fain think, is indeed the *"panis cœlestis,"* the bread of angels, or, robed in the garments of the Passion of Christ, breaking the Host into the chalice, and smiting his breast for his sins. The fuming censers, that the grave boys, in their lace and scarlet, tossed into the air like great gilt flowers, had their subtle fascination for him. As he passed out, he used to look with wonder at the black confessionals, and long to sit in the dim shadow of one of them and listen to men and women whispering through the worn grating the true story of their lives.

But he never fell into the error of arresting his intellectual development by any formal acceptance of creed or system, or of mistaking, for a house in which to live, an inn that is but suitable for the sojourn of a night, or for a few hours of a night in which there are no stars and the moon is in travail. Mysticism, with its marvellous power of making common things strange to us, and the subtle anti-nomianism that always seems to accompany it, moved him for a season; and for a season he inclined to the materialistic doctrines of the *Darwinismus* movement in Germany, and found a curious pleasure in tracing the thoughts and passions of men to some pearly cell in the brain, or some white nerve in the body, delighting in the conception of the absolute dependence of the spirit on certain physical conditions, morbid or healthy, normal or diseased. Yet, as has been said of him before, no theory of life seemed to him to be of any importance compared with life itself. He felt keenly conscious of how barren all intellectual speculation is when separated from action and experiment. He knew that the senses, no less than the soul, have their spiritual mysteries to reveal.

And so he would now study perfumes, and the secrets of their manufacture, distilling heavily-scented oils, and burning odorous gums from the East. He saw that there was no mood of the mind that had not its counterpart in the sensuous life, and set himself to discover their true relations, wondering what there was in frankincense that made one mystical, and in ambergris that stirred one's passions, and in violets that woke the memory of dead romances, and in musk that troubled the brain, and in champak that stained the imagination; and seeking often to elaborate a real psychology of perfumes, and to estimate the several influences of sweet-smelling roots, and scented pollen-laden flowers, or aromatic balms, and of dark and fragrant woods, of spikenard that sickens, of hovenia that makes men mad, and of aloes that are said to be able to expel melancholy from the soul.

At another time he devoted himself entirely to music, and in a long latticed room, with a vermilion-and-gold ceiling and walls of olive-green lacquer, he used to give curious concerts, in which mad gypsies tore wild music from little zithers, or grave yellow-shawled Tunisians plucked at the strained strings of monstrous lutes, while grinning negroes beat monotonously upon copper drums, and, crouching upon scarlet mats, slim turbaned Indians blew through long pipes of reed or brass, and charmed, or feigned to charm, great hooded snakes and horrible horned adders. The harsh intervals and shrill discords of barbaric music stirred him at times when Schubert's grace, and Chopin's beautiful sorrows, and the mighty harmonies of Beethoven himself, fell unheeded on his ear. He collected together from all parts of the world the strangest instruments that could be found, either in the tombs of dead nations or among the few savage tribes that have survived contact with Western civilisations, and loved to touch and try them. He had the mysterious *juruparis* of the Rio Negro Indians, that women are not allowed to look at, and that even youths may not see till they have been subjected to fasting and scourging, and the earthen jars of the Peruvians that have the shrill cries of birds, and flutes of human bones such as Alfonso de Ovalle heard in Chili, and the sonorous green jaspers that are found near Cuzco and give forth a note of singular sweetness. He had painted gourds filled with pebbles that rattled when they were shaken; the long *clarin* of the Mexicans, into which the performer does not blow, but through which he inhales the air; the harsh *ture* of the Amazon tribes, that is sounded by the sentinels who sit all day long in high trees, and can be heard, it is said, at a distance of three leagues; the *teponaztli,* that has two vibrating tongues of wood, and is beaten with sticks that are smeared with an elastic gum obtained from the milky juice of plants; the *yotl*-bells of the Aztecs, that are hung in clusters like grapes; and a huge cylindrical drum, covered with the skins of great serpents, like the one that Bernal Diaz saw when he went with Cortes into the Mexican temple, and of whose doleful sound he has left us so vivid a description. The fantastic character of these instruments fascinated him, and he felt a curious delight in the thought that Art, like Nature, has her monsters, things of bestial shape and with hideous voices. Yet, after some time, he wearied of them, and would sit in his box at the Opera, either alone or with Lord Henry, listening in rapt pleasure to "Tannhäuser," and seeing in the prelude to that great work of art a presentation of the tragedy of his own soul.

On one occasion he took up the study of jewels, and appeared at a costume ball as Anne de Joyeuse, Admiral of France, in a dress covered with five hundred and sixty pearls. This taste enthralled him for years, and, indeed, may be said never to have left him. He would often spend a whole day settling and resettling in their cases the various stones that he had collected, such as the olive-green chrysoberyl that turns red by lamplight, the cymophane with its wire-like line of silver, the pistachio-coloured peridot, rose-pink and wine-yellow topazes, carbuncles of fiery scarlet with tremulous four-rayed stars, flame-red cinnamon-stones, orange and violet spinels, and amethysts with their alternate layers of ruby and sapphire. He loved the red gold of the sunstone, and the moonstone's pearly whiteness, and the broken rainbow of the milky opal. He procured from Amsterdam three emeralds of extraordinary size and richness of colour, and had a turquoise *de la vieille roche* that was the envy of all the connoisseurs.

He discovered wonderful stories, also, about jewels. In Alphonso's "Clericalis Disciplina" a serpent was mentioned with eyes of real jacinth, and in the romantic history of Alexander, the Conqueror of Emathia was said to have found in the vale of Jordan snakes "with collars of real emeralds growing on their backs." There was a gem in the brain of the dragon, Philostratus told us, and "by the exhibition of golden letters and a scarlet robe" the monster could be thrown into a magical sleep, and slain. According to the great alchemist, Pierre de Boniface, the diamond rendered a man invisible, and the agate of India made him eloquent. The cornelian appeased anger, and the hyacinth provoked sleep, and the amethyst drove away the fumes of wine. The garnet cast out demons, and the hydropicus deprived the moon of her

colour. The selenite waxed and waned with the moon, and
the meloceus, that discovers thieves, could be affected only
by the blood of kids. Leonardus Camillus had seen a white
stone taken from the brain of a newly-killed toad, that was a
certain antidote against poison. The bezoar, that was found
in the heart of the Arabian deer, was a charm that could cure
the plague. In the nests of Arabian birds was the aspilates,
that, according to Democritus, kept the wearer from any
danger by fire.

The King of Ceilan rode through his city with a large ruby
in his hand, at the ceremony of his coronation. The gates of
the palace of John the Priest were "made of sardius, with the
horn of the horned snake inwrought, so that no man might
bring poison within." Over the gable were "two golden
apples, in which were two carbuncles," so that the gold might
shine by day, and the carbuncles by night. In Lodge's strange
romance "A Margarite of America" it was stated that in the
chamber of the queen one could behold "all the chaste ladies
of the world, inchased out of silver, looking through fair
mirrours of chrysolites, carbuncles, sapphires, and greene
emeraults." Marco Polo had seen the inhabitants of Zipangu
place rose-coloured pearls in the mouths of the dead. A sea-
monster had been enamoured of the pearl that the diver
brought to King Prozes, and had slain the thief, and mourned
for seven moons over its loss. When the Huns lured the king
into the great pit, he flung it away—Procopius tells the story
—nor was it ever found again, though the Emperor Anas-
tasius offered five hundred-weight of gold pieces for it. The
King of Malabar had shown to a certain Venetian a rosary of
three hundred and four pearls, one for every god that he
worshipped.

When the Duke of Valentinois, son of Alexander VI.,
visited Louis XII. of France, his horse was loaded with gold
leaves, according to Brantôme, and his cap had double rows

of rubies that threw out a great light. Charles of England had ridden in stirrups hung with four hundred and twenty-one diamonds. Richard II. had a coat, valued at thirty thousand marks, which was covered with balas rubies. Hall described Henry VIII., on his way to the Tower previous to his corona tion, as wearing "a jacket of raised gold, the placard em broidered with diamonds and other rich stones, and a great bauderike about his neck of large balasses." The favourites of James I. wore earrings of emeralds set in gold filigrane. Edward II. gave to Piers Gaveston a suit of red-gold armour studded with jacinths, a collar of gold roses set with tur- quoise-stones, and a skull-cap *parsemé* with pearls. Henry II. wore jewelled gloves reaching to the elbow, and had a hawk-glove sewn with twelve rubies and fifty-two great orients. The ducal hat of Charles the Rash, the last Duke of Burgundy of his race, was hung with pear-shaped pearls, and studded with sapphires.

How exquisite life had once been! How gorgeous in its pomp and decoration! Even to read of the luxury of the dead was wonderful.

Then he turned his attention to embroideries, and to the tapestries that performed the office of frescoes in the chill rooms of the Northern nations of Europe. As he investigated the subject—and he always had an extraordinary faculty of becoming absolutely absorbed for the moment in what- ever he took up—he was almost saddened by the reflection of the ruin that Time brought on beautiful and wonderful things. He, at any rate, had escaped that. Summer followed summer, and the yellow jonquils bloomed and died many times, and nights of horror repeated the story of their shame, but he was unchanged. No winter marred his face or stained his flower-like bloom. How different it was with material things! Where had they passed to? Where was the great cro- cus-coloured robe, on which the gods fought against the giants, that had been worked by brown girls for the pleasure of Athena? Where, the huge velarium that Nero had stretched across the Colosseum at Rome, that Titan sail of purple on which was represented the starry sky, and Apollo driving a chariot drawn by white gilt-reined steeds? He longed to see the curious table-napkins wrought for the Priest of the Sun, on which were displayed all the dainties and viands that could be wanted for a feast; the mortuary cloth of King Chilperic, with its three hundred golden bees; the fantastic robes that excited the indignation of the Bishop of Pontus, and were figured with "lions, panthers, bears, dogs, forests, rocks, hunters—all, in fact, that a painter can copy from nature;" and the coat that Charles of Orleans once wore, on the sleeves of which were embroidered the verses of a song beginning *"Madame, je suis tout joyeux,"* the musical accompaniment of the words being wrought in gold thread, and each note, of square shape in those days, formed with four pearls. He read of the room that was prepared at the palace at Rheims for the use of Queen Joan of Burgundy, and was decorated with "thirteen hundred and twenty-one parrots, made in broidery, and blazoned with the king's arms, and five hundred and sixty-one butterflies, whose wings were similarly ornamented with the arms of the queen, the whole worked in gold." Catherine de Médicis had a mourning-bed made for her of black velvet powdered with crescents and suns. Its curtains were of damask, with leafy wreaths and garlands, figured upon a gold and silver ground, and fringed along the edges with broideries of pearls, and it stood in a room hung with rows of the queen's devices in cut black velvet upon cloth of silver. Louis XIV. had gold embroidered caryatides fifteen feet high in his apartment. The state bed of Sobieski, King of Poland, was made of Smyrna gold brocade embroidered in turquoises with verses from the Koran. Its supports were of silver gilt, beautifully chased, and profusely set with enamelled and jewelled medallions. It had been taken from the Turkish camp before Vienna, and the standard of Mohammed had stood beneath the tremulous gilt of its canopy.

And so, for a whole year, he sought to accumulate the most exquisite specimens that he could find of textile and embroidered work, getting the dainty Delhi muslins, finely wrought with gold-thread palmates, and stitched over with iridescent beetles' wings; the Dacca gauzes, that from their transparency are known in the East as "woven air," and "running water," and "evening dew"; strange figured cloths from Java; elaborate yellow Chinese hangings; books bound in tawny satins or fair blue silks, and wrought with *fleurs de lys,* birds, and images; veils of *lacis* worked in Hungary point; Sicilian brocades, and stiff Spanish velvets; Georgian work with its gilt coins, and Japanese *Foukousas* with their green-toned golds and their marvellously-plumaged birds.

He had a special passion, also, for ecclesiastical vestments, as indeed he had for everything connected with the service of the Church. In the long cedar chests that lined the west gallery of his house he had stored away many rare and beautiful specimens of what is really the raiment of the Bride of Christ, who must wear purple and jewels and fine linen that she may hide the pallid macerated body that is worn by the suffering that she seeks for, and wounded by self-inflicted pain. He possessed a gorgeous cope of crimson silk and gold-thread damask, figured with a repeating pattern of golden pomegranates set in six-petalled formal blossoms, beyond which on either side was the pine-apple device wrought in seed-pearls. The orphreys were divided into panels representing scenes from the life of the Virgin, and the coronation of the Virgin was figured in coloured silks upon the hood. This was Italian work of the fifteenth century. Another cope was of green velvet, embroidered with

heart-shaped groups of acanthus-leaves, from which spread
long-stemmed white blossoms, the details of which were
picked out with silver-thread and coloured crystals. The
morse bore a seraph's head in gold-thread raised work. The
orphreys were woven in a diaper of red and gold silk, and
were starred with medallions of many saints and martyrs,
among whom was St. Sebastian. He had chasubles, also, of
amber-coloured silk and blue silk and gold brocade, and yellow silk damask and cloth of gold figured with representa-
tions of the Passion and Crucifixion of Christ, and embroidered with lions and peacocks and other emblems; dalmatics
of white satin and pink silk damask, decorated with tulips
and dolphins and *fleurs de lys;* altar frontals of crimson velvet and blue linen; and many corporals, chalice-veils, and
sudaria. In the mystic offices to which such things were put,
there was something that quickened his imagination.

For these treasures, and everything that he collected in his
lovely house, were to be to him means of forgetfulness, modes
by which he could escape, for a season, from the fear that
seemed to him at times to be almost too great to be borne.
Upon the walls of the lonely locked room where he had spent
so much of his boyhood, he had hung with his own hands
the terrible portrait whose changing features showed him the
real degradation of his life, and in front of it had
draped the purple-and-gold pall as a curtain. For weeks
he would not go there, would forget the hideous painted
thing, and get back his light heart, his wonderful joyousness, his passionate absorption in mere existence. Then, suddenly, some night he would creep out of the house, go down
to dreadful places near Blue Gate Fields, and stay there, day
after day, until he was driven away. On his return he would
sit in front of the picture, sometimes loathing it and himself,
but filled, at other times, with that pride of individualism
that is half the fascination of sin, and smiling with secret

pleasure, at the misshapen shadow that had to bear the burden that should have been his own.

After a few years he could not endure to be long out of England, and gave up the villa that he had shared at Trouville with Lord Henry, as well as the little white walled-in house at Algiers where they had more than once spent the winter. He hated to be separated from the picture that was such a part of his life, and was also afraid that during his absence someone might gain access to the room, in spite of the elaborate bars that he had caused to be placed upon the door.

He was quite conscious that this would tell them nothing. It was true that the portrait still preserved, under all the foulness and ugliness of the face, its marked likeness to himself; but what could they learn from that? He would laugh at anyone who tried to taunt him. He had not painted it. What was it to him how vile and full of shame it looked? Even if he told them, would they believe it?

Yet he was afraid. Sometimes when he was down at his great house in Nottinghamshire, entertaining the fashionable young men of his own rank who were his chief companions, and astounding the county by the wanton luxury and gorgeous splendour of his mode of life, he would suddenly leave his guests and rush back to town to see that the door had not been tampered with, and that the picture was still there. What if it should be stolen? The mere thought made him cold with horror. Surely the world would know his secret then. Perhaps the world already suspected it.

For, while he fascinated many, there were not a few who distrusted him. He was very nearly black-balled at a West End club of which his birth and social position fully entitled him to become a member, and it was said that on one occasion when he was brought by a friend into the smoking-room of the Churchill, the Duke of Berwick and another gentleman got up in a marked manner and went out. Curious stories became current about him after he had passed his twenty-fifth year. It was rumoured that he had been seen brawling with foreign sailors in a low den in the distant parts of Whitechapel, and that he consorted with thieves and coiners and knew the mysteries of their trade. His extraordinary absences became notorious, and, when he used to reappear again in society, men would whisper to each other in corners, or pass him with a sneer, or look at him with cold searching eyes, as though they were determined to discover his secret.

Of such insolences and attempted slights he, of course, took no notice, and in the opinion of most people his frank debonair manner, his charming boyish smile, and the infinite grace of that wonderful youth that seemed never to leave him, were in themselves a sufficient answer to the calumnies, for so they termed them, that were circulated about him. It was remarked, however, that some of those who had been most intimate with him appeared, after a time, to shun him. Women who had wildly adored him, and for his sake had braved all social censure and set convention at defiance, were seen to grow pallid with shame or horror if Dorian Gray entered the room.

Yet these whispered scandals only increased, in the eyes of many, his strange and dangerous charm. His great wealth was a certain element of security. Society, civilised society at least, is never very ready to believe anything to the detriment of those who are both rich and fascinating. It feels instinctively that manners are of more importance than morals, and, in its opinion, the highest respectability is of much less value than the possession of a good chef. And, after all, it is a very poor consolation to be told that the man who has given one a bad dinner, or poor wine, is irreproachable in his private life. Even the cardinal virtues cannot atone for half-cold entrées, as Lord Henry remarked once, in a discussion on the subject; and there is possibly a good deal to be said for his view. For the canons of good society are, or should be, the same as the canons of art. Form is absolutely essential to it. It should have the dignity of a ceremony, as well as its unreality, and should combine the insincere character of a romantic play with the wit and beauty that make such plays delightful to us. Is insincerity such a terrible thing? I think not. It is merely a method by which we can multiply our personalities.

Such, at any rate, was Dorian Gray's opinion. He used to wonder at the shallow psychology of those who conceive the Ego in man as a thing simple, permanent, reliable, and of one essence. To him, man was a being with myriad lives and myriad sensations, a complex multiform creature that bore within itself strange legacies of thought and passion, and whose very flesh was tainted with the monstrous maladies of the dead. He loved to stroll through the gaunt cold picture-gallery of his country house and look at the various portraits of those whose blood flowed in his veins. Here was Philip Herbert, described by Francis Osborne, in his "Memoirs on the Reigns of Queen Elizabeth and King James," as one who was "caressed by the Court for his handsome face, which kept him not long company." Was it young Herbert's life that he sometimes led? Had some strange poisonous germ crept from body to body till it had reached his own? Was it some dim sense of that ruined grace that had made him so suddenly, and almost without cause, give utterance, in Basil Hallward's studio, to the mad prayer that had so changed his life? Here, in gold-embroidered red doublet, jewelled surcoat, and gilt-edged ruff and wrist-bands, stood Sir Anthony Sherard, with his silver-and-black armour piled at his feet. What had this man's legacy been? Had the lover of Giovanna of Naples bequeathed him some inheritance of sin and shame? Were his own actions merely the dreams that the dead man had not dared to realise? Here, from the fading canvas, smiled Lady Elizabeth Devereux, in her gauze hood, pearl stomacher, and pink slashed sleeves. A flower was in her right hand, and her left clasped an enamelled collar of white and damask roses. On a table by her side lay a mandolin and an apple. There were large green rosettes upon her little pointed shoes. He knew her life, and the strange stories that were told about her lovers. Had he something of her temperament in him? These oval-heavy-lidded eyes seemed to look curiously at him. What of George Willoughby, with his powdered hair and fantastic patches? How evil he looked! The face was saturnine and swarthy, and the sensual lips seemed to be twisted with disdain. Delicate lace ruffles fell over the lean yellow hands that were so over-laden with rings. He had been a macaroni of the eighteenth century, and the friend, in his youth, of Lord Ferrars. What of the second Lord Beckenham, the companion of the Prince Regent in his wildest days, and one of the witnesses at the secret marriage with Mrs. Fitzherbert? How proud and handsome he was, with his chestnut curls and insolent pose! What passions had he bequeathed? The world had looked upon him as infamous. He had led the orgies at Carlton House. The Star of the Garter glittered upon his breast. Beside him hung the portrait of his wife, a pallid, thin-lipped woman in black. Her blood, also, stirred within him. How curious it all seemed! And his mother with her Lady Hamilton face, and her moist wine-dashed lips—he knew what he had got from her. He had got from her his beauty, and his passion for the beauty of others. She laughed at him in her loose Bacchante dress. There were vine leaves in her hair. The purple spilled from the cup she was holding. The carnations of the painting had withered, but the eyes were still

wonderful in their depth and brilliancy of colour. They
seemed to follow him wherever he went.

Yet one had ancestors in literature, as well as in one's own
race, nearer perhaps in type and temperament, many of them,
and certainly with an influence of which one was more absolutely conscious. There were times when it appeared to
Dorian Gray that the whole of history was merely the record
of his own life, not as he had lived it in act and circumstance,
but as his imagination had created it for him, as it had been
in his brain and in his passions. He felt that he had known
them all, those strange terrible figures that had passed across
the stage of the world and made sin so marvellous, and evil
so full of subtlety. It seemed to him that in some mysterious
way their lives had been his own.

The hero of the wonderful novel that had so influenced
his life had himself known this curious fancy. In the seventh
chapter he tells how, crowned with laurel, lest lightning
might strike him, he had sat, as Tiberius, in a garden at
Capri, reading the shameful books of Elephantis, while
dwarfs and peacocks strutted round him, and the flute-
player mocked the swinger of the censer; and, as Caligula,
had caroused with the green-shirted jockeys in their stables
and supped in an ivory manger with a jewel-frontleted horse;
and, as Domitian had wandered through a corridor lined
with marble mirrors, looking round with haggard eyes for
the reflection of the dagger that was to end his days, and sick
with that ennui, that terrible *tædium vitæ,* that comes on
those to whom life denies nothing; and had peered through
a clear emerald at the red shambles of the Circus, and then,
in a litter of pearl and purple drawn by sliver-shod mules,
been carried through the Street of Pomegranates to a House
of Gold, and heard men cry on Nero Cæsar as he passed by;
and, as Elagabulus, had painted his face with colours, and
plied the distaff among the women, and brought the Moon

from Carthage, and given her in mystic marriage to the Sun.

Over and over again Dorian used to read this fantastic chapter, and the two chapters immediately following, in which, as in some curious tapestries or cunningly-wrought enamels, were pictured the awful and beautiful forms of those whom Vice and Blood and Weariness had made monstrous or mad: Filippo, Duke of Milan, who slew his wife, and painted her lips with scarlet poison that her lover might suck death from the dead thing he fondled; Pietro Barbi, the Venetian, known as Paul the Second, who sought in his vanity to assume the title of Formosus, and whose tiara, valued at two hundred thousand florins, was bought at the price of a terrible sin; Gian Maria Visconti, who used hounds to chase living men, and whose murdered body was covered with roses by a harlot who had loved him; the Borgia on his white horse, with Fratricide riding beside him, and his mantle stained with the blood of Perotto; Pietro Riario, the young Cardinal Archbishop of Florence, child and minion of Sixtus IV., whose beauty was equalled only by his debauchery, and who received Leonora of Aragon in a pavilion of white and crimson silk, filled with nymphs and centaurs, and gilded a boy that he might serve at the feast as Ganymede or Hylas; Ezzelin, whose melancholy could be cured only by the spectacle of death, and who had a passion for red blood, as other men have for red wine—the son of the Fiend, as was reported, and one who had cheated his father at dice when gambling with him for his own soul; Giambattista Cibo, who in mockery took the name of Innocent, and into whose torpid veins the blood of three lads was infused by a Jewish doctor; Sigismondo Malatesta, the lover of Isotta, and the lord of Rimini, whose effigy was burned at Rome as the enemy of God and man, who strangled Polyssena with a napkin, and gave poison to Ginevra d'Este in a cup of emerald, and in honour of a shameful pas-

sion built a pagan church for Christian worship; Charles VI.,
who had so wildly adored his brother's wife that a leper had
warned him of the insanity that was coming on him, and
who, when his brain had sickened and grown strange, could
only be soothed by Saracen cards painted with the images of
Love and Death and Madness; and, in his trimmed jerkin
and jewelled cap and acanthus-like curls, Grifonetto Bag-
lioni, who slew Astorre with his bride, and Simonetto with
his page, and whose comeliness was such that, as he lay dying
in the yellow piazza of Perugia, those who had hated him
could not choose but weep, and Atalanta, who had cursed
him, blessed him.

There was a horrible fascination in them all. He saw them
at night, and they troubled his imagination in the day. The
Renaissance knew of strange manners of poisoning—poisoning by a helmet and a lighted torch, by an embroidered glove
and a jewelled fan, by a gilded pomander and by an amber
chain. Dorian Gray had been poisoned by a book. There
were moments when he looked on evil simply as a mode
through which he could realise his conception of the beautiful.

CHAPTER XII

IT was on the ninth of November, the eve of his own thirty-eighth birthday, as he often remembered afterwards.

He was walking home about eleven o'clock from Lord Henry's, where he had been dining, and was wrapped in heavy furs, as the night was cold and foggy. At the corner of Grosvenor Square and South Audley Street a man passed him in the mist, walking very fast, and with the collar of his grey ulster turned up. He had a bag in his hand. Dorian recognised him. It was Basil Hallward. A strange sense of fear, for which he could not account, came over him. He made no sign of recognition, and went on quickly in the direction of his own house.

But Hallward had seen him. Dorian heard him first stopping on the pavement, and then hurrying after him. In a few moments his hand was on his arm.

"Dorian! What an extraordinary piece of luck! I have been waiting for you in your library ever since nine o'clock. Finally I took pity on your tired servant, and told him to go to bed, as he let me out. I am off to Paris by the midnight train, and I particularly wanted to see you before I left. I thought it was you, or rather your fur coat, as you passed me. But I wasn't quite sure. Didn't you recognise me?"

"In this fog, my dear Basil? Why, I can't even recognise Grosvenor Square. I believe my house is somewhere about here, but I don't feel at all certain about it. I am sorry you are going away, as I have not seen you for ages. But I suppose you will be back soon?"

"No: I am going to be out of England for six months. I intend to take a studio in Paris, and shut myself up till I have finished a great picture I have in my head. However, it wasn't about myself I wanted to talk. Here we are at your door. Let me come in for a moment. I have something to say to you."

"I shall be charmed. But won't you miss your train?" said Dorian Gray, languidly, as he passed up the steps and opened the door with his latchkey.

The lamp-light struggled out through the fog, and Hallward looked at his watch. "I have heaps of time," he answered. "The train doesn't go till twelve-fifteen, and it is only just eleven. In fact, I was on my way to the club to look for you, when I met you. You see, I shan't have any delay about luggage, as I have sent on my heavy things. All I have with me is in this bag, and I can easily get to Victoria in twenty minutes."

Dorian looked at him and smiled. "What a way for a fashionable painter to travel! A Gladstone bag, and an ulster! Come in, or the fog will get into the house. And mind you don't talk about anything serious. Nothing is serious nowadays. At least nothing should be."

Hallward shook his head as he entered, and followed Dorian into the library. There was a bright wood fire blazing in the large open hearth. The lamps were lit, and an open Dutch silver spirit-case stood, with some siphons of soda-water and large cut-glass tumblers, on a little marqueterie table.

"You see your servant made me quite at home, Dorian. He gave me everything I wanted, including your best gold-tipped cigarettes. He is a most hospitable creature. I like him much better than the Frenchman you used to have. What has become of the Frenchman, by the bye?"

Dorian shrugged his shoulders. "I believe he married

Lady Radley's maid, and has established her in Paris as an English dressmaker. *Anglomanie* is very fashionable over there now, I hear. It seems silly of the French, doesn't it? But—do you know?—he was not at all a bad servant. I never liked him, but I had nothing to complain about. One often imagines things that are quite absurd. He was really very devoted to me, and seemed quite sorry when he went away. Have another brandy-and-soda? Or would you like hock-and-seltzer? I always take hock-and-seltzer myself. There is sure to be some in the next room."

"Thanks, I won't have anything more," said the painter, taking his cap and coat off, and throwing them on the bag that he had placed in the corner. "And now, my dear fellow, I want to speak to you seriously. Don't frown like that. You make it so much more difficult for me."

"What is it all about?" cried Dorian, in his petulant way, flinging himself down on the sofa. "I hope it is not about myself. I am tired of myself to-night. I should like to be somebody else."

"It is about yourself," answered Hallward, in his grave, deep voice, "and I must say it to you. I shall only keep you half an hour."

Dorian sighed, and lit a cigarette. "Half an hour!" he murmured.

"It is not much to ask of you, Dorian, and it is entirely for your own sake that I am speaking. I think it right that you should know that the most dreadful things are being said against you in London."

"I don't wish to know anything about them. I love scandals about other people, but scandals about myself don't interest me. They have not got the charm of novelty."

"They must interest you, Dorian. Every gentleman is interested in his good name. You don't want people to talk of you as something vile and degraded. Of course you have

your position, and your wealth, and all that kind of thing.
But position and wealth are not everything. Mind you, I
don't believe these rumours at all. At least, I can't believe
them when I see you. Sin is a thing that writes itself across
a man's face. It cannot be concealed. People talk sometimes
of secret vices. There are no such things. If a wretched man
has a vice, it shows itself in the lines of his mouth, the droop
of his eyelids, the moulding of his hands even. Somebody—
I won't mention his name, but you know him—came to me
last year to have his portrait done. I had never seen him
before, and had never heard anything about him at the
time, though I have heard a good deal since. He offered an
extravagant price. I refused him. There was something in
the shape of his fingers that I hated. I know now that I was
quite right in what I fancied about him. His life is dreadful. But you, Dorian, with your pure, bright, innocent face,
and your marvellous untroubled youth—I can't believe anything against you. And yet I see you very seldom, and you
never come down to the studio now, and when I am away
from you, and I hear all these hideous things that people
are whispering about you, I don't know what to say. Why is
it, Dorian, that a man like the Duke of Berwick leaves the
room of a club when you enter it? Why is it that so many
gentlemen in London will neither go to your house nor
invite you to theirs? You used to be a friend of Lord Staveley.
I met him at dinner last week. Your name happened to come
up in conversation, in connection with the miniatures you
have lent to the exhibition at the Dudley. Staveley curled his
lip, and said that you might have the most artistic tastes,
but that you were a man whom no pure-minded girl should
be allowed to know, and whom no chaste woman should sit
in the same room with. I reminded him that I was a friend
of yours, and asked him what he meant. He told me. He
told me right out before everybody. It was horrible! Why

is your friendship so fatal to young men? There was that wretched boy in the Guards who committed suicide. You were his great friend. There was Sir Henry Ashton, who had to leave England, with a tarnished name. You and he were inseparable. What about Adrian Singleton, and his dreadful end? What about Lord Kent's only son, and his career? I met his father yesterday in St. James's Street. He seemed broken with shame and sorrow. What about the young Duke of Perth? What sort of life has he got now? What gentleman would associate with him?"

"Stop, Basil. You are talking about things of which you know nothing," said Dorian Gray, biting his lip, and with a note of infinite contempt in his voice. "You ask me why Berwick leaves a room when I enter it. It is because I know everything about his life, not because he knows anything about mine. With such blood as he has in his veins, how could his record be clean? You ask me about Henry Ashton and young Perth. Did I teach the one his vices, and the other his debauchery? If Kent's silly son takes his wife from the streets what is that to me? If Adrian Singleton writes his friend's name across a bill, ^m I his keeper? I know how people chatter in England. The middle classes air their moral prejudices over their gross dinner-tables, and whisper about what they call the profligacies of their betters in order to try and pretend that they are in smart society, and on intimate terms with the people they slander. In this country it is enough for a man to have distinction and brains for every common tongue to wag against him. And what sort of lives do these people, who pose as being moral, lead themselves? My dear fellow, you forget that we are in the native land of the hypocrite."

"Dorian," cried Hallward, "that is not the question. England is bad enough, I know, and English society is all wrong. That is the reason why I want you to be fine. You have not been fine. One has a right to judge of a man by the effect he has over his friends. Yours seem to lose all sense of honour, of goodness, of purity. You have filled them with a madness for pleasure. They have gone down into the depths. You led them there. Yes you led them there, and yet you can smile, as you are smiling now. And there is worse behind. I know you and Harry are inseparable. Surely for that reason, if for none other, you should not have made his sister's name a by-word."

"Take care, Basil. You go too far."

"I must speak, and you must listen. You shall listen. When you met Lady Gwendolen, not a breath of scandal had ever touched her. Is there a single decent woman in London now who would drive with her in the Park? Why, even her children are not allowed to live with her. Then there are other stories—stories that you have been seen creeping at dawn out of dreadful houses and slinking in disguise into the foulest dens in London. Are they true? Can they be true? When I first heard them, I laughed. I hear them now, and they make me shudder. What about your country house, and the life that is led there? Dorian, you don't know what is said about you. I won't tell you that I don't want to preach to you. I remember Harry saying once that every man who turned himself into an amateur curate for the moment always began by saying that, and then proceeded to break his word. I do want to preach to you. I want you to lead such a life as will make the world respect you. I want you to have a clean name and a fair record. I want you to get rid of the dreadful people you associate with. Don't shrug your shoulders like that. Don't be so indifferent. You have a wonderful influence. Let it be for good, not for evil. They say that you corrupt everyone with whom you become intimate, and that it is quite sufficient for you to enter a house, for shame of some kind to follow after. I don't know whether it is so or not. How should I know? But it is said of you. I am told things that it seems impossible to doubt. Lord Gloucester was one of my greatest friends at Oxford. He showed me a letter that his wife had written to him when she was dying alone in her villa at Mentone. Your name was implicated in the most terrible confession I ever read. I told him that it was absurd—that I knew you thoroughly, and that you were incapable of anything of the kind. Know you? I wonder do I know you? Before I could answer that, I should have to see your soul."

"To see my soul!" muttered Dorian Gray, starting up from the sofa and turning almost white from fear.

"Yes," answered Hallward, gravely, and with deep-toned sorrow in his voice—"to see your soul. But only God can do that."

A bitter laugh of mockery broke from the lips of the younger man. "You shall see it yourself, to-night!" he cried, seizing a lamp from the table. "Come: it is your own handi-work. Why shouldn't you look at it? You can tell the world all about it afterwards, if you choose. Nobody would believe you. If they did believe you, they would like me all the better for it. I know the age better than you do, though you will prate about it so tediously. Come, I tell you. You have chat-tered enough about corruption. Now you shall look on it face to face."

There was the madness of pride in every word he uttered. He stamped his foot upon the ground in his boyish insolent manner. He felt a terrible joy at the thought that someone else was to share his secret, and that the man who had painted the portrait that was the origin of all his shame was to be burdened for the rest of his life with the hideous memory of what he had done.

"Yes." he continued, coming closer to him, and looking

steadfastly into his stern eyes, "I shall show you my soul. You shall see the thing that you fancy only God can see."

Hallward started back. "This is blasphemy, Dorian!" he cried. "You must not say things like that. They are horrible, and they don't mean anything."

"You think so?" He laughed again.

"I know so. As for what I said to you to-night, I said it for your good. You know I have been always a staunch friend to you."

"Don't touch me. Finish what you have to say."

A twisted flash of pain shot across the painter's face. He paused for a moment, and a wild feeling of pity came over him. After all, what right had he to pry into the life of Dorian Gray? If he had done a tithe of what was rumoured about him, how much he must have suffered! Then he straightened himself up, and walked over to the fireplace, and stood there, looking at the burning logs with their frost-like ashes and their throbbing cores of flame.

"I am waiting, Basil," said the young man, in a hard, clear voice.

He turned round. "What I have to say is this," he cried. "You must give me some answer to these horrible charges that are made against you. If you tell me that they are absolutely untrue from beginning to end, I shall believe you. Deny them, Dorian, deny them! Can't you see what I am going through? My God! don't tell me that you are bad, and corrupt, and shameful."

Dorian Gray smiled. There was a curl of contempt on his lips. "Come upstairs, Basil," he said, quietly. "I keep a diary of my life from day to day, and it never leaves the room in which it is written. I shall show it to you if you come with me."

"I shall come with you, Dorian, if you wish it. I see I have missed my train. That makes no matter. I can go to-morrow. But don't ask me to read anything to-night. All I want is a plain answer to my question."

"That shall be given to you upstairs. I could not give it here. You will not have to read long."

CHAPTER XIII

WE passed out of the room, and began the ascent, Basil Hallward following close behind. They walked softly, as men do instinctively at night. The lamp cast fantastic shadows on the wall and staircase. A rising wind made some of the windows rattle.

When they reached the top landing, Dorian set the lamp down on the floor, and taking out the key turned it in the lock. "You insist on knowing, Basil?" he asked, in a low voice.

"Yes."

"I am delighted," he answered, smiling. Then he added, somewhat harshly, "you are the one man in the world who is entitled to know everything about me. You have had more to do with my life than you think:" and, taking up the lamp, he opened the door and went in. A cold current of air passed them, and the light shot up for a moment in a flame of murky orange. He shuddered. "Shut the door behind you," he whispered, as he placed the lamp on the table.

Hallward glanced round him, with a puzzled expression. The room looked as if it had not been lived in for years. A faded Flemish tapestry, a curtained picture, an old Italian *cassone,* and an almost empty bookcase—that was all that it seemed to contain, besides a chair and a table. As Dorian Gray was lighting a half-burned candle that was standing on the mantelshelf, he saw that the whole place was covered with dust, and that the carpet was in holes. A mouse ran scuffling behind the wainscoting. There was a damp odour of mildew.

"So you think that it is only God who sees the soul, Basil? Draw that curtain back, and you will see mine."

The voice that spoke was cold and cruel. "You are mad, Dorian, or playing a part," muttered Hallward, frowning.

"You won't? Then I must do it myself," said the young man; and he tore the curtain from its rod, and flung it on the ground.

An exclamation of horror broke from the painter's lips as he saw in the dim light the hideous face on the canvas grinning at him. There was something in its expression that filled him with disgust and loathing. Good heavens! it was Dorian Gray's own face that he was looking at! The horror, whatever it was, had not yet entirely spoiled that marvellous beauty. There was still some gold in the thinning hair and some scarlet on the sensual mouth. The sodden eyes had kept something of the loveliness of their blue, the noble curves had not yet completely passed away from chiselled nostrils and from plastic throat. Yes, it was Dorian himself. But who had done it? He seemed to recognise his own brush-work, and the frame was his own design. The idea was monstrous, yet he felt afraid. He seized the lighted candle, and held it to the picture. In the left-hand corner was his own name, traced in long letters of bright vermilion.

It was some foul parody, some infamous, ignoble satire. He had never done that. Still, it was his own picture. He knew it, and he felt as if his blood had changed in a moment from fire to sluggish ice. His own picture! What did it mean? Why had it altered? He turned, and looked at Dorian Gray with the eyes of a sick man. His mouth twitched, and his parched tongue seemed unable to articulate. He passed his hand across his forehead. It was dank with clammy sweat.

The young man was leaning against the mantelshelf, watching him with that strange expression that one sees on the faces of those who are absorbed in a play when some great artist is acting. There was neither real sorrow in it nor real joy. There was simply the passion of the spectator, with perhaps a flicker of triumph in his eyes. He had taken the flower out of his coat, and was smelling it, or pretending to do so.

"What does this mean?" cried Hallward, at last. His own voice sounded shrill and curious in his ears.

"Years ago, when I was a boy," said Dorian Gray, crushing the flower in his hand, "you met me, flattered me, and taught me to be vain of my good looks. One day you introduced me to a friend of yours, who explained to me the wonder of youth, and you finished the portrait of me that revealed to me the wonder of beauty. In a mad moment, that, even now, I don't know whether I regret or not, I made a wish, perhaps you would call it a prayer . . ."

"I remember it! Oh, how well I remember it! No! the thing is impossible. The room is damp. Mildew has got into the canvas. The paints I used had some wretched mineral poison in them. I tell you the thing is impossible."

"Ah, what is impossible?" murmured the young man, going over to the window, and leaning his forehead against the cold, mist-stained glass.

"You told me you had destroyed it."

"I was wrong. It has destroyed me."

"I don't believe it is my picture."

"Can't you see your ideal in it?" said Dorian, bitterly.

"My ideal, as you call it . . ."

"As you called it."

"There was nothing evil in it, nothing shameful. You were to me such an ideal as I shall never meet again. This is the face of a satyr."

"It is the face of my soul."

"Christ! what a thing I must have worshipped! It has the eyes of a devil."

"Each of us has Heaven and Hell in him, Basil," cried Dorian, with a wild gesture of despair.

Hallward turned again to the portrait, and gazed at it. "My God! if it is true," he exclaimed, "and this is what you have done with your life, why, you must be worse even than those who talk against you fancy you to be!" He held the light up again to the canvas, and examined it. The surface seemed to be quite undisturbed, and as he had left it It was from within, apparently, that the foulness and horror had come. Through some strange quickening of inner life the leprosies of sin were slowly eating the thing away. The rotting of a corpse in a watery grave was not so fearful.

His hand shook, and the candle fell from its socket on the floor, and lay there sputtering. He placed his foot on it and put it out. Then he flung himself into the rickety chair that was standing by the table and buried his face in his hands.

"Good God, Dorian, what a lesson! what an awful lesson!" There was no answer, but he could hear the young man sobbing at the window. "Pray, Dorian, pray," he murmured. "What is it that one was taught to say in one's boyhood? 'Lead us not into temptation. Forgive us our sins. Wash away our iniquities.' Let us say that together. The prayer of your pride has been answered. The prayer of your repentance will be answered also. I worshipped you too much. I am punished for it. You worshipped yourself too much. We are both punished."

Dorian Gray turned slowly around, and looked at him with tear-dimmed eyes. "It is too late, Basil," he faltered.

"It is never too late, Dorian. Let us kneel down and try if we cannot remember a prayer. Isn't there a verse somewhere: 'Though your sins be as scarlet, yet I will make them as white as snow'?"

"Those words mean nothing to me now."

"Hush! don't say that. You have done enough evil in your

life. My God! don't you see that accursed thing leering at us?"

Dorian Gray glanced at the picture, and suddenly an uncontrollable feeling of hatred for Basil Hallward came over him, as though it had been suggested to him by the image on the canvas, whispered into his ear by those grinning lips. The mad passions of a hunted animal stirred within him, and he loathed the man who was seated at the table, more than in his whole life he had ever loathed anything. He glanced wildly around. Something glimmered on the top of the painted chest that faced him. His eye fell on it. He knew what it was. It was a knife that he had brought up, some days before, to cut a piece of cord, and had forgotten to take away with him. He moved slowly towards it, passing Hallward as he did so. As soon as he got behind him, he seized it, and turned round. Hallward stirred in his chair as if he was going to rise. He rushed at him, and dug the knife into the great vein that is behind the ear, crushing the man's head down on the table, and stabbing again and again.

There was a stifled groan, and the horrible sound of someone choking with blood. Three times the outstretched arms shot up convulsively, waving grotesque stiff-fingered hands in the air. He stabbed him twice more, but the man did not move. Something began to trickle on the floor. He waited for a moment, still pressing the head down. Then he threw the knife on the table, and listened.

He could hear nothing but the drip, drip on the threadbare carpet. He opened the door and went out on the landing. The house was absolutely quiet. No one was about. For a few seconds he stood bending over the balustrade, and peering down into the black seething well of darkness. Then he took out the key and returned to the room, locking himself in as he did so.

The thing was still seated in the chair, straining over the table with bowed head, and humped back, and long fantastic arms. Had it not been for the red jagged tear in the neck, and the clotted black pool that was slowly widening on the table, one would have said that the man was simply asleep.

How quickly it had all been done! He felt strangely calm, and, walking over to the window, opened it, and stepped out on the balcony. The wind had blown the fog away, and the sky was like a monstrous peacock's tail, starred with myriads of golden eyes. He looked down, and saw the policeman going his rounds and flashing the long beam of his lantern on the doors of the silent houses. The crimson spot of a prowling hansom gleamed at the corner, and then vanished. A woman in a fluttering shawl was creeping slowly by the railings, staggering as she went. Now and then she stopped, and peered back. Once, she began to sing in a hoarse voice. The policeman strolled over and said something to her. She stumbled away, laughing. A bitter blast swept across the Square. The gas-lamps flickered, and became blue, and the leafless trees shook their black iron branches to and fro. He shivered, and went back, closing the window behind him.

Having reached the door, he turned the key, and opened it. He did not even glance at the murdered man. He felt that the secret of the whole thing was not to realise the situation. The friend who had painted the fatal portrait to which all his misery had been due, had gone out of his life. That was enough.

Then he remembered the lamp. It was a rather curious one of Moorish workmanship, made of dull silver inlaid with arabesques of burnished steel, and studded with coarse turquoises. Perhaps it might be missed by his servant, and questions would be asked. He hesitated for a moment, then he turned back and took it from the table. He could not help seeing the dead thing. How still it was! How horribly white the long hands looked! It was like a dreadful wax image.

Having locked the door behind him, he crept quietly downstairs. The woodwork creaked, and seemed to cry out as if in pain. He stopped several times, and waited. No: everything was still. It was merely the sound of his own footsteps.

When he reached the library, he saw the bag and coat in the corner. They must be hidden away somewhere. He unlocked a secret press that was in the wainscoting, a press in which he kept his own curious disguises, and put them into it. He could easily burn them afterwards. Then he pulled out his watch. It was twenty minutes to two.

He sat down, and began to think. Every year—every month, almost—men were strangled in England for what he had done. There had been a madness of murder in the air. Some red star had come too close to the earth. . . . And yet what evidence was there against him? Basil Hallward had left the house at eleven. No one had seen him come in again. Most of the servants were at Selby Royal. His valet had gone to bed. . . . Paris! Yes. It was to Paris that Basil had gone, and by the midnight train, as he had intended. With his curious reserved habits, it would be months before any suspicions would be aroused. Months! Everything could be destroyed long before then.

A sudden thought struck him. He put on his fur coat and hat, and went out into the hall. There he paused, hearing the slow heavy tread of the policeman on the pavement outside, and seeing the flash of the bull's-eye reflected in the window. He waited, and held his breath.

After a few moments he drew back the latch, and slipped out, shutting the door very gently behind him. Then he began ringing the bell. In about five minutes his valet appeared half dressed, and looking very drowsy.

"I am sorry to have had to wake you up, Francis," he

said, stepping in; "but I had forgotten my latchkey. What time is it?"

"Ten minutes past two, sir," answered the man, looking at the clock and blinking.

"Ten minutes past two? How horribly late! You must wake me at nine to-morrow. I have some work to do."

"All right, sir."

"Did anyone call this evening?"

"Mr. Hallward, sir. He stayed here till eleven, and then he went away to catch his train."

"Oh! I am sorry I didn't see him. Did he leave any message?"

"No, sir, except that he would write to you from Paris, if he did not find you at the club."

"That will do, Francis. Don't forget to call me at nine to-morrow."

"No, sir."

The man shambled down the passage in his slippers.

Dorian Gray threw his hat and coat upon the table, and passed into the library. For a quarter of an hour he walked up and down the room biting his lip, and thinking. Then he took down the Blue Book from one of the shelves, and began to turn over the leaves. "Alan Campbell, 152, Hertford Street, Mayfair." Yes; that was the man he wanted.

CHAPTER XIV

AT nine o'clock the next morning his servant came in with a cup of chocolate on a tray, and opened the shutters. Dorian was sleeping quite peacefully, lying on his right side, with one hand underneath his cheek. He looked like a boy who had been tired out with play, or study.

The man had to touch him twice on the shoulder before he awoke, and as he opened his eyes a faint smile passed across his lips, as though he had been lost in some delightful dream. Yet he had not dreamed at all. His night had been untroubled by any images of pleasure or of pain. But youth smiles without any reason. It is one of its chiefest charms.

He turned round, and, leaning upon his elbow, began to sip his chocolate. The mellow November sun came streaming into the room. The sky was bright, and there was a genial warmth in the air. It was almost like a morning in May.

Gradually the events of the preceding night crept with silent blood-stained feet into his brain, and reconstructed themselves there with terrible distinctness. He winced at the memory of all that he had suffered, and for a moment the same curious feeling of loathing for Basil Hallward that had made him kill him as he sat in the chair, came back to him, and he grew cold with passion. The dead man was still sitting there, too, and in the sunlight now. How horrible that was! Such hideous things were for the darkness, not for the day.

He felt that if he brooded on what he had gone through he would sicken or grow mad. There were sins whose fascination was more in the memory than in the doing of them; strange triumphs that gratified the pride more than the passions, and gave to the intellect a quickened sense of joy, greater than joy they brought, or could ever bring, to the senses. But this was not of them. It was a thing to be driven out of the mind, to be drugged with poppies, to be strangled lest it might strangle one itself.

When the half-hour struck, he passed his hand across his forehead, and then got up hastily, and dressed himself with even more than his usual care, giving a good deal of attention to the choice of his necktie and scarf-pin, and changing his rings more than once. He spent a long time also over breakfast, tasting the various dishes, talking to his valet about some new liveries that he was thinking of getting made for the servants at Selby, and going through his correspondence. At some of the letters he smiled. Three of them bored him. One he read several times over, and then tore up with a slight look of annoyance on his face. "That awful thing, a woman's memory!" as Lord Henry once said.

After he had drunk his cup of black coffee, he wiped his lips slowly with a napkin, motioned to his servant to wait, and going over to the table sat down and wrote two letters. One he put in his pocket, the other he handed to the valet.

"Take this round to 152, Hertford Street, Francis, and if Mr. Campbell is out of town, get his address."

As soon as he was alone, he lit a cigarette, and began sketching upon a piece of paper, drawing first flowers, and bits of architecture, and then human faces. Suddenly, he remarked that every face that he drew seemed to have a fantastic likeness to Basil Hallward. He frowned, and, getting up, went over to the bookcase and took out a volume at hazard. He was determined that he would not think about what had happened until it became absolutely necessary that he should do so.

When he had stretched himself on the sofa, he looked at the title-page of the book. It was Gautier's "Emaux et Camées," Charpentier's Japanese-paper edition, with the Jacquemart etching. The binding was of citron-green leather, with a design of gilt trellis-work and dotted pomegranates. It had been given to him by Adrian Singleton. As he turned over the pages his eye fell on the poem about the hand of Lacenaire, the cold yellow hand *"du supplice encore mal lavée,"* with its downy red hairs and its *"doigts de faune."* He glanced at his own white taper fingers, shuddering slightly in spite of himself, and passed on, till he came to those lovely stanzas upon Venice—

> "Sur une gamme chromatique,
> Le sein de perles ruisselant,
> La Vénus de l'Adriatique
> Sort de l'eau son corps rose et blanc.

> "Les dômes, sur l'azur des ondes
> Suivant la phrase au pur contour,
> S'enflent comme des gorges rondes
> Que soulève un soupir d'amour.

> "L'esquif aborde et me dépose,
> Jetant son amarre au pilier,
> Devant une façade rose,
> Sur le marbre d'un escalier."

How exquisite they were! As one read them, one seemed to be floating down the green waterways of the pink and pearl city, seated in a black gondola with silver prow and trailing curtains. The mere lines looked to him like those straight lines of turquoise-blue that follow one as one pushes out to the Lido. The sudden flashes of colour reminded him of the gleam of the opal-and-iris-throated birds that flutter round the tall honeycombed Campanile, or stalk, with such stately grace, through the dim, dust-stained arcades. Leaning back with half-closed eyes, he kept saying over and over to himself—

> "Devant une façade rose,
>   Sur le marbre d'un escalier."

The whole of Venice was in those two lines. He remembered the autumn he had passed there, and a wonderful love that had stirred him to mad, delightful follies. There was romance in every place. But Venice, like Oxford, had kept the background for romance, and, to the true romantic, background was everything, or almost everything. Basil had been with him part of the time, and had gone wild over Tintoret. Poor Basil! what a horrible way for a man to die!

He sighed, and took up the volume again, and tried to forget. He read of the swallows that fly in and out of the little café at Smyrna where the Hadjis sit counting their amber beads and the turbaned merchants smoke their long tasselled pipes and talk gravely to each other; he read of the Obelisk in the Place de la Concorde that weeps tears of granite in its lonely sunless exile, and longs to be back by the hot lotus-covered Nile, where there are Sphinxes, and rose-red ibises, and white vultures with gilded claws, and crocodiles, with small beryl eyes, that crawl over the green steaming mud; he began to brood over those verses which, drawing music from kiss-stained marble, tell of that curious statue that Gautier compares to a contralto voice, the *"monstre charmant"* that couches in the porphyry-room of the Louvre. But after a time the book fell from his hand. He grew nervous, and a horrible fit of terror came over him. What if Alan Campbell should be out of England? Days would elapse before he could come back. Perhaps he might refuse to come. What could he do then? Every moment was of vital importance. They had been great friends once, five years before—almost inseparable, indeed. Then the intimacy had come suddenly to an end. When they met in society now, it was only Dorian Gray who smiled; Alan Campbell never did.

He was an extremely clever young man, though he had no real appreciation of the visible arts, and whatever little sense of the beauty he possessed he had gained entirely from Dorian. His dominant intellectual passion was for science. At Cambridge he had spent a great deal of his time working in the Laboratory, and had taken a good class in the Natural Science Tripos of his year. Indeed, he was still devoted to the study of chemistry, and had a laboratory of his own, in which he used to shut himself up all day long, greatly to the annoyance of his mother, who had set her heart on his standing for Parliament, and had a vague idea that a chemist is a person who made up prescriptions. He was an excellent musician, however, as well, and played both the violin and the piano better than most amateurs. In fact, it was music that had first brought him and Dorian Gray together—music and that indefinable attraction that Dorian seemed to be able to exercise whenever he wished, and indeed exercised often without being conscious of it. They had met at Lady Berkshire's the night that Rubenstein played there, and after that used to be always seen together at the Opera, and wherever good music was going on. For eighteen months their intimacy lasted. Campbell was always either at Selby Royal or in Grosvenor Square. To him, as to many others, Dorian Gray was the type of everything that is wonderful and fascinating in life. Whether or not a quarrel had taken place between them no one ever knew. But suddenly people remarked that they scarcely spoke when they met, and that Campbell seemed always to go away early from any party at which Dorian Gray was present. He had changed, too—was strangely melancholy at times, appeared almost to dislike hearing music, and would never himself play, giving as his excuse, when he was called upon, that he was so absorbed in science that he had no time left in which to practise. And this was certainly true. Every day he seemed to become more interested in biology, and his name appeared once or twice in some of the scientific reviews, in connection with certain curious experiments.

This was the man Dorian Gray was waiting for. Every second he kept glancing at the clock. As the minutes went by he became horribly agitated. At last he got up, and began to pace up and down the room, looking like a beautiful caged thing. He took long stealthy strides. His hands were curiosly cold.

The suspense became unbearable. Time seemed to him to be crawling with feet of lead, while he by monstrous winds was being swept towards the jagged edge of some black precipice. He knew what was waiting for him there: saw it indeed, and, shuddering, crushed with dank hands his burning lids as though he would have robbed the very brain of sight, and driven the eyeballs back into their cave. It was useless. The brain had its own food on which it battened, and the imagination, made grotesque by terror, twisted and distorted as a living thing by pain, danced like some foul puppet on a stand, and grinned through moving masks. Then, suddenly, Time stopped for him. Yes: that blind, slow-breathing thing crawled no more, and horrible thoughts, Time being dead, raced nimbly on in front, and dragged a hideous future from its grave, and showed it to him. He stared at it. Its very horror made him stone.

At last the door opened, and his servant entered. He turned glazed eyes upon him.

"Mr. Campbell, sir," said the man.

A sigh of relief broke from his parched lips, and the colour came back to his cheeks.

"Ask him to come in at once, Francis." He felt that he was himself again. His mood of cowardice had passed away.

The man bowed, and retired. In a few moments Alan Campbell walked in, looking very stern and rather pale, his pallor being intensified by his coal-black hair and dark eyebrows.

"Alan! this is kind of you! I thank you for coming."

"I had intended never to enter your house again, Gray. But you said it was a matter of life and death." His voice was hard and cold. He spoke with slow deliberation. There was a look of contempt in the steady searching gaze that he turned on Dorian. He kept his hands in the pockets of his Astrakhan coat, and seemed not to have noticed the gesture with which he had been greeted.

"Yes: it is a matter of life and death, Alan, and to more than one person. Sit down."

Campbell took a chair by the table, and Dorian sat opposite to him. The two men's eyes met. In Dorian's there was infinite pity. He knew that what he was going to do was dreadful.

After a strained moment of silence, he leaned across and said, very quietly, but watching the effect of each word upon the face of him he had sent for: "Alan, in a locked room at the top of this house, a room to which nobody but myself has access, a dead man is seated at a table. He has been dead ten hours now. Don't stir, and don't look at me like that. Who the man is, why he died, how he died, are matters that do not concern you. What you have to do is this——"

"Stop, Gray. I don't want to know anything further. Whether what you have told me is true or not true, doesn't concern me. I entirely decline to be mixed up in your life. Keep your horrible secrets to yourself. They don't interest me any more."

"Alan, they will have to interest you. This one will have

to interest you. I am awfully sorry for you, Alan. But I can't help myself. You are the one man who is able to save me. I am forced to bring you into the matter. I have no option. Alan, you are scientific. You know about chemistry, and things of that kind. You have made experiments. What you have got to do is to destroy the thing that is upstairs—to destroy it so that not a vestige of it will be left. Nobody saw this person come into the house. Indeed, at the present moment he is supposed to be in Paris. He will not be missed for months. When he is missed, there must be no trace of him found here. You, Alan, you must change him, and everything that belongs to him, into a handful of ashes that I may scatter in the air."

"You are mad, Dorian."

"Ah, I was waiting for you to call me Dorian."

"You are mad, I tell you—mad to imagine that I would raise a finger to help you, mad to make this monstrous confession. I will have nothing to do with this matter, whatever it is. Do you think I am going to peril my reputation for you? What is it to me what devil's work you are up to?"

"It was suicide, Alan."

"I am glad of that. But who drove him to it? You, I should fancy."

"Do you still refuse to do this for me?"

"Of course I refuse. I will have absolutely nothing to do with it. I don't care what shame comes on you. You deserve it all. I should not be sorry to see you disgraced, publicly disgraced. How dare you ask me, of all men in the world, to mix myself up in this horror? I should have thought you knew more about people's characters. Your friend Lord Henry Wotton can't have taught you much about psychology, whatever else he has taught you. Nothing will induce me to stir a step to help you. You have come to the wrong man. Go to some of your friends. Don't come to me."

"Alan, it was murder. I killed him. You don't know what he had made me suffer. Whatever my life is, he had more to do with the making or the marring of it than poor Harry has had. He may not have intended it, the result was the same."

"Murder! Good God, Dorian, is that what you have come to? I shall not inform upon you. It is not my business. Besides, without my stirring in the matter, you are certain to be arrested. Nobody ever commits a crime without doing something stupid. But I will have nothing to do with it."

"You must have something to do with it. Wait, wait a moment; listen to me. Only listen, Alan. All I ask of you is to perform a certain scientific experiment. You go to hospitals and dead-houses, and the horrors that you do there don't affect you. If in some hideous dissecting-room or fetid laboratory you found this man lying on a leaden table with red gutters scooped out in it for the blood to flow through, you would simply look upon him as an admirable subject. You would not turn a hair. You would not believe that you were doing anything wrong. On the contrary, you would probably feel that you were benefiting the human race, or increasing the sum of knowledge in the world, or gratifying intellectual curiosity, or something of that kind. What I want you to do is merely what you have often done before. Indeed, to destroy a body must be far less horrible than what you are accustomed to work at. And, remember, it is the only piece of evidence against me. If it is discovered, I am lost; and it is sure to be discovered unless you help me."

"I have no desire to help you. You forget that. I am simply indifferent to the whole thing. It has nothing to do with me."

"Alan, I entreat you. Think of the position I am in. Just before you came I almost fainted with terror. You may know terror yourself some day. No! don't think of that. Look at the matter purely from the scientific point of view. You don't inquire where the dead things on which you experiment come from. Don't inquire now. I have told you too much as it is. But I beg of you to do this. We were friends once, Alan."

"Don't speak about those days, Dorian: they are dead."

"The dead linger sometimes. The man upstairs will not go away. He is sitting at the table with bowed head and outstretched arms. Alan! Alan! if you don't come to my assistance I am ruined. Why, they will hang me, Alan! Don't you understand? They will hang me for what I have done."

"There is no good in prolonging this scene. I absolutely refuse to do anything in the matter. It is insane of you to ask me."

"You refuse?"

"Yes."

"I entreat you, Alan."

"It is useless."

The same look of pity came into Dorian Gray's eyes. Then he stretched out his hand, took a piece of paper, and wrote something on it. He read it over twice, folded it carefully, and pushed it across the table. Having done this, he got up, and went over to the window.

Campbell looked at him in surprise, and then took up the paper and opened it. As he read it, his face became ghastly pale, and he fell back in his chair. A horrible sense of sickness came over him. He felt as if his heart was beating itself to death in some empty hollow.

After two or three minutes of terrible silence, Dorian turned round, and came and stood behind him putting his hand upon his shoulder.

"I am so sorry for you, Alan," he murmured, "but you leave me no alternative. I have a letter written already. Here it is. You see the address. If you don't help me, I must send it.

If you don't help me, I will send it. You know what the result will be. But you are going to help me. It is impossible for
you to refuse now. I tried to spare you. You will do me the
justice to admit that. You were stern, harsh, offensive. You
treated me as no man has ever dared to treat me—no living
man, at any rate. I bore it all. Now it is for me to dictate
terms."

Campbell buried his face in his hands, and a shudder
passed through him.

"Yes, it is my turn to dictate terms, Alan. You know what
they are. The thing is quite simple. Come, don't work yourself into this fever. The thing has to be done. Face it, and
do it."

A groan broke from Campbell's lips, and he shivered all
over. The ticking of the clock on the mantelpiece seemed
to him to be dividing Time into separate atoms of agony,
each of which was too terrible to be borne. He felt as if an
iron ring was being slowly tightened round his forehead,
as if the disgrace with which he was threatened had already
come upon him. The hand upon his shoulder weighed like
a hand of lead. It was intolerable. It seemed to crush him.

"Come, Alan, you must decide at once."

"I cannot do it," he said, mechanically, as though words
could alter things.

"You must. You have no choice. Don't delay."

He hesitated a moment. "Is there a fire in the room upstairs?"

"Yes, there is a gas-fire with asbestos."

"I shall have to go home and get some things from the
laboratory."

"No, Alan, you must not leave the house. Write out on a
sheet of note-paper what you want, and my servant will take
a cab and bring the things back to you."

Campbell scrawled a few lines, blotted them, and addressed an envelope to his assistant. Dorian took the note up and read it carefully. Then he rang the bell, and gave it to his valet, with orders to return as soon as possible, and to bring the things with him.

As the hall door shut, Campbell started nervously, and, having got up from the chair, went over to the chimney-piece. He was shivering with a kind of ague. For nearly twenty minutes, neither of the men spoke. A fly buzzed noisily about the room, and the ticking of the clock was like the beat of a hammer.

As the chime struck one, Campbell turned round, and, looking at Dorian Gray, saw that his eyes were filled with tears. There was something in the purity and refinement of that sad face that seemed to enrage him. "You are infamous, absolutely infamous!" he muttered.

"Hush, Alan: you have saved my life," said Dorian.

"Your life? Good heavens! what a life that is! You have gone from corruption to corruption, and now you have culminated in crime. In doing what I am going to do, what you force me to do, it is not of your life that I am thinking."

"Ah, Alan," murmured Dorian, with a sigh. "I wish you had a thousandth part of the pity for me that I have for you." He turned away as he spoke, and stood looking out at the garden. Campbell made no answer.

After about ten minutes a knock came to the door, and the servant entered, carrying a large mahogany chest of chemicals, with a long coil of steel and platinum wire and two rather curiously-shaped iron clamps.

"Shall I leave the things here, sir?" he asked Campbell.

"Yes," said Dorian. "And I am afraid, Francis, that I have another errand for you. What is the name of the man at Richmond who supplies Selby with orchids?"

"Harden, sir."

"Yes—Harden. You must go down to Richmond at once,

see Harden personally, and tell him to send twice as many orchids as I ordered, and to have as few white ones as possible. In fact, I don't want any white ones. It is a lovely day, Francis, and Richmond is a very pretty place, otherwise I wouldn't bother you about it."

"No trouble, sir. At what time shall I be back?"

Dorian looked at Campbell. "How long will your experiment take, Alan?" he said, in a calm, indifferent voice. The presence of a third person in the room seemed to give him extraordinary courage.

Campbell frowned, and bit his lip. "It will take about five hours," he answered.

"It will be time enough, then, if you are back at half-past seven, Francis. Or stay; just leave my things out for dressing. You can have the evening to yourself. I am not dining at home, so I shall not want you."

"Thank you, sir," said the man, leaving the room.

"Now, Alan, there is not a moment to be lost. How heavy this chest is! I'll take it for you. You bring the other things." He spoke rapidly, and in an authoritative manner. Campbell felt dominated by him. They left the room together.

When they reached the top landing, Dorian took out the key and turned it in the lock. Then he stopped, and a troubled look came into his eyes. He shuddered. "I don't think I can go in, Alan," he murmured.

"It is nothing to me. I don't require you," said Campbell, coldly.

Dorian half opened the door. As he did so, he saw the face of his portrait leering in the sunlight. On the floor in front of it the torn curtain was lying. He remembered that the night before he had forgotten, for the first time in his life, to hide the fatal canvas, and was about to rush forward, when he drew back with a shudder.

What was that loathsome red dew that gleamed, wet and

glistening, on one of the hands, as though the canvas had sweated blood? How horrible it was!—more horrible, it seemed to him for the moment, than the silent thing that he knew was stretched across the table, the thing whose grotesque misshapen shadow on the spotted carpet showed him that it had not stirred, but was still there, as he had left it.

He heaved a deep breath, opened the door a little wider, and with half-closed eyes and averted head walked quickly in, determined that he would not look even once upon the dead man. Then, stooping down, and taking up the gold and purple hanging, he flung it right over the picture.

There he stopped, feeling afraid to turn round, and his eyes fixed themselves on the intricacies of the pattern before him. He heard Campbell bringing in the heavy chest, and the irons, and the other things that he had required for his dreadful work. He began to wonder if he and Basil Hallward had ever met, and, if so, what they had thought of each other.

"Leave me now," said a stern voice behind him.

He turned and hurried out, just conscious that the dead man had been thrust back into the chair, and that Campbell was gazing into a glistening yellow face. As he was going downstairs he heard the key being turned in the lock.

It was long after seven when Campbell came back into the library. He was pale, but absolutely calm. "I have done what you asked me to do," he muttered. "And now, good-bye. Let us never see each other again."

"You have saved me from ruin, Alan. I cannot forget that," said Dorian, simply.

As soon as Campbell had left, he went upstairs. There was a horrible smell of nitric acid in the room. But the thing that had been sitting at the table was gone.

CHAPTER XV

THAT evening, at eight-thirty, exquisitely dressed and wearing a large buttonhole of Parma violets, Dorian Gray was ushered into Lady Narborough's drawing-room by bowing servants. His forehead was throbbing with maddened nerves, and he felt wildly excited, but his manner as he bent over his hostess's hand was as easy and graceful as ever. Perhaps one never seems so much at one's ease as when one has to play a part. Certainly no one looking at Dorian Gray that night could have believed that he had passed through a tragedy as horrible as any tragedy of our age. Those finely-shaped fingers could never have clutched a knife for sin, nor those smiling lips have cried out on God and goodness. He himself could not help wondering at the calm of his demeanour, and for a moment felt keenly the terrible pleasure of a double life.

It was a small party, got up rather in a hurry by Lady Narborough, who was a very clever woman, with what Lord Henry used to describe as the remains of really remarkable ugliness. She had proved an excellent wife to one of our most tedious ambassadors, and having buried her husband properly in a marble mausoleum, which she had herself designed, and married off her daughters to some rich, rather elderly men, she devoted herself now to the pleasures of French fiction, French cookery, and French *esprit* when she could get it.

Dorian was one of her special favourites, and she always told him that she was extremely glad she had not met him in early life. "I know, my dear, I should have fallen madly in love with you," she used to say, and thrown my bonnet right over the mills for your sake. It is most fortunate that you were not thought of at the time. As it was, our bonnets were so unbecoming, and the mills were so occupied in trying to raise the wind, that I never had even a flirtation with anybody. However, that was all Narborough's fault. He was dreadfully short-sighted, and there is no pleasure in taking in a husband who never sees anything."

Her guests this evening were rather tedious. The fact was, as she explained to Dorian, behind a very shabby fan, one of her married daughters had come up quite suddenly to stay with her, and, to make matters worse, had actually brought her husband with her. "I think it is most unkind of her, my dear," she whispered. "Of course I go and stay with them every summer after I come from Homburg, but then an old woman like me must have fresh air sometimes, and besides, I really wake them up. You don't know what an existence they lead down there. It is pure unadulterated country life. They get up early, because they have so much to do, and go to bed early because they have so little to think about. There has not been a scandal in the neighbourhood since the time of Queen Elizabeth, and consequently they all fall asleep after dinner. You shan't sit next to either of them. You shall sit by me and amuse me."

Dorian murmured a graceful compliment, and looked round the room. Yes: it was certainly a tedious party. Two of the people he had never seen before, and the others consisted of Ernest Harrowden, one of those middle-aged mediocrities so common in London clubs who have no enemies, but are thoroughly disliked by their friends; Lady Ruxton, an overdressed woman of forty-seven, with a hooked nose, who was always trying to get herself compromised, but was so peculiarly plain that to her great disappointment no one would ever believe anything against her; Mrs. Erlynne, a pushing nobody, with a delightful lisp, and Venetian-red hair; Lady Alice Chapman, his hostess's daughter, a dowdy dull girl, with one of those characteristic British faces, that, once seen, are never remembered; and her husband, a red-cheeked, white-whiskered creature who, like so many of his class, was under the impression that inordinate joviality can atone for an entire lack of ideas.

He was rather sorry he had come, till Lady Narborough, looking at the great ormolu gilt clock that sprawled in gaudy curves on the mantelshelf, exclaimed: "How horrid of Henry Wotton to be so late! I sent round to him this morning on chance, and he promised faithfully not to disappoint me."

It was some consolation that Harry was to be there, and when the door opened and he heard his slow musical voice lending charm to some insincere apology, he ceased to feel bored.

But at dinner he could not eat anything. Plate after plate went away untasted. Lady Narborough kept scolding him for what she called "an insult to poor Adolphe, who invented the *menu* specially for you," and now and then Lord Henry looked across at him, wondering at his silence and abstracted manner. From time to time the butler filled his glass with champagne. He drank eagerly, and his thirst seemed to increase.

"Dorian," said Lord Henry, at last, as the *chaudfroid* was being handed round, "what is the matter with you to-night? You are quite out of sorts."

"I believe he is in love," cried Lady Narborough, "and that he is afraid to tell me for fear I should be jealous. He is quite right. I certainly should."

"Dear Lady Narborough," murmured Dorian, smiling, "I have not been in love for a whole week—not, in fact, since Madame de Ferrol left town."

"How you men can fall in love with that woman!" ex-claimed the old lady. "I really cannot understand it."

"It is simply because she remembers you when you were a little girl, Lady Narborough," said Lord Henry. "She is the one link between us and your short frocks."

"She does not remember my short frocks at all, Lord Henry. But I remember her very well at Vienna thirty years ago, and how *décolletée* she was then."

"She is still *décolletée*," he answered, taking an olive in his long fingers; "and when she is in a very smart gown she looks like an *édition de luxe* of a bad French novel. She is really wonderful, and full of surprises. Her capacity for family affection is extraordinary. When her third husband died, her hair turned quite gold from grief."

"How can you, Harry!" cried Dorian.

"It is a most romantic explanation," laughed the hostess. "But her third husband, Lord Henry! You don't mean to say Ferrol is the fourth."

"Certainly, Lady Narborough."

"I don't belive a word of it."

"Well, ask Mr. Gray. He is one of her most intimate friends."

"Is it true, Mr. Gray?"

"She assures me so, Lady Narborough," said Dorian. "I asked her whether, like Marguerite de Navarre, she had their hearts embalmed and hung at her girdle. She told me she didn't, because none of them had any hearts at all."

"Four husbands! Upon my word that is *trop de zèle*."

"*Trop d'audace*, I tell her," said Dorian.

"Oh! she is audacious enough for anything, my dear. And what is Ferrol like? I don't know him."

"The husbands of very beautiful women belong to the criminal classes," said Lord Henry, sipping his wine.

Lady Narborough hit him with her fan. "Lord Henry,

I am not at all surprised that the world says that you are extremely wicked."

"But what world says that?" asked Lord Henry, elevating his eyebrows. "It can only be the next world. This world and I are on excellent terms."

"Everybody I know says you are very wicked," cried the old lady, shaking her head.

Lord Henry looked serious for some moments. "It is perfectly monstrous," he said, at last, "the way people go about nowadays saying things against one behind one's back that are absolutely and entirely true."

"Isn't he incorrigible?" cried Dorian, leaning forward in his chair.

"I hope so," said his hostess, laughing. "But really if you all worship Madame de Ferrol in this ridiculous way, I shall have to marry again so as to be in the fashion."

"You will never marry again, Lady Narborough," broke in Lord Henry. "You were far too happy. When a woman marries again it is because she detested her first husband. When a man marries again, it is because he adored his first wife. Women try their luck; men risk theirs."

"Narborough wasn't perfect," cried the old lady.

"If he had been, you would not have loved him, my dear lady," was the rejoinder. "Women love us for our defects. If we have enough of them they will forgive us everything, even our intellects. You will never ask me to dinner again, after saying this, I am afraid, Lady Narborough; but it is quite true."

"Of course it is true, Lord Henry. If we women did not love you for your defects, where would you all be? Not one of you would ever be married. You would be a set of unfortunate bachelors, Not, however, that that would alter you much. Nowadays all the married men live like bachelors, and all the bachelors live like married men."

"*Fin de siècle*," murmured Lord Henry.

"*Fin du globe*," answered his hostess.

"I wish it were *fin du globe*," said Dorian, with a sigh. "Life is a great disappointment."

"Ah, my dear," cried Lady Narborough, putting on her gloves, "don't tell me that you have exhausted Life. When a man says that, one knows that Life has exhausted him. Lord Henry is very wicked, and I sometimes wish that I had been; but you are made to be good—you look so good. I must find you a nice wife. Lord Henry, don't you think that Mr. Gray should get married?"

"I am always telling him so, Lady Narborough," said Lord Henry, with a bow.

"Well, we must look out for a suitable match for him. I shall go through Debrett carefully to-night, and draw out a list of all the eligible young ladies."

"With their ages, Lady Narborough?" asked Dorian.

"Of course, with their ages, slightly edited. But nothing must be done in a hurry. I want it to be what 'The Morning Post' calls a substantial alliance, and I want you both to be happy."

"What nonsense people talk about happy marriages!" exclaimed Lord Henry. "A man can be happy with any woman, as long as he does not love her."

"Ah! what a cynic you are!" cried the old lady, pushing back her chair, and nodding to Lady Ruxton. "You must come and dine with me soon again. You are really an admirable tonic, much better than what Sir Andrew prescribes for me. You must tell me what people you would like to meet, though. I want it to be a delightful gathering."

"I like men who have a future, and women who have a past," he answered. "Or do you think that would make a petticoat party?"

"I fear so," she said, laughing, as she stood up. "A thousand pardons, my dear Lady Ruxton," she added. "I didn't see you hadn't finished your cigarette."

"Never mind, Lady Narborough. I smoke a great deal too much. I am going to limit myself, for the future."

"Pray don't, Lady Ruxton," said Lord Henry. Moderation is a fatal thing. Enough is as bad as a meal. More than enough is as good as a feast."

Lady Ruxton glanced at him curiously. "You must come and explain that to me some afternoon, Lord Henry. It sounds a fascinating theory," she murmured, as she swept out of the room.

"Now, mind you don't stay too long over your politics and scandal," cried Lady Narborough from the door. "If you do, we are sure to squabble upstairs."

The men laughed, and Mr. Chapman got up solemnly from the foot of the table and came up to the top. Dorian Gray changed his seat, and went and sat by Lord Henry. Mr. Chapman began to talk in a loud voice about the situation in the House of Commons. He guffawed at his adversaries. The word *doctrinaire*—word full of terror to the British mind—reappeared from time to time between his explosions. An alliterative prefix served as an ornament of oratory. He hoisted the Union Jack on the pinnacles of Thought. The inherited stupidity of the race—sound English common sense he jovially termed it—was shown to be the proper bulwark for Society.

A smile curved over Lord Henry's lips, and he turned round and looked at Dorian.

"Are you better, my dear fellow?" he asked. "You seemed rather out of sorts at dinner."

"I am quite well, Harry. I am tired. That is all."

"You were charming last night. The little Duchess is quite devoted to you. She tells me she is going down to Selby."

"She has promised to come on the twentieth."

"Is Monmouth to be there too?"

"Oh, yes, Harry."

"He bores me dreadfully, almost as much as he bores her. She is very clever, too clever for a woman. She lacks the indefinable charm of weakness. It is the feet of clay that makes the gold of the image precious. Her feet are very pretty, but they are not feet of clay. White porcelain feet, if you like. They have been through the fire, and what fire does not destroy it hardens. She has had experiences."

"How long has she been married?" asked Dorian.

"An eternity, she tells me. I believe, according to the peerage, it is ten years, but ten years with Monmouth must have been like eternity, with time thrown in. Who else is coming?"

"Oh, the Willoughbys, Lord Rugby and his wife, our hostess, Geoffrey, Clouston, the usual set. I have asked Lord Grotrian."

"I like him," said Lord Henry. "A great many people don't, but I find him charming. He atones for being occasionally somewhat overdressed, by being always absolutely over-educated. He is a very modern type."

"I don't know if he will be able to come, Harry. He may have to go to Monte Carlo with his father."

"Ah! what a nuisance people's people are! Try and make him come. By the way, Dorian, you ran off very early last night. You left before eleven. What did you do afterwards? Did you go straight home?"

Dorian glanced at him hurriedly, and frowned. "No, Harry," he said at last, "I did not get home till nearly three."

"Did you go to the club?"

"Yes," he answered. Then he bit his lip. "No, I don't mean that. I didn't go to the club. I walked about. I forget what I did. . . . How inquisitive you are, Harry! You always want to know what one has been doing. I always

want to forget what I have been doing. I came in
at half-past two, if you wish to know the exact time. I had
left my latch-key at home, and my servant had to let me in.
If you want any corroborative evidence on the subject you
can ask him."

Lord Henry shrugged his shoulders. "My dear fellow,
as if I cared! Let us go up to the drawing-room. No sherry,
thank you, Mr. Chapman. Something has happened to you,
Dorian. Tell me what it is. You are not yourself to-night."

"Don't mind me, Harry. I am irritable, and out of temper.
I shall come round and see you to-morrow or next day.
Make my excuses to Lady Narborough. I shan't go upstairs.
I shall go home. I must go home."

"All right, Dorian. I daresay I shall see you to-morrow
at tea-time. The Duchess is coming."

"I will try to be there, Harry," he said, leaving the room.
As he drove back to his own house he was conscious that
the sense of terror he thought he had strangled had come
back to him. Lord Henry's casual questioning had made
him lose his nerves for the moment, and he wanted his nerve
still. Things that were dangerous had to be destroyed. He
winced. He hated the idea of even touching them.

Yet it had to be done. He realised that, and when he had
locked the door of his library, he opened the secret press into
which he had thrust Basil Hallward's coat and bag. A huge
fire was blazing. He piled another log on it. The smell of the
singeing clothes and burning leather was horrible. It took
him three-quarters of an hour to consume everything. At
the end he felt faint and sick, and having lit some Algerian
pastilles in a pierced copper brazier, he bathed his hands
and forehead with a cool musk-scented vinegar.

Suddenly he started. His eyes grew strangely bright, and
he gnawed nervously at his under-lip. Between two of the
windows stood a large Florentine cabinet, made out of ebony,

and inlaid with ivory and blue lapis. He watched it as though
it were a thing that could fascinate and make afraid, as
though it held something that he longed for and yet almost
loathed. His breath quickened. A mad craving came over
him. He lit a cigarette and then threw it away. His eyelids
drooped till the long fringed lashes almost touched his cheek.
But he still watched the cabinet. At last he got up from the
sofa on which he had been lying, went over to it, and, having
unlocked it, touched some hidden spring. A triangular
drawer passed slowly out. His fingers moved instinctively
towards it, dipped in, and closed on something. It was a
small Chinese box of black and gold-dust lacquer, elaborately wrought, the sides patterned with curved waves, and
the silken cords hung with round crystals and tasselled in
plaited metal threads. He opened it. Inside was a green paste,
waxy in lustre, the odour curiously heavy and persistent.

He hesitated for some moments, with a strangely immobile smile upon his face. Then shivering, though the atmosphere of the room was terribly hot, he drew himself up, and
glanced at the clock. It was twenty minutes to twelve. He
put the box back, shutting the cabinet doors as he did so, and
went into his bedroom.

As midnight was striking bronze blows upon the dusky
air, Dorian Gray dressed commonly, and with a muffler
wrapped round his throat, crept quietly out of the house.
In Bond Street he found a hansom with a good horse. He
hailed it, and in a low voice gave the driver an address.

The man shook his head. "It is too far for me," he muttered.

"Here is a sovereign for you," said Dorian. "You shall
have another if you drive fast."

"All right, sir," answered the man, "you will be there in
an hour," and after his fare had got in he turned his horse
round, and drove rapidly towards the river.

CHAPTER XVI

A COLD rain began to fall, and the blurred street-lamps looked ghastly in the dripping mist. The public-houses were just closing, and dim men and women were clustering in broken groups round their doors. From some of the bars came the sound of horrible laughter. In others, drunkards brawled and screamed.

Lying back in the hansom, with his hat pulled over his forehead, Dorian Gray watched with listless eyes the sordid shame of the great city, and now and then he repeated to himself the words that Lord Henry had said to him on the first day they had met: "To cure the soul by means of the senses, and the senses by means of the soul." Yes, that was the secret. He had often tried it, and would try it again now. There were opium-dens, where one could buy oblivion, dens of horror where the memory of old sins could be destroyed by the madness of sins that were new.

The moon hung low in the sky like a yellow skull. From time to time a huge misshapen cloud stretched a long arm across and hid it. The gas-lamps grew fewer, and the streets more narrow and gloomy. Once the man lost his way, and had to drive back half a mile. A steam rose from the horse as it splashed up the puddles. The side-windows of the hansom were clogged with a grey-flannel mist.

"To cure the soul by means of the senses, and the senses by means of the soul!" How the words rang in his ears! His soul, certainly, was sick to death. Was it true that the senses could cure it? Innocent blood had been spilt. What could atone for that? Ah! for that there was no atonement; but though forgiveness was impossible, forgetfulness was possible still, and he was determined to forget, to stamp the thing out, to crush it as one would crush the adder that had stung one. Indeed, what right had Basil to have spoken to him as he had done? Who had made him a judge over others? He had said things that were dreadful, horrible, not to be endured.

On and on plodded the hansom, going slower, it seemed to him, at each step. He thrust up the trap, and called to the man to drive faster. The hideous hunger for opium began to gnaw at him. His throat burned, and his delicate hands twitched nervously together. He struck at the horse madly with his stick. The driver laughed, and whipped up. He laughed in answer, and the man was silent.

The way seemed interminable, and the streets like the black web of some sprawling spider. The monotony became unbearable, and, as the mist thickened, he felt afraid.

Then they passed by lonely brickfields. The fog was lighter here, and he could see the strange bottle-shaped kilns with their orange fan-like tongues of fire. A dog barked as they went by, and far away in the darkness some wandering sea-gull screamed. The horse stumbled in a rut, then swerved aside, and broke into a gallop.

After some time they left the clay road, and rattled again over rough-paven streets. Most of the windows were dark, but now and then fantastic shadows were silhouetted against some lamp-lit blind. He watched them curiously. They moved like monstrous marionettes, and made gestures like live things. He hated them. A dull rage was in his heart. As they turned a corner a woman yelled something at them from an open door, and two men ran after the hansom for about a hundred yards. The driver beat at them with his whip.

It is said that passion makes one think in a circle. Certainly

with hideous iteration the bitten lips of Dorian Gray shaped
and reshaped those subtle words that dealt with soul and
sense, till he had found in them the full expression, as it
were, of his mood, and justified, by intellectual approval,
passions that without such justification would still have
dominated his temper. From cell to cell of his brain crept
the one thought; and the wild desire to live, most terrible of
all man's appetites, quickened into force each trembling
nerve and fibre. Ugliness that had once been hateful to him
because it made things real, became dear to him now for
that very reason. Ugliness was the one reality. The coarse
brawl, the loathsome den, the crude violence of disordered
life, the very vileness of thief and outcast, were more vivid,
in their intense actuality of impression, than all the gracious
shapes of Art, the dreamy shadows of Song. They were what
he needed for forgetfulness. In three days he would be free.

Suddenly the man drew up with a jerk at the top of a
dark lane. Over the low roofs and jagged chimney stacks of
the houses rose the black masts of ships. Wreaths of white
mist clung like ghostly sails to the yards.

"Somewhere about here, sir, ain't it?" he asked huskily
through the trap.

Dorian started, and peered round. "This will do," he answered, and, having got out hastily, and given the driver the
extra fare he had promised him, he walked quickly in the
direction of the quay. Here and there a lantern gleamed at
the stern of some huge merchantman. The light shook and
splintered in the puddles. A red glare came from an outward-
bound steamer that was coaling. The slimy pavement looked
like a wet mackintosh.

He hurried on towards the left, glancing back now and
then to see if he was being followed. In about seven or eight
minutes he reached a small shabby house, that was wedged

in between two gaunt factories. In one of the top-windows stood a lamp. He stopped, and gave a peculiar knock.

After a little time he heard steps in the passage, and the chain being unhooked. The door opened quietly, and he went in without saying a word to the squat misshapen figure that flattened itself into the shadow as he passed. At the end of the hall hung a tattered green curtain that swayed and shook in the gusty wind which had followed him in from the street. He dragged it aside, and entered a long, low room which looked as if it had once been a third-rate dancing-saloon. Shrill flaring gas-jets, dulled and distorted in the fly-blown mirrors that faced them, were ranged round the walls. Greasy reflectors of ribbed tin backed them, making quivering discs of light. The floor was covered with ochre-coloured sawdust, trampled here and there into mud, and stained with dark rings of spilt liquor. Some Malays were crouching by a little charcoal stove playing with bone counters, and showing their white teeth as they chattered. In one corner, with his head buried in his arms, a sailor sprawled over a table, and by the tawdrily-painted bar that ran across one complete side stood two haggard women mocking an old man who was brushing the sleeves of his coat with an expression of disgust. "He thinks he's got red ants on him," laughed one of them, as Dorian passed by. The man looked at her in terror and began to whimper.

At the end of the room there was a little staircase, leading to a darkened chamber. As Dorian hurried up its three rickety steps, the heavy odour of opium met him. He heaved a deep breath, and his nostrils quivered with pleasure. When he entered, a young man with smooth yellow hair, who was bending over a lamp, lighting a long thin pipe, looked up at him, and nodded in a hesitating manner.

"You here, Adrian?" muttered Dorian.

"Where else should I be?" he answered, listlessly. "None of the chaps will speak to me now."

"I thought you had left England."

"Darlington is not going to do anything. My brother paid the bill at last. George doesn't speak to me either. . . . I don't care," he added, with a sigh. "As long as one has this stuff, one doesn't want friends. I think I have had too many friends."

Dorian winced, and looked round at the grotesque things that lay in such fantastic postures on the ragged mattresses. The twisted limbs, the gaping mouths, the staring lustreless eyes, fascinated him. He knew in what strange heavens they were suffering, and what dull hells were teaching them the secret of some new joy. They were better off than he was. He was prisoned in thought. Memory, like a horrible malady, was eating his soul away. From time to time he seemed to see the eyes of Basil Hallward looking at him. Yet he felt he could not stay. The presence of Adrian Singleton troubled him. He wanted to be where no one would know who he was. He wanted to escape from himself.

"I am going on to the other place," he said, after a pause.

"On the wharf?"

"Yes."

"That mad-cat is sure to be there. They won't have her in this place now."

Dorian shrugged his shoulders. "I am sick of women who love one. Women who hate one are much more interesting. Besides, the stuff is better."

"Much the same."

"I like it better. Come and have something to drink. I must have something."

"I don't want anything," murmured the young man.

"Never mind."

Adrian Singleton rose up wearily, and followed Dorian to

the bar. A half-caste, in a ragged turban and a shabby ulster, grinned a hideous greeting as he thrust a bottle of brandy and two tumblers in front of them. The women sidled up, and began to chatter. Dorian turned his back on them, and said something in a low voice to Adrian Singleton.

A crooked smile, like a Malay crease, writhed across the face of one of the women. "We are very proud to-night," she sneered.

"For God's sake don't talk to me," cried Dorian, stamping his foot on the ground. "What do you want? Money? Here it is. Don't ever talk to me again."

Two red sparks flashed for a moment in the woman's sodden eyes, then flickered out, and left them dull and glazed. She tossed her head, and raked the coins off the counter with greedy fingers. Her companion watched her enviously.

"It's no use," sighed Adrian Singleton. "I don't care to go back. What does it matter? I am quite happy here."

"You will write to me if you want anything, won't you?" said Dorian, after a pause.

"Perhaps."

"Good-night, then."

"Good-night," answered the young man, passing up the steps, and wiping his parched mouth with a handkerchief.

Dorian walked to the door with a look of pain in his face. As he drew the curtain aside a hideous laugh broke from the painted lips of the woman who had taken his money. "There goes the devil's bargain!" she hiccoughed, in a hoarse voice.

"Curse you!" he answered, "don't call me that."

She snapped her fingers. "Prince Charming is what you like to be called, ain't it?" she yelled after him.

The drowsy sailor leapt to his feet as she spoke, and looked wildly round. The sound of the shutting of the hall door fell on his ear. He rushed out as if in pursuit.

Dorian Gray hurried along the quay through the drizzling rain. His meeting with Adrian Singleton had strangely moved him, and he wondered if the ruin of that young life was really to be laid at his door, as Basil Hallward had said to him with such infamy of insult. He bit his lip, and for a few seconds his eyes grew sad. Yet, after all, what did it matter to him? One's days were too brief to take the burden of another's errors on one's shoulders. Each man lived his own life, and paid his own price for living it. The only pity was one had to pay so often for a single fault. One had to pay over and over again, indeed. In her dealings with man Destiny never closed her accounts.

There are moments, psychologists tell us, when the passion for sin, or for what the world calls sin, so dominates a nature, that every fibre of the body, as every cell of the brain, seems to be instinct with fearful impulses. Men and women at such moments lose the freedom of their will. They move to their terrible end as automatons move. Choice is taken from them, and conscience is either killed, or, if it lives at all, lives but to give rebellion its fascination, and disobedience its charm. For all sins, as theologians weary not of reminding us, are sins of disobedience. When that high spirit, that morning-star of evil, fell from heaven, it was as a rebel that he fell.

Callous, concentrated on evil, with stained mind, and soul hungry for rebellion, Dorian Gray hastened on, quickening his step as he went, but as he darted aside into a dim arch-way, that had served him often as a short cut to the ill-famed place where he was going, he felt himself suddenly seized from behind, and before he had time to defend himself he was thrust back against the wall, with a brutal hand round his throat.

He struggled madly for life, and by a terrible effort wrenched the tightening fingers away. In a second he heard the click of a revolver, and saw the gleam of a polished barrel pointing straight at his head, and the dusky form of a short thick-set man facing him.

"What do you want?" he gasped.

"Keep quiet," said the man. "If you stir, I shoot you."

"You are mad. What have I done to you?"

"You wrecked the life of Sibyl Vane," was the answer, "and Sibyl Vane was my sister. She killed herself. I know it. Her death is at your door. I swore I would kill you in return. For years I have sought you. I had no clue, no trace. The two people who could have described you were dead. I knew nothing of you but the pet name she used to call you. I heard it to-night by chance. Make your peace with God, for to-night you are going to die."

Dorian Gray grew sick with fear. "I never knew her," he stammered. "I never heard of her. You are mad."

"You had better confess your sin, for as sure as I am James Vane, you are going to die." There was a horrible moment. Dorian did not know what to say or do. "Down on your knees!" growled the man. "I give you one minute to make your peace—no more. I go on board to-night for India, and I must do my job first. One minute. That's all."

Dorian's arms fell to his side. Paralysed with terror, he did not know what to do. Suddenly a wild hope flashed across his brain. "Stop," he cried. "How long ago is it since your sister died? Quick, tell me!"

"Eighteen years," said the man. "Why do you ask me? What do years matter?"

"Eighteen years," laughed Dorian Gray, with a touch of triumph in his voice. "Eighteen years! Set me under the lamp and look at my face!"

James Vane hesitated for a moment, not understanding what was meant. Then he seized Dorian Gray and dragged him from the archway.

Dim and wavering as was the wind-blown light, yet it

served to show him the hideous error, as it seemed, into which he had fallen, for the face of the man he had sought to kill had all the bloom of boyhood, all the unstained purity of youth. He seemed little more than a lad of twenty summers, hardly older, if older indeed at all, than his sister had been when they had parted so many years ago. It was obvious that this was not the man who had destroyed her life.

He loosened his hold and reeled back. "My God! my God!" he cried, "and I would have murdered you!"

Dorian Gray drew a long breath. "You have been on the brink of committing a terrible crime, my man," he said, looking at him sternly. "Let this be a warning to you not to take vengeance into your own hands."

"Forgive me, sir," muttered James Vane. "I was deceived. A chance word I heard in that damned den set me on the wrong track."

"You had better go home, and put that pistol away, or you may get into trouble," said Dorian, turning on his heel, and going slowly down the street.

James Vane stood on the pavement in horror. He was trembling from head to foot. After a little while a black shadow that had been creeping along the dripping wall, moved out into the light and came close to him with stealthy footsteps. He felt a hand laid on his arm and looked round with a start. It was one of the women who had been drinking at the bar.

"Why didn't you kill him?" she hissed out, putting her haggard face quite close to his. "I knew you were following him when you rushed out from Daly's. You fool! You should have killed him. He has lots of money, and he's as bad as bad."

"He is not the man I am looking for," he answered, "and I want no man's money. I want a man's life. The man whose life I want must be nearly forty now. This one is little more than a boy. Thank God, I have not got his blood upon my hands."

The woman gave a bitter laugh. "Little more than a boy!" she sneered. "Why, man, it's nigh on eighteen years since Prince Charming made me what I am."

"You lie!" cried James Vane.

She raised her hand up to heaven. "Before God I am telling the truth," she cried.

"Before God?"

"Strike me dumb if it ain't so. He is the worst one that comes here. They say he has sold himself to the devil for a pretty face. It's nigh on eighteen years since I met him. He hasn't changed much since then. I have though," she added, with a sickly leer.

"You swear this?"

"I swear it," came in hoarse echo from her flat mouth. "But don't give me away to him," she whined; "I am afraid of him. Let me have some money for my night's lodging."

He broke from her with an oath, and rushed to the corner of the street, but Dorian Gray had disappeared. When he looked back, the woman had vanished also.

CHAPTER XVII

A WEEK later Dorian Gray was sitting in the conservatory at Selby Royal talking to the pretty Duchess of
Monmouth, who with her husband, a jaded-looking man
of sixty, was amongst his guests. It was tea-time, and the
mellow light of the huge lace-covered lamp that stood on
the table lit up the delicate china and hammered silver of
the service at which the Duchess was presiding. Her white
hands were moving daintily among the cups, and her full
red lips were smiling at something that Dorian had whispered to her. Lord Henry was lying back in a silk-draped
wicker chair looking at them. On a peach-coloured divan
sat Lady Narborough pretending to listen to the Duke's
description of the last Brazilian beetle that he had added to
his collection. Three young men in elaborate smoking-suits
were handing tea-cakes to some of the women. The house
party consisted of twelve people, and there were more expected to arrive on the next day.

"What are you two talking about?" said Lord Henry,
strolling over to the table, and putting his cup down. "I
hope Dorian has told you about my plan for rechristening
everything, Gladys. It is a delightful idea."

"But I don't want to be rechristened, Harry," rejoined the
Duchess, looking up at him with her wonderful eyes. "I
am quite satisfied with my own name, and I am sure Mr.
Gray should be satisfied with his."

"My dear Gladys, I would not alter either name for the
world. They are both perfect. I was thinking chiefly of
flowers. Yesterday I cut an orchid, for my button-hole. It

was a marvellous spotted thing, as effective as the seven deadly sins. In a thoughtless moment I asked one of the gardeners what it was called. He told me it was a fine specimen of 'Robinsoniana,' or something dreadful of that kind. It is a sad truth, but we have lost the faculty of giving lovely names to things. Names are everything. I never quarrel with actions. My one quarrel is with words. That is the reason I hate vulgar realism in literature. The man who could call a spade a spade should be compelled to use one. It is the only thing he is fit for."

"Then what should we call you, Harry?" she asked.

"His name is Prince Paradox," said Dorian.

"I recognise him in a flash," exclaimed the Duchess.

"I won't hear of it," laughed Lord Henry, sinking into a chair. "From a label there is no escape! I refuse the title."

"Royalties may not abdicate," fell as a warning from pretty lips.

"You wish me to defend my throne, then?"

"Yes."

"I give the truths of to-morrow."

"I prefer the mistakes of to-day," she answered.

"You disarm me, Gladys," he cried, catching the wilfulness of her mood.

"Of your shield, Harry: not of your spear."

"I never tilt against Beauty," he said, with a wave of his hand.

"That is your error, Harry, believe me. You value beauty far too much."

"How can you say that? I admit that I think that it is better to be beautiful than to be good. But on the other hand no one is more ready than I am to acknowledge that it is better to be good than to be ugly."

"Ugliness is one of the seven deadly sins, then?" cried the Duchess. "What becomes of your simile about the orchid?"

"Ugliness is one of the seven deadly virtues, Gladys. You, as a good Tory, must not underrate them. Beer, the Bible, and the seven deadly virtues have made our England what she is."

"You don't like your country, then?" she asked.

"I live in it."

"That you may censure it the better."

"Would you have me take the verdict of Europe on it?" he inquired.

"What do they say of us?"

"That Tartuffe has emigrated to England and opened a shop."

"Is that yours, Harry?"

"I give it to you."

"I could not use it. It is too true."

"You need not be afraid. Our countrymen never recognise a description."

"They are practical."

"They are more cunning than practical. When they make up their ledger, they balance stupidity by wealth, and vice by hypocrisy."

"Still, we have done great things."

"Great things have been thrust on us, Gladys."

"We have carried their burden."

"Only as far as the Stock Exchange."

She shook her head. "I believe in the race," she cried.

"It represents the survival of the pushing."

"It has development."

"Decay fascinates me more."

"What of Art?" she asked.

"It is a malady."

"Love?"

"An illusion."

"Religion?"

"The fashionable substitute for Belief."

"You are a sceptic."

"Never! Scepticism is the beginning of Faith."

"What are you?"

"To define is to limit."

"Give me a clue."

"Threads snap. You would lose your way in the labyrinth."

"You bewilder me. Let us talk of something else."

"Our host is a delightful topic. Years ago he was christened Prince Charming."

"Ah! don't remind me of that," cried Dorian Gray.

"Our host is rather horrid this evening," answered the Duchess, colouring. "I believe he thinks that Monmouth married me on purely scientific principles as the best speci-men he could find of a modern butterfly."

"Well, I hope he won't stick pins into you, Duchess," laughed Dorian.

"Oh! my maid does that already, Mr. Gray, when she is annoyed with me."

"And what does she get annoyed with you about, Duchess?"

"For the most trivial things, Mr. Gray, I assure you. Usually because I come in at ten minutes to nine and tell her that I must be dressed by half-past eight."

"How unreasonable of her! You should give her warning."

"I daren't, Mr. Gray. Why, she invents hats for me. You remember the one I wore at Lady Hilstone's garden-party? You don't, but it is nice of you to pretend that you do? Well, she made it out of nothing. All good hats are made out of nothing."

"Like all good reputations, Gladys," interrupted Lord Henry. "Every effect that one produces gives one an enemy. To be popular one must be a mediocrity."

"Not with women," said the Duchess, shaking her head;

"and women rule the world. I assure you we can't bear mediocrities. We women, as someone says, love with our ears, just as you men love with your eyes, if you ever love at all."

"It seems to me that we never do anything else," murmured Dorian.

"Ah! then, you never really love, Mr. Gray," answered the Duchess, with mock sadness.

"My dear Gladys!" cried Lord Henry. "How can you say that? Romance lives by repetition, and repetition converts an appetite into an art. Besides, each time that one loves is the only time one has ever loved. Difference of object does not alter singleness of passion. It merely intensifies it. We can have in life but one great experience at best, and the secret of life is to reproduce that experience as often as possible."

"Even when one has been wounded by it, Harry?" asked the Duchess, after a pause.

"Especially when one has been wounded by it," answered Lord Henry.

The Duchess turned and looked at Dorian Gray with a curious expression in her eyes. "What do you say to that, Mr. Gray?" she inquired.

Dorian hesitated for a moment. Then he threw his head back and laughed. "I always agree with Harry, Duchess."

"Even when he is wrong?"

"Harry is never wrong, Duchess."

"And does his philosophy make you happy?"

"I have never searched for happiness. Who wants happiness? I have searched for pleasure."

"And found it, Mr. Gray?"

"Often. Too often."

The Duchess sighed. "I am searching for peace," she said, "and if I don't go and dress, I shall have none this evening."

"Let me get you some orchids, Duchess," cried Dorian, starting to his feet, and walking down the conservatory.

"You are flirting disgracefully with him," said Lord Henry to his cousin. "You had better take care. He is very fascinating."

"If he were not, there would be no battle."

"Greek meets Greek, then?"

"I am on the side of the Trojans. They fought for a woman."

"They were defeated."

"There are worse things than capture," she answered.

"You gallop with a loose rein."

"Pace gives life," was the *riposte*.

"I shall write it in my diary to-night."

"What?"

"That a burnt child loves the fire."

"I am not even singed. My wings are untouched."

"You use them for everything, except flight."

"Courage has passed from men to women. It is a new experience for us."

"You have a rival."

"Who?"

He laughed. "Lady Narborough," he whispered. "She perfectly adores him."

"You fill me with apprehension. The appeal to Antiquity is fatal to us who are romanticists."

"Romanticists! You have all the methods of science."

"Men have educated us."

"But not explained you."

"Describe us as a sex," was her challenge.

"Sphinxes without secrets."

She looked at him, smiling. "How long Mr. Gray is!" she said. "Let us go and help him. I have not yet told him the colour of my frock."

"Ah! you must suit your frock to his flowers, Gladys."

"That would be a premature surrender."

"Romantic Art begins with its climax."

"I must keep an opportunity for retreat."

"In the Parthian manner?"

"They found safety in the desert. I could not do that."

"Women are not always allowed a choice," he answered, but hardly had he finished the sentence before from the far end of the conservatory came a stifled groan, followed by the dull sound of a heavy fall. Everybody started up. The Duchess stood motionless in horror. And with fear in his eyes Lord Henry rushed through the flapping palms to find Dorian Gray lying face downward on the tiled floor in a death-like swoon.

He was carried at once into the blue drawing-room and laid upon one of the sofas. After a short time he came to himself, and looked round with a dazed expression.

"What has happened?" he asked. "Oh! I remember. Am I safe here, Harry?" He began to tremble.

"My dear Dorian," answered Lord Henry, "you merely fainted. That was all. You must have overtired yourself. You had better not come down to dinner. I will take your place."

"No, I will come down," he said, struggling to his feet. "I would rather come down. I must not be alone."

He went to his room and dressed. There was a wild recklessness of gaiety in his manner as he sat at table, but now and then a thrill of terror ran through him when he remembered that, pressed against the window of the conservatory, like a white handkerchief, he had seen the face of James Vane watching him.

CHAPTER XVIII

THE next day he did not leave the house, and, indeed, spent most of the time in his own room, sick with a wild terror of dying, and yet indifferent to life itself. The consciousness of being hunted, snared, tracked down, had begun to dominate him. If the tapestry did but tremble in the wind, he shook. The dead leaves that were blown against the leaded panes seemed to him like his own wasted resolutions and wild regrets. When he closed his eyes, he saw again the sailor's face peering through the mist-stained glass, and horror seemed once more to lay its hand upon his heart.

But perhaps it had been only his fancy that had called vengeance out of the night, and set the hideous shapes of punishment before him. Actual life was chaos, but there was something terribly logical in the imagination. It was the imagination that set remorse to dog the feet of sin. It was the imagination that made each crime bear its misshapen brood. In the common world of fact the wicked were not punished, nor the good rewarded. Success was given to the strong, failure thrusts upon the weak. That was all. Besides, had any stranger been prowling round the house he would have been seen by the servants or the keepers. Had any footmarks been found on the flower-beds, the gardeners would have reported it. Yes: it had been merely fancy. Sibyl Vane's brother had not come back to kill him. He had sailed away in his ship to founder in some winter sea. From him, at any rate, he was safe. Why, the man did not know who he was, could not know who he was. The mask of youth had saved him.

And yet if it had been merely an illusion, how terrible it was to think that conscience could raise such fearful phantoms, and give them visible form, and make them move before one! What sort of life would his be, if day and night, shadows of his crime were to peer at him from silent corners, to mock him from secret places, to whisper in his ear as he sat at the feast, to wake him with icy fingers as he lay asleep! As the thought crept through his brain, he grew pale with terror, and the air seemed to him to have become suddenly colder. Oh! in what a wild hour of madness he had killed his friend! How ghastly the mere memory of the scene! He saw it all again. Each hideous detail came back to him with added horror. Out of the black cave of Time, terrible and swathed in scarlet, rose the image of his sin. When Lord Henry came in at six o'clock, he found him crying as one whose heart will break.

It was not till the third day that he ventured to go out. There was something in the clear, pine-scented air of that winter morning that seemed to bring him back his joyousness and his ardour for life. But it was not merely the physical conditions of environment that had caused the change. His own nature had revolted against the excess of anguish that had sought to maim and mar the perfection of its calm. With subtle and finely-wrought temperaments it is always so. Their strong passions must either bruise or bend. They either slay the man, or themselves die. Shallow sorrows and shallow loves live on. The loves and sorrows that are great are destroyed by their own plenitude. Besides, he had convinced himself that he had been the victim of a terror-stricken imagination, and looked back now on his fears with something of pity and not a little of contempt.

After breakfast he walked with the Duchess for an hour in the garden, and then drove across the park to join the shooting-party. The crisp frost lay like salt upon the grass.

The sky was an inverted cup of blue metal. A thin film of ice bordered the flat reed-grown lake.

At the corner of the pine-wood he caught sight of Sir Geoffrey Clouston, the Duchess's brother, jerking two spent cartridges out of his gun. He jumped from the cart, and having told the groom to take the mare home, made his way towards his guest through the withered bracken and rough undergrowth.

"Have you had good sport, Geoffrey?" he asked.

"Not very good, Dorian. I think most of the birds have gone to the open. I dare say it will be better after lunch, when we get to new ground."

Dorian strolled along by his side. The keen aromatic air, the brown and red lights that glimmered in the wood, the hoarse cries of the beaters ringing out from time to time, and the sharp snaps of the guns that followed, fascinated him, and filled him with a sense of delightful freedom. He was dominated by the carelessness of happiness, by the high indifference of joy.

Suddenly from a lumpy tussock of old grass, some twenty yards in front of them, with black-tipped ears erect, and long hinder limbs throwing it forward, started a hare. It bolted for a thicket of alders. Sir Geoffrey put his gun to his shoulder, but there was something in the animal's grace of movement that strangely charmed Dorian Gray, and he cried out at once: "Don't shoot it, Geoffrey. Let it live."

"What nonsense, Dorian!" laughed his companion, and as the hare bounded into the thicket he fired. There were two cries heard, the cry of a hare in pain, which is dreadful, the cry of a man in agony, which is worse.

"Good heavens! I have hit a beater!" exclaimed Sir Geoffrey. "What an ass the man was to get in front of the guns! Stop shooting there!" he called out at the top of his voice. "A man is hurt."

The head-keeper came running up with a stick in his hand.

"Where, sir? Where is he?" he shouted. At the same time the firing ceased along the line.

"Here," answered Sir Geoffrey, angrily, hurrying towards the thicket. "Why on earth don't you keep your men back? Spoiled my shooting for the day."

Dorian watched them as they plunged into the alder-clump, brushing the lithe, swinging branches aside. In a few moments they emerged, dragging a body after them into the sunlight. He turned away in horror. It seemed to him that misfortune followed wherever he went. He heard Sir Geoffrey ask if the man was really dead, and the affirmative answer of the keeper. The wood seemed to him to have become suddenly alive with faces. There was the trampling of myriad feet, and the low buzz of voices. A great copper-breasted pheasant came beating through the boughs overhead.

After a few moments, that were to him, in his perturbed state, like endless hours of pain, he felt a hand laid on his shoulder. He started, and looked round.

"Dorian," said Lord Henry, "I had better tell them that the shooting is stopped for to-day. It would not look well to go on."

"I wish it were stopped for ever, Harry," he answered, bitterly. "The whole thing is hideous and cruel. Is the man . . . ?"

He could not finish the sentence.

"I am afraid so," rejoined Lord Henry. "He got the whole charge of shot in his chest. He must have died almost instantaneously. Come; let us go home."

They walked side by side in the direction of the avenue for nearly fifty yards without speaking. Then Dorian looked at Lord Henry, and said, with a heavy sigh: "It is a bad omen, Harry, a very bad omen."

"What is?" asked Lord Henry. "Oh! this accident, I suppose. My dear fellow, it can't be helped. It was the man's own fault. Why did he get in front of the guns? Besides, it's nothing to us. It is rather awkward for Geoffrey, of course. It does not do to pepper beaters. It makes people think that one is a wild shot. And Geoffrey is not; he shoots very straight. But there is no use talking about the matter."

Dorian shook his head. "It is a bad omen, Harry. I feel as if something horrible were going to happen to some of us. To myself, perhaps," he added, passing his hand over his eyes, with a gesture of pain.

The elder man laughed. "The only horrible thing in the world is ennui, Dorian. That is the one sin for which there is no forgiveness. But we are not likely to suffer from it, unless these fellows keep chattering about this thing at dinner. I must tell them that the subject is to be tabooed. As for omens, there is no such thing as an omen. Destiny does not send us heralds. She is too wise or too cruel for that. Besides, what on earth could happen to you, Dorian? You have everything in the world that a man can want. There is no one who would not be delighted to change places with you."

"There is no one with whom I would not change places, Harry. Don't laugh like that. I am telling you the truth. The wretched peasant who has just died is better off than I am. I have no terror of Death. It is the coming of Death that terrifies me. Its monstrous wings seem to wheel in the leaden air around me. Good heavens! don't you see a man moving behind the trees there, watching me, waiting for me?"

Lord Henry looked in the direction in which the trembling gloved hand was pointing. "Yes," he said, smiling, "I see the gardener waiting for you. I suppose he wants to ask you what flowers you wish to have on the table to-night. How absurdly nervous you are, my dear fellow! You must come and see my doctor, when we get back to town."

Dorian heaved a sigh of relief as he saw the gardener approaching. The man touched his hat, glanced for a moment at Lord Henry in a hesitating manner, and then produced a letter, which he handed to his master. "Her Grace told me to wait for an answer," he murmured.

Dorian put the letter into his pocket. "Tell her Grace that I am coming in," he said, coldly. The man turned round, and went rapidly in the direction of the house.

"How fond women are of doing dangerous things!" laughed Lord Henry. "It is one of the qualities in them that I admire most. A woman will flirt with anybody in the world as long as other people are looking on."

"How fond you are of saying dangerous things, Harry! In the present instance you are quite astray. I like the Duchess very much, but I don't love her."

"And the Duchess loves you very much, but she likes you less, so you are excellently matched."

"You are talking scandal, Harry, and there is never any basis for scandal."

"The basis of every scandal is an immoral certainty," said Lord Henry, lighting a cigarette.

"You would sacrifice anybody, Harry, for the sake of an epigram."

"The world goes to the altar of its own accord," was the answer.

"I wish I could love," cried Dorian Gray, with a deep note of pathos in his voice. "But I seem to have lost the passion, and forgotten the desire. I am too much concentrated on myself. My own personality has become a burden to me. I want to escape, to go away, to forget. It was silly of me to come down here at all. I think I shall send a wire to Harvey to have the yacht got ready. On a yacht one is safe."

"Safe from what, Dorian? You are in some trouble. Why not tell me what it is? You know I would help you."

"I can't tell you, Harry," he answered, sadly. "And I dare say it is only a fancy of mine. This unfortunate accident has upset me. I have a horrible presentiment that something of the kind may happen to me."

"What nonsense!"

"I hope it is, but I can't help feeling it. Ah! here is the Duchess, looking like Artemis in a tailor-made gown. You see we have come back, Duchess."

"I have heard all about it, Mr. Gray," she answered, "Poor Geoffrey is terribly upset. And it seems that you asked him not to shoot the hare. How curious!"

"Yes, it was very curious. I don't know what made me say it. Some whim, I suppose. It looked the loveliest of little live things. But I am sorry they told you about the man. It is a hideous subject."

"It is an annoying subject," broke in Lord Henry. "It has no psychological value at all. Now if Geoffrey had done the thing on purpose, how interesting he would be! I should like to know someone who had committed a real murder."

"How horrid of you, Harry!" cried the Duchess. "Isn't it, Mr. Gray? Harry, Mr. Gray is ill again. He is going to faint."

Dorian drew himself up with an effort, and smiled. "It is nothing, Duchess," he murmured; "my nerves are dreadfully out of order. That is all. I am afraid I walked too far this morning. I didn't hear what Harry said. Was it very bad? You must tell me some other time. I think I must go and lie down. You will excuse me, won't you?"

They had reached the great flight of steps that led from the conservatory on to the terrace. As the glass door closed behind Dorian, Lord Henry turned and looked at the Duchess with his slumberous eyes. "Are you very much in love with him?" he asked.

She did not answer for some time, but stood gazing at the landscape. "I wish I knew," she said at last.

He shook his head. "Knowledge would be fatal. It is the uncertainty that charms one. A mist makes things wonderful."

"One may lose one's way."

"All ways end at the same point, my dear Gladys."

"What is that?"

"Disillusion."

"It was my début in life," she sighed.

"It came to you crowned."

"I am tired of strawberry leaves."

"They become you."

"Only in public."

"You would miss them," said Lord Henry.

"I will not part with a petal."

"Monmouth has ears."

"Old age is dull of hearing."

"Has he never been jealous?"

"I wish he had been."

He glanced about as if in search of something. "What are you looking for?" she inquired.

"The button from your foil," he answered. "You have dropped it."

She laughed. "I have still the mask."

"It makes your eyes lovelier," was his reply.

She laughed again. Her teeth showed like white seeds in a scarlet fruit.

Upstairs, in his own room, Dorian Gray was lying on a sofa, with terror in every tingling fibre of his body. Life had suddenly become too hideous a burden for him to bear.

The dreadful death of the unlucky beater, shot in the thicket like a wild animal, had seemed to him to prefigure death for himself also. He had nearly swooned at what Lord Henry had said in a chance mood of cynical jesting.

At five o'clock he rang his bell for his servant and gave him orders to pack his things for the night-express to town, and to have the brougham at the door by eight-thirty. He was determined not to sleep another night at Selby Royal. It was an ill-omened place. Death walked there in the sunlight. The grass of the forest had been spotted with blood.

Then he wrote a note to Lord Henry, telling him that he was going up to town to consult his doctor, and asking him to entertain his guests in his absence. As he was putting it into the envelope, a knock came to the door, and his valet informed him that the head-keeper wished to see him. He frowned, and bit his lip. "Send him in," he muttered, after some moments' hesitation.

As soon as the man entered Dorian pulled his cheque-book out of a drawer, and spread it out before him.

"I suppose you have come about the unfortunate accident of this morning, Thornton?" he said, taking up a pen.

"Yes, sir," answered the gamekeeper.

"Was the poor fellow married? Had he any people dependent on him?" asked Dorian, looking bored. "If so, I should not like them to be left in want, and will send them any sum of money you may think necessary."

"We don't know who he is, sir. That is what I took the liberty of coming to you about."

"Don't know who he is?" said Dorian, listlessly. "What do you mean? Wasn't he one of your men?"

"No, sir. Never saw him before. Seems like a sailor, sir."

The pen dropped from Dorian Gray's hand, and he felt as if his heart had suddenly stopped beating. "A sailor?" he cried out. "Did you say a sailor?"

"Yes, sir. He looks as if he had been a sort of sailor; tattooed on both arms, and that kind of thing."

"Was there anything found on him?" said Dorian, leaning forward and looking at the man with startled eyes. "Anything that would tell his name?"

"Some money, sir—not much, and a six-shooter. There was no name of any kind. A decent-looking man, sir, but rough-like. A sort of sailor, we think."

Dorian started to his feet. A terrible hope fluttered past him. He clutched at it madly. "Where is the body?" he exclaimed. "Quick! I must see it at once."

"It is in an empty stable in the Home Farm, sir. The folk don't like to have that sort of thing in their houses. They say a corpse brings bad luck."

"The Home Farm! Go there at once and meet me. Tell one of the grooms to bring my horse round. No, never mind. I'll go to the stables myself. It will save time."

In less than a quarter of an hour Dorian Gray was galloping down the long avenue as hard as he could go. The trees seemed to sweep past him in spectral procession, and wild shadows to fling themselves across his path. Once the mare swerved at a white gate-post and nearly threw him. He lashed her across the neck with his crop. She cleft the dusky air like an arrow. The stones flew from her hoofs.

At last he reached the Home Farm. Two men were loitering in the yard. He leapt from the saddle and threw the reins to one of them. In the farthest stable a light was glimmering. Something seemed to tell him that the body was there, and he hurried to the door, and put his hand upon the latch.

There he paused for a moment, feeling that he was on the brink of discovery that would either make or mar his life. Then he thrust the door open, and entered.

On a heap of sacking in the far corner was lying the dead body of a man dressed in a coarse shirt and a pair of blue trousers. A spotted handkerchief had been placed over the face. A coarse candle, stuck in a bottle, sputtered beside it.

Dorian Gray shuddered. He felt that his could not be the hand to take the handkerchief away, and called out to one of the farm-servants to come to him.

"Take that thing off the face. I wish to see it," he said, clutching at the doorpost for support.

When the farm-servant had done so, he stepped forward. A cry of joy broke from his lips. The man who had been shot in the thicket was James Vane.

He stood there for some minutes looking at the dead body. As he rode home, his eyes were full of tears, for he knew he was safe.

CHAPTER XIX

"THERE is no use your telling me that you are going to be good," cried Lord Henry, dipping his white fingers into a red copper bowl filled with rose-water. "You're quite perfect. Pray, don't change."

Dorian Gray shook his head. "No, Harry, I have done too many dreadful things in my life. I am not going to do any more. I began my good actions yesterday."

"Where were you yesterday?"

"In the country, Harry. I was staying at a little inn by myself."

"My dear boy," said Lord Henry, smiling, "anybody can be good in the country. There are no temptations there. That is the reason why people who live out of town are so absolutely uncivilised. Civilisation is not by any means an easy thing to attain to. There are only two ways by which man can reach it. One is by being cultured, the other by being corrupt. Country people have no opportunity of being either, so they stagnate."

"Culture and corruption," echoed Dorian. "I have known something of both. It seems terrible to me now that they should ever be found together. For I have a new ideal, Harry. I am going to alter. I think I have altered."

"You have not yet told me what your good action was. Or did you say you had done more than one?" asked his companion, as he spilt into his plate a little crimson pyramid of seeded strawberries, and through a perforated shell-shaped spoon snowed white sugar upon them.

"I can tell you, Harry. It is not a story I could tell to anyone else. I spared somebody. It sounds vain, but you understand what I mean. She was quite beautiful, and wonderfully like Sibyl Vane. I think it was that which first attracted me to her. You remember Sibyl, don't you? How long ago that seems! Well, Hetty was not one of our own class of course. She was simply a girl in a village. But I really loved her. I am quite sure that I loved her. All during this wonderful May that we have been having, I used to run down and see her two or three times a week. Yesterday she met me in a little orchard. The apple-blossoms kept tumbling down on her hair, and she was laughing. We were to have gone away together this morning at dawn. Suddenly I determined to leave her as flower-like as I had found her."

"I should think the novelty of the emotion must have given you a thrill of real pleasure, Dorian," interrupted Lord Henry. "But I can finish your idyll for you. You gave her good advice, and broke her heart. That was the beginning of your reformation."

"Harry, you are horrible! You mustn't say these dreadful things. Hetty's heart is not broken. Of course she cried, and all that. But there is no disgrace upon her. She can live, like Perdita, in her garden of mint and marigold."

"And weep over a faithless Florizel," said Lord Henry, laughing, as he leant back in his chair. "My dear Dorian, you have the most curiously boyish moods. Do you think this girl will ever be really contented now with anyone of her own rank? I suppose she will be married some day to a rough carter or a grinning ploughman. Well, the fact of having met you, and loved you, will teach her to despise her husband, and she will be wretched. From a moral point of view, I cannot say that I think much of your great renunciation. Even as a beginning, it is poor. Besides, how do you know that Hetty isn't floating at the present moment in some starlit mill-pond, with lovely water-lilies round her, like Ophelia?"

"I can't bear this, Harry! You mock at everything, and then suggest the most serious tragedies. I am sorry I told you now. I don't care what you say to me. I know I was right in acting as I did. Poor Hetty! As I rode past the farm this morning, I saw her white face at the window, like a spray of jasmine. Don't let us talk about it any more, and don't try to persuade me that the first good action I have done for years, the first little bit of self-sacrifice I have ever known, is really a sort of sin. I want to be better. I am going to be better. Tell me something about yourself. What is going on in town? I have not been to the club for days."

"The people are still discussing poor Basil's disappearance."

"I should have thought they had got tired of that by this time," said Dorian, pouring himself out some wine, and frowning slightly.

"My dear boy, they have only been talking about it for six weeks, and the British public are really not equal to the mental strain of having more than one topic every three months. They have been very fortunate lately, however. They have had my own divorce-case, and Alan Campbell's suicide. Now they have got the mysterious disappearance of an artist. Scotland Yard still insists that the man in the grey ulster who left for Paris by the midnight train on the ninth of November was poor Basil, and the French police declare that Basil never arrived in Paris at all. I suppose in about a fortnight we shall be told that he has been seen in San Francisco. It is an odd thing, but everyone who disappears is said to be seen at San Francisco. It must be a delightful city, and possess all the attractions of the next world."

"What do you think has happened to Basil?" asked Dorian,

holding up his Burgundy against the light, and wondering how it was that he could discuss the matter so calmly.

"I have not the slightest idea. If Basil chooses to hide himself, it is no business of mine. If he is dead, I don't want to think about him. Death is the only thing that ever terrifies me. I hate it."

"Why?" said the younger man, wearily.

"Because," said Lord Henry, passing beneath his nostrils the gilt trellis of an open vinaigrette box, "one can survive everything nowadays except that. Death and vulgarity are the only two facts in the nineteenth century that one cannot explain away. Let us have our coffee in the music-room, Dorian. You must play Chopin to me. The man with whom my wife ran away played Chopin exquisitely. Poor Victoria! I was very fond of her. The house is rather lonely without her. Of course married life is merely a habit, a bad habit. But then one regrets the loss even of one's worst habits. Perhaps one regrets them the most. They are such an essential part of one's personality."

Dorian said nothing, but rose from the table and, passing into the next room, sat down to the piano and let his fingers stray across the white and black ivory of the keys. After the coffee had been brought in, he stopped, and, looking over at Lord Henry, said· "Harry, did it ever occur to you that Basil was murdered?"

Lord Henry yawned. "Basil was very popular, and always wore a Waterbury watch. Why should he have been murdered? He was not clever enough to have enemies. Of course he had a wonderful genius for painting. But a man can paint like Velasquez and yet be as dull as possible. Basil was really rather dull. He only interested me once, and that was when he told me, years ago, that he had a wild adoration for you, and that you were the dominant motive of his art."

"I was very fond of Basil," said Dorian, with a note of

sadness in his voice. "But don't people say that he was **mur-dered**?"

"Oh, some of the papers do. It does not seem to me to be at all probable. I know there are dreadful places in Paris, but Basil was not the sort of man to have gone to them. He had no curiosity. It was his chief defect."

"What would you say, Harry, if I told you that I had murdered Basil?" said the younger man. He watched him intently after he had spoken.

"I would say, my dear fellow, that you were posing for a character that doesn't suit you. All crime is vulgar, just as all vulgarity is crime. It is not in you, Dorian, to commit a murder. I am sorry if I hurt your vanity by saying so, but I assure you it is true. Crime belongs exclusively to the lower orders. I don't blame them in the smallest degree. I should fancy that crime was to them what art is to us, simply a method of procuring extraordinary sensations."

"A method of procuring sensations? Do you think, then, that a man who has once committed murder could possibly do the same crime again? Don't tell me that."

"Oh! anything becomes a pleasure if one does it too often," cried Lord Henry, laughing. "That is one of the most important secrets of life. I should fancy, however, that murder is always a mistake. One should never do anything that one cannot talk about after dinner. But let us pass from poor Basil. I wish I could believe that he had come to such a really romantic end as you suggest; but I can't. I dare say he fell into the Seine off an omnibus, and that the conductor hushed up the scandal. Yes: I should fancy that was his end. I see him lying now on his back under those dull-green waters with the heavy barges floating over him, and long weeds catching in his hair. Do you know, I don't think he would have done much more good work. During the last ten years his painting has gone off very much."

Dorian heaved a sigh, and Lord Henry strolled across the room and began to stroke the head of a curious Java parrot, a large grey-plumaged bird, with pink crest and tail, that was balancing itself upon a bamboo perch. As his pointed fingers touched it, it dropped the white scurf of crinkled lids over black glass-like eyes, and began to sway backwards and forwards.

"Yes," he continued, turning round, and taking his hand-kerchief out of his pocket; "his painting had quite gone off. It seemed to me to have lost something. It had lost an ideal. When you and he ceased to be great freinds, he ceased to be a great artist. What was it separated you? I suppose he bored you. If so, he never forgave you. It's a habit bores have. By the way, what has become of that wonderful portrait he did of you? I don't think I have ever seen it since he finished it. Oh! I remember your telling me years ago that you had sent it down to Selby, and that it had got mislaid or stolen on the way. You never got it back? What a pity! It was really a masterpiece. I remember I wanted to buy it. I wish I had now. It belonged to Basil's best period. Since then, his work was that curious mixture of bad painting and good intentions that always entitles a man to be called a repre-sentative British artist. Did you advertise for it? You should."

"I forget," said Dorian. "I suppose I did. But I never really liked it. I am sorry I sat for it. The memory of the thing is hateful to me. Why do you talk of it? It used to remind me of those curious lines in some play—'Hamlet,' I think—how do they run?—

> " 'Like the painting of a sorrow,
> A face without a heart.'

Yes: that is what it was like."

Lord Henry laughed. "If a man treats life artistically, his

brain is his heart," he answered, sinking into an arm-chair.

Dorian Gray shook his head, and struck some soft chords on the piano. " 'Like the painting of a sorrow,' " he repeated, " 'a face without a heart.' "

The elder man lay back and looked at him with half-closed eyes. "By the way, Dorian," he said, after a pause, " 'what does it profit a man if he gain the whole world and lose'—how does the quotation run?—'his own soul'?"

The music jarred and Dorian Gray started, and stared at his friend. "Why do you ask me that, Harry?"

"My dear fellow," said Lord Henry, elevating his eyebrows in surprise, "I asked you because I thought you might be able to give me an answer. That is all. I was going through the Park last Sunday, and close by the Marble Arch there stood a little crowd of shabby-looking people listening to some vulgar street-preacher. As I passed by, I heard the man yelling out that question to his audience. It struck me as being rather dramatic. London is very rich in curious effects of that kind. A wet Sunday, an uncouth Christian in a mackintosh, a ring of sickly white faces under a broken roof of dripping umbrellas, and a wonderful phrase flung into the air by shrill, hysterical lips—it was really very good in its way, quite a suggestion. I thought of telling the prophet that Art had a soul, but that man had not. I am afraid, however, he would not have understood me."

"Don't, Harry. The soul is a terrible reality. It can be bought, and sold, and bartered away. It can be poisoned, or made perfect. There is a soul in each one of us. I know it."

"Do you feel quite sure of that, Dorian?"

"Quite sure."

"Ah! then it must be an illusion. The things one feels absolutely certain about are never true. That is the fatality of Faith, and the lesson of Romance. How grave you are! Don't be so serious. What have you or I to do with the superstitions

of our age? No: we have given up our belief in the soul.
Play me something. Play me a nocturne, Dorian, and, as
you play, tell me, in a low voice, how you have kept your
youth. You must have some secret. I am only ten years older
than you are, and I am wrinkled, and worn, and yellow.
You are really wonderful, Dorian. You have never looked
more charming than you do to-night. You remind me of
the day I saw you first. You were rather cheeky, very shy,
and absolutely extraordinary. You have changed, of course,
but not in appearance. I wish you would tell me your secret.
To get back my youth I would do anything in the world,
except take exercise, get up early, or be respectable. Youth!
There is nothing like it. It's absurd to talk of the ignorance
of youth. The only people to whose opinions I listen now
with any respect are people much younger than myself.
They seem in front of me. Life has revealed to them her
latest wonder. As for the aged, I always contradict the aged.
I do it on principle. If you ask them their opinion on something that happened yesterday, they solemnly give you the
opinions current in 1820, when people wore high stocks, believed in everything, and knew absolutely nothing. How
lovely that thing you are playing is! I wonder did Chopin
write it at Majorca, with the sea weeping round the villa,
and the salt spray dashing against the panes? It is marvel-
lously romantic. What a blessing it is that there is one art
left to us that is not imitative! Don't stop. I want music
to-night. It seems to me that you are the young Apollo, and
that I am Marsyas listening to you. I have sorrows, Dorian,
of my own, that even you know nothing of. The tragedy of
old age is not that one is old, but that one is young. I am
amazed sometimes at my own sincerity. Ah, Dorian, how
happy you are! What an exquisite life you have had! You
have drunk deeply of everything. You have crushed the
grapes against your palate. Nothing has been hidden from

you. And it has all been to you no more than the sound of music. It has not marred you. You are still the same."

"I am not the same, Harry."

"Yes: you are the same. I wonder what the rest of your life will be. Don't spoil it by renunciations. At present you are a perfect type. Don't make yourself incomplete. You are quite flawless now. You need not shake your head: you know you are. Besides, Dorian, don't deceive yourself. Life is not governed by will or intention. Life is a question of nerves, and fibres, and slowly built-up cells in which thought hides itself and passion has its dreams. You may fancy yourself safe, and think yourself strong. But a chance tone of colour in a room or a morning sky, a particular perfume that you had once loved and that brings subtle memories with it, a line from a forgotten poem that you had come across again, a cadence from a piece of music that you had ceased to play—I tell you, Dorian, that it is on things like these that our lives depend. Browning writes about that somewhere; but our own senses will imagine them for us. There are moments when the odour of *lilas blanc* passes suddenly across me, and I have to live the strangest month of my life over again. I wish I could change places with you, Dorian. The world has cried out against us both, but it has always worshipped you. It always will worship you. You are the type of what the age is searching for, and what it is afraid it has found. I am so glad that you have never done anything, never carved a statue, or painted a picture, or produced anything outside of yourself! Life has been your art. You have set yourself to music. Your days are your sonnets."

Dorian rose up from the piano, and passed his hand through his hair. "Yes, life has been exquisite," he murmured, "but I am not going to have the same life, Harry. And you must not say these extravagant things to me. You don't know everything about me. I think that if you did, even you would turn from me. You laugh. Don't laugh."

"Why have you stopped playing, Dorian? Go back and give me the nocturne over again. Look at that great honey-coloured moon that hangs in the dusky air. She is waiting for you to charm her, and if you play she will come closer to the earth. You won't? Let us go to the club, then. It has been a charming evening, and we must end it charmingly. There is some one at White's who wants immensely to know you—young Lord Poole, Bournemouth's eldest son. He has already copied your neckties, and has begged me to introduce him to you. He is quite delightful, and rather reminds me of you."

"I hope not," said Dorian, with a sad look in his eyes. "But I am tired to-night, Harry. I shan't go to the club. It is nearly eleven, and I want to go to bed early."

"Do stay. You have never played so well as to-night. There was something in your touch that was wonderful. It had more expression than I had ever heard from it before."

"It is because I am going to be good," he answered, smiling. "I am a little changed already."

"You cannot change to me, Dorian," said Lord Henry. "You and I will always be friends."

"Yet you poisoned me with a book once. I should not forgive that. Harry, promise me that you will never lend that book to any one. It does harm."

"My dear boy, you are really beginning to moralise. You will soon be going about like the converted, the revivalist, warning people against all the sins of which you have grown tired. You are much too delightful to do that. Besides, it is no use. You and I are what we are, and will be what we will be. As for being poisoned by a book, there is no such thing as that. Art has no influence upon action. It annihilates the desire to act. It is superbly sterile. The books that the world calls immoral are books that show the world its own shame.

That is all. But we won't discuss literature. Come round to-morrow. I am going to ride at eleven. We might go together, and I will take you to lunch afterwards with Lady Brank-some. She is a charming woman, and wants to consult you about some tapestries she is thinking of buying. Mind you come. Or shall we lunch with our little Duchess? She says she never sees you now. Perhaps you are tired of Gladys? I thought you would be. Her clever tongue gets on one's nerves. Well, in any case, be here at eleven."

"Must I really come, Harry?"

"Certainly. The Park is quite lovely now. I don't think there have been such lilacs since the year I met you."

"Very well. I shall be here at eleven," said Dorian. "Good-night, Harry." As he reached the door he hesitated for a moment, as if he had something more to say. Then he sighed and went out.

CHAPTER XX

IT was a lovely night, so warm that he threw his coat over his arm, and did not even put his silk scarf round his throat. As he strolled home, smoking his cigarette, two young men in evening dress passed him. He heard one of them whisper to the other: "That is Dorian Gray." He remembered how pleased he used to be when he was pointed out, or stared at, or talked about. He was tired of hearing his own name now. Half the charm of the little village where he had been so often lately was that no one knew who he was. He had often told the girl whom he had lured to love him that he was poor, and she had believed him. He had told her once that he was wicked, and she had laughed at him, and answered that wicked people were always very old and very ugly. What a laugh she had!—just like a thrush singing. And how pretty she had been in her cotton dresses and her large hats! She knew nothing, but she had everything that he had lost.

When he reached home, he found his servant waiting up for him. He sent him to bed, and threw himself down on the sofa in the library, and began to think over some of the things that Lord Henry had said to him.

Was it really true that one could never change? He felt a wild longing for the unstained purity of his boyhood—his rose-white boyhood, as Lord Henry had once called it. He knew that he had tarnished himself, filled his mind with corruption, and given horror to his fancy; that he had been an evil influence to others, and had experienced a terrible joy in being so; and that, of the lives that had crossed his own, it had been the fairest and the most full of promise that he had brought to shame. But was it all irretrievable? Was there no hope for him?

Ah! in what a monstrous moment of pride and passion he had prayed that the portrait should bear the burden of his days, and he keep the unsullied splendour of eternal youth! All his failure had been due to that. Better for him that each sin of his life had brought its sure, swift penalty along with it. There was purification in punishment. Not "Forgive us our sins," but "Smite us for our iniquities" should be the prayer of a man to a most just God.

The curiously carved mirror that Lord Henry had given to him, so many years ago now, was standing on the table, and the white-limbed Cupids laughed round it as of old. He took it up, as he had done on that night of horror, when he had first noted the change in the fatal picture, and with wild, tear-dimmed eyes looked into its polished shield. Once, some one who had terribly loved him had written to him a mad letter, ending with these idolatrous words: "The world is changed because you are made of ivory and gold. The curves of your lips rewrite history." The phrases came back to his memory, and he repeated them over and over to himself. Then he loathed his own beauty, and, flinging the mirror on the floor, crushed it into silver splinters beneath his heel. It was his beauty that had ruined him, his beauty and the youth that he had prayed for. But for those two things, his life might have been free from stain. His beauty had been to him but a mask, his youth but a mockery. What was youth at best? A green, unripe time, a time of shallow moods and sickly thoughts. Why had he worn its livery? Youth had spoiled him.

It was better not to think of the past. Nothing could alter that. It was of himself, and of his own future, that he had to think. James Vane was hidden in a nameless grave in Selby churchyard. Alan Campbell had shot himself one night in his laboratory, but had not revealed the secret that he had been forced to know. The excitement, such as it was, over Basil Hallward's disappearance would soon pass away. It was already waning. He was perfectly safe there. Nor, indeed, was it the death of Basil Hallward that weighed most upon his mind. It was the living death of his own soul that troubled him. Basil had painted the portrait that had marred his life. He could not forgive him that. It was the portrait that had done everything. Basil had said things to him that were unbearable, and that he had yet borne with patience. The murder had been simply the madness of a moment. As for Alan Campbell, his suicide had been his own act. He had chosen to do it. It was nothing to him.

A new life! That was what he wanted. That was what he was waiting for. Surely he had begun it already. He had spared one innocent thing, at any rate. He would never again tempt innocence. He would be good.

As he thought of Hetty Merton, he began to wonder if the portrait in the locked room had changed. Surely it was not still so horrible as it had been? Perhaps if his life became pure, he would be able to expel every sign of evil passion from the face. Perhaps the signs of evil had already gone away. He would go and look.

He took the lamp from the table and crept upstairs. As he unbarred the door a smile of joy flitted across his strangely young-looking face and lingered for a moment about his lips. Yes, he would be good, and the hideous thing that he had hidden away would no longer be a terror to him. He felt as if the load had been lifted from him already.

He went in quietly, locking the door behind him, as was his custom, and dragged the purple hanging from the portrait. A cry of pain and indignation broke from him. He could see no change, save that in the eyes there was a look of cunning, and in the mouth the curved wrinkle of the hypocrite. The thing was still loathsome—more loathsome, if possible, than before—and the scarlet dew that spotted the hand seemed brighter, and more like blood newly spilt. Then he trembled. Had it been merely vanity that had made him do his one good deed? Or the desire for a new sensation, as Lord Henry had hinted, with his mocking laugh? Or that passion to act a part that sometimes makes us do things finer than we are ourselves? Or, perhaps, all these? And why was the red stain larger than it had been? It seemed to have crept like a horrible disease over the wrinkled fingers. There was blood on the painted feet, as though the thing had dripped—blood even on the hand that had not held the knife. Confess? Did it mean that he was to confess? To give himself up, and be put to death? He laughed. He felt that the idea was monstrous. Besides, even if he did confess, who would believe him? There was no trace of the murdered man anywhere. Everything belonging to him had been destroyed. He himself had burned what had been below-stairs. The world would simply say that he was mad. They would shut him up if he persisted in his story. . . . Yet it was his duty to confess, to suffer public shame, and to make public atonement. There was a God who called upon men to tell their sins to earth as well as to heaven. Nothing that he could do would cleanse him till he had told his own sin. His sin? He shrugged his shoulders. The death of Basil Hall-ward seemed very little to him. He was thinking of Hetty Merton. For it was an unjust mirror, this mirror of his soul that he was looking at. Vanity? Curiosity? Hypocrisy? Had there been nothing more in his renunciation than that? There had been something more. At least he thought so. But who could tell? . . . No. There had been nothing more. Through vanity he had spared her. In hypocrisy he had worn the mask of goodness. For curiosity's sake he had tried the denial of self. He recognised that now.

But this murder—was it to dog him all his life? Was he always to be burdened by his past? Was he really to confess? Never. There was only one bit of evidence left against him. The picture itself—that was evidence. He would destroy it. Why had he kept it so long? Once it had given him pleasure to watch it changing and growing old. Of late he had felt no such pleasure. It had kept him awake at night. When he had been away, he had been filled with terror lest other eyes should look upon it. It had brought melancholy across his passions. Its mere memory had marred many moments of joy. It had been like conscience to him. Yes, it had been conscience. He would destroy it.

He looked round, and saw the knife that had stabbed Basil Hallward. He had cleaned it many times, till there was no stain left upon it. It was bright, and glistened. As it had killed the painter, so it would kill the painter's work, and all that that meant. It would kill the past, and when that was dead he would be free. It would kill this monstrous soul-life, and, without its hideous warnings, he would be at peace. He seized the thing, and stabbed the picture with it.

There was a cry heard, and a crash. The cry was so horrible in its agony that the frightened servants woke, and crept out of their rooms. Two gentlemen, who were passing in the Square below, stopped, and looked up at the great house. They walked on till they met a policeman, and brought him back. The man rang the bell several times, but there was no answer. Except for a light in one of the top windows, the house was all dark. After a time, he went away and stood in an adjoining portico and watched.

"Whose house is that, constable?" asked the elder of the two gentlemen.

"Mr. Dorian Gray's, sir," answered the policeman.

They looked at each other, as they walked away and sneered. One of them was Sir Henry Ashton's uncle.

Inside, in the servants' part of the house, the half-clad domestics were talking in low whispers to each other. Old Mrs. Leaf was crying and wringing her hands. Francis was as pale as death.

After about a quarter of an hour, he got the coachman and one of the footmen and crept upstairs. They knocked, but there was no reply. They called out. Everything was still. Finally, after vainly trying to force the door, they got on the roof, and dropped down on to the balcony. The windows yielded easily: their bolts were old.

When they entered they found, hanging upon the wall, a splendid portrait of their master as they had last seen him, in all the wonder of his exquisite youth and beauty. Lying on the floor was a dead man, in evening dress, with a knife in his heart. He was withered, wrinkled, and loathsome of visage. It was not till they had examined the rings that they recognised who it was.

DE PROFUNDIS

INTRODUCTION

FIVE and twenty years ago Oscar Wilde died in Paris, with his friends, Bobbie Ross and Reggio Turner, by his bed-side. In the last four or six months in Reading prison he had written "De Profundis, an Epistola," as he called it, *in carcera et vincula*: "a letter written in prison and in fetters."

When Robert Ross first published part of it, only two or three privileged people knew that it was a letter addressed to Lord Alfred Douglas, who had spurred him on to attack the Marquis of Queensberry, and so brought him to disaster and a prison cell.

We know that Lord Alfred Douglas did this, hoping all the while to revenge himself thereby on his father, the prize-fighting Marquis whom he hated, and with little or no sympathy for the man whom he called his friend, and whom he thus drove to ruin.

Lord Alfred Douglas still thinks he was perfectly justified in using his friend to beat his father, even though the operation brought the man he pretended to love, to shame and misery and an untimely death.

The book falls naturally into two parts: the reflections of Oscar Wilde in prison, his reactions to punishment and suffering, humiliation and disgrace, and his opinion of the man whom he holds mainly responsible for his stupendous fall.

Knowing something of the weak and cunning vanity of human nature, we shall not look in "De Profundis" for a fair and sympathetic portrait of Lord Alfred Douglas; before we read a word we expect that the portrait will be blocked in with deep shadows, and the lights used sparingly, if at all.

But no one can doubt that the portrait is the work of a real artist, and Wilde's insistence on the singular selfishness and rank malignance of his friend is curiously justified by Douglas' subsequent writings.

In my book "The Life and Confessions of Oscar Wilde", I have given in the appendix, that part of "De Profundis" which concerns Lord Alfred Douglas most intimately: it is a passionate and terrible indictment. I have indicated the passages, in which, in my opinion, Oscar Wilde has allowed his personal animosity and disappointment to deform the facts: he poses as a sort of lord of life brought to ruin through the imperious will and almost insane temper of a youth half his age. Wilde says:

"I blame myself for the entire ethical degradation I allowed you to bring on me. The basis of character is will power and my will power became absolutely subject to yours. It sounds a grotesque thing to say, but it is none the less true. Those incessant scenes that seemed to be almost physically necessary to you, and in which your mind and body grew distorted, and you became a thing as terrible to look at as to listen to: that dreadful mania you inherit from your father, the mania for writing revolting and loathsome letters; your entire lack of any control over your emotions as displayed in your long resentful moods of sullen silence, no less than in the sudden fits of almost epileptic rage; all these things, in reference to which one of my letters to you, left by you about in the Savoy or some other hotel, and so produced in court by your father's counsel, contained an entreaty not devoid of pathos, had you at that time been able to recognize pathos either in the elements or in its expression—these, I say, were the origin and causes of my fatal yielding to you in your daily increasing demands. You wore me out. It was the triumph of the smaller over the bigger nature. . . ."

He continues:

"At a time when I should have been in London taking wise counsel and calmly considering the hideous trap in which I had allowed myself to be caught—the booby trap, as your father calls it to the present day—you insisted on my taking you to Monte Carlo, of all revolting places on God's earth, that all day and all night as well, you might gamble as long as the Casino remained open. As for me, baccarat having no charms for me—I was left alone outside by myself. You refused to discuss even for five minutes the position to which you and your father had brought me. My business was merely to pay your hotel expenses and your losses.

" . . . The slightest allusion to the ordeal awaiting me was regarded as a bore. A new brand of champagne that was recommended to us had more interest for you. On my return to London those of my friends who really desired my welfare implored me to retire abroad, and not to face an impossible trial. You imputed mean motives to them for giving such advice and cowardice to me for listening to them.

"You forced me to brazen it out, if possible, in the box by absurd and silly perjuries. At the end, of course, I was arrested, and your father became the hero of the hour. . . .

"As far as I can make out, I ended my friendship with you every three months regularly. And each time that I did so, you managed by means of entreaties, telegrams, letters, the interposition of your friends, the interposition of mine, and the like to induce me to allow you back.

"But the froth and folly of our new life grew often very wearisome to me; it was only in the mire that we met: and though fascinating, terribly fascinating, the one topic round which your talk invariably centered, was, still at the end it became quite monotonous. I was often bored to death by it, and accepted it as I accepted your passion for music halls, and your mania for absurd extravagance in eating and drinking, or any other of your to me less attractive characteristics, as a thing, that is to say, that one simply had to put up with, a part of the high price one had to pay for knowing you. . . ."

Here follows the cost of this strange friendship:

"When I tell you that between the autumn of 1892 and the date of my imprisonment, I spent with you and on you, more than £5000 in actual money, irrespective of the bills I incurred, you will have some idea of the sort of life on which you insisted.

"Do you think I exaggerate? My ordinary expenses with you for an ordinary day in London—for luncheon, dinner, supper, amusements, hansoms and the rest of it—ranged from £12 to £20 and the week's expenses were naturally in proportion and ranged from £80 to £130. For our three months at Goring my expenses (rent, of course, included) were £1,340. Step by step, with the Bankruptcy Receiver I had to go over every item of my life. It was horrible. 'Plain living and high thinking,' was, of course, an ideal you could not at that time have appreciated, but such extravagance was a disgrace to both of us."

Then the summing up:

"The gods are strange. It is not of our vices only they make instruments to scourge us. They bring us to ruin through what in us is good, gentle, humane, loving. But for my pity and affection for you and yours, I would not now be weeping in this terrible place."

And finally the explanation:

"You, like myself, had a terrible tragedy in your life, though one of an entirely opposite character to mine. Do you want to learn what it was? It was this; in you hate was always stronger than love. Your hatred of your father was of such stature that it entirely outstripped, overgrew and overshadowed your love for me. There was no struggle between them at all, or but little; of such dimensions was your hatred and of such monstrous growth. . . .

"You did not realize there was no room for both passions

in the same soul; they cannot live together in that fair carven house. Love is fed by the imagination, by which we become wiser than we know, better than we feel, nobler than we are; by which we can see life as a whole, by which, and by which alone, we can understand others in their real as in their ideal relations. Only what is fine and finely conceived can feed love. But anything will feed hate. There was not a glass of champagne that you drank, not a rich dish that you ate of in all those years, that did not feed your hate and make it fat. So, to gratify it, you gambled with my life, as you gambled with my money, carelessly, recklessly indifferent to consequences. If you lost, the loss would not, you fancied, be yours. If you won, yours you knew would be the exultation and the advantage of victory. Hate blinds people."

The portrait here and there is deformed almost out of human likeness: Wilde talks of Douglas' "low stature" though he is about five feet nine in height, and of a "very nice poem of the Undergraduate school of verse" which Douglas sent him. He insists that "his brain was undeveloped; his imagination—dead; his heart—not yet born."

And he signs himself: "Your affectionate friend, Oscar Wilde."

But with all his affection and critical acumen, he never realised or would never admit that Lord Alfred Douglas was a greater poet than himself. Douglas has written, as I stated at the time, two or three sonnets as fine as anything in English. Strange to say, only two or three, and all produced in this period when Wilde's intellectuality lifted him to enthusiasm: but still there they are.

After the publication of this personal part of "De Profundis" Lord Alfred Douglas replied in a book entitled: "Oscar Wilde and Myself," which almost demonstrates the truth of Wilde's most bitter criticism. It is an appalling production, livid with hate, from start to finish, and even falser to fact, than Oscar's extravagant disdain.

The main point in this sordid dispute is that Lord Alfred Douglas admits that he was directed all through by hatred of his father, and not by affection for Wilde. And worse than this admission is the fact that he knew that the charges which his father brought against Wilde were true, and were, therefore, considering his father's position and influence, almost certain to be established in court.

He was, therefore, mainly responsible for Oscar Wilde's ruin.

Now what is the impartial judgment on this bitter drama of love turned to hate? Vinegar, they tell us, is strong in proportion to the strength of the wine from which it is made. It must be admitted that all through Oscar has the better part: he knows that in spite of his ruin and shame and most bitter disappointment, he must blame himself as well as his friend and keep affection in his heart at all costs and the soul-vivifying tenderness of love. Even when dying in the pillory he will try to help his friend to this deeper understanding that sanctifies life.

Douglas on the other hand sees himself as perfection perfected: never was there more complete self-deception: he hates and sulks and rages, says Oscar; why not? He had cause, good cause; his self-love is invincible: he lives at his lover's expense for years, wastes his friend's hard-earned thousands and when he comes into his fortune doles him out a few hundreds ("four hundred", he says) with insults and jibes: Wilde, he declares, is like "an old prostitute" in his constant begging for help. In Lord Alfred Douglas' book there is not one sweet page; no thrill of affectionate admiration; he never even tries to describe Wilde's incomparable gift as a talker; he has no gratitude for intellectual stimulus; no realisation even of the fact that the friendship of Oscar Wilde was the ladder which lifted him to fame.

Let no one think that I am misled by Wilde's misery and

disappointment though at the time it brought tears to my eyes. But the self-righteous defence of Douglas, written ten years later, is infinitely baser than anything in "De Profundis." At the end of the second chapter, Douglas tells us that it has always been his "fatal habit to idealise my friends", and he puts it on record that he has suffered for this, adding in choice phrase: "This is got by casting pearls to hogs." Douglas calls his friendship with Wilde "a harmless and proper friendship . . . if, perhaps, somewhat extravagantly lived", and does not scruple to write of "the loathsome depths in which Wilde was taken redhanded . . ." and in which "no sane person could flounder."

What English for a master-poet to write: "redhanded" indeed. How appropriate! and "flounder"; what an image!

When Alfred Douglas writes of the technique of English poetry, he is worth reading: but otherwise there is nothing of the slightest value in what he has written and the spirit of his book is simply poisonous: Douglas seems to hate everyone he meets. He sneers at everyone, even those like Shaw who stand on the forehead of the time to come. He is consumed with the envy of gifted mediocrity.

Shakespeare speaks of this "all-hating world": I had never realised the dreadful significance of the phrase except in my acquaintance with Lord Alfred Douglas.

He professes now loudly that he is a devout Christian, but he knows nothing of repentance and believes firmly that lies will carry him through even the final judgment of posterity, triumphantly.

I have written "The Life and Confessions of Oscar Wilde"; now it appears almost a duty to write "The Life and Confessions of Lord Alfred Douglas", and so complete the greatest tragi-comedy of this age.

FRANK HARRIS.

February, 1926.

A PREFATORY DEDICATION

*M*Y *DEAR DR. MEYERFELD,—It is a great pleasure to dedicate this new edition of* De Profundis *to yourself. But for you I do not think the book would have ever been published. When first you asked me about the manuscript which you heard Wilde wrote in prison, I explained to you vaguely that some day I hoped to issue portions of it, in accordance with the writer's wishes; though I thought it would be premature to do so at that moment. You begged however that Germany (which already held Wilde's plays in the highest esteem) should have the opportunity of seeing a new work by one of her favourite authors. I rather reluctantly consented to your proposal; and promised, at a leisured opportunity, to extract such portions of the work as might be considered of general public interest. I fear that I postponed what was to me a rather painful task; it was only your visits and more importunate correspondence (of which I frankly began to hate the sight) that brought about the fulfilment of your object. There was no idea of issuing the work in England; but after despatching to you a copy for translation in* Die Neue Rundschau, *it occurred to me that a simultaneous publication of the original might gratify Wilde's English friends and admirers who had expressed curiosity on the subject. The decision was not reached without some misgiving, for reasons which need only be touched upon here. Wilde's name unfortunately did not bring very agreeable memories to English ears: his literary position, hardly recognised even in the zenith of his successful dramatic career, had come to be ignored by Mr. Ruskin's countrymen, unable to separate* *the man and the artist; how rightly or wrongly it is not for me to say. In Germany and France, where tolerance and literary enthusiasm are more widely distributed, Wilde's works were judged independently of the author's career.* Salomé, *prohibited by the English censor in the author's lifetime, had become part of the repertoire of the European stage, long before that finest of all his dramas inspired the great opera of Dr. Strauss; whilst the others, performed occasionally in the English provinces without his name, were still banned in the London theatres. His great intellectual endowments were either denied or forgotten. Wilde (who in* De Profundis, *exaggerates his lost contemporary position in England and shows no idea of his future European reputation) gauges fairly accurately the nadir he had reached when he says that his name was become a synonym for folly.*

In sending copy to Messrs. Methuen (to whom alone I submitted it) I anticipated refusal, as though the work were my own. A very distinguished man of letters who acted as their reader advised, however, its acceptance, and urged, in view of the uncertainty of its reception, the excision of certain passages, to which I readily assented. Since there has been a demand to see these passages, already issued in German, they are here replaced along with others of minor importance. I have added besides some of those letters written to me from Reading, which though they were brought out by you in Germany I did not, at first, contemplate publishing in this country. They illustrate Wilde's varying moods in prison. Owing to a foolish error in transcription, I sent you these letters with wrong dates—dates of other unpublished letters. The error is here rectified. By the courtesy of the editor and the proprietors of the Daily Chronicle *I have included the two remarkable contributions to their paper on the subject of prison life: these and* The Ballad of Reading Gaol *being all*

that Wilde wrote after his release other than private cor-
respondence. The generous reception accorded to De Profundis *has justified the preparation of a new and fuller edi-*
tion. The most sanguine hopes have been realised; English
critics have shown themselves ready to estimate the writer,
whether favourably or unfavourably, without emphasising
their natural prejudice against his later career, even in refer-
ence to this book where the two things occasion synchronous
comment. The work has met of course with some severe criti-
cisms, chiefly from "narrow natures and hectic-brains."

But in justice to the author and myself there are two points
which I ought to make clear: the title De Profundis, *against*
which some have cavilled, is, as you will remember from our
correspondence, my own; for this I do not make any apology.
Then, certain people (among others a well-known French
writer) have paid me the compliment of suggesting that the
text was an entire forgery by myself or a cento *of Wilde's*
letters to myself. Were I capable either of the requisite art,
or the requisite fraud, I should have made a name in literature
ere now. I need only say here that De Profundis *is a manu-*
script of eighty close-written pages on twenty folio sheets;
that it is cast in the form of a letter to a friend not *myself; that*
it was written at intervals during the last six months of the
author's imprisonment on blue stamped prison foolscap
paper. Reference to it and directions in regard to it occur in
the letters addressed to myself and printed in this volume.
Wilde handed me the document on the day of his release; he
was not allowed to send it to me from prison. With the excep-
tion of Major Nelson then Governor of Reading Gaol, my-
self, and a confidential typewriter no one has read the whole
of it. Contrary to a general impression it contains nothing
scandalous. There is no definite scheme or plan in the work;
as he proceeded the writer's intention obviously and con-
stantly changed; it is desultory; a large portion of it is taken

up with business and private matters of no interest whatever. The manuscript has, however, been seen and authenticated by yourself, by Mr. Methuen, and Mr. Hamilton Fyfe, when editor of The Daily Mirror, where a leaf of it was facsimiled.

Editorial egoism has led me to make this introduction longer than was intended, but I must answer one question: both you and other friends have asked why I do not write any life of Wilde. I can give you two reasons: I am not capable of doing so; and Mr. Robert Sherard has ably supplied the deficiency. Mr. Sherard's book contains all the important facts of his career; the errors are of minor importance, except in regard to certain gallant exaggerations about myself. His view of Wilde, however, is not MY view, especially in reference to the author's unhappiness after his release. That Wilde suffered at times from extreme poverty and intensely from social ostracism I know very well; but his temperament was essentially a happy one, and I think his good spirits and enjoyment of life far outweighed any bitter recollections or realisation of an equivocal and tragic position. No doubt he felt the latter keenly, but he concealed his feeling as a general rule, and his manifestations of it only lasted a very few days. He was, however, a man with many facets to his character; and he left in regard to that character, and to his attainments, both before and after his downfall, curiously different impressions on professing judges of their fellowmen. To give the whole man would require the art of Boswell, Purcell, or Robert Browning. My friend Mr. Sherard will only, I think, claim the biographical genius of Dr. Johnson; and I, scarcely the talent of Theophrastus.—Believe me, dear Dr. Meyerfeld, yours very truly,

                                        ROBERT ROSS

CONTENTS

	PAGE
INTRODUCTION—BY FRANK HARRIS	251
A PREFATORY DEDICATION TO DR. MAX MEYERFELD, BY THE EDITOR	259
FOUR LETTERS WRITTEN FROM READING PRISON	265
De Profundis, WITH ADDITIONAL MATTER	281
TWO LETTERS TO THE *Daily Chronicle* ON PRISON LIFE	339

LETTERS FROM READING PRISON

LETTER I

10th March 1896.

MY DEAR ROBBIE,—I want you to have a letter written at once to Mr. —— the solicitor, stating that as my wife has promised to settle a third on me, in the case of her predeceasing me, I do not wish any opposition to be made to her purchasing my life interest. I feel that I have brought such unhappiness on her, and such ruin on my children, that I have no right to go against her wishes in anything. She was gentle and good to me here, when she came to see me. I have full trust in her. Please have this done at once, and thank my friends for their kindness. I feel I am acting rightly leaving this to my wife.

Please write to Stuart Merrill in Paris, or Robert Sherard, to say how gratified I was at the performance of my play, and have my thanks conveyed to Lugne-Poë,[1] it is something that at a time of disgrace and shame I should be still regarded as an artist: I wish I could feel more pleasure, but I seem dead to all emotions except those of anguish and despair. However, please let Lugne-Poë know that I am sensible of the honour he has done me. He is a poet himself. I fear you will find it difficult to read this, but as I am not allowed writing materials I seem to have forgotten how to write—you must excuse me. Thank More for exerting himself for books; unluckily I suffer from headaches when I read my Greek and

[1] The first impersonator of Herod and first producer of *Salomé* in Paris, 1896.

Roman poets—so they have not been of much use—but his kindness was great in getting the set. Ask him to express my gratitude to the lady who lives at Wimbledon. Write to me please in answer to this, and tell me about literature, what new books, etc.—also Jones's play and Forbes-Robertson's management:—about any new tendency in the stage of Paris or London. Also try and see what Lemaître, Bauër, and Sarcey said of *Salomé,* and give me a little *résumé;* please write to Henri Bauër, and say I am touched at his writing nicely; Robert Sherard knows him. It was sweet of you to come and see me. You must come again next time. Here I have the horror of death with the still greater horror of living, and in silence and misery. . . .

. . . . : .[1]

I always remember you with deep affection.

I wish Ernest would get from Oakley Street my portman-teau, fur coat, clothes, and the books of my own writing which I gave my dear mother—ask . . . in whose name the burial ground of my mother was taken.

Always your friend,

OSCAR WILDE.

LETTER II

H.M. PRISON, READING,
after September 1896 [N.D.].

. . . To these purely business matters. perhaps More Adey will kindly reply. His letter dealing purely with business, I shall be allowed to receive. It will not, I mean, interfere with your literary letter, with regard to which the Governor has just now read me your kind message.

For myself, my dear Robbie, I have little to say that can

---

[1] The hiatus here is due to the scissors of Major Isacson, then Governor of Reading Gaol. He was succeeded by Major Nelson.

please you. The refusal to commute my sentence has been like a blow from a leaden sword. I am dazed with a dull sense of pain. I had fed on hope, and now anguish, grown hungry, feeds her fill on me as though she had been starved of her proper appetite. There are, however, kinder elements in this evil prison air than before: sympathies have been shown to me, and I no longer feel entirely isolated from human influences, which was before a source of terror and trouble to me. And I read Dante, and make excerpts and notes for the pleasure of using a pen and ink. And it seems as if I were better in many ways, and I am going to take up the study of German. Indeed, prison seems to be the proper place for such a study. There is a thorn, however—as bitter as that of St. Paul, though different—that I must pluck out of my flesh in this letter. It is caused by a message you wrote on a piece of paper for me to see. I feel that if I kept it secret it might grow in my mind (as poisonous things grow in the dark) and take its place with other terrible thoughts that gnaw me. . . . Thought, to those that sit alone and silent and in bonds, being no "winged living thing," as Plato feigned it, but a thing dead, breeding what is horrible like a slime that shows monsters to the moon.

I mean, of course, what you said about the sympathies of others being estranged from me, or in danger of being so, by the deep bitterness of my feelings: and I believe that my letter was lent and shown to others. . . . Now, I don't like my letters shown about as curiosities: it is most distasteful to me. I write to you freely as to one of the dearest friends I have, or have ever had: and, with a few exceptions, the sympathy of others touches me, as far as its loss goes, very little. No man of my position can fall into the mire of life without getting a great deal of pity from his inferiors; and I know that when plays last too long, spectators tire. My tragedy has lasted far too long; its climax is over; its end is mean; and I am quite

conscious of the fact that when the end does come I shall return an unwelcome visitant to a world that does not want me;
a *revenant,* as the French say, and one whose face is grey with
long imprisonment and crooked with pain. Horrible as are
the dead when they rise from their tombs, the living who
come out from tombs are more horrible still. Of all this I am
only too conscious. When one has been for eighteen terrible
months in a prison cell, one sees things and people as they
really are. The sight turns one to stone. Do not think that I
would blame any one for my vices. My friends had as little
to do with them as I had with theirs. Nature was in this matter a stepmother to all of us. I blame them for not appreciat-
ing the man they ruined. As long as my table was red with
wine and roses, what did they care? My genius, my life as an
artist, my work, and the quiet I needed for it, were nothing
to them. I admit I lost my head. I was bewildered, incapable
of judgment. I made the one fatal step. And now I sit here
on a bench in a prison cell. In all tragedies there is a grotesque
element. You know the grotesque element in mine. Do not
think I do not blame myself. I curse myself night and day
for my folly in allowing something to dominate my life. If
there was an echo in these walls, it would cry "Fool" for ever.
I am utterly ashamed of my friendships. . . . For by their
friendships men can be judged. It is a test of every man. And
I feel poignant abasement of shame for my friendships . . .
of which you may read a full account in my trial.

It is to me a daily source of mental humiliation. Of some of
them I never think. They trouble me not. It is of no
importance. . . . Indeed my entire tragedy seems to be
grotesque and nothing else. For as a result of my having
suffered myself to be thrust into a trap . . . in the lowest
mire of Malebolge, I sit between Gilles de Retz and the Marquis de Sade. In certain places no one, except those actually
insane, is allowed to laugh: and indeed, even in their case, it

is against the regulations for conduct; otherwise I think I would laugh at that. . . . For the rest, do not let any one suppose that I am crediting others with unworthy motives. They really had no motives in life at all. Motives are intellectual things. They had passions merely, and such passions are false gods that will have victims at all costs and in the present case have had one wreathed with bay. Now I have plucked the thorn out—that little scrawled line of yours rankled terribly. I now think merely of your getting quite well again, and writing at last the wonderful story of . . . Pray remember me with my thanks to your dear mother, and also to Aleck. The "Gilded Sphinx" [1] is, I suppose, wonderful as ever. And send from me all that in my thoughts and feelings is good, and whatever of remembrance and reverence she will accept, to the lady of Wimbledon, whose soul is a sanctuary for those who are wounded and a house of refuge for those in pain. Do not show this letter to others—nor discuss what I have written in your answer. Tell me about that world of shadows I loved so much. And about the life and the soul tell me also. I am curious of the things that stung me; and in my pain there is pity.

Yours,

OSCAR.

LETTER III

April 1st, 1897.

MY DEAR ROBBIE,—I send you a MS. separate from this, which I hope will arrive safely. As soon as you have read it, I want you to have it carefully copied for me. There are many causes why I wish this to be done. One will suffice. I want

---

[1] The "Gilded Sphinx" is a nickname given to the clever author of *The Twelfth Hour*. She became acquainted with Wilde through her amusing parodies of his work in *Punch*. She received him hospitably at her house in 1895 when he was released on bail between his trials.

you to be my literary executor in case of my death, and to have complete control of my plays, books, and papers. As soon as I find I have a legal right to make a will, I will do so. My wife does not understand my art, nor could be expected to have any interest in it, and Cyril is only a child. So I turn naturally to you, as indeed I do for everything, and would like you to have all my works. The deficit that their sale will produce may be lodged to the credit of Cyril and Vivian. Well, if you are my literary executor, you must be in possession of the only document that gives any explanation of my extraordinary behaviour. . . . When you have read the letter, you will see the psychological explanation of a course of conduct that from the outside seems a combination of absolute idiocy with vulgar bravado. Some day the truth will have to be known—not necessarily in my lifetime . . . but I am not prepared to sit in the grotesque pillory they put me into, for all time; for the simple reason that I inherited from my father and mother a name of high distinction in literature and art, and I cannot for eternity allow that name to be degraded. I don't defend my conduct. I explain it. Also there are in my letter certain passages which deal with my mental development in prison, and the inevitable evolution of my character and intellectual attitude towards life that has taken place: and I want you and others who still stand by me and have affection for me to know exactly in what mood and manner I hope to face the world. Of course from one point of view I know that on the day of my release I shall be merely passing from one prison into another, and there are times when the whole world seems to me no larger than my cell and as full of terror for me. Still I believe that at the beginning God made a world for each separate man, and in that world which is within us we should seek to live. At any rate you will read those parts of my letter with less pain than the others. Of course I need not remind you how fluid a thing thought is with me—with us all—and of what an evanescent substance are our emotions made. Still I do see a sort of possible goal towards which, through art, I may progress. It is not unlikely that you may help me.

As regards the mode of copying: of course it is too long for any amanuensis to attempt: and your own handwriting, dear Robbie, in your last letter seems specially designed to remind me that the task is not to be yours. I think that the only thing to do is to be thoroughly modern and to have it typewritten. Of course the MS. should not pass out of your control, but could you not get Mrs. Marshall to send down one of her typewriting girls—women are the most reliable as they have no memory for the important—to Hornton Street or Phillimore Gardens, to do it under your supervision? I assure you that the typewriting machine, when played with expression, is not more annoying than the piano when played by a sister or near relation. Indeed many among those most devoted to domesticity prefer it. I wish the copy to be done not on tissue paper but on good paper such as is used for plays, and a wide rubricated margin should be left for corrections. . . . If the copy is done at Hornton Street the lady typewriter might be fed through a lattice in the door, like the Cardinals when they elect a Pope; till she comes out on the balcony and can say to the world: "Habet Mundus Epistolam"; for indeed it is an Encyclical letter, and as the Bulls of the Holy Father are named from their opening words, it may be spoken of as the *"Epistola: in Carcere et Vinculis."* . . . In point of fact, Robbie, prison life makes one see people and things as they really are. That is why it turns one to stone. It is the people outside who are deceived by the illusions of a life in constant motion. They revolve with life and contribute to its unreality. We who are immobile both see and know. Whether or not the letter does good to narrow natures and hectic brains, to me it has done good. I have "cleansed my bosom of much perilous stuff"; to borrow a phrase from the poet whom you and I once thought of rescuing from the Philistines. I need not remind you that mere expression is to an artist the supreme and only mode of life. It is by utterance that we live. Of the many, many things for which I have to thank the Governor there is none for which I am more grateful than for his permission to write fully and at as great a length as I desire. For nearly two years I had within a growing burden of bitterness, of much of which I have now got rid. On the other side of the prison wall there are some poor black soot-besmirched trees that are just breaking out into buds of an almost shrill green. I know quite well what they are going through. They are finding expression.

Ever yours,

OSCAR

LETTER IV

April 6th, 1897.

. . . Consider now, my dear Robbie, my proposal. I think my wife, who in money matters is most honourable and high-minded, will refund the £— paid for my share. I have no doubt she will. But I think it should be offered from me and that I should not accept anything in the way of income from her; I can accept what is given in love and affection to me, but I could not accept what is doled out grudgingly or with conditions. I would sooner let my wife be quite free. She may marry again. In any case I think that if free she would allow me to see my children from time to time. That is what I want. But I must set her free first, and had better do it as a gentleman by bowing my head and accepting everything. You must consider the whole question, as it is to you and your ill-advised action it is due: and let me know what you and others think. Of course you acted for the best. But you were wrong in your view. I may say candidly that I am getting gradually to a state of mind when I think that everything that happens is for the best. This may be philosophy or a broken heart, or religion, or the dull apathy of despair. But, whatever its origin, the feeling is strong with me. To tie my wife to me against her will would be wrong. She has a full right to her freedom. And not to be supported by her would be a pleasure to me. It is an ignominious position to be a pensioner on her. Talk over this with More Adey. Get him to show you the letter I have written to him. Ask your brother Aleck to give me his advice. He has excellent wisdom on things.

Now to other points.

I have never had the chance of thanking you for the books. They were most welcome. Not being allowed the magazines was a blow, but Meredith's novel charmed me. What a sane artist in temper! He is quite right in his assertion of sanity as the essential in romance. Still up to the present only the abnormal has found expression in life and literature. Rossetti's letters are dreadful; obviously forgeries by his brother. I was interested, however, to see how my grand-uncle's *Melmoth* and my mother's *Sidonia* have been two of the books that fascinated his youth. As regards the conspiracy against him in later years, I believe it really existed, and that the funds for it came out of Hake's[1] Bank. The conduct of a thrush in Cheyne Walk seems to be most suspicious, though William Rossetti says: "I could discern nothing in the thrush's song at all out of the common." Stevenson's letters are most disappointing also—I see that romantic surroundings are the worst surroundings possible for a romantic writer. In Gower Street Stevenson could have written a new *Trois Mousquetaires*. In Samoa he wrote letters to the *Times* about Germans. I see also the traces of a terrible strain to lead

---

[1] Egmont Hake, author of *Free Trade in Capital* and advocate of a new scheme of banking which amused Wilde very much.

a natural life. To chop wood with any advantage to oneself
or profit to others, one should not be able to describe the
process. In point of fact the natural life is the unconscious life.
Stevenson merely extended the sphere of the artificial by
taking to digging. The whole dreary book has given me a
lesson. If I spend my future life reading Baudelaire in a café
I shall be leading a more natural life than if I take to hedger's
work or plant cacao in mud-swamps. *En Route* is most over-
rated. It is sheer journalism. It never makes one hear a note
of the music it describes. The subject is delightful, but the
style is of course worthless, slipshod, flaccid. It is worse French
than Ohnet's. Ohnet tries to be commonplace and succeeds.
Huysmans tries not to be, and is. Hardy's novel is pleasant, and the style perfect; and Harold Frederic's very interesting in matter. Later on, there being hardly any novels
in the prison library for the poor imprisoned fellows I live
with, I think of presenting the Library with about a dozen
good novels: Stevenson's (none here but the *Black Arrow*),
some of Thackeray's (none here), Jane Austen (none here),
and some good Dumas-*père*-like books, by Stanley Weyman,
for instance, and any modern young man. You mentioned
Henley had a *protégé*? [1] Also the Anthony Hope man. After
Easter you might make out a list of about fourteen and apply
to let me have them. They would please the few who do not
care about De Goncourt's journal.[2] Don't forget I would pay
myself for them. I have a horror myself of going out into a
world without a single book of my own. I wonder would
there be any of my friends, such as C—— L——, Reggie
Turner, G—— B——, Max, and the like, who would give me
a few books? You know the sort of books I want: Flaubert,
Stevenson, Baudelaire, Maeterlinck, Dumas *père,* Keats,

[1] This is Mr. H. G. Wells.
[2] De Goncourt's journal, of which a new volume had been published, contained references to Wilde. It was one of the books sent to him in prison.

Marlowe, Chatterton, Coleridge, Anatole France, Gautier, Dante and all Dante literature: Goethe and Goethe literature, and so on. I should feel it a great compliment to have books waiting for me—and perhaps there may be some friends who would like to be kind to me. One is really very grateful, though I fear I often seem not to be. But then remember I have had incessant worries besides prison-life.

In answer to this you can send me a long letter all about plays and books. Your handwriting, in your last, was so dreadful that it looked as if you were writing a three volume novel on the terrible spread of communistic ideas among the rich, or in some other way wasting a youth that always has been, and always will remain, quite full of promise. If I wrong you in ascribing it to such a cause, you must make allowances for the morbidity produced by long imprisonment. But do write clearly. Otherwise it looks as if you had something to conceal.

There is much that is horrid, I suppose, in this letter. But I had to blame you to yourself, not to others. Read my letter to More. Harris comes to see me on Saturday, I hope. Remember me to Arthur Clifton and his wife, who, I find, is so like Rossetti's wife—the same lovely hair—but of course a sweeter nature, though Miss Siddal is fascinating and her poem A1.

Yours ever,

OSCAR.

DE PROFUNDIS

PREFACE TO THE FIRST EDITION

FOR a long time considerable curiosity has been expressed about the manuscript of DE PROFUNDIS, which was known to be in my possession, the author having mentioned its existence to many other friends. The book requires little introduction, and scarcely any explanation. I have only to record that it was written by my friend during the last months of his imprisonment, that it was the only work he wrote while in prison, and the last work in prose he ever wrote. (*The Ballad of Reading Gaol* was not composed or even planned until he had regained his liberty.)

I venture to hope that this fragment, which renders so vividly, perhaps painfully, the effect of social *débâcle* and imprisonment on a highly intellectual and artificial nature will give many readers a different impression of the witty and delightful writer from any they may have hitherto received.

ROBERT ROSS.

DE PROFUNDIS

. . . . .

MY place would be between Gilles de Retz and the Marquis de Sade. I daresay it is best so. I have no desire to complain. One of the many lessons that one learns in prison is, that things are what they are and will be what they will be. Nor have I any doubt that the leper of mediævalism and the author of *Justine* will prove better company than *Sandford and Merton*. . . .

All this took place in the early part of November of the year before last. A great river of life flows between me and a date so distant. Hardly, if at all, can you see across so wide a waste. But to me it seems to have occurred, I will not say yesterday, but to-day. Suffering is one very long moment. We can not divide it by seasons. We can only record its moods, and chronicle their return. With us time itself does not progress. It revolves. It seems to circle round one centre of pain. The paralysing immobility of a life every circumstance of which is regulated after an unchangeable pattern, so that we eat and drink and lie down and pray, or kneel at least for prayer, according to the inflexible laws of an iron formula: this immobile quality, that makes each dreadful day in the very minutest detail like its brother, seems to communicate itself to those external forces, the very essence of whose existence is ceaseless change. Of seed-time or harvest, of the reapers bending over the corn, or the grape gatherers threading through the vines, of the grass in the orchard made white with broken blossoms or strewn with fallen fruit: of these we know nothing, and can know nothing.

For us there is only one season, the season of sorrow. The very sun and moon seem taken from us. Outside, the day may be blue and gold, but the light that creeps down through the thickly-muffled glass of the small iron-barred window beneath which one sits is grey and niggard. It is always twilight in one's cell, as it is always twilight in one's heart. And in the sphere of thought, no less than in the sphere of time, motion is no more. The thing that you personally, have long ago forgotten, or can easily forget, is happening to me now, and will happen to me again to-morrow. Remember this, and you will be able to understand a little of why I am writing, and in this manner writing. . . .

A week later, I am transferred here. Three more months go over and my mother dies. No one knew how deeply I loved and honoured her. Her death was terrible to me; but I, once a lord of language, have no words in which to express my anguish and my shame. Never even in the most perfect days of my development as an artist could I have found words fit to bear so august a burden; or to move with sufficient stateliness of music through the purple pageant of my incommunicable woe. She and my father had bequeathed me a name they had made noble and honoured, not merely in literature, art, archæology, and science, but in the public history of my own country, in its evolution as a nation. I had disgraced that name eternally. I had made it a low byword among low people. I had dragged it through the very mire. I had given it to brutes that they might make it brutal, and to fools that they might turn it into a synonym for folly. What I suffered then, and still suffer, is not for pen to write or paper to record. My wife, always kind and gentle to me, rather than that I should hear the news from indifferent lips, travelled, ill as she was, all the way from Genoa to England to break to me herself the tidings of so irreparable, so irredeemable, a loss. Messages of sympathy reached me from all who had still affection for me. Even people who had not known me personally, hearing that a new sorrow had broken into my life, wrote to ask that some expression of their condolence should be conveyed to me. . . .

Three months go over. The calendar of my daily conduct and labour that hangs on the outside of my cell door, with my name and sentence written upon it, tells me that it is May. . . .

Prosperity, pleasure and success, may be rough of grain and common in fibre, but sorrow is the most sensitive of all created things. There is nothing that stirs in the whole world of thought to which sorrow does not vibrate in terrible and exquisite pulsation. The thin beaten-out leaf of tremulous gold that chronicles the direction of forces the eye cannot see is in comparison coarse. It is a wound that bleeds when any hand but that of love touches it, and even then must bleed again, though not in pain.

Where there is sorrow there is holy ground. Some day people will realise what that means. They will know nothing of life till they do. —— and natures like his can realise it. When I was brought down from my prison to the Court of Bankruptcy, between two policemen, —— waited in the long dreary corridor that, before the whole crowd, whom an action so sweet and simple hushed into silence, he might gravely raise his hat to me, as, handcuffed and with bowed head, I passed him by. Men have gone to heaven for smaller things than that. It was in this spirit, and with this mode of love, that the saints knelt down to wash the feet of the poor, or stooped to kiss the leper on the cheek. I have never said one single word to him about what he did. I do not know to the present moment whether he is aware that I was even conscious of his action. It is not a thing for which one can render formal thanks in formal words. I store it in the treasure-house of my heart. I keep it there as a secret debt that I am glad to think I can never possibly repay. It is embalmed and kept sweet by the myrrh and cassia of many tears. When wisdom has been profitless to me, philosophy barren, and the proverbs and phrases of those who have sought to give me consolation as dust and ashes in my mouth, the memory of that little, lovely, silent act of love has unsealed for me all the wells of pity: made the desert blossom like a rose, and brought me out of the bitterness of lonely exile into harmony with the wounded, broken, and great heart of the world. When people are able to understand, not merely how beautiful ———'s action was, but why it meant so much to me, and always will mean so much, then, perhaps, they will realise how and in what spirit they should approach me. . . .

.   .   .   .   .

The first volume of Poems that in the very springtide of his manhood a young man sends forth to the world should be like a blossom or flower of spring, like the white thorn in the meadow at Magdalen or the cowslips in the Cumnor fields. It should not be burdened by the weight of a terrible and revolting tragedy; a terrible revolting scandal. If I had allowed my name to serve as herald to such a book, it would have been a grave artistic error; it would have brought a wrong atmosphere round the whole work and in modern art atmosphere counts for so much. Modern life is complex and relative; those are its two distinguishing notes; to render the first we require atmosphere with its subtlety of *nuances,* of suggestion, of strange perspectives; as for the second we require background. That is why sculpture has ceased to be a representative art and why music is a representative art and why literature is, and has been and always will remain the supreme representative art. . . .

.   .   .   .   .

Every twelve weeks R——— writes to me a little budget of literary news. Nothing can be more charming than his letters, in their wit, their clever concentrated criticism, their light touch: they are real letters, they are like a person talking to one; they have the quality of a French *causerie intime:* and in his delicate mode of deference to me, appealing at one time to my judgment, at another to my sense of humour, at another to my instinct for beauty or to my culture, and reminding me in a hundred subtle ways that once I was to many arbiter of style in art; the supreme arbiter to some; he shows how he has the tact of love as well as the tact of literature. His letters have been the messengers between me and that beautiful unreal world of art where once I was King, and would have remained King indeed, had I not let myself be lured into the imperfect world of coarse uncompleted passion, of appetite without distinction, desire without limit, and formless greed. Yet when all is said surely ——— might have been able to understand or conceive, at any rate that on the ordinary grounds of mere psychological curiosity it would have been more interesting to me to hear from ——— than to learn that Alfred Austin was trying to bring out a volume of poems; that George Street was writing dramatic criticism for the *Daily Chronicle;* or that by one who cannot speak a panegyric without stammering, Mrs. Meynell had been pronounced to be the new Sibyl of style. . . .

.   .   .   .

Other miserable men when they are thrown into prison, if they are robbed of the beauty of the world are at least safe in some measure from the world's most deadly slings, most awful arrows. They can hide in the darkness of their cells and of their very disgrace make a mode of sanctuary. The world having had its will goes its way, and they are left to suffer undisturbed. With me it has been different. Sorrow after sorrow has come beating at the prison doors in search of me; they have opened the gates wide and let them in. Hardly if at all have my friends been suffered to see me. But my enemies have had full access to me always; twice in my public appearances in the Bankruptcy Court; twice again in my public transferences from one prison to another have I been shown under conditions of unspeakable humiliation to the gaze and mockery of men. The messenger of Death has brought me his tidings and gone his way; and in entire solitude and isolated from all that could give me comfort or suggest relief I have had to bear the intolerable burden of misery and remorse, which the memory of my mother placed upon me and places on me still. Hardly has that wound been dulled, not healed, by time, when violent and bitter and harsh letters come to me from solicitors. I am at once taunted and threatened with poverty. That I can bear. I can school myself to worse than that; but my two children are taken from me by legal procedure. That is, and always will remain to me a source of infinite distress, of infinite pain, of grief without end or limit. That the law should decide and take upon itself to decide that I am one unfit to be with my own children is something quite horrible to me. The disgrace of prison is as nothing compared with it. I envy the other men who tread the yard along with me. I am sure that their children wait for them, look for their coming, will be sweet to them.

The poor are wiser, more charitable, more kind, more sensitive than we are. In their eyes prison is a tragedy in a man's life, a misfortune, a casualty, something that calls for sympathy in others. They speak of one who is in prison as of one who is "in trouble" simply. It is the phrase they always use, and the expression has the perfect wisdom of love in it. With people of our own rank it is different. With us, prison makes a man a pariah. I, and such as I am, have hardly any right to air and sun. Our presence taints the pleasures of others. We are unwelcome when we reappear. To revisit the glimpses of the moon is not for us. Our very children are taken away. Those lovely links with humanity are broken. We are doomed to be solitary, while our sons still live. We are denied the one thing that might heal us and keep us, that might bring balm to the bruised heart, and peace to the soul in pain. . . .

I must say to myself that I ruined myself, and that nobody great or small can be ruined except by his own hand. I am quite ready to say so. I am trying to say so, though they may not think it at the present moment. This pitiless indictment I bring without pity against myself. Terrible as was what the world did to me, what I did to myself was far more terrible still.

I was a man who stood in symbolic relations to the art and culture of my age. I had realised this for myself at the very dawn of my manhood, and had forced my age to realise it afterwards. Few men hold such a position in their own life-time, and have it so acknowledged. It is usually discerned, if discerned at all, by the historian, or the critic, long after both the man and his age have passed away. With me it was different. I felt it myself, and made others feel it. Byron was a symbolic figure, but his relations were to the passion of his age and its weariness of passion. Mine were to something more noble, more permanent, of more vital issue, of larger scope.

The gods had given me almost everything. I had genius, a distinguished name, high social position, brilliancy, intel-lectual daring; I made art a philosophy and philosophy an art: I altered the minds of men and the colours of things: there was nothing I said or did that did not make people wonder. I took the drama, the most objective form known to art, and made it as personal a mode of expression as the

lyric or sonnet; at the same time I widened its range and en-
riched its characterisation. Drama, novel, poem in prose,
poem in rhyme, subtle or fantastic dialogue, whatever I
touched, I made beautiful in a new mode of beauty: to truth
itself I gave what is false no less than what is true as its right-
ful province, and showed that the false and the true are merely
forms of intellectual existence. I treated art as the supreme
reality and life as a mere mode of fiction. I awoke the imagination of my century so that it created myth and legend around
me. I summed up all systems in a phrase and all existence in an epigram. Along with these things I had things
that were different. But I let myself be lured into long spells
of senseless and sensual ease. I amused myself with being a
flâneur, a dandy, a man of fashion. I surrounded myself with
the smaller natures and the meaner minds. I became the
spendthrift of my own genius, and to waste an eternal youth
gave me a curious joy. Tired of being on the heights, I de-
liberately went to the depths in the search for new sensation.
What the paradox was to me in the sphere of thought, perversity became to me in the sphere of passion. Desire, at the
end, was a malady, or a madness, or both. I grew careless of
the lives of others. I took pleasure where it pleased me, and
passed on. I forgot that every little action of the common day
makes or unmakes character, and that therefore what one
has done in the secret chamber one has some day to cry aloud
on the housetops. I ceased to be lord over myself. I was no
longer the captain of my soul, and did not know it. I allowed
pleasure to dominate me. I ended in horrible disgrace. There
is only one thing for me now, absolute humility.

I have lain in prison for nearly two years. Out of my nature
has come wild despair; an abandonment to grief that was
piteous even to look at; terrible and impotent rage; bitterness and scorn; anguish that wept aloud; misery that could
find no voice; sorrow that was dumb. I have passed through

every possible mood of suffering. Better than Wordsworth himself I know what Wordsworth meant when he said—

"Suffering is permanent, obscure, and dark,
And has the nature of infinity."

But while there were times when I rejoiced in the idea that my sufferings were to be endless, I could not bear them to be without meaning. Now I find hidden somewhere away in my nature something that tells me that nothing in the whole world is meaningless, and suffering least of all. That some-thing hidden away in my nature, like a treasure in a field, is Humility.

It is the last thing left in me, and the best: the ultimate dis-covery at which I have arrived, the starting-point for a fresh development. It has come to me right out of myself, so I know that it has come at the proper time. It could not have come before, nor later. Had any one told me of it, I would have rejected it. Had it been brought to me, I would have refused it. As I found it, I want to keep it. I must do so. It is the one thing that has in it the elements of life, of a new life, a *Vita Nuova* for me. Of all things it is the strangest; one cannot give it away and another may not give it to one. One cannot acquire it except by surrendering everything that one has. It is only when one has lost all things, that one knows that one possesses it.

Now I have realised that it is in me, I see quite clearly what I ought to do; in fact, must do. And when I use such a phrase as that, I need not say that I am not alluding to any external sanction or command. I admit none. I am far more of an in-dividualist than I ever was. Nothing seems to me of the smallest value except what one gets out of oneself. My nature is seeking a fresh mode of self-realisation. That is all I am concerned with. And the first thing that I have got to do is to free myself from any possible bitterness of feeling against the world.

I am completely penniless, and absolutely homeless. Yet there are worse things in the world than that. I am quite candid when I say that rather than go out from this prison with bitterness in my heart against the world, I would gladly and readily beg my bread from door to door. If I got nothing from the house of the rich I would get something at the house of the poor. Those who have much are often greedy; those who have little always share. I would not a bit mind sleeping in the cool grass in summer, and when winter came on sheltering myself by the warm close-thatched rick, or under the penthouse of a great barn, provided I had love in my heart. The external things of life seem to me now of no importance at all. You can see to what intensity of individualism I have arrived—or am arriving rather, for the journey is long, and "where I walk there are thorns."

Of course I know that to ask alms on the highway is not to be my lot, and that if ever I lie in the cool grass at night-time it will be to write sonnets to the moon. When I go out of prison, R———— will be waiting for me on the other side of the big iron-studded gate, and he is the symbol, not merely of his own affection, but of the affection of many others besides. I believe I am to have enough to live on for about eighteen months at any rate, so that if I may not write beautiful books, I may at least read beautiful books; and what joy can be greater? After that, I hope to be able to recreate my creative faculty.

But were things different: had I not a friend left in the world; were there not a single house open to me in pity; had I to accept the wallet and ragged cloak of sheer penury: as long as I am free from all resentment, hardness, and scorn, I would be able to face the life with much more calm and confidence than I would were my body in purple and fine linen and the soul within me sick with hate.

And I really shall have no difficulty. When you really want love you will find it waiting for you.

I need not say that my task does not end there. It would be comparatively easy if it did. There is much more before me. I have hills far steeper to climb, valleys much darker to pass through. And I have to get it all out of myself. Neither religion, morality, nor reason can help me at all.

Morality does not help me. I am a born antinomian. I am one of those who are made for exceptions, not for laws. But while I see that there is nothing wrong in what one does, I see that there is something wrong in what one becomes. It is well to have learned that.

Religion does not help me. The faith that others give to what is unseen, I give to what one can touch, and look at. My gods dwell in temples made with hands; and within the circle of actual experience is my creed made perfect and complete: too complete, it may be, for like many or all of those who have placed their heaven in this earth, I have found in it not merely the beauty of heaven, but the horror of hell also. When I think about religion at all, I feel as if I would like to found an order for those who *cannot* believe: the Confraternity of the Fatherless [1] one might call it, where on an altar, on which no taper burned, a priest, in whose heart peace had no dwelling, might celebrate with unblessed bread and a chalice empty of wine. Every thing to be true must become a religion. And agnosticism should have its ritual no less than faith. It has sown its martyrs, it should reap its saints, and praise God daily for having hidden Himself from man. But whether it

---

[1] In the early editions the word read *Faithless*. Wilde's writing, usually so clear, was sometimes cramped in the MSS. of *De Profundis*. I read it, however, *Faithless* until some one pointed out to me that from the context it must be *Fatherless;* an expert on handwriting has decided in favour of the new reading.

be faith or agnosticism, it must be nothing external to me. Its symbols must be of my own creating. Only that is spiritual which makes its own form. If I may not find its secret within myself, I shall never find it: if I have not got it already, it will never come to me.

Reason does not help me. It tells me that the laws under which I am convicted are wrong and unjust laws, and the system under which I have suffered a wrong and unjust system. But, somehow, I have got to make both of these things just and right to me. And exactly as in Art one is only concerned with what a particular thing is at a particular moment to oneself, so it is also in the ethical evolution of one's character. I have got to make everything that has happened to me good for me. The plank bed, the loathsome food, the hard ropes shredded into oakum till one's finger-tips grow dull with pain, the menial offices with which each day begins and finishes, the harsh orders that routine seems to necessitate, the dreadful dress that makes sorrow grotesque to look at, the silence, the solitude, the shame—each and all of these things I have to transform into a spiritual experience. There is not a single degradation of the body which I must not try and make into a spiritualising of the soul.

I want to get to the point when I shall be able to say quite simply, and without affectation, that the two great turning-points in my life were when my father sent me to Oxford, and when society sent me to prison. I will not say that prison is the best thing that could have happened to me; for that phrase would savour of too great bitterness towards myself. I would sooner say, or hear it said of me, that I was so typical a child of my age, that in my perversity, and for that perversity's sake, I turned the good things of my life to evil, and the evil things of my life to good.

What is said, however, by myself or by others, matters little. The important thing, the thing that lies before me, the thing that I have to do, if the brief remainder of my days is not to be maimed, marred, and incomplete, is to absorb into my nature all that has been done to me, to make it part of me, to accept it without complaint, fear, or reluctance. The supreme vice is shallowness. Whatever is realised is right.

When first I was put into prison some people advised me to try and forget who I was. It was ruinous advice. It is only by realising what I am that I have found comfort of any kind. Now I am advised by others to try on my release to forget that I have ever been in a prison at all. I know that would be equally fatal. It would mean that I would always be haunted by an intolerable sense of disgrace, and that those things that are meant for me as much as for anybody else—the beauty of the sun and moon, the pageant of the seasons, the music of daybreak and the silence of great nights, the rain falling through the leaves, or the dew creeping over the grass and making it silver—would all be tainted for me, and lose their healing power and their power of communicating joy. To regret one's own experiences is to arrest one's own development. To deny one's own experiences is to put a lie into the lips of one's own life. It is no less than a denial of the soul.

For just as the body absorbs things of all kinds, things common and unclean no less than those that the priest or a vision has cleansed, and converts them into swiftness or strength, into the play of beautiful muscles and the moulding of fair flesh, into the curves and colours of the hair, the lips, the eye; so the soul in its turn has its nutritive functions also, and can transform into noble moods of thought and passions of high import what in itself is base, cruel, and degrading; nay, more, may find in these its most august modes of assertion, and can often reveal itself most perfectly through what was intended to desecrate or destroy.

The fact of my having been the common prisoner of a common gaol I must frankly accept, and, curious as it may seem, one of the things I shall have to teach myself is not to be ashamed of it. I must accept it as a punishment, and if one is ashamed of having been punished, one might just as well never have been punished at all. Of course there are many things of which I was convicted that I had not done, but then there are many things of which I was convicted that I had done, and a still greater number of things in my life for which I was never indicted at all. And as the gods are strange, and punish us for what is good and humane in us as much as for what is evil and perverse, I must accept the fact that one is punished for the good as well as for the evil that one does. I have no doubt that it is quite right one should be. It helps one, or should help one, to realise both, and not to be too conceited about either. And if I then am not ashamed of my punishment, as I hope not to be, I shall be able to think, and walk, and live with freedom.

Many men on their release carry their prison about with them into the air, and hide it as a secret disgrace in their hearts, and at length, like poor poisoned things, creep into some hole and die. It is wretched that they should have to do so, and it is wrong, terribly wrong, of society that it should force them to do so. Society takes upon itself the right to inflict appalling punishment on the individual, but it also has the supreme vice of shallowness, and fails to realise what it has done. When the man's punishment is over, it leaves him to himself; that is to say, it abandons him at the very moment when its highest duty towards him begins. It is really ashamed of its own actions, and shuns those whom it has punished, as people shun a creditor whose debt they cannot pay, or one on whom they have inflicted an irreparable, an irredeemable wrong. I can claim on my side that if I realise what I have suffered, society should realise what it has inflicted on me; and that there should be no bitterness or hate on either side.

Of course I know that from one point of view things will

be made different for me than for others; must indeed, by the very nature of the case, be made so. The poor thieves and outcasts who are imprisoned here with me are in many respects more fortunate than I am. The little way in grey city or green field that saw their sin is small; to find those who know nothing of what they have done they need go no further than a bird might fly between the twilight at dawn and dawn itself: but for me the world is shrivelled to a handsbreadth, and everywhere I turn my name is written on the rocks in lead. For I have come, not from obscurity into the momentary notoriety of crime, but from a sort of eternity of fame to a sort of eternity of infamy, and sometimes seem to myself to have shown, if indeed it required showing, that between the famous and the infamous there is but one step, if as much as one.

Still, in the very fact that people will recognise me wherever I go, and know all about my life, as far as its follies go, I can discern something good for me. It will force on me the necessity of again asserting myself as an artist, and as soon as I possibly can. If I can produce only one beautiful work of art I shall be able to rob malice of its venom, and cowardice of its sneer, and to pluck out the tongue of scorn by the roots.

And if life be, as it surely is, a problem to me, I am no less a problem to life. People must adopt some attitude towards me, and so pass judgment both on themselves and me. I need not say I am not talking of particular individuals. The only people I would care to be with now are artists and people who have suffered: those who know what beauty is, and those who know what sorrow is: nobody else interests me. Nor am I making any demands on life. In all that I have said I am simply concerned with my own mental attitude towards life as a whole; and I feel that not to be ashamed of having been punished is one of the first points I must attain to, for the sake of my own perfection, and because I am so imperfect.

Then I must learn how to be happy. Once I knew it, or thought I knew it, by instinct. It was always springtime once in my heart. My temperament was akin to joy. I filled my life to the very brim with pleasure, as one might fill a cup to the very brim with wine. Now I am approaching life from a completely new standpoint, and even to conceive happiness is often extremely difficult for me. I remember during my first term at Oxford reading in Pater's *Renaissance*—that book which has had such strange influence over my life—how Dante places low in the Inferno those who wilfully live in sadness; and going to the college library and turning to the passage in the *Divine Comedy* where beneath the dreary marsh lie those who were "sullen in the sweet air," saying for ever and ever through their sighs—

"Tristi fummo
Nell aer dolce che dal sol s'allegra."

I knew the Church condemned *accidia,* but the whole idea seemed to me quite fantastic, just the sort of sin, I fancied, a priest who knew nothing about real life would invent. Nor could I understand how Dante, who says that "sorrow remarries us to God," could have been so harsh to those who were enamoured of melancholy, if any such there really were. I had no idea that some day this would become to me one of the greatest temptations of my life.

While I was in Wandsworth prison I longed to die. It was my one desire. When after two months in the infirmary I was transferred here, and found myself growing gradually better in physical health, I was filled with rage. I determined to commit suicide on the very day on which I left prison. After a time that evil mood passed away, and I made up my mind to live, but to wear gloom as a king wears purple; never to smile again; to turn whatever house I entered into a house of mourning: to make my friends walk slowly in sadness with me: to teach them that melancholy is the true secret of life: to maim them with an alien sorrow: to mar them with my own pain. Now I feel quite differently. I see it would be both ungrateful and unkind of me to pull so long a face that when my friends came to see me they would have to make their faces still longer in order to show their sympathy; or, if I desired to entertain them, to invite them to sit down silently to bitter herbs and funeral baked meats. I must learn how to be cheerful and happy.

The last two occasions on which I was allowed to see my friends here, I tried to be as cheerful as possible, and to show my cheerfulness, in order to make them some slight return for their trouble in coming all the way from town to see me. It is only a slight return, I know, but it is the one, I feel certain, that pleases them most. I saw R—— for an hour on Saturday week, and I tried to give her the fullest possible expression of the delight I really felt at our meeting. And that, in the views and ideas I am here shaping for myself, I am quite right is shown to me by the fact that now for the first time since my imprisonment I have a real desire for life.

There is before me so much to do that I would regard it as a terrible tragedy if I died before I was allowed to complete at any rate a little of it. I see new developments in art and life, each one of which is a fresh mode of perfection. I long to live so that I can explore what is no less than a new world to me. Do you want to know what this new world is? I think you can guess what it is. It is the world in which I have been living. Sorrow, then, and all that it teaches one, is my new world.

I used to live entirely for pleasure. I shunned suffering and sorrow of every kind. I hated both. I resolved to ignore them as far as possible: to treat them, that is to say, as modes of imperfection. They were not part of my scheme of life. They had no place in my philosophy. My mother, who knew life as a whole, used often to quote to me Goethe's lines—written by

Carlyle in a book he had given her years ago, and translated by him, I fancy, also:—

> "Who never ate his bread in sorrow,
>   Who never spent the midnight hours
> Weeping and waiting for the morrow,—
>   He knows you not, ye heavenly powers."

They were the lines which that noble Queen of Prussia, whom Napoleon treated with such coarse brutality, used to quote in her humiliation and exile; they were the lines my mother often quoted in the troubles of her later life. I absolutely declined to accept or admit the enormous truth hidden in them. I could not understand it. I remember quite well how I used to tell her that I did not want to eat my bread in sorrow, or to pass any night weeping and watching for a more bitter dawn.

I had no idea that it was one of the special things that the Fates had in store for me: that for a whole year of my life, indeed, I was to do little else. But so has my portion been meted out to me; and during the last few months I have, after terrible difficulties and struggles, been able to comprehend some of the lessons hidden in the heart of pain. Clergymen and people who use phrases without wisdom sometimes talk of suffering as a mystery. It is really a revelation. One discerns things one never discerned before. One approaches the whole of history from a different standpoint. What one had felt dimly, through instinct, about art, is intellectually and emotionally realised with perfect clearness of vision and absolute intensity of apprehension.

I now see that sorrow, being the supreme emotion of which man is capable, is at once the type and test of all great art. What the artist is always looking for is the mode of existence in which soul and body are one and indivisible: in which the outward is expressive of the inward: in which form reveals.

Of such modes of existence there are not a few: youth and the arts preoccupied with youth may serve as a model for us at one moment: at another we may like to think that in its subtlety and sensitiveness of impression, its suggestion of a spirit dwelling in external things and making its raiment of earth and air, of mist and city alike, and in its morbid sympathy of its moods, and tones, and colours, modern landscape art is realising for us pictorially what was realised in such plastic perfection by the Greeks. Music, in which all subject is absorbed in expression and cannot be separated from it, is a complex example, and a flower or a child a simple example, of what I mean; but sorrow is the ultimate type both in life and art.

Behind you and laughter there may be a temperament, coarse, hard, and callous. But behind sorrow there is always sorrow. Pain, unlike pleasure, wears no mask. Truth in art is not any correspondence between the essential idea and the accidental existence; it is not the resemblance of shape to shadow, or of the form mirrored in the crystal to the form itself; it is no echo coming from a hollow hill, any more than it is a silver well of water in the valley that shows the moon to the moon and Narcissus to Narcissus. Truth in art is the unity of a thing with itself: the outward rendered expressive of the inward: the soul made incarnate: the body instinct with spirit. For this reason there is no truth comparable to sorrow. There are times when sorrow seems to me to be the only truth. Other things may be illusions of the eye or the appetite, made to blind the one and cloy the other, but out of sorrow have the worlds been built, and at the birth of a child or a star there is pain.

More than this, there is about sorrow an intense, an extraordinary reality. I have said of myself that I was one who stood in symbolic relations to the art and culture of my age. There is not a single wretched man in this wretched place along with me who does not stand in symbolic relation to the very secret of life. For the secret of life is suffering. It is what is hidden behind everything. When we begin to live, what is sweet is so sweet to us, and what is bitter is so bitter that we inevitably direct all our desires towards pleasures, and seek not merely for a "month or twain to feed on honeycomb," but for all our years to taste no other food, ignorant all the while that we may really be starving the soul.

I remember talking once on this subject to one of the most beautiful personalities I have ever known [1]: a woman, whose sympathy and noble kindness to me, both before and since the tragedy of my imprisonment, have been beyond power and description; one who has really assisted me, though she does not know it, to bear the burden of my troubles more than any one else in the whole world has, and all through the mere fact of her existence, through her being what she is— partly an ideal and partly an influence: a suggestion of what one might become as well as a real help towards becoming it; a soul that renders the common air sweet, and makes what is spiritual seem as simple and natural as sunlight or the sea: one for whom beauty and sorrow walk hand in hand, and have the same message. On the occasion of which I am thinking I recall distinctly how I said to her that there was enough suffering in one narrow London lane to show that God did not love man, and that wherever there was any sorrow, though but that of a child in some little garden weeping over a fault that it had or had not committed, the whole face of creation was completely marred. I was entirely wrong. She told me so, but I could not believe her. I was not in the sphere in which such belief was to be attained to. Now it seems to me that love of some kind is the only possible explanation of the extraordinary amount of suffering that there is in the

---

[1] This is the lady at Wimbledon to whom reference is made in Letter II. and to whom the editor has dedicated the *Duchess of Padua*.

world. I cannot conceive of any other explanation. I am convinced that there is no other, and that if the world has indeed,
as I have said, been built of sorrow, it has been built by the
hands of love, because in no other way could the soul of man,
for whom the world was made, reach the full stature of its
perfection. Pleasure for the beautiful body, but pain for the
beautiful soul.

When I say that I am convinced of these things I speak
with too much pride. Far off, like a perfect pearl, one can see
the city of God. It is so wonderful that it seems as if a child
could reach it in a summer's day. And so a child could. But
with me and such as me it is different. One can realise a thing
in a single moment, but one loses it in the long hours that
follow with leaden feet. It is so difficult to keep "heights that
the soul is competent to gain." We think in eternity, but we
move slowly through time; and how slowly time goes with
us who lie in prison I need not tell again, nor of the weariness
and despair that creep back into one's cell, and into the cell
of one's heart, with such strange insistence that one has, as it
were, to garnish and sweep one's house for their coming, as
for an unwelcome guest, or a bitter master, or a slave whose
slave it is one's chance or choice to be.

And, though at present my friends may find it a hard thing
to believe, it is true none the less, that for them living in freedom and idleness and comfort it is more easy to learn the
lessons of humility that it is for me, who begin the day by
going down on my knees and washing the floor of my cell.
For prison life with its endless privations and restrictions
makes one rebellious. The most terrible thing about it is not
that it breaks one's heart—hearts are made to be broken—
but that it turns one's heart to stone. One sometimes feels that
it is only with a front of brass and a lip of scorn that one can
get through the day at all. And he who is in a state of rebellion cannot receive grace, to use the phrase of which the

Church is so fond—so rightly fond, I dare say—for in life as in art the mood of rebellion closes up the channels of the soul, and shuts out the airs of heaven. Yet I must learn these lessons here if I am to learn them anywhere, and must be filled with joy if my feet are on the right road and my face set towards "the gate which is called beautiful," though I may fall many times in the mire and often in the mist go astray.

This New Life, as through my love of Dante I like sometimes to call it, is of course no new life at all, but simply the continuance by means of development and evolution, of my former life. I remember when I was at Oxford saying to one of my friends as we were strolling round Magdalen's narrow bird-haunted walks one morning in the year before I took my degree, that I wanted to eat of the fruit of all the trees in the garden of the world, and that I was going out into the world with that passion in my soul. And so, indeed, I went out, and so I lived. My only mistake was that I confined myself so exclusively to the trees of what seemed to me the sun-lit side of the garden, and shunned the other side for its shadow and its gloom. Failure, disgrace, poverty, sorrow, despair, suffering, tears even, the broken words that come from lips in pain, remorse that makes one walk on thorns, conscience that condemns, self-abasement that punishes, the misery that puts ashes on its head, the anguish that chooses sackcloth for its raiment and into its own drink puts gall:—all these were things of which I was afraid. And as I had determined to know nothing of them, I was forced to taste each of them in turn, to feed on them, to have for a season, indeed, no other food at all.

I don't regret for a single moment having lived for pleasure. I did it to the full, as one should do everything that one does. There was no pleasure I did not experience. I threw the pearl of my soul into a cup of wine. I went down the primrose path to the sound of flutes. I lived on honeycomb. But to have continued the same life would have been wrong because it would have been limiting. I had to pass on. The other half of the garden had its secrets for me also. Of course all this is fore-shadowed and prefigured in my books. Some of it is in *The Happy Prince,* some of it in *The Young King,* notably in the passage where the bishop says to the kneeling boy, "Is not He who made misery wiser than thou art?" a phrase which when I wrote it seemed to me little more than a phrase; a great deal of it is hidden away in the note of doom that like a purple thread runs through the texture of *Dorian Gray;* in *The Critic as Artist* it is set forth in many colours; in *The Soul of Man* it is written down, and in letters too easy to read; it is one of the refrains whose recurring *motifs* make *Salomé* so like a piece of music and bind it together as a ballad; in the prose poem of the man who from the bronze of the image of the "Pleasure that liveth for a moment" has to make the image of the "Sorrow that abideth for ever" it is incarnate. It could not have been otherwise. At every single moment of one's life one is what one is going to be no less than what one has been. Art is a symbol, because man is a symbol.

It is, if I can fully attain to it, the ultimate realisation of the artistic life. For the artistic life is simply self-development. Humility in the artist is his frank acceptance of all experi-ences, just as love in the artist is simply the sense of beauty that reveals to the world its body and its soul. In *Marius the Epicurean* Pater seeks to reconcile the artistic life with the life of religion, in the deep, sweet, and austere sense of the word. But Marius is a little more than a spectator: an ideal spectator indeed, and one to whom it is given "to contemplate the spectacle of life with appropriate emotions," which Wordsworth defines as the poet's true aim; yet a spectator merely, and perhaps a little too much occupied with the come-liness of the benches of the sanctuary to notice that it is the sanctuary of sorrow that he is gazing at.

I see a far more intimate and immediate connection between the true life of Christ and the true life of the artist; and I take a keen pleasure in the reflection that long before sorrow had made my days her own and bound me to her wheel I had written in *The Soul of Man* that he who would lead a Christ-like life must be entirely and absolutely himself, and had taken as my types not merely the shepherd on the hillside and the prisoner in his cell, but also the painter to whom the world is a pageant and the poet for whom the world is a song. I remember saying once to André Gide, as we sat together in some Paris *café,* that while metaphysics had but little real interest for me, and morality absolutely none, there was nothing that either Plato or Christ had said that could not be transferred immediately into the sphere of Art and there find its complete fulfilment.

Nor is it merely that we can discern in Christ that close union of personality with perfection which forms the real distinction between the classical and romantic movement in life, but the very basis of his nature was the same as that of the nature of the artist—an intense and flamelike imagination. He realised in the entire sphere of human relations that imaginative sympathy which in the sphere of Art is the sole secret of creation. He understood the leprosy of the leper, the darkness of the blind, the fierce misery of those who live for pleasure, the strange poverty of the rich. Some one wrote to me in trouble, "When you are not on your pedestal you are not interesting." How remote was the writer from what Matthew Arnold calls "the Secret of Jesus." Either would have taught him that whatever happens to another happens to oneself, and if you want an inscription to read at dawn and at night-time, and for pleasure or for pain, write up on the walls of your house in letters for the sun to gild and the moon to silver, "Whatever happens to oneself happens to another."

Christ's place indeed is with the poets. His whole conception of Humanity sprang right out of the imagination and can only be realised by it. What God was to the pantheist, man was to Him. He was the first to conceive the divided races as a unity. Before his time there had been gods and men, and, feeling through the mysticism of sympathy that in himself each had been made incarnate, he calls himself the Son of the one or the Son of the other, according to his mood. More than any one else in history he wakes in us that temper of wonder to which romance always appeals. There is still something to me almost incredible in the idea of a young Galilean peasant imagining that he could bear on his own shoulders the burden of the entire world: all that had already been done and suffered, and all that was yet to be done and suffered: the sins of Nero, of Cæsar Borgia, of Alexander VI., and of him who was Emperor of Rome and Priest of the Sun: the sufferings of those whose names are legion and whose dwelling is among the tombs: oppressed nationalities, factory children, thieves, people in prison, outcasts, those who are dumb under oppression and whose silence is heard only of God; and not merely imagining this but actually achieving it, so that at the present moment all who come in contact with his personality, even though they may neither bow to his altar nor kneel before his priest, in some way find that the ugliness of their sin is taken away and the beauty of their sorrow revealed to them.

I had said of Christ that He ranks with the poets. That is true. Shelley and Sophocles are of his company. But his entire life also is the most wonderful of poems. For "pity and terror" there is nothing in the entire cycle of Greek tragedy to touch it. The absolute purity of the protagonist raises the entire scheme to a height of romantic art from which the sufferings of Thebes and Pelops' line are by their very horror excluded, and shows how wrong Aristotle was when he said in his treatise on the drama that it would be impossible to bear the

spectacle of one blameless in pain. Nor in Æschylus nor
Dante, those stern masters of tenderness, in Shakespeare, the
most purely human of all the great artists, in the whole of
Celtic myth and legend, where the loveliness of the world is
shown through a mist of tears, and the life of a man is no
more than the life of a flower, is there anything that, for sheer
simplicity of pathos wedded and made one with sublimity
of tragic effect, can be said to equal or even approach
the last act of Christ's passion. The little supper with
his companions, one of whom has already sold him for a
price; the anguish in the quiet moon-lit garden; the false
friend coming close to him so as to betray him with a kiss;
the friend who still believed in him, and on whom as on a
rock he had hoped to build a house of refuge for Man, denying him as the bird cried to the dawn; his own utter loneli-
ness, his submission, his acceptance of everything; and along
with it all such scenes as the high priest of orthodoxy rending
his raiment in wrath, and the magistrate of civil justice calling for water in the vain hope of cleansing himself of that
stain of innocent blood that makes him the scarlet figure of
history; the coronation ceremony of sorrow, one of the most
wonderful things in the whole of recorded time; the crucifixion of the Innocent One before the eyes of his mother and
of the disciple whom he loved; the soldiers gambling and
throwing dice for his clothes; the terrible death by which he
gave the world its most eternal symbol; and his final burial
in the tomb of the rich man, his body swathed in Egyptian
linen with costly spices and perfumes as though he had been
a king's son. When one contemplates all this from the point
of view of art alone one cannot but be grateful that the supreme office of the Church should be playing of the tragedy
without the shedding of blood: the mystical presentation, by
means of dialogue and costume and gesture even, of the Passion of her Lord; and it is always a source of pleasure and awe

to me to remember that the ultimate survival of the Greek chorus, lost elsewhere to art, is to be found in the servitor answering the priest at Mass.

Yet the whole life of Christ—so entirely may sorrow and beauty be made one in their meaning and manifestation—is really an idyll, though it ends with the veil of the temple being rent, and the darkness coming over the face of the earth, and the stone rolled to the door of the sepulchre. One always thinks of him as a young bridegroom with his companions, as indeed he somewhere describes himself; as a shepherd straying through a valley with his sheep in search of green meadow or cool stream; as a singer trying to build out of the music the walls of the City of God; or as a lover for whose love the whole world was too small. His miracles seem to me to be as exquisite as the coming of spring, and quite as natural. I see no difficulty at all in believing that such was the charm of his personality that his mere presence could bring peace to souls in anguish, and that those who touched his garments or his hands forgot their pain; or that as he passed by on the highway of life people who had seen nothing of life's mystery saw it clearly, and others who had been deaf to every voice but that of pleasure heard for the first time the voice of love and found it as "musical as Apollo's lute"; or that evil passions fled at his approach, and men whose dull unimaginative lives had been but a mode of death rose as it were from the grave when he called them; or that when he taught on the hillside the multitude forgot their hunger and thirst and the cares of this world, and that to his friends who listened to him as he sat at meat the coarse food seemed delicate, and the water had the taste of good wine, and the whole house became full of the odour and sweetness of nard.

Renan in his *Vie de Jésus*—that gracious fifth gospel, the gospel according to St. Thomas, one might call it—says somewhere that Christ's great achievement was that he had made himself as much loved after his death as he had been during his lifetime. And certainly, if his place is among the poets, he is the leader of all the lovers. He saw that love was the first secret of the world for which the wise men had been looking, and that it was only through love that one could approach either the heart of the leper or the feet of God.

And above all, Christ is the most supreme of individualists. Humility, like the artistic acceptance of all experiences, is merely a mode of manifestation. It is man's soul that Christ is always looking for. He calls it "God's Kingdom," and finds it in every one. He compares it to little things, to a tiny seed, to a handful of leaven, to a pearl. That is because one realises one's soul only by getting rid of all alien passions, all acquired culture, and all external possessions, be they good or evil.

I bore up against everything with some stubbornness of will and much rebellion of nature, till I had absolutely nothing left in the world but one thing. I had lost my name, my position, my happiness, my freedom, my wealth. I was a prisoner and a pauper. But I still had my children left. Suddenly they were taken away from me by the law. It was a blow so appalling that I did not know what to do, so I flung myself on my knees, and bowed my head, and wept, and said, "The body of a child is as the body of the Lord: I am not worthy of either." That moment seemed to save me. I saw then that the only thing for me was to accept everything. Since then— curious as it will no doubt sound—I have been happier. It was of course my soul in its ultimate essence that I had reached. In many ways I had been its enemy, but I found it waiting for me as a friend. When one comes in contact with the soul it makes one simple as a child, as Christ said one should be.

It is tragic how few people ever "possess their souls" before they die. "Nothing is more rare in any man," says Emerson, "than an act of his own." It is quite true. Most people are other people. Their thoughts are some one else's opinions,

their lives a mimicry, their passions a quotation. Christ was
not merely the supreme individualist, but he was the first individualist in history. People have tried to make him out an
ordinary philanthropist, or ranked him as an altruist with the
unscientific and sentimental. But he was really neither one
nor the other. Pity he has, of course, for the poor, for those
who are shut up in prisons, for the lowly, for the wretched;
but he has far more pity for the rich, for the hard hedonists,
for those who waste their freedom in becoming slaves to
things, for those who wear soft raiment and live in king's
houses. Riches and pleasure seemed to him to be really greater
tragedies than poverty or sorrow. And as for altruism, who
know better than he that it is vocation not volition that de-
termines us, and that one cannot gather grapes of thorns or
figs from thistles?

To live for others as a definite self-conscious aim was not
his creed. It was not the basis of his creed. When he says, "Forgive your enemies." is it not for the sake of the enemy, but
for one's own sake that he says so, and because love is more
beautiful than hate. In his own entreaty to the young man,
"Sell all that thou hast and give to the poor," it is not of the
state of the poor that he is thinking, but of the soul of the
young man, the soul that wealth was marring. In his view of
life he is one with the artist who knows that by the inevitable
law of self-perfection, the poet must sing, and the sculptor
think in bronze, and the painter make the world a mirror
for his moods, as surely and as certainly as the hawthorn must
blossom in spring, and the corn turn to gold at harvest-time,
and the moon in her ordered wanderings change from shield
to sickle, and from sickle to shield.

But while Christ did not say to men, "Live for others," he
pointed out that there was no difference at all between the
lives of others and one's own life. By this means he gave to
man an extended, a Titan personality. Since his coming the

history or each separate individual is, or can be made, the history of the world. Of course, culture has intensified the personality of man. Art has made us myriad-minded. Those who have the artistic temperament go into exile with Dante and learn how salt is the bread of others, and how steep their stairs; they catch for a moment the serenity and calm of Goethe, and yet know but too well that Baudelaire cried to God:

"O Seigneur, donnez-moi la force et le courage
De contempler mon corps et mon cœur sans dégoût."

Out of Shakespeare's sonnets they draw, to their own hurt it may be, the secret of his love and make it their own; they look with new eyes on modern life, because they have listened to one of Chopin's nocturnes, or handled Greek things, or read the story of the passion of some dead man for some dead woman whose hair was like threads of fine gold, and whose mouth was as a pomegranate. But the sympathy of the artistic temperament is necessarily with what has found expression. In words or in colours, in music or in marble, behind the painted masks of an Æschylean play, or through some Sicilian shepherds' pierced and jointed reeds, the man and his message must have been revealed.

To the artist, expression is the only mode under which he can conceive life at all. To him what is dumb is dead. But to Christ it was not so. With a width and wonder of imagination that fills one almost with awe, he took the entire world of the inarticulate, the voiceless world of pain, as his kingdom, and made of himself its external mouthpiece. Those of whom I have spoken, who are dumb under oppression and "whose silence is heard only of God," he chose as his brothers. He sought to become eyes to the blind, ears to the deaf, and a cry in the lips of those whose tongues had been tied. His desire was to be to the myriads who had found no utterance a very trumpet through which they might call to heaven. And feeling, with the artistic nature of one to whom suffering and sorrow were modes through which he could realise his conception of the beautiful, that an idea is of no value till it becomes incarnate and is made an image, he made of himself the image of the Man of Sorrows, and as such has fascinated and dominated art as no Greek god ever succeeded in doing.

For the Greek gods, in spite of the white and red of their fair fleet limbs, were not really what they appeared to be. The curved brow of Apollo was like the sun's disc over a hill at dawn, and his feet were as the wings of the morning, but he himself had been cruel to Marsyas and had made Niobe childless. In the steel shields of Athena's eyes there had been no pity for Arachne; the pomp and peacocks of Hera were all that was really noble about her: and the Father of the Gods himself had been too fond of the daughters of men. The two most deeply suggestive figures of Greek mythology were, for religion, Demeter, an earth goddess, not one of the Olympians, and for art, Dionysos, the son of a mortal woman to whom the moment of his birth had proved also the moment of her death.

But Life itself from its lowliest and most humble sphere produced one far more marvellous than the mother of Proserpina or the son of Semele. Out of the Carpenter's shop at Nazareth had come a personality infinitely greater than any made by myth and legend, and one, strangely enough, destined to reveal to the world the mystical meaning of wine and the real beauties of the lilies of the field as none, either on Cithaeron or at Enna, had ever done.

The song of Isaiah, "He is despised and rejected of men, a man of sorrows and acquainted with grief: and we hid as it were our faces from him," had seemed to him to prefigure himself, and in him the prophecy was fulfilled. We must not be afraid of such a phrase. Every single work of art is the

fulfilment of a prophecy: for every work of art is the conversion of an idea into an image. Every single human being
should be the fulfilment of a prophecy: for every human being should be the realisation of some ideal, either in the mind
of God or in the mind of man. Christ found the type and
fixed it, and the dream of a Virgilian poet either at Jerusalem
or at Babylon, became in the long progress of the centuries
incarnate in him for whom the world was "waiting." "His
visage was marred more than any man's, and his form was
more than the sons of men," are among the signs noted by
Isaiah as distinguishing the new ideal, and as soon as art
understood what was meant it opened like a flower at the
presence of one in whom truth in art was set forth as it had
never been before. For is not truth in art, as I have said, "that
in which the outward is expressive of the inward; in which
the soul is made flesh and the body instinct with spirit in
which form reveals."

To me one of the things in history the most to be regretted,
is that the Christ's own renaissance which has produced the
Cathedral at Chartres, the Arthurian cycle of legends, the life
of St. Francis of Assisi, the art of Giotto, and Dante's *Divine
Comedy,* was not allowed to develop on its own lines, but was
interrupted and spoiled by the dreary classical Renaissance
that gave us Petrarch, and Raphael's frescoes, and Palladian
architecture, and formal French tragedy, and St. Paul's
Cathedral, and Pope's poetry, and everything that is made
from without and by dead rules, and does not spring from
within through some spirit informing it. But wherever there
is a romantic movement in art there somehow, and under
some form, is Christ, or the soul of Christ. He is in *Romeo
and Juliet,* in the *Winter's Tale,* in Provençal poetry, in the
Ancient Mariner, in *La Belle Dame sans merci,* and in Chatterton's *Ballad of Charity.*

We owe to him the most diverse things and people. Hugo's

Les Misérables, Baudelaire's *Fleurs du Mal,* the note of pity
in Russian novels, Verlaine and Verlaine's poems, the stained
glass and tapestries and the quattro-cento work of Burne-
Jones and Morris, belong to him no less than the tower of
Giotto, Lancelot and Guinevere, Tannhäuser, the troubled
romantic marbles of Michael Angelo, pointed architecture,
and the love of children and flowers—for both of which,
indeed, in classical art there was but little place, hardly
enough for them to grow or play in, but which, from the
twelfth century down to our own day, have been continually
making their appearances in art, under various modes and
at various times, coming fitfully and wilfully, as children,
as flowers, are apt to do: spring always seeming to one as
if the flowers had been in hiding, and only came out into
the sun because they were afraid that grown-up people would
grow tired of looking for them and give up the search; and
the life of a child being no more than an April day on
which there is both rain and sun for the narcissus.

It is the imaginative quality of Christ's own nature that
makes him this palpitating centre of romance. The strange
figures of poetic drama and ballad are made by the imagination of others, but out of his own imagination entirely did
Jesus of Nazareth create himself. The cry of Isaiah had really
no more to do with his coming than the song of the night-
ingale has to do with the rising of the moon—no more,
though perhaps no less. He was the denial as well as the
affirmation of prophecy. For every expectation that he fulfilled there was another that he destroyed. "In all beauty,"
says Bacon, "there is some strangeness of proportion," and
of those who are born of the spirit—of those, that is to say,
who like himself are dynamic forces—Christ says that they
are like the wind that "bloweth where it listeth, and no man
can tell whence it cometh and whither it goeth." That is
why he is so fascinating to artists. He has all the colour

elements of life: mystery, strangeness, pathos, suggestion, ecstasy, love. He appeals to the temper of wonder, and creates that mood in which alone he can be understood.

And to me it is a joy to remember that if he is "of imagination all compact," the world itself is of the same substance. I said in *Dorian Gray* that the great sins of the world take place in the brain: but it is in the brain that everything takes place. We know now that we do not see with the eyes or hear with the ears. They are really channels for the transmission, adequate or inadequate, of sense impressions. It is in the brain that the poppy is red, that the apple is odorous, that the skylark sings.

Of late I have been studying with diligence the four prose poems about Christ. At Christmas I managed to get hold of a Greek Testament, and every morning, after I had cleaned my cell and polished my tins, I read a little of the Gospels, a dozen verses taken by chance anywhere. It is a delightful way of opening the day. Every one, even in a turbulent, ill-disciplined life, should do the same. Endless repetition, in and out of season, has spoiled for us the freshness, the naïveté, the simple romantic charm of the Gospels. We hear them read far too often and far too badly, and all repetition is anti-spiritual. When one returns to the Greek, it is like going into a garden of lilies out of some narrow and dark house.

And to me, the pleasure is doubled by the reflection that it is extremely probable that we have the actual terms, the *ipsissima verba,* used by Christ. It was always supposed that Christ talked in Aramaic. Even Renan thought so. But now we know that the Galilean peasants, like the Irish peasants of our own day, were bilingual, and that Greek was the ordinary language of intercourse all over Palestine, as indeed all over the Eastern world. I never liked the idea that we knew of Christ's own words only through a translation of a translation. It is a delight to me to think that as far as his conversation was concerned, Charmides might have listened to him, and Socrates reasoned with him, and Plato understood him: That he really said ἐγώ εἰμι ὁ ποιμὴν ὁ καλός, that when the thought of the lilies of the field and how they neither toil nor spin, his absolute expression was καταμάθετε τὰ κρίνα τοῦ ἀγροῦ πως αὐξάνει οὐ κοπιᾷ οὐδὲ νήθει, and that his last word when he cried out "my life has been completed, has reached its fulfilment, has been perfected," was exactly as St. John tells us it was: τετέλεσται—no more.

While in reading the Gospels—particularly that of St. John himself, or whatever early Gnostic took his name and mantle—I see the continual assertion of the imagination as the basis of all spiritual and material life, I see also that to Christ imagination was simply a form of love, and that to him love was lord in the fullest meaning of the phrase. Some six weeks ago I was allowed by the doctor to have white bread to eat instead of the coarse black or brown bread of ordinary prison fare. It is a great delicacy. It will sound strange that dry bread could possibly be a delicacy to any one. To me it is so much so that at the close of each meal I carefully eat whatever crumbs may be left on my tin plate, or have fallen on the rough towel that one uses as a cloth so as not to soil one's table; and I do so not from hunger— I get now quite sufficient food—but simply in order that nothing should be wasted of what is given to me. So one should look on love.

Christ, like all fascinating personalities, had the power of not merely saying beautiful things himself, but of making other people say beautiful things to him; and I love the story St. Mark tells us about the Greek woman, who, when as a trial of her faith he said to her that he could not give her the bread of the children of Israel, answered him that the little dogs—(κυνάρια, "little dogs" it should be rendered)—who are under the table eat of the crumbs that the children let fall. Most people live for love and admiration. But it is by love and admiration that we should live. If any love is shown us we should recognise that we are quite unworthy of it. Nobody is worthy to be loved. The fact that God loves man shows us that in the divine order of ideal things it is written that eternal love is to be given to what is eternally unworthy. Or if that phrase seems to be a bitter one to bear, let us say that every one is worthy of love, except him who thinks that he is. Love is a sacrament that should be taken kneeling, and *Domine, non sum dignus* should be on the lips and in the hearts of those who receive it.

If ever I write again, in the sense of producing artistic work, there are just two subjects on which and through which I desire to express myself: one is "Christ as the precursor of the romantic movement in life": the other is "The artistic life considered in its relation to conduct." The first is, of course, intensely fascinating, for I see in Christ not merely the essentials of the supreme romantic type, but all the accidents, the wilfulness even, of the romantic temperament also. He was the first person who ever said to people that they should live "flower-like lives." He fixed the phrase. He took children as the type of what people should try to become. He held them up as examples to their elders, which I myself have always thought the chief use of children, if what is perfect should have a use. Dante describes the soul of a man as coming from the hand of God "weeping and laughing like a little child," and Christ also saw that the soul of each one should be a *guisa di fanciulla che piangendo e ridendo pargoleggia.* He felt that life was changeful, fluid, active, and that to allow it to be stereotyped into any form was death. He saw that people should not be too serious over material, common interests: that to be unpractical was to be a great thing: that one should not bother too much over affairs. "The birds didn't, why should man?" He is charming when he says, "Take no thought for the morrow; is not the soul more than meat? is not the body more than raiment?" A Greek might have used the latter phrase. It is full of Greek feeling. But only Christ could have said both, and so summed up life perfectly for us.

His morality is all sympathy, just what morality should be. If the only thing that he ever said had been, "Her sins are forgiven her because she loved much," it would have been worth while dying to have said it. His justice is all poetical justice, exactly what justice should be. The beggar goes to heaven because he has been unhappy. I cannot conceive a better reason for his being sent there. The people who work for an hour in the vineyard in the cool of the evening receive just as much reward as those who have toiled there all day long in the hot sun. Why shouldn't they? Probably no one deserved anything. Or perhaps they were a different kind of people. Christ had no patience with the dull lifeless mechanical systems that treat people as if they were things, and so treat everybody alike: for him there were no laws: there were exceptions merely, as if anybody, or anything, for that matter, was like aught else in the world!

That which is the very keynote of romantic art was to him the proper basis of natural life. He saw no other basis. And when they brought him one taken in the very act of sin and showed him her sentence written in the law, and asked him what was to be done, he wrote with his finger on the ground as though he did not hear them, and finally, when they pressed him again, looked up and said, "Let him of you who has never sinned be the first to throw the stone at her." It was worth while living to have said that.

Like all poetical natures he loved ignorant people. He knew that in the soul of one who is ignorant there is always room for a great idea. But he could not stand stupid people, especially those who are made stupid by education: people who are full of opinions not one of which they even understand, a peculiarly modern type, summed up by Christ when he describes it as the type of one who has the key of knowledge, cannot use it himself, and does not allow other people to use it, though it may be made to open the gate of God's Kingdom. His chief war was against the Philistines. That is the war every child of light has to wage. Philistinism was the note of the age and community in which he lived. In their heavy inaccessibility to ideas, their dull respectability, their tedious orthodoxy, their worship of vulgar success, their entire preoccupation with the gross materialistic side of life, and their ridiculous estimate of themselves and their importance, the Jews of Jerusalem in Christ's day were the exact counterpart of the British Philistine of our own. Christ mocked at the "whited sepulchre" of respectability, and fixed that phrase for ever. He treated worldly success as a thing absolutely to be despised. He saw nothing in it at all. He looked on wealth as an encumbrance to a man. He would not hear of life being sacrificed to any system of thought or morals. He pointed out that forms and ceremonies were made for man, not man for forms and ceremonies. He took sabbatarianism as a type of the things that should be set at nought. The cold philanthropies, the ostentatious public charities, the tedious formalisms so dear to the middle-class mind, he exposed with utter and relentless scorn. To us, what is termed orthodoxy is merely a facile unintelligent acquiescence; but to them, and in their hands, it was a terrible and paralysing tyranny. Christ swept it aside. He showed that the spirit alone was of value. He took a keen pleasure in pointing out to them that though they were always reading the law and the prophets, they had not really the smallest idea of what either of them meant. In opposition to their

tithing of each separate day into the fixed routine of pre-
scribed duties, as they tithe mint and rue, he preached the
enormous importance of living completely for the moment.

Those whom he saved from their sins are saved simply
for beautiful moments in their lives. Mary Magdalen, when
she sees Christ, breaks the rich vase of alabaster that one
of her seven lovers had given her, and spills the odorous
spices over his tired dusty feet, and for that one moment's
sake sits for ever with Ruth and Beatrice in the tresses of the
snow-white rose of Paradise. All that Christ says to us by
the way of a little warning is that every moment should be
beautiful, that the soul should always be ready for the coming of the bridegroom, always waiting for the voice of the
lover, Philistinism being simply that side of man's nature
that is not illumined by the imagination. He sees all the
lovely influences of life as modes of light: the imagination
itself is the world of light. The world is made by it, and yet
the world cannot understand it: that is because the imagination is simply a manifestation of love, and it is love and
the capacity for it that distinguishes one human being from
another.

But it is when he deals with a sinner that Christ is most
romantic, in the sense of most real. The world had always
loved the saint as being the nearest possible approach to the
perfection of God. Christ, through some divine instinct in
him, seems to have always loved the sinner as being the nearest possible approach to the perfection of man. His primary
desire was not to reform people, any more than his primary
desire was to relieve suffering. To turn an interesting thief
into a tedious honest man was not his aim. He would have
thought little of the Prisoners' Aid Society and other modern
movements of the kind. The conversion of a publican into a
Pharisee would not have seemed to him a great achievement.
But in a manner not yet understood of the world he re-

garded sin and suffering as being in themselves beautiful
holy things and modes of perfection.

It seems a very dangerous idea. It is—all great ideas are
dangerous. That it was Christ's creed admits of no doubt.
That it is the true creed I don't doubt myself.

Of course the sinner must repent. But why? Simply because otherwise he would be unable to realise what he had
done. The moment of repentance is the moment of initia-
tion. More than that: it is the means by which one alters
one's past. The Greeks thought that impossible. They often
say in their Gnomic aphorisms, "Even the Gods cannot alter
the past." Christ showed that the commonest sinner could
do it, that it was the one thing he could do. Christ, had he
been asked, would have said—I feel quite certain about it—
that the moment the prodigal son fell on his knees and wept,
he made his having wasted his substance with harlots, his
swine-herding and hungering for the husks they ate, beautiful and holy moments in his life. It is difficult for most
people to grasp the idea. I dare say one has to go to prison
to understand it. If so, it may be worth while going to
prison.

There is something so unique about Christ. Of course just
as there are false dawns before the dawn itself, and winter
days so full of sudden sunlight that they will cheat the wise
crocus into squandering its gold before its time, and make
some foolish bird call to its mate to build on barren boughs,
so there were Christians before Christ. For that we should
be grateful. The unfortunate thing is that there have been
none since. I make one exception, St. Francis of Assisi. But
then God had given him at his birth the soul of a poet,
as he himself when quite young had in mystical marriage
taken poverty as his bride: and with the soul of a poet and
the body of a beggar he found the way to perfection not difficult. He understood Christ, and so he became like him. We

do not require the Liber Conformitatum to teach us that the life of St. Francis was the true *Imitatio Christi,* a poem compared to which the book of that name is merely prose.

Indeed, that is the charm about Christ, when all is said: he is just like a work of art. He does not really teach one anything, but by being brought into his presence one becomes something. And everybody is predestined to his presence. Once at least in his life each man walks with Christ to Emmaus.

As regards the other subject, the Relation of the Artistic Life to Conduct, it will no doubt seem strange to you that I should select it. People point to Reading Gaol and say, "That is where the artistic life leads a man." Well, it might lead to worse places. The more mechanical people to whom life is a shrewd speculation depending on a careful calculation of ways and means, always know where they are going, and go there. They start with the ideal desire of being the parish beadle, and in whatever sphere they are placed they succeed in being the parish beadle and no more. A man whose desire is to be something separate from himself, to be a member of Parliament, or a successful grocer, or a prominent solicitor, or a judge, or something equally tedious, invariably succeeds in being what he wants to be. That is his punishment. Those who want a mask have to wear it.

But with the dynamic forces of life, and those in whom those dynamic forces become incarnate, it is different. People whose desire is solely for self-realisation never know where they are going. They can't know. In one sense of the word it is of course necessary as the Greek oracle said, to know oneself: that is the first achievement of knowledge. But to recognise that the soul of a man is unknowable, is the ultimate achievement of wisdom. The final mystery is oneself. When one has weighed the sun in the balance, and measured the steps of the moon, and mapped out the seven heavens star by star, there still remains oneself. Who can calculate the orbit of his own soul? When the son went out to look for his father's asses, he did not know that a man of God was waiting for him with the very chrism of coronation, and that his own soul was already the soul of a king.

I hope to live long enough and to produce work of such a character that I shall be able at the end of my days to say, "Yes! this is just where the artistic life leads a man!" Two of the most perfect lives I have come across in my own experience are the lives of Verlaine and of Prince Kropotkin: both of them men who have passed years in prison: the first, the one Christian poet since Dante; the other, a man with a soul of that beautiful white Christ which seems coming out of Russia. And for the last seven or eight months, in spite of a succession of great troubles reaching me from the outside world almost without intermission, I have been placed in direct contact with a new spirit working in this prison through man and things, that has helped me beyond any possibility of expression in words: so that while for the first year of my imprisonment I did nothing else, and can remember doing nothing else, but wring my hands in impotent despair, and say, "What an ending, what an appalling ending!" now I try to say to myself, and sometimes when I am not torturing myself do really and sincerely say, "What a beginning, what a wonderful beginning!" It may really be so. It may become so. If it does I shall owe much to this new personality that has altered every man's life in this place.

You may realise it when I say that had I been released last May, as I tried to be, I would have left this place loathing it and every official in it with a bitterness of hatred that would have poisoned my life. I have had a year longer of imprisonment, but humanity has been in the prison along with us all, and now when I go out I shall always remember great kindnesses that I have received here from almost everybody, and on the day of my release I shall give many thanks to many people, and ask to be remembered by them in turn.

The prison style is absolutely and entirely wrong. I would give anything to be able to alter it when I go out. I intend to try. But there is nothing in the world so wrong but that the spirit of humanity, which is the spirit of love, the spirit of the Christ who is not in churches, may make it, if not right, at least possible to be borne without too much bitterness of heart.

I know also that much is waiting for me outside that is very delightful, from what St. Francis of Assisi calls "my brother the wind, and my sister the rain," lovely things both of them, down to the shop-windows and sunsets of great cities. If I made a list of all that still remains to me, I don't know where I should stop; for, indeed, God made the world just as much for me as for any one else. Perhaps I may go out with something that I had not got before. I need not tell you that to me reformations in morals are as meaningless and vulgar as reformations in theology. But while to propose to be a better man is a piece of unscientific cant, to have become a deeper man is the privilege of those who have suffered. And such I think I have become.

If after I am free a friend of mine gave a feast, and did not invite me to it, I should not mind a bit. I can be perfectly happy by myself. With freedom, flowers, books, and the moon, who could not be perfectly happy? Besides, feasts are not for me any more. I have given too many to care about them. That side of life is over for me, very fortunately, I dare say. But if after I am free a friend of mine had a sorrow and refused to allow me to share it, I should feel it most bitterly. If he shut the doors of the house of mourning against me, I would come back again and again and beg to be admitted, so that I might share in what I was entitled to share in. If he thought me unworthy, unfit to weep with him, I should feel it as the most poignant humiliation, as the most terrible mode in which disgrace could be inflicted on me. But that could not be. I have a right to share in sorrow, and he who can look at the loveliness of the world and share its sorrow, and realise something of the wonder of both, is in immediate contact with divine things, and has got as near to God's secret as any one can get.

Perhaps there may come into my art also, no less than into my life, a still deeper note, one of greater unity of passion, and directness of impulse. Not width but intensity is the true aim of modern art. We are no longer in art concerned with the type. It is with the exception that we have to do. I cannot put my sufferings into any form they took, I need hardly say. Art only begins where Imitation ends, but something must come into my work, of fuller memory of words perhaps, of richer cadences, of more curious effects, of simpler architectural order, of some æsthetic quality at any rate.

When Marsyas was "torn from the scabbard of his limbs" —*della vagina della membra sue,* to use one of Dante's most terrible Tacitean phrases—he had no more song, the Greek said. Apollo had been victor. The lyre had vanquished the reed. But perhaps the Greeks were mistaken. I hear in much modern Art the cry of Marsyas. It is bitter in Baudelaire, sweet and plaintive in Lamartine, mystic in Verlaine. It is in the deferred resolutions of Chopin's music. It is in the discontent that haunts Burne-Jones's women. Even Matthew Arnold, whose song of Callicles tells of "the triumph of the sweet persuasive lyre," and the "famous final victory," in such a clear note of lyrical beauty, has not a little of it; in the troubled undertone of doubt and distress that haunts his verses, neither Goethe nor Wordsworth could help him, though he followed each in turn, and when he seeks to mourn for *Thyrsis* or to sing of the *Scholar Gipsy,* it is the reed that he has to take for the rendering of his strain. But whether or not the Phrygian Faun was silent, I cannot be. Expression is as necessary to me as leaf and blossoms are to the black branches of the trees that show themselves about the prison walls and are so restless in the wind. Between my art and the world there is now a wide gulf, but between art and myself there is none. I hope at least that there is none.

To each of us different fates are meted out. My lot has been one of public infamy, of long imprisonment, of misery, of ruin, of disgrace, but I am not worthy of it—not yet, at any rate. I remember that I used to say that I thought I could bear a real tragedy if it came to me with purple pall and a mask of noble sorrow, but that the dreadful thing about modernity was that it put tragedy into the raiment of comedy, so that the great realities seemed commonplace or grotesque or lacking in style. It is quite true about modernity. It has probably always been true about actual life. It is said that all martyrdoms seemed mean to the looker on. The nineteenth century is no exception to the rule.

Everything about my tragedy has been hideous, mean, repellent, lacking in style; our very dress makes us grotesque. We are the zanies of sorrow. We are clowns whose hearts are broken. We are specially designed to appeal to the sense of humour. On November 13th, 1895, I was brought down here from London. From two o'clock till half-past two on that day I had to stand on the centre platform of Clapham Junction in convict dress, and handcuffed, for the world to look at. I had been taken out of the hospital ward without a moment's notice being given to me. Of all possible objects I was the most grotesque. When people saw me they laughed. Each train as it came up swelled the audience. Nothing could exceed their amusement. That was, of course, before they knew who I was. As soon as they had been informed they laughed still more. For half an hour I stood there in the grey November rain surrounded by a jeering mob.

For a year after that was done to me I wept every day at the same hour and for the same space of time. That is not such a tragic thing as possibly it sounds to you. To those who are in prison tears are a part of every day's experience. A day in prison on which one does not weep is a day on which one's heart is hard, not a day on which one's heart is happy.

Well, now I am really beginning to feel more regret for the people who laughed than for myself. Of course when they saw me I was not on my pedestal, I was in the pillory. But it is a very unimaginative nature that only cares for people on their pedestals. A pedestal may be a very unreal thing. A pillory is a terrific reality. They should have known also how to interpret sorrow better. I have said that behind sorrow there is always sorrow. It were wiser still to say that behind sorrow there is always a soul. And to mock at a soul in pain is a dreadful thing. In the strangely simple economy of the world people only get what they give, and to those who have not enough imagination to penetrate the mere outward of things, and feel pity, what pity can be given save that of scorn?

I write this account of the mode of my being transferred here simply that it should be realised how hard it has been for me to get anything out of my punishment but bitterness and despair. I have, however, to do it, and now and then I have moments of submission and acceptance. All the spring may be hidden in the single bud, and the low ground nest of the lark may hold the joy that is to herald the feet of many rose-red dawns. So perhaps whatever beauty of life still remains to me is contained in some moment of surrender, abasement, and humiliation. I can, at any rate, merely proceed on the lines of my own development, and, accepting all that has happened to me, make myself worthy of it.

People used to say of me that I was too individualistic. I must be far more of an individualist than ever I was. I must get far more out of myself than ever I got, and ask for less of the world than ever I asked. Indeed, my ruin came not from too great individualism of life, but from too little. The one disgraceful, unpardonable, and to all time contemptible action of my life was to allow myself to appeal to society for help and protection. To have made such an appeal would have been from the individualist point of view bad enough, but what excuse can there ever be put forward for having made it? Of course once I had put into motion the forces of society, society turned on me and said, "Have you been living all this time in defiance of my laws, and do you now appeal to those laws for protection? You shall have those laws exercised to the full. You shall abide by what you have appealed to." The result is I am in gaol. Certainly no man ever fell so ignobly, and by such ignoble instruments, as I did. I say in *Dorian Gray* somewhere that "A man cannot be too careful in the choice of his enemies." I little thought that it was by a pariah I was to be made a pariah myself.

The Philistine element in life is not the failure to understand art. Charming people such as fishermen, shepherds, ploughboys, peasants and the like, know nothing about art, and are the very salt of the earth. He is the Philistine who upholds and aids the heavy, cumbrous, blind, mechanical forces of society, and who does not recognise dynamic force when he meets it either in a man or a movement.

People thought it dreadful of me to have entertained at dinner the evil things of life, and to have found pleasure in their company. But then, from the point of view through which I, as an artist in life, approach them they were delightfully suggestive and stimulating. It was like feasting with panthers; the danger was half the excitement. I used to feel as a snake-charmer must feel when he lures the cobra to stir from the painted cloth or reed basket that holds it and makes it spread its hood at his bidding and sway to and fro in the air as a plant sways restfully in a stream. They were to me the brightest of gilded snakes, their poison was part of their perfection. I did not know that when they were to strike at me it was to be at another's piping and at another's pay. I don't feel at all ashamed at having known them, they were intensely interesting; what I do feel ashamed of is the horrible Philistine atmosphere into which I was brought. My business as an artist was with Ariel, I set myself to wrestle with Caliban. Instead of making beautiful coloured musical things such as *Salomé* and *The Florentine Tragedy* and *La Sainte Courtisane* I forced myself to send long lawyer's letters and was constrained to appeal to the very things against which I had always protested. Clibborn and Atkins were wonderful in their infamous war against life. To entertain them was an astounding adventure; Dumas *père,* Cellini, Goya, Edgar Allan Poe, or Baudelaire would have done just the same. What is loathsome to me is the memory of interminable visits paid by me to the solicitor H——, when in the ghastly glare of a bleak room I would sit with a serious face telling serious lies to a bald man till I really groaned and yawned with ennui. There is where I found myself, right in the centre of Philistia. away from everything that was beautiful or brilliant or wonderful or daring. I had come forward as the champion of respectability in conduct, of puritanism in life, and of morality in art. *Voilà où menent les mauvais chemins* . . . but I can think with gratitude of those who by kindness without stint, devotion without limit, cheerfulness and joy in giving have lightened my black burden for me, have visited me again and again, have written to me beautiful and sympathetic letters, have managed my affairs for me arranged my future life. and stood by me in the teeth of

obloquy, taunt and open sneer, or insult even. I owe every·
thing to them. The very books in my cell are paid for by
——— out of his pocket-money; from the same sources are to
come clothes for me when I am released. I am not ashamed
of taking a thing that is given in love and affection; I am
proud of it. Yes, I think of my friends, such as More Adey,
R——, Robert Sherard, Frank Harris, Arthur Clifton, and
what they have been to me, in giving me help, affection, and
sympathy. I think of every single person who has been kind
to me in my prison life down to the warder who gives me a
"Good-morning" and a "Good-night" (not one of his pre-
scribed duties) down to the common policemen who, in their
homely, rough way strove to comfort me on my journeys to
and fro from the Bankruptcy Court under conditions of
terrible mental distress—down to the poor thief who recog-
nising me as we tramped round the yard at Wandsworth,
whispered to me in the hoarse prison voice men get from
long and compulsory silence: "I am sorry for you; it is
harder for the likes of you than it is for the likes of us."

A great friend of mine—a friend of ten years' standing—
came to see me some time ago, and told me that he did not
believe a single word of what was said against me, and
wished me to know that he considered me quite innocent,
and the victim of a hideous plot. I burst into tears at what
he said, and told him that while there was much amongst
the definite charges that was quite untrue and transferred to
me by revolting malice, still that my life had been full of
perverse pleasures, and that unless he accepted that as a
fact about me and realised it to the full I could not possibly
be friends with him any more, or ever be in his company.
It was a terrible shock to him, but we are friends, and I
have not got his friendship on false pretences. I have said
to you to speak the truth is a painful thing. To be forced
to tell lies is much worse.

I remember that as I was sitting in the Dock on the occasion of my last trial listening to Lockwood's appalling denunciation of me—like a thing out of Tacitus, like a passage in Dante, like one of Savonarola's indictments of the Popes of Rome—and being sickened with horror at what I heard. Suddenly it occurred to me, *How splendid it would be, if I was saying all this about myself.* I saw then at once that what is said of a man is nothing. The point is, who says it. A man's very highest moment is, I have no doubt at all, when he kneels in the dust, and beats his breast, and tells all the sins of his life.

Emotional forces, as I say somewhere in *Intentions,* are as limited in extent and duration as the forces of physical energy. The little cup that is made to hold so much can hold so much and no more, though all the purple vats of Burgundy be filled with wine to the brim, and the treaders stand knee-deep in the gathered grapes of the stony vineyards of Spain. There is no error more common than that of thinking that those who are the causes or occasions of great tragedies share in the feelings suitable to the tragic mood: no error more fatal than expecting it of them. The martyr in his "shirt of flame" may be looking on the face of God, but to him who is piling the faggots or loosening the logs for the blast the whole scene is no more than the slaying of an ox is to the butcher, or the felling of a tree to the charcoal burner in the forest, or the fall of a flower to one who is mowing down the grass with a scythe. Great passions are for the great of soul, and great events can be seen only by those who are on a level with them. We think we can have our emotions for nothing. We cannot. Even the finest and the most self-sacrificing emotions have to be paid for. Strangely enough, that is what makes them fine. The intellectual and emotional life of ordinary people is a very contemptible affair. Just as they borrow their ideas from a sort of circulating library of thought—the *Zeitgeist* of an age that has no soul and send them back soiled at the end of each week—so they always try to get their emotions on credit, or refuse to pay the bill when it comes in. We must pass out of that conception of life; as soon as we have to pay for an emotion we shall know its quality and be the better for such knowledge. Remember that the sentimentalist is always a cynic at heart. Indeed sentimentality is merely the Bank-holiday of cynicism. And delightful as cynicism is from its intellectual side, now that it has left the tub for the club, it never can be more than the perfect philosophy for a man who has no soul. It has its social value; and to an artist all modes of expression are interesting, but in itself it is a poor affair, for to the true cynic nothing is ever revealed.

. . . . .

I know of nothing in all drama more incomparable from the point of view of art, nothing more suggestive in its sub-tlety of observation, than Shakespeare's drawing of Rosen-crantz and Guildenstern. They are Hamlet's college friends. They have been his companions. They bring with them memories of pleasant days together. At the moment when they come across him in the play he is staggering under the weight of a burden intolerable to one of his temperament. The dead have come armed out of the grave to impose on him a mission at once too great and too mean for him. He is a dreamer, and he is called upon to act. He has the nature of the poet, and he is asked to grapple with the common com-plexity of cause and effect, with life in its practical realisa-tion, of which he knows nothing, not with life in its ideal essence, of which he knows so much. He has no conception of what to do, and his folly is to feign folly. Brutus used mad-ness as a cloak to conceal the sword of his purpose, the dagger of his will, but the Hamlet madness is a mere mask for the hiding of weakness. In the making of fancies and jests he sees a chance of delay. He keeps playing with action as an artist plays with a theory. He makes himself the spy of his proper actions and listening to his own words knows them to be but "words, words, words." Instead of trying to be the hero of his own history, he seeks to be the spectator of his own tragedy. He disbelieves in everything including himself, and yet his doubt helps him not, as it comes not from scepticism but from a divided will.

Of all this Guildenstern and Rosencrantz realise nothing. They bow and smirk and smile, and what the one says the other echoes with sickliest intonation. When, at last, by means of the play within the play, and the puppets in their dalliance, Hamlet "catches the conscience" of the King, and drives the wretched man in terror from his throne, Guildenstern and Rosencrantz see no more in his conduct than a rather painful breach of Court etiquette. That is as far as they can attain to in "the contemplation of the spectacle of life with appropriate emotions." They are close to his very secret and know nothing of it. Nor would there be any use in telling them. They are the little cups that can hold so much and no more. Towards the close it is suggested that, caught in a cunning spring set for another, they have met, or may meet, with a violent and sudden death. But a tragic ending of this kind, though touched by Hamlet's humour with something of the surprise and justice of comedy, is really not for such as they. They never die. Horatio, who in order to "report Hamlet and his cause aright to the unsatisfied,"

"Absents him from felicity a while,
  And in this harsh world draws his breath in pain,"

dies, though not before an audience and leaves no brother. But Guildenstern and Rosencrantz are as immortal as Angelo and Tartuffe, and should rank with them. They are what

THE PICTURE OF DORIAN GRAY

AND

DE PROFUNDIS

BY OSCAR WILDE

A quarter of a century ago *The Picture of Dorian Gray* was discussed furtively and in whispers as a book of sinister meaning and frightening moral consequences. Today, when its theme of decadence is a matter of general knowledge, it is regarded as Oscar Wilde's most scintillating, and certainly his most popular, work. Dealing as it does with the radiance and corruption of a pampered youth, it is written in Oscar Wilde's most dazzling manner, full of stinging epigrams, shrewd observations and a nimble, sharp-barbed wit.

LOOK INSIDE JACKET ▶

BRON, FRANCIS, *Selected Writings of* 296

BALZAC, *Droll Stories* 193
BALZAC, *Père Goriot and Eugénie Grandet* 245
BEERBOHM, MAX, *Zuleika Dobson* 116
BELLAMY, EDWARD, *Looking Backward* 22
BENNETT, ARNOLD, *The Old Wives' Tale* 184
BERGSON, HENRI, *Creative Evolution* 231
BLAKE, WILLIAM, *Selected Poetry and Prose of* 285
BOCCACCIO, *The Decameron* 71
BOSWELL, JAMES, *Life of Samuel Johnson* 282
BRONTË, CHARLOTTE, *Jane Eyre* 64
BRONTË, EMILY, *Wuthering Heights* 106
BROWNING, ROBERT, *Selected Poetry of* 198
BUCK, PEARL, *The Good Earth* 15
BURCKHARDT, JACOB, *The Civilization of the Renaissance in Italy* 32
BURK, JOHN N., *Life and Works of Beethoven* 241
BUTLER, SAMUEL, *Erewhon & Erewhon Revisited* 136
BUTLER, SAMUEL, *The Way of All Flesh* 13
BYRON, LORD, *The Selected Poetry of* 195
BYRON, LORD, *Don Juan* 24
CAESAR, JULIUS, *The Gallic War and Other Writings of* 295
CALDWELL, ERSKINE, *God's Little Acre* 51
CALDWELL, ERSKINE, *Tobacco Road* 249
CANFIELD, DOROTHY, *The Deepening Stream* 200
CARROLL, LEWIS, *Alice in Wonderland, etc.* 79
CASANOVA, JACQUES, *Memoirs of* 165
CELLINI, BENVENUTO, *Autobiography* 150
CERVANTES, *Don Quixote* 174
CHAUCER, *The Canterbury Tales* 161
CHEKHOV, ANTON, *Best Plays by* 171
CHEKHOV, ANTON, *The Short Stories of* 50
CICERO, *The Basic Works of* 272
COLERIDGE, *Selected Poetry and Prose of* 279
COMMAGER, HENRY STEELE & NEVINS, ALLAN, *A Short History of the United States* 235
CONFUCIUS, *The Wisdom of* 7
CONRAD, JOSEPH, *Lord Jim* 186
CONRAD, JOSEPH, *Nostromo* 275
CONRAD, JOSEPH, *Victory* 34
COOPER, JAMES FENIMORE, *The Pathfinder* 105
CORNEILLE & RACINE, *Six Plays of* 194
CORVO, FREDERICK BARON, *A History of the Borgias* 192
CRANE, STEPHEN, *The Red Badge of Courage* 130
CUMMINGS, E. E., *The Enormous Room* 214
DANA, RICHARD HENRY, *Two Years Before the Mast* 236
DANTE, *The Divine Comedy* 208
DA VINCI, LEONARDO, *The Notebooks of* 156
DEFOE, DANIEL, *Moll Flanders* 122
DEFOE, DANIEL, *Robinson Crusoe & A Journal of the Plague Year* 92
DESCARTES, RENE, *Philosophical Writings* 43
DEWEY, JOHN, *Human Nature and Conduct* 173
DICKENS, CHARLES, *David Copperfield* 110
DICKENS, CHARLES, *Pickwick Papers* 204
DICKENS, CHARLES, *A Tale of Two Cities* 189
DICKINSON, EMILY, *Selected Poems of* 25

This Is a Complete

modern life has contributed to the antique ideal of friendship. He who writes a new *De Amicitia* must find a niche for them, and praise them in Tusculan prose. They are types fixed for all time. To censure them would show "a lack of appreciation." They are merely out of their sphere: that is all. In sublimity of soul there is no contagion. High thoughts and high emotions are by their very existence isolated.

I am to be released, if all goes well with me, towards the end of May, and hope to go at once to some little seaside village abroad with R—— and M——.

The sea, as Euripides says in one of his plays about Iphigenia, washes away the stains and wounds of the world.

I hope to be at least a month with my friends, and to gain peace and balance, and a less troubled heart, and a sweeter mood; and then if I feel able I shall arrange through R—— to go to some quiet foreign town like Bruges whose grey houses and green canals and cool still ways had a charm for me years ago. I have a strange longing for the great simple primeval things, such as the sea, to me no less of a mother than the Earth. It seems to me that we all look at Nature too much, and live with her too little. I discern great sanity in the Greek attitude. They never chattered about sunsets, or discussed whether the shadows on the grass were really mauve or not. But they saw that the sea was for the swimmer, and the sand for the feet of the runner. They loved the trees for the shadow that they cast, and the forest for its silence at noon. The vineyard-dresser wreathed his hair with ivy that he might keep off the rays of the sun as he stooped over the young shoots, and for the artist and the athlete, the two types that Greece gave us, they plaited with garlands the leaves of the bitter laurel and of the wild parsley, which else had been of no service to men.

We call ours a utilitarian age, and we do not know the uses of any single thing. We have forgotten that water can cleanse, and fire purify, and that the Earth is mother to us all. As a consequence our art is of the moon and plays with shadows, while Greek art is of the sun and deals directly with things. I feel sure that in elemental forces there is purification, and I want to go back to them and live in their presence.

.   .   .   .   .

It is not for nothing or to no purpose that in my lifelong cult of literature I have made myself

"Miser of sound and syllable, no less
Than Midas of his coinage."

I must not be afraid of the past; if people tell me that it is irrevocable I shall not believe them; the past, the present, and the future are one moment in the sight of God, in whose sight we should try to live. Time and space, succession and extension, are merely accidental conditions of thought, the imagination can transcend them and move in a free sphere of ideal existences. Things also are in their essence of what we choose to make them; a thing *is* according to the mode in which we look at it. "Where others," says Blake, "see but the dawn coming over the hill, I see the sons of God shouting for joy." What seemed to the world and to myself my future I lost when I allowed myself to be taunted into taking action against Queensberry; I daresay I lost it really long before that. What lies before me is my past. I have got to make myself look on that with different eyes, to make God look on it with different eyes. This I cannot do by ignoring it, or slighting it, or praising it, or denying it; it is only to be done by accepting it as an inevitable part of the evolution of my life and character: by bowing my head to everything I have suffered. How far I am away from the true temper of soul, this letter in its changing uncertain moods, its scorn and bitterness, its aspirations and its failure to realise those aspirations, show quite clearly; but do not forget in what a terrible school I am sitting at my task, and incomplete, imperfect as I am, my friends have still much to gain. They came to me to learn the pleasure of life and the pleasure of art. Perhaps I am chosen to teach them something more wonderful, the meaning of sorrow and its beauty.

Of course to one so modern as I am, "enfant de mon siècle," merely to look at the world will be always lovely. I tremble with pleasure when I think that on the very day of my leaving prison both the laburnum and the lilac will be blooming in the gardens, and that I shall see the wind stir into restless beauty the swaying gold of the one, and make the other toss the pale purple of its plumes so that all the air shall be Arabia for me. Linnæus fell on his knees and wept for joy when he saw for the first time the long heath of some English upland made yellow with the tawny aromatic blossoms of the common furze; and I know that for me, to whom flowers are part of desire, there are tears waiting in the petals of some rose. It has always been so with me from my boyhood. There is not a single colour hidden away in the chalice of a flower, or the curve of a shell, to which, by some subtle sympathy with the very soul of things, my nature does not answer. Like Gautier, I have always been one of those "pour qui le monde visible existe."

Still, I am conscious now that behind all this beauty, satisfying though it may be, there is some spirit hidden of which the painted forms and shapes are but modes of manifestation, and it is with this spirit that I desire to become in harmony. I have grown tired of the articulate utterances of men and things. The Mystical in Art, the Mystical in Life, the Mystical in Nature—this is what I am looking for. It is absolutely necessary for me to find it somewhere.

All trials are trials for one's life, just as all sentences are

sentences of death; and three times have I been tried. The first
time I left the box to be arrested, the second time to be led
back to the house of detention, the third time to pass into a
prison for two years. Society, as we have constituted it, will
have no place for me, has none to offer; but Nature, whose
sweet rains fall on unjust and just alike, will have clefts in
the rocks where I may hide, and secret valleys in whose silence
I may weep undisturbed. She will hang the night with stars
so that I may walk abroad in the darkness without stumbling,
and send the wind over my footprints so that none may track
me to my hurt: she will cleanse me in great waters, and with
bitter herbs make me whole.

TWO LETTERS TO THE "DAILY CHRONICLE" ON PRISON LIFE

I. THE CASE OF WARDER MARTIN: SOME CRUELTIES OF PRISON LIFE [1]

The Editor of the "Daily Chronicle"

SIR,—I learn with great regret, through the columns of your paper, that the warder Martin, of Reading Prison, has been dismissed by the Prison Commissioners for having given some sweet biscuits to a little hungry child. I saw the three children myself on the Monday preceding my release. They had just been convicted, and were standing in a row in the central hall in their prison dress, carrying their sheets under their arms previous to their being sent to the cells allotted to them. I happened to be passing along one of the galleries on my way to the reception room, where I was to have an interview with a friend. They were quite small children, the youngest—the one to whom the warder gave the biscuits—being a tiny little chap, for whom they had evidently been unable to find clothes small enough to fit. I had, of course, seen many children in prison during the two years during which I was myself confined. Wandsworth Prison especially contained always a large number of children. But the little child I saw on the afternoon of Monday, the 17th, at Reading, was tinier than any one of them. I need not say how utterly distressed I was to see these children at Reading, for I knew the treatment in store for them. The cruelty that is practised by day and night on children in English prisons is

[1] May 28, 1897.

incredible, except to those that have witnessed it and are aware of the brutality of the system.

People nowadays do not understand what cruelty is. They regard it as a sort of terrible mediæval passion, and connect it with the race of men like Eccelin da Romano, and others, to whom the deliberate infliction of pain gave a real madness of pleasure. But men of the stamp of Eccelin are merely abnormal types of perverted individualism. Ordinary cruelty is simply stupidity. It is the entire want of imagination. It is the result in our days of stereotyped systems, of hard-and-fast rules, and of stupidity. Wherever there is centralisation there is stupidity. What is inhuman in modern life is officialism. Authority is as destructive to those who exercise it as it is to those on whom it is exercised. It is the Prison Board, and the system that it carries out, that is the primary source of the cruelty that is exercised on a child in prison. The people who uphold the system have excellent intentions. Those who carry it out are humane in intention also. Responsibility is shifted on to the disciplinary regulations. It is supposed that because a thing is the rule it is right.

The present treatment of children is terrible, primarily from people not understanding the peculiar psychology of a child's nature. A child can understand a punishment inflicted by an individual, such as a parent or guardian, and bear it with a certain amount of acquiescence. What it cannot understand is a punishment inflicted by society. It cannot realise what society is. With grown people it is, of course, the reverse. Those of us who are either in prison or have been sent there, can understand, and do understand, what that collective force called society means, and whatever we may think of its methods or claims, we can force ourselves to accept it. Punishment inflicted on us by an individual, on the other hand, is a thing that no grown person endures, or is expected to endure.

The child consequently, being taken away from its parents by people whom it has never seen, and of whom it knows nothing, and finding itself in a lonely and unfamiliar cell, waited on by strange faces, and ordered about and punished by the representatives of a system that it cannot understand, becomes an immediate prey to the first and most prominent emotion produced by modern prison life—the emotion of terror. The terror of a child in prison is quite limitless. I remember once in Reading, as I was going out to exercise, seeing in the dimly lit cell right opposite my own a small boy. Two warders—not unkindly men—were talking to him, with some sternness apparently, or perhaps giving him some useful advice about his conduct. One was in the cell with him, the other was standing outside. The child's face was like a white wedge of sheer terror. There was in his eyes the terror of a hunted animal. The next morning I heard him at breakfast-time crying, and calling to be let out. His cry was for his parents. From time to time I could hear the deep voice of the warder on duty telling him to keep quiet. Yet he was not even convicted of whatever little offence he had been charged with. He was simply on remand. That I knew by his wearing his own clothes, which seemed neat enough. He was, however, wearing prison socks and shoes. This showed that he was a very poor boy, whose own shoes, if he had any, were in a bad state. Justices and magistrates, an entirely ignorant class as a rule, often remand children for a week, and then perhaps remit whatever sentence they are entitled to pass. They call this "not sending a child to prison." It is, of course, a stupid view on their part. To a little child, whether he is in prison on remand or after conviction is not a subtlety of social position he can comprehend. To him the horrible thing is to be there at all. In the eyes of humanity it should be a horrible thing for him to be there at all.

This terror that seizes and dominates the child, as it seizes the grown man also, is of course intensified beyond power of expression by the solitary cellular system of our prisons. Every child is confined to its cell for twenty-three hours out of the twenty-four. This is the appalling thing. To shut up a child in a dimly lit cell, for twenty-three hours out of the twenty-four, is an example of the cruelty of stupidity. If an individual, parent or guardian, did this to a child, he would be severely punished. The Society for the Prevention of Cruelty to Children would take the matter up at once. There would be on all hands the utmost detestation of whomsoever had been guilty of such cruelty. A heavy sentence would, undoubtedly, follow conviction. But our own actual society does worse itself, and to the child to be so treated by a strange abstract force, of whose claims it has no cognisance, is much worse than it would be to receive the same treatment from its father or mother, or some one it knew. The inhuman treatment of a child is always inhuman, by whomsoever it is inflicted. But inhuman treatment by society is to the child the more terrible because there is no appeal. A parent or guardian can be moved, and let out a child from the dark lonely room in which it is confined. But a warder cannot. Most warders are very fond of children. But the system prohibits them from rendering the child any assistance. Should they do so, as Warder Martin did, they are dismissed.

The second thing from which a child suffers in prison is hunger. The food that is given to it consists of a piece of usually badly-baked prison bread and a tin of water for breakfast at half-past seven. At twelve o'clock it gets dinner, composed of a tin of coarse Indian meal stirabout; and at half-past five it gets a piece of dry bread and a tin of water for its supper. This diet in the case of a strong grown man is always productive of illness of some kind, chiefly, of course, diarrhœa, with its attendant weakness. In fact, in a big prison astringent medicines are served out regularly by the warders as a matter of course. In the case of a child, the child is, as a rule, incapable of eating the food at all. Any one who knows anything about children knows how easily a child's digestion is upset by a fit of crying, or trouble and mental distress of any kind. A child who has been crying all day long, and perhaps half the night, in a lonely dimly lit cell, and is preyed upon by terror, simply cannot eat food of this coarse, horrible kind. In the case of the little child to whom Warder Martin gave the biscuits, the child was crying with hunger on Tuesday morning, and utterly unable to eat the bread and water served to it for its breakfast. Martin went out after the breakfasts had been served, and bought the few sweet biscuits for the child rather than see it starving. It was a beautiful action on his part, and was so recognised by the child, who, utterly unconscious of the regulation of the Prison Board, told one of the senior warders how kind this junior warder had been to him. The result was, of course, a report and a dismissal.

I know Martin extremely well, and I was under his charge for the last seven weeks of my imprisonment. On his appointment at Reading he had charge of Gallery C, in which I was confined, so I saw him constantly. I was struck by the singular kindness and humanity of the way in which he spoke to me and to the other prisoners. Kind words are much in prison, and a pleasant "Good-morning" or "Good-evening" will make one as happy as one can be in a prison. He was always gentle and considerate. I happen to know another case in which he showed great kindness to one of the prisoners, and I have no hesitation in mentioning it. One of the most horrible things in prison is the badness of the sanitary arrangements. No prisoner is allowed under any circumstances to leave his cell after half-past five P. M. If, consequently, he is suffering from diarrhœa, he has to use his cell as a latrine, and pass the night in a most fetid and unwholesome atmosphere. Some days before my release Martin was going the rounds at half-past seven with one of the senior warders for the purpose of collecting the oakum and tools of the prisoners. A man just convicted, and suffering from violent diarrhœa in consequence of the food, as is always the case, asked the senior warder to allow him to empty the slops in his cell on account of the horrible odour of the cell and the possibility of illness again in the night. The senior warder refused absolutely; it was against the rules. The man had to pass the night in this dreadful condition. Martin, however, rather than see this wretched man in such a loathsome pre-dicament, said he would empty the man's slops himself, and did so. A warder emptying a prisoner's slops is, of course, against the rules, but Martin did this act of kindness to the man out of the simple humanity of his nature, and the man was naturally most grateful.

As regards the children, a great deal has been talked and written lately about the contaminating influence of prison on young children. What is said is quite true. A child is utterly contaminated by prison life. But the contaminating influence is not that of the prisoners. It is that of the whole prison sys-tem—of the governor, the chaplain, the warders, the lonely cell, the isolation, the revolting food, the rules of the Prison Commissioners, the mode of discipline as it is termed, of the life. Every care is taken to isolate a child from the sight even of all prisoners over sixteen years of age. Children sit behind a curtain in chapel, and are sent to take exercise in small sun-less yards—sometimes a stone-yard, sometimes a yard at the back of the mills—rather than that they should see the elder prisoners at exercise. But the only really humanising influ-ence in prison is the influence of the prisoners. Their cheer-fulness under terrible circumstances, their sympathy for each other, their humility, their gentleness, their pleasant smiles of greeting when they meet each other, their complete acquiescence in their punishments, are all quite wonderful, and I myself learnt many sound lessons from them. I am not proposing that the children should not sit behind a curtain in chapel, or that they should take exercise in a corner of the common yard. I am merely pointing out that the bad influence on children is not, and could never be, that of the prisoners, but is, and will always remain, that of the prison system itself. There is not a single man in Reading Gaol that would not gladly have done the three children's punishment for them. When I saw them last it was on the Tuesday following their conviction. I was taking exercise at half-past eleven with about twelve other men, as the three children passed near us, in charge of a warder, from the damp, dreary stoneyard in which they had been at their exercise. I saw the greatest pity and sympathy in the eyes of my companions as they looked at them. Prisoners are, as a class, extremely kind and sympathetic to each other. Suffering and the community of suffering makes people kind, and day after day as I tramped the yard I used to feel with pleasure and comfort what Carlyle calls somewhere "the silent rhythmic charm of human companionship." In this, as in all other things, philanthropists and people of that kind are astray. It is not the prisoners who need reformation. It is the prisons.

Of course no child under fourteen years of age should be sent to prison at all. It is an absurdity, and, like many absurdities, of absolutely tragic results. If, however, they are to be sent to prison, during the daytime they should be in a workshop or schoolroom with a warder. At night they should sleep in a dormitory, with a night-warder to look after them. They should be allowed exercise for at least three hours a day. The dark, badly ventilated, ill-smelling prison cells are dreadful for a child, dreadful indeed for any one. One is always breathing bad air in prison. The food given to children should consist of tea and bread-and-butter and soup

Prison soup is very good and wholesome. A resolution of the House of Commons could settle the treatment of children in half an hour. I hope you will use your influence to have this done. The way that children are treated at present is really an outrage on humanity and common sense. It comes from stupidity.

Let me draw attention now to another terrible thing that goes on in English prisons, indeed in prisons all over the world where the system of silence and cellular confinement is practised. I refer to the large number of men who become insane or weak-minded in prison. In convict prisons this is, of course, quite common; but in ordinary gaols also, such as that I was confined in, it is to be found.

About three months ago I noticed amongst the prisoners who took exercise with me a young man who seemed to me to be silly or half-witted. Every prison, of course, has its half-witted clients, who return again and again, and may be said to live in the prison. But this young man struck me as being more than usually half-witted on account of his silly grin and idiotic laughter to himself, and the peculiar restlessness of his eternally twitching hands. He was noticed by all the other prisoners on account of the strangeness of his conduct. From time to time he did not appear at exercise, which showed me that he was being punished by confinement to his cell. Finally, I discovered that he was under observation, and being watched night and day by warders. When he did appear at exercise he always seemed hysterical, and used to walk round crying or laughing. At chapel he had to sit right under the observation of two warders, who carefully watched him all the time. Sometimes he would bury his head in his hands, an offence against the chapel regulations, and his head would be immediately struck up by a warder so that he should keep his eyes fixed permanently in the direction of the Communion-table. Sometimes he would cry—not making any disturbance—but with tears streaming down his face and a hysterical throbbing in the throat. Sometimes he would grin idiot-like to himself and make faces. He was on more than one occasion sent out of chapel to his cell, and of course he was continually punished. As the bench on which I used to sit in chapel was directly behind the bench at the end of which this unfortunate man was placed I had full opportunity of observing him. I also saw him, of course, at exercise continually, and I saw that he was becoming insane, and was being treated as if he was shamming.

On Saturday week last I was in my cell at about one o'clock occupied in cleaning and polishing the tins I had been using for dinner. Suddenly I was startled by the prison silence being broken by the most horrible and revolting shrieks, or rather howls, for at first I thought some animal like a bull or a cow was being unskilfully slaughtered outside the prison walls. I soon realised, however, that the howls proceeded from the basement of the prison, and I knew that some wretched man was being flogged. I need not say how hideous and terrible it was for me, and I began to wonder who it was who was being punished in this revolting manner. Suddenly it dawned upon me that they might be flogging this unfortunate lunatic. My feelings on the subject need not be chronicled; they have nothing to do with the question.

The next day, Sunday 16th, I saw the poor fellow at exercise, his weak, ugly, wretched face bloated by tears and hysteria almost beyond recognition. He walked in the centre ring along with the old men, the beggars, and the lame people, so that I was able to observe him the whole time. It was my last Sunday in prison, a perfectly lovely day, the finest day we had had the whole year, and there, in the beautiful sunlight, walked this poor creature—made once in the image of God—grinning like an ape, and making with his hands the most fantastic gestures, as though he was playing in the air on some invisible stringed instrument, or arranging and dealing counters in some curious game. All the while these hysterical tears, without which none of us ever saw him, were making soiled runnels on his white swollen face. The hideous and deliberate grace of his gestures made him like an antic. He was a living grotesque. The other prisoners all watched him, and not one of them smiled. Everybody knew what had happened to him, and that he was being driven insane—was insane already. After half an hour he was ordered in by the warder, and I supposed punished. At least he was not at exercise on Monday, though I think I caught sight of him at the corner of the stone-yard, walking in charge of a warder.

On the Tuesday—my last day in prison—I saw him at exercise. He was worse than before, and again was sent in. Since then I know nothing of him, but I found out from one of the prisoners who walked with me at exercise that he had had twenty-four lashes in the cookhouse on Saturday afternoon, by order of the visiting justices on the report of the doctor. The howls that had horrified us all were his.

This man is undoubtedly becoming insane. Prison doctors have no knowledge of mental disease of any kind. They are as a class ignorant men. The pathology of the mind is unknown to them. When a man grows insane, they treat him as shamming. They have him punished again and again. Naturally the man becomes worse. When ordinary punishments are exhausted, the doctor reports the case to the justices. The result is flogging. Of course the flogging is not done with a cat-of-nine-tails. It is what is called birching. The instrument is a rod; but the result on the wretched half-witted man may be imagined.

His number is, or was, A. 2.11. I also managed to find out his name. It is Prince. Something should be done at once for him. He is a soldier, and his sentence is one of court-martial. The term is six months. Three have yet to run.

May I ask you to use your influence to have this case examined into, and to see that the lunatic prisoner is properly treated?

No report by the Medical Commissioners is of any avail. It is not to be trusted. The medical inspectors do not seem to understand the difference between idiocy and lunacy—between the entire absence of a function or organ and the diseases of a function or organ. This man A. 2.11. will, I have no doubt, be able to tell his name, the nature of his offence, the day of the month, the date of the beginning and expiration of his sentence, and answer any ordinary simple question; but that his mind is diseased admits of no doubt. At present it is a horrible duel between himself and the doctor. The doctor is fighting for a theory. The man is fighting for his life. I am anxious that the man should win. But let the whole case be examined into by experts who understand brain-disease, and by people of humane feelings who have still some common sense and some pity. There is no reason that the sentimentalist should be asked to interfere. He always does harm.

The case is a special instance of the cruelty inseparable from a stupid system, for the present Governor of Reading is a man of gentle and humane character, greatly liked and respected by all the prisoners. He was appointed in July last, and though he cannot alter the rules of the prison system he has altered the spirit in which they used to be carried out under his predecessor. He is very popular with the prisoners and with the warders. Indeed he has quite altered the whole tone of the prison life. Upon the other hand, the system is, of course, beyond his reach as far as altering its rules is concerned. I have no doubt that he sees daily much of what he knows to be unjust, stupid, and cruel. But his hands are tied. Of course I have no knowledge of his real views of the

case of A. 2.11, nor, indeed, of his views on our present system. I merely judge him by the complete change he brought
about in Reading Prison. Under his predecessor the system
was carried out with the greatest harshness and stupidity.—I
remain, Sir, your obedient servant,

OSCAR WILDE.

May 27.

PRISON REFORM[1]

THE EDITOR OF THE *Daily Chronicle*

SIR,—I understand, that the Home Secretary's Prison Reform Bill is to be read this week for the first or second time, and as your journal has been the one paper in England that has taken a real and vital interest in this important question, I hope that you will allow me, as one who has had long personal experience of life in an English gaol, to point out what reforms in our present stupid and barbarous system are urgently necessary.

From a leading article that appeared in your columns about a week ago, I learn that the chief reform proposed is an increase in the number of inspectors and official visitors, that are to have access to our English prisons.

Such a reform as this is entirely useless. The reason is extremely simple. The inspectors and justices of the peace that visit prisons come there for the purpose of seeing that the prison regulations are duly carried out. They come for no other purpose, nor have they any power, even if they had the desire, to alter a single clause in the regulations. No prisoner has ever had the smallest relief, or attention, or care from any of the official visitors. The visitors arrive not to help the prisoners, but to see that the rules are carried out. Their object in coming is to ensure the enforcement of a foolish and inhuman code. And, as they must have some occupation, they take very good care to do it. A prisoner who has been allowed the smallest privilege dreads the arrival of the inspectors.

[1] March 24, 1898.

And on the day of any prison inspection the prison officials
are more than usually brutal to the prisoners. Their object is,
of course, to show the splendid discipline they maintain.

The necessary reforms are very simple. They concern the
needs of the body and the needs of the mind of each unfortunate prisoner.

With regard to the first, there are three permanent punishments authorised by law in English prisons:—

1. Hunger.
2. Insomnia.
3. Disease.

The food supplied to prisoners is entirely inadequate. Most
of it is revolting in character. All of it is insufficient. Every
prisoner suffers day and night from hunger. A certain
amount of food is carefully weighed out ounce by ounce for
each prisoner. It is just enough to sustain, not life exactly, but
existence. But one is always racked by the pain and sickness
of hunger.

The result of the food—which in most cases consists of
weak gruel, suet, and water—is disease in the form of incessant diarrhœa. This malady, which ultimately with most
prisoners becomes a permanent disease, is a recognised insti-
tution in every prison. At Wandsworth Prison, for instance—
where I was confined for two months, till I had to be carried
into hospital, where I remained for another two months—
the warders go round twice or three times a day with astringent medicines, which they serve out to the prisoners as
a matter of course. After about a week of such treatment it is
unnecessary to say that the medicine produces no effect at all.
The wretched prisoner is then left a prey to the most weaken-
ing, depressing, and humiliating malady that can be conceived: and if, as often happens, he fails, from physical
weakness, to complete his required revolutions at the crank

or the mill he is reported for idleness, and punished with the greatest severity and brutality. Nor is this all.

Nothing can be worse than the sanitary arrangements of English prisons. In old days each cell was provided with a form of latrine. These latrines have now been suppressed. They exist no longer. A small tin vessel is supplied to each prisoner instead. Three times a day a prisoner is allowed to empty his slops. But he is not allowed to have access to the prison lavatories, except during the one hour when he is at exercise. And after five o'clock in the evening he is not allowed to leave his cell under any pretence, or for any reason. A man suffering from diarrhœa is consequently placed in a position so loathsome that it is unnecessary to dwell on it, that it would be unseemly to dwell on it. The misery and tortures that prisoners go through in consequence of the revolting sanitary arrangements are quite indescribable. And the foul air of the prison cells, increased by a system of ventilation that is utterly ineffective, is so sickening and unwholesome that it is no uncommon thing for warders, when they come in the morning out of fresh air and open and inspect each cell, to be violently sick. I have seen this myself on more than three occasions, and several of the warders have mentioned it to me as one of the disgusting things that their office entails on them.

The food supplied to prisoners should be adequate and wholesome. It should not be of such a character as to produce the incessant diarrhœa that, at first a malady, becomes a permanent disease.

The sanitary arrangements in English prisons should be entirely altered. Every prisoner should be allowed to have access to the lavatories when necessary, and to empty his slops when necessary. The present system of ventilation in each cell is utterly useless. The air comes through choked-up gratings, and through a small ventilator in the tiny barred window, which is far too small, and too badly constructed, to admit any adequate amount of fresh air. One is only allowed out of one's cell for one hour out of the twenty-four that compose the long day, and so for twenty-three hours one is breathing the foulest possible air.

With regard to the punishment of insomnia, it only exists in Chinese and in English prisons. In China it is inflicted by placing the prisoner in a small bamboo cage; in England by means of the plank bed. The object of the plank bed is to produce insomnia. There is no other object in it, and it invariably succeeds. And even when one is subsequently allowed a hard mattress, as happens in the course of imprisonment, one still suffers from insomnia. For sleep, like all wholesome things, is a habit. Every prisoner who has been on a plank bed suffers from insomnia. It is a revolting and ignorant punishment.

With regard to the needs of the mind, I beg that you will allow me to say something.

The present prison system seems almost to have for its aim the wrecking and the destruction of the mental faculties. The production of insanity is, if not its object, certainly its result. That is a well-ascertained fact. Its causes are obvious. Deprived of books, of all human intercourse, isolated from every humane and humanising influence, condemned to eternal silence, robbed of all intercourse with the external world, treated like an unintelligent animal, brutalised below the level of any of the brute creation, the wretched man who is confined in an English prison can hardly escape becoming insane. I do not wish to dwell on these horrors; still less to excite any momentary sentimental interest in these matters. So I will merely, with your permission, point out what should be done.

Every prisoner should have an adequate supply of good books. At present, during the first three months of imprisonment, one is allowed no books at all, except a Bible, Prayer-book, and hymn-book. After that one is allowed one book a week. That is not merely inadequate, but the books that compose an ordinary prison library are perfectly useless. They consist chiefly of third-rate, badly written, religious books so-called, written apparently for children, and utterly unsuitable for children or for any one else. Prisoners should be encouraged to read, and should have whatever books they want, and the books should be well chosen. At present the selection of books is made by the prison chaplain.

Under the present system a prisoner is only allowed to see his friends four times a year, for twenty minutes each time. This is quite wrong. A prisoner should be allowed to see his friends once a month, and for a reasonable time. The mode at present in vogue of exhibiting a prisoner to his friends should be altered. Under the present system, the prisoner is either locked up in a large iron cage or in a large wooden box, with a small aperture, covered with wire netting, through which he is allowed to peer. His friends are placed in a similar cage, some three or four feet distant, and two warders stand between to listen to, and, if they wish, stop or interrupt the conversation, such as it may be. I propose that a prisoner should be allowed to see his relatives or friends in a room. The present regulations are inexpressively revolting and harassing. A visit from (our) relatives or friends is to every prisoner an intensification of humiliation and mental distress. Many prisoners, rather than support such an ordeal, refuse to see their friends at all. And I cannot say I am surprised. When one sees one's solicitor, one sees him in a room with a glass door, on the other side of which stands the warder. When a man sees his wife and children, or his parents, or his friends, he should be allowed the same privilege. To be exhibited, like an ape in a cage, to people who are fond of one, and of whom one is fond, is a needless and horrible degradation.

Every prisoner should be allowed to write and receive a letter at least once a month. At present one is allowed to write only four times a year. This is quite inadequate. One of the tragedies of prison life is that it turns a man's heart to stone. The feelings of natural affection, like all other feelings, require to be fed. They die easily of inanition. A brief letter, four times a year, is not enough to keep alive the gentler and more humane affections by which ultimately the nature is kept sensitive to any fine or beautiful influences that may heal a wrecked and ruined life.

The habit of mutilating and expurgating prisoners' letters should be stopped. At present, if a prisoner in a letter makes any complaint of the prison system, that portion of his letter is cut out with a pair of scissors. If, upon the other hand, he makes any complaint when he speaks to his friends through the bars of the cage, or the aperture of the wooden box, he is brutalised by the warders, and reported for punishment every week till his next visit comes round, by which time he is expected to have learned, not wisdom, but cunning, and one always learns that. It is one of the few things that one does learn in prison. Fortunately, the other things are, in some instances, of higher import.

If I may trespass for a little longer, may I say this? You suggested in your leading article that no prison chaplain should be allowed to have any care or employment outside the prison itself. But this is a matter of no moment. The prison chaplains are entirely useless. They are, as a class, well-meaning, but foolish, indeed, silly men. They are of no help to any prisoner. Once every six weeks or so a key turns in the lock of one's cell door, and the chaplain enters. One stands, of course, at attention. He asks one whether one has been reading the Bible. One answers "Yes" or "No," as the case may be. He then quotes a few texts, and goes out and locks the door. Sometimes he leaves a tract.

The officials who should not be allowed to hold any employment outside the prison, or to have any private practice, are the prison doctors. At present the prison doctors have usually, if not always, a large private practice, and hold appointments in other institutions. The consequence is that the health of the prisoners is entirely neglected, and the sanitary condition of the prison entirely overlooked. As a class, I regard, and have always from my earliest youth regarded, doctors as by far the most humane profession in the community. But I must make an exception for prison doctors. They are, as far as I came across them, and from what I saw of them in hospital and elsewhere, brutal in manner, coarse in temperament, and utterly indifferent to the health of the prisoners or their comfort. If prison doctors were prohibited from private practice they would be compelled to take some interest in the health and sanitary condition of the people under their charge. I have tried to indicate in my letter a few of the reforms necessary to our English prison system. They are simple, practical, and humane. They are, of course, only a beginning. But it is time that a beginning should be made, and it can only be started by a strong pressure of public opinion formularised in your powerful paper, and fostered by it.

But to make even these reforms effectual, much has to be done. And the first, and perhaps the most difficult task is to humanise the governors of prisons, to civilise the warders and to Christianise the chaplains—Yours, etc.

THE AUTHOR OF THE "BALLAD
OF READING GAOL."

March 23.

The Best of the World's Best Books
COMPLETE LIST OF TITLES IN
THE MODERN LIBRARY

For convenience in ordering use number at right of title

ADAMS, HENRY	The Education of Henry Adams 76
AIKEN, CONRAD (Editor)	A Comprehensive Anthology of American Poetry 101
AIKEN, CONRAD (Editor)	20th-Century American Poetry 127
ALEICHEM, SHOLOM	Selected Stories of 145
ANDERSON, SHERWOOD	Winesburg, Ohio 104
AQUINAS, ST. THOMAS	Introduction to St. Thomas Aquinas 259
ARISTOTLE	Introduction to Aristotle 248
ARISTOTLE	Politics 228
ARISTOTLE	Rhetoric and Poetics 246
AUGUSTINE, ST.	The Confessions of 263
AUSTEN, JANE	Pride and Prejudice and Sense and Sensibility 264
BACON, FRANCIS	Selected Writings of 256
BALZAC	Droll Stories 193
BALZAC	Père Goriot and Eugénie Grandet 245
BEERBOHM, MAX	Zuleika Dobson 116
BELLAMY, EDWARD	Looking Backward 22
BENNETT, ARNOLD	The Old Wives' Tale 184
BERGSON, HENRI	Creative Evolution 231
BLAKE, WILLIAM	Selected Poetry & Prose of 285
BOCCACCIO	The Decameron 71
BOSWELL, JAMES	The Life of Samuel Johnson 282
BRONTË, CHARLOTTE	Jane Eyre 64
BRONTË, EMILY	Wuthering Heights 106
BROWNING, ROBERT	Selected Poetry of 198
BUCK, PEARL	The Good Earth 15
BURCKHARDT, JACOB	The Civilization of the Renaissance in Italy 32
BURK, JOHN N.	The Life and Works of Beethoven 241
BUTLER, SAMUEL	Erewhon and Erewhon Revisited 136
BUTLER, SAMUEL	The Way of All Flesh 13
BYRON, LORD	The Selected Poetry of 195
BYRON, LORD	Don Juan 24
CAESAR, JULIUS	The Gallic War and Other Writings of 295
CALDWELL, ERSKINE	God's Little Acre 51
CALDWELL, ERSKINE	Tobacco Road 249
CANFIELD, DOROTHY	The Deepening Stream 200
CARROLL, LEWIS	Alice in Wonderland, etc. 79
CASANOVA, JACQUES	Memoirs of Casanova 165
CELLINI, BENVENUTO	Autobiography of Cellini 150
CERVANTES	Don Quixote 174
CHAUCER	The Canterbury Tales 161
CHEKHOV, ANTON	Best Plays by 171
CHEKHOV, ANTON	The Short Stories of 50
CICERO	The Basic Works of 272
COLERIDGE	Selected Poetry and Prose of 279

COMMAGER, HENRY STEELE & NEVINS, ALLAN	A Short History of the United States 235
CONFUCIUS	The Wisdom of Confucius 7
CONRAD, JOSEPH	Lord Jim 186
CONRAD, JOSEPH	Nostromo 275
CONRAD, JOSEPH	Victory 34
COOPER, JAMES FENIMORE	The Pathfinder 105
CORNEILLE & RACINE	Six Plays of Corneille and Racine 194
CORVO, FREDERICK BARON	A History of the Borgias 192
CRANE, STEPHEN	The Red Badge of Courage 130
CUMMINGS, E. E.	The Enormous Room 214
DANA, RICHARD HENRY	Two Years Before the Mast 236
DANTE	The Divine Comedy 208
DA VINCI, LEONARDO	The Notebooks of 156
DEFOE, DANIEL	Moll Flanders 122
DEFOE, DANIEL	Robinson Crusoe and A Journal of the Plague Year 92
DESCARTES, RENE	Philosophical Writings 43
DEWEY, JOHN	Human Nature and Conduct 173
DICKENS, CHARLES	David Copperfield 110
DICKENS, CHARLES	Pickwick Papers 204
DICKENS, CHARLES	A Tale of Two Cities 189
DICKINSON, EMILY	Selected Poems of 25
DINESEN, ISAK	Out of Africa 23
DINESEN, ISAK	Seven Gothic Tales 54
DONNE, JOHN	Complete Poetry and Selected Prose of 12
DOS PASSOS, JOHN	Three Soldiers 205
DOSTOYEVSKY, FYODOR	The Best Short Stories of 293
DOSTOYEVSKY, FYODOR	The Brothers Karamazov 151
DOSTOYEVSKY, FYODOR	Crime and Punishment 199
DOSTOYEVSKY, FYODOR	The Possessed 55
DOUGLAS, NORMAN	South Wind 5
DOYLE, SIR ARTHUR CONAN	The Adventures and Memoirs of Sherlock Holmes 206
DREISER, THEODORE	Sister Carrie 8
DUMAS, ALEXANDRE	Camille 69
DUMAS, ALEXANDRE	The Three Musketeers 143
DU MAURIER, DAPHNE	Rebecca 227
ELLIS, HAVELOCK	The Dance of Life 160
EMERSON, RALPH WALDO	Essays and Other Writings 91
FAULKNER, WILLIAM	Absalom, Absalom! 271
FAULKNER, WILLIAM	Go Down, Moses 175
FAULKNER, WILLIAM	Light in August 88
FAULKNER, WILLIAM	Sanctuary 61
FAULKNER, WILLIAM	The Sound and the Fury and As I Lay Dying 187
FIELDING, HENRY	Joseph Andrews 117
FIELDING, HENRY	Tom Jones 185
FLAUBERT, GUSTAVE	Madame Bovary 28
FORESTER, C. S.	The African Queen 102
FRANCE, ANATOLE	Penguin Island 210
FRANKLIN, BENJAMIN	Autobiography, etc. 39
FREUD, SIGMUND	The Interpretation of Dreams 96
FROST, ROBERT	The Poems of 242
GALSWORTHY, JOHN	The Apple Tree (in Great Modern Short Stories 168)
GEORGE, HENRY	Progress and Poverty 36
GOETHE	Faust 177

GOGOL, NIKOLAI	Dead Souls 40
GOLDSMITH, OLIVER	The Vicar of Wakefield and other Writings 291
GRAVES, ROBERT	I, Claudius 20
GUNTHER, JOHN	Death Be Not Proud 286
HACKETT, FRANCIS	The Personal History of Henry the Eighth 265
HAGGARD, H. RIDER	She and King Solomon's Mines 163
HARDY, THOMAS	Jude the Obscure 135
HARDY, THOMAS	The Mayor of Casterbridge 17
HARDY, THOMAS	The Return of the Native 121
HARDY, THOMAS	Tess of the D'Urbervilles 72
HART & KAUFMAN	Six Plays by 233
HARTE, BRET	The Best Stories of 250
HAWTHORNE, NATHANIEL	The Scarlet Letter 93
HEGEL	The Philosophy of 239
HELLMAN, LILLIAN	Four Plays by 223
HENRY, O.	Best Short Stories of 4
HERODOTUS	The Persian Wars 255
HOFFENSTEIN, SAMUEL	The Complete Poetry of 225
HOMER	The Iliad 166
HOMER	The Odyssey 167
HORACE	The Complete Works of 141
HOWELLS, WILLIAM DEAN	The Rise of Silas Lapham 277
HUDSON, W. H.	Green Mansions 89
HUGO, VICTOR	The Hunchback of Notre Dame 35
HUXLEY, ALDOUS	Antic Hay 209
HUXLEY, ALDOUS	Brave New World 48
HUXLEY, ALDOUS	Point Counter Point 180
IBSEN, HENRIK	Six Plays by 6
IRVING, WASHINGTON	Selected Writings of 240
JAMES, HENRY	The Bostonians 16
JAMES, HENRY	The Portrait of a Lady 107
JAMES, HENRY	The Turn of the Screw 169
JAMES, HENRY	Washington Square 269
JAMES, HENRY	The Wings of the Dove 244
JAMES, WILLIAM	The Philosophy of William James 114
JAMES, WILLIAM	The Varieties of Religious Experience 70
JEFFERS, ROBINSON	Roan Stallion; Tamar and Other Poems 118
JEFFERSON, THOMAS	The Life and Selected Writings of 234
JOYCE, JAMES	Dubliners 124
KAFKA, FRANZ	Selected Stories of 283
KANT	The Philosophy of 266
KAUFMAN & HART	Six Plays by 233
KEATS	The Complete Poetry and Selected Prose of 273
KIPLING, RUDYARD	Kim 99
KOESTLER, ARTHUR	Darkness at Noon 74
LAOTSE	The Wisdom of 262
LAWRENCE, D. H.	The Rainbow 128
LAWRENCE, D. H.	Sons and Lovers 109
LAWRENCE, D. H.	Women in Love 68
LEWIS, SINCLAIR	Dodsworth 252
LEWIS, SINCLAIR	Cass Timberlane 221
LONGFELLOW, HENRY W.	Poems 56
LOUYS, PIERRE	Aphrodite 77
LUDWIG, EMIL	Napoleon 95

MACHIAVELLI	The Prince and The Discourses 65
MALRAUX, ANDRE	Man's Fate 33
MANN, THOMAS	Death in Venice (in Great German Short Novels and Stories 108)
MARQUAND, JOHN P.	The Late George Apley 182
MARX, KARL	Capital and Other Writings 202
MAUGHAM, W. SOMERSET	The Best Short Stories of 14
MAUGHAM, W. SOMERSET	Cakes and Ale 270
MAUGHAM, W. SOMERSET	The Moon and Sixpence 27
MAUGHAM, W. SOMERSET	Of Human Bondage 176
MAUPASSANT, GUY DE	Best Short Stories 98
MAUROIS, ANDRÉ	Disraeli 46
McCORD, DAVID (Editor)	What Cheer: An Anthology of Humorous and Witty Verse 190
MEAD, MARGARET	Coming of Age in Samoa 126
MELVILLE, HERMAN	Moby Dick 119
MEREDITH, GEORGE	The Egoist 253
MEREDITH, GEORGE	The Ordeal of Richard Feverel 134
MEREJKOWSKI, DMITRI	The Romance of Leonardo da Vinci 138
MICHENER, JAMES A.	Selected Writings of 296
MILTON, JOHN	The Complete Poetry and Selected Prose of John Milton 132
MOLIÈRE	Eight Plays by 78
MONTAIGNE	Selected Essays of 218
MORIER, JAMES	The Adventures of Hajji Baba of Ispahan 289
NASH, OGDEN	The Selected Verse of Ogden Nash 191
NEVINS, ALLAN & COMMAGER, HENRY STEELE	A Short History of the United States 235
NEWMAN, CARDINAL JOHN H.	Apologia Pro Vita Sua 113
NIETZSCHE, FRIEDRICH	Thus Spake Zarathustra 9
NOSTRADAMUS	Oracles of 81
ODETS, CLIFFORD	Six Plays of 67
O'HARA, JOHN	Appointment in Samarra 42
O'HARA, JOHN	Selected Short Stories of 211
O'NEILL, EUGENE	The Emperor Jones, Anna Christie and The Hairy Ape 146
O'NEILL, EUGENE	The Long Voyage Home: Seven Plays of the Sea 111
PALGRAVE, FRANCIS (Editor)	The Golden Treasury 232
PARKER, DOROTHY	The Collected Short Stories of 123
PARKER, DOROTHY	The Collected Poetry of 237
PARKMAN, FRANCIS	The Oregon Trail 267
PASCAL, BLAISE	Pensées and The Provincial Letters 164
PATER, WALTER	Marius the Epicurean 90
PATER, WALTER	The Renaissance 86
PEPYS, SAMUEL	Passages from the Diary of 103
PERELMAN, S. J.	The Best of 247
PLATO	The Republic 153
PLATO	The Works of Plato 181
POE, EDGAR ALLAN	Selected Poetry and Prose 82
POLO, MARCO	The Travels of Marco Polo 196
POPE, ALEXANDER	Selected Works of 257
PORTER, KATHERINE ANNE	Flowering Judas 284
PORTER, KATHERINE ANNE	Pale Horse, Pale Rider 45
PROUST, MARCEL	The Captive 120
PROUST, MARCEL	Cities of the Plain 220
PROUST, MARCEL	The Guermantes Way 213

PROUST, MARCEL   The Past Recaptured 278
PROUST, MARCEL   Swann's Way 59
PROUST, MARCEL   The Sweet Cheat Gone 260
PROUST, MARCEL   Within a Budding Grove 172
RACINE & CORNEILLE   Six Plays by 194
READE, CHARLES   The Cloister and the Hearth 62
REED, JOHN   Ten Days that Shook the World 215
RENAN, ERNEST   The Life of Jesus 140
RICHARDSON, SAMUEL   Clarissa 10
ROSTAND, EDMOND   Cyrano de Bergerac 154
ROUSSEAU, JEAN JACQUES The Confessions of 243
RUNYON, DAMON   Famous Stories 53
RUSSELL, BERTRAND   Selected Papers of Bertrand Russell 137
SAKI   The Short Stories of 280
SANTAYANA, GEORGE   The Sense of Beauty 292
SCHOPENHAUER   The Philosophy of Schopenhauer 52
SCHULBERG, BUDD   What Makes Sammy Run? 281
SHAKESPEARE, WILLIAM   Tragedies, 1, 1A—complete, 2 vols.
SHAKESPEARE, WILLIAM   Comedies, 2, 2A—complete, 2 vols.
SHAKESPEARE, WILLIAM   Histories, 3
                        Histories, Poems, 3A } complete, 2 vols.
SHAW, BERNARD   Four Plays by 19
SHAW, BERNARD   Saint Joan, Major Barbara, and
                            Androcles and the Lion 294
SHAW, IRWIN   The Young Lions 112
SHELLEY   The Selected Poetry & Prose of 274
SMOLLETT, TOBIAS   Humphry Clinker 159
SPINOZA   The Philosophy of Spinoza 60
STEINBECK, JOHN   In Dubious Battle 115
STEINBECK, JOHN   The Grapes of Wrath 148
STEINBECK, JOHN   Of Mice and Men 29
STEINBECK, JOHN   Tortilla Flat 216
STENDHAL   The Red and the Black 157
STERNE, LAURENCE   Tristram Shandy 147
STEWART, GEORGE R.   Storm 254
STOKER, BRAM   Dracula 31
STONE, IRVING   Lust for Life 11
STOWE, HARRIET BEECHER Uncle Tom's Cabin 261
STRACHEY, LYTTON   Eminent Victorians 212
SUETONIUS   Lives of the Twelve Caesars 188
SWIFT, JONATHAN   Gulliver's Travels and Other Writings
                            100
SYMONDS, JOHN A.   The Life of Michelangelo 49
TACITUS   The Complete Works of 222
TENNYSON   Selected Poetry of 230
THACKERAY, WILLIAM   Henry Esmond 80
THACKERAY, WILLIAM   Vanity Fair 131
THOMPSON, FRANCIS   Complete Poems 38
THOREAU, HENRY DAVID   Walden and Other Writings 155
THUCYDIDES   The Complete Writings of 58
THURBER, JAMES   The Thurber Carnival 85
TOLSTOY, LEO   Anna Karenina 37
TROLLOPE, ANTHONY   Barchester Towers and The Warden 41
TROLLOPE, ANTHONY   The Eustace Diamonds 251
TURGENEV, IVAN   Fathers and Sons 21
TWAIN, MARK   A Connecticut Yankee in King Arthur's
                            Court 162
VEBLEN, THORSTEIN   The Theory of the Leisure Class 63

VIRGIL	The Aeneid, Eclogues & Georgics 75
VOLTAIRE	Candide and Other Writings 47
WALPOLE, HUGH	Fortitude 178
WALTON, IZAAK	The Compleat Angler 26
WARREN, ROBERT PENN	All The King's Men 170
WEBB, MARY	Precious Bane 219
WELLS, H. G.	Tono Bungay 197
WELTY, EUDORA	Selected Stories of 290
WHARTON, EDITH	The Age of Innocence 229
WHITMAN, WALT	Leaves of Grass 97
WILDE, OSCAR	Dorian Gray, De Profundis 125
WILDE, OSCAR	The Plays of Oscar Wilde 83
WILDE, OSCAR	Poems and Fairy Tales 84
WORDSWORTH	Selected Poetry of 268
YEATS, W. B. (Editor)	Irish Fairy and Folk Tales 44
YOUNG, G. F.	The Medici 179
ZIMMERN, ALFRED	The Greek Commonwealth 207
ZOLA, EMILE	Nana 142
MISCELLANEOUS	An Anthology of Irish Literature 288
	The Arabian Nights' Entertainments 201
	Best Amer. Humorous Short Stories 87
	Best Russian Short Stories 18
	Best Spanish Stories 129
	A Comprehensive Anthology of American Poetry 101
	The Consolation of Philosophy 226
	Eight Famous Elizabethan Plays 94
	Eighteenth-Century Plays 224
	Famous Ghost Stories 73
	The Federalist 139
	Five Great Modern Irish Plays 30
	Fourteen Great Detective Stories 144
	Great German Short Novels and Stories 108
	Great Modern Short Stories 168
	Great Tales of the American West 238
	The Greek Poets 203
	The Latin Poets 217
	The Making of Man: An Outline of Anthropology 149
	The Making of Society: An Outline of Sociology 183
	Medieval Romances 133
	New Voices in the American Theatre 258
	Outline of Abnormal Psychology 152
	Outline of Psychoanalysis 66
	Restoration Plays 287
	Seven Famous Greek Plays 158
	The Short Bible 57
	Six Modern American Plays 276
	Twentieth-Century Amer. Poetry 127

MODERN LIBRARY GIANTS

*A series of full-sized library editions of books that formerly
were available only in cumbersome and expensive sets.*
THE MODERN LIBRARY GIANTS REPRESENT A
SELECTION OF THE WORLD'S GREATEST BOOKS

These volumes contain from 600 to 1,400 pages each

G1. TOLSTOY, LEO. War and Peace.
G2. BOSWELL, JAMES. Life of Samuel Johnson.
G3. HUGO, VICTOR. Les Miserables.
G4. THE COMPLETE POEMS OF KEATS AND SHELLEY.
G5. PLUTARCH'S LIVES (The Dryden Translation).
G6.
G7. } GIBBON, EDWARD. The Decline and Fall of the Roman
G8. Empire (Complete in three volumes).
G9. GREAT VOICES OF THE REFORMATION.
G10. TWELVE FAMOUS RESTORATION PLAYS (1660-1820)
    (Congreve, Wycherley, Gay, Goldsmith, Sheridan, etc.)
G11. JAMES, HENRY. The Short Stories of
G12. THE MOST POPULAR NOVELS OF SIR WALTER
    SCOTT (Quentin Durward, Ivanhoe and Kenilworth).
G13. CARLYLE, THOMAS. The French Revolution.
G14. BULFINCH'S MYTHOLOGY (Illustrated).
G15. CERVANTES. Don Quixote (Illustrated).
G16. WOLFE, THOMAS. Look Homeward, Angel.
G17. THE POEMS AND PLAYS OF ROBERT BROWNING.
G18. ELEVEN PLAYS OF HENRIK IBSEN.
G19. THE COMPLETE WORKS OF HOMER.
G20. THE LIFE AND WRITINGS OF ABRAHAM LINCOLN.
G21. SIXTEEN FAMOUS AMERICAN PLAYS.
G22. THIRTY FAMOUS ONE-ACT PLAYS.
G23. TOLSTOY, LEO. Anna Karenina.
G24. LAMB, CHARLES. The Complete Works and Letters of
G25. THE COMPLETE PLAYS OF GILBERT AND SULLIVAN.
G26. MARX, KARL. Capital.
G27. DARWIN, CHARLES. Origin of Species & The Descent of Man.
G28. THE COMPLETE WORKS OF LEWIS CARROLL.
G29. PRESCOTT, WILLIAM H. The Conquest of Mexico and
    The Conquest of Peru.
G30. MYERS, GUSTAVUS. History of the Great American
    Fortunes.
G31. FAMOUS SCIENCE-FICTION STORIES: ADVENTURES IN
    TIME AND SPACE
G32. SMITH, ADAM. The Wealth of Nations.
G33. COLLINS, WILKIE. The Moonstone and The Woman in White.
G34. NIETZSCHE, FRIEDRICH. The Philosophy of Nietzsche.
G35. BURY, J. B. A History of Greece.
G36. DOSTOYEVSKY, FYODOR. The Brothers Karamazov.
G37. THE COMPLETE NOVELS AND SELECTED TALES OF
    NATHANIEL HAWTHORNE.
G38. ROLLAND, ROMAIN. Jean-Christophe.

G39. THE BASIC WRITINGS OF SIGMUND FREUD.
G40. THE COMPLETE TALES AND POEMS OF EDGAR
      ALLAN POE.
G41. FARRELL, JAMES T. Studs Lonigan.
G42. THE POEMS AND PLAYS OF TENNYSON.
G43. DEWEY, JOHN. Intelligence in the Modern World: John
      Dewey's Philosophy.
G44. DOS PASSOS, JOHN. U. S. A.
G45. STOIC AND EPICUREAN PHILOSOPHERS
G46. A NEW ANTHOLOGY OF MODERN POETRY.
G47. THE ENGLISH PHILOSOPHERS FROM BACON TO
      MILL.
G48. THE METROPOLITAN OPERA GUIDE.
G49. TWAIN, MARK. Tom Sawyer and Huckleberry Finn.
G50. WHITMAN, WALT. Leaves of Grass.
G51. THE BEST-KNOWN NOVELS OF GEORGE ELIOT.
G52. JOYCE, JAMES. Ulysses.
G53. SUE, EUGENE. The Wandering Jew.
G54. AN ANTHOLOGY OF FAMOUS BRITISH STORIES.
G55. O'NEILL, EUGENE. Nine Plays by
G56. THE WISDOM OF CATHOLICISM.
G57. MELVILLE. Selected Writings of Herman Melville.
G58. THE COMPLETE NOVELS OF JANE AUSTEN.
G59. THE WISDOM OF CHINA AND INDIA.
G60. DOSTOYEVSKY, FYODOR. The Idiot.
G61. SPAETH, SIGMUND. A Guide to Great Orchestral Music.
G62. THE POEMS, PROSE AND PLAYS OF PUSHKIN.
G63. SIXTEEN FAMOUS BRITISH PLAYS.
G64. MELVILLE, HERMAN. Moby Dick.
G65. THE COMPLETE WORKS OF RABELAIS.
G66. THREE FAMOUS MURDER NOVELS
      Before the Fact, Francis Iles.
      Trent's Last Case, E. C. Bentley.
      The House of the Arrow, A. E. W. Mason.
G67. ANTHOLOGY OF FAMOUS ENGLISH AND AMERI-
      CAN POETRY.
G68. THE SELECTED WORK OF TOM PAINE.
G69. ONE HUNDRED AND ONE YEARS' ENTERTAIN-
      MENT.
G70. THE COMPLETE POETRY OF JOHN DONNE AND
      WILLIAM BLAKE.
G71. SIXTEEN FAMOUS EUROPEAN PLAYS.
G72. GREAT TALES OF TERROR AND THE SUPERNATURAL.
G73. A SUB-TREASURY OF AMERICAN HUMOR.
G74. ST. AUGUSTINE. The City of God.
G75. SELECTED WRITINGS OF ROBERT LOUIS STEVENSON.
G76. GRIMM AND ANDERSEN, TALES OF
G77. AN ANTHOLOGY OF FAMOUS AMERICAN STORIES.
G78. HOLMES, OLIVER WENDELL. The Mind and Faith of
      Justice Holmes.
G79. THE WISDOM OF ISRAEL.
G80. DREISER, THEODORE. An American Tragedy.
G81. AN ENCYCLOPEDIA OF MODERN AMERICAN HUMOR